AURO.

A Humorous Regency Novel

by D. G. Rampton

Book 3, Regency Goddesses Series

Foreword

It has been a real pleasure to spend time with Aurora and the Duke of Rothworth over the last year. I have thoroughly enjoyed writing their story and seeing them come to life. They are charmingly demanding characters, and I was often at their whim while they steered my pen! I hope you fall in love with them, as I did.

The novels in the Regency Goddesses series are standalone and can be enjoyed in any order. They share only one minor character (have you spotted them yet?).

Chronological order:

Artemisia – Book 1 (1812)
Aphrodite – Book 2 (1820)
Aurora – Book 3 (1821)

Acknowledgments

Andy
Always my love and my secret weapon.

Francesca
The light of my life.

Ingrid
Friend, editor, wise soul, and a talent in her own right.

This book is dedicated to Jane and Georgette.
Thank you for the memories!

One

"Percy, for goodness sake, go quickly and hide yourself! He'll be riding through here at any moment! Or better still, if you can't reconcile yourself to what I must do, ride back and wait with John at the inn," Miss Aurora Wesley told her brother with a tinge of exasperation.

"John is perfectly capable of watching over our luggage without my assistance," replied Percy, frowning down at her. "I've no intention of going off and leaving you alone in this madness!"

"I know perfectly well what I'm about. And, besides, it is not as if we have any choice in the matter, so there is really no point in attempting to dissuade me."

Percy studied her where she sat on the grass verge, by the side of a narrow country lane. By the resolute tilt of her chin, he knew he would not win this argument.

He turned his attention to her horse, feasting placidly on a crop of daisies a few feet away, and cast his eyes over it critically. As with his own mount, the animal had been hired from the coaching inn where they had spent the night and could hardly be considered a prime specimen.

"If there is a need for you to get away quickly," he said, "that pile of bones will be of little use to you! Had I known what you planned, I'd have insisted we bring our own horses on this ill-fated journey."

"But I didn't know it myself! The plan only came to me once my purse was stolen at that horrid posting house in Cambridge yesterday. Also stabling is expensive in London, from what I have heard, so we couldn't have afforded it. Pray, don't worry, dearest! You must trust me on this."

"I seem to have little choice in the matter," he grumbled, his handsome face creased in consternation.

Walking over to his horse, he took hold of the pummel and swung himself up into the saddle with athletic grace.

"I'll keep an eye on you from that copse of trees over there. You have only to scream if things go awry . . . which, God knows, is more than likely!

I have to say, Rory, this is the most addlebrained thing you've done yet. That we should sink so low as to . . . "

"Dearest, you can tell me all your reservations again shortly. But for now, please, just *go!*"

Percy was her darling and she was in the habit of spoiling him, particularly since their parents' untimely death four years ago, but though he had recently attained his majority and in the eyes of the world was a man capable of handling his own affairs, she knew him to still be young and idealistic, and quite incapable of dealing with the exigencies of the situation they found themselves in.

And so, she shooed him away with an impatient hand.

When he had reluctantly ridden off, she arranged the skirt of her pale-blue riding habit in a way that showed off her petticoats and finely shaped ankles, repositioned the tall-crowned hat on her blonde curls so that it sat forward over one eye, and leaned back against the rise of the verge, giving all the appearance of a young lady who had recently been tossed from her horse.

There was no denying that she felt some trepidation for what she was about to do, but there was no room for scruples at this late stage; not when so much depended on this trip to London.

It was a lovely spring afternoon, and she could have enjoyed basking in the sunshine, amongst the wildflowers, had not the sound of clip-clopping hoofs reached her ears and made her tense in anticipation.

A few moments later, a rider came cantering around the bend in the road.

She let out a sigh of relief to see it was the gentleman she had been expecting. Over lunch at the inn, she had overheard him ask the innkeeper about a back route to Peterborough that avoided the busy Great North Road, however, there had always been a possibility that he would change his mind and take the main road after all, rather than this conveniently quiet lane.

Seeing her lying prostrate on the grass, the gentleman urged his horse towards her.

She raised herself up on her elbows, then dropped back to the ground with a low moan.

"Can I be of assistance?" he asked, dismounting.

Her unobstructed eye looked him over as he approached.

His lean build, muscled thighs and broad shoulders, as well as a riding coat and buff breeches tailored for comfort rather than fashion, all gave him the appearance of a country gentleman addicted to sporting activities.

Back at the inn she had felt confident in categorising him as a well-to-do squire, but she now realised she had not given proper consideration to the air of authority that clung to him. This was not a man used to deferring to others.

His expression was one of unruffled composure, as if he chanced upon ladies in distress on most days, and she was happy to find her judgement on that point at least had been correct. He would not be an easy man to fluster; one of the key factors in her selection of him.

What she had not surmised, for she had kept her face averted when he had turned in her direction, was that his dark, wavy hair framed a countenance of such masculine beauty any female over the age of eighteen must fear for her peace of mind.

He was several shades darker than the customary paleness that was in fashion throughout the aristocracy, a remainder, little though she knew it, of his Indian heritage from a long-ago Punjabi princess great-grandmother, and with his prominent cheekbones, strong jaw, and a nose that had been broken yet somehow made more attractive by its imperfection, he was an arresting sight.

As for his beautiful eyes, they reminded her of the North Sea: blue-grey and impenetrable. She sensed they were capable of flashes of passion . . . and retribution (but that must simply be her guilt colouring her reasoning).

Giving herself a mental shake to dispel such fanciful thoughts, she offered him a guileless look.

"Oh, thank you ever so much for stopping, sir!" she said, assuming a higher pitched tone than her naturally husky voice and imprinting it with a country inflection.

"Are you hurt, ma'am?"

"Only my pride! I don't believe anything is broken, though I feel shockingly bruised and will no doubt be limping around tomorrow. Papa will say it is no more than I deserve for being such a goose as to allow my horse to unseat me! And over nothing more than a rabbit crossing my path."

She pushed herself up into a sitting position so that the velvet of her riding habit strained provocatively against her bosom, and smiled up at him in a manner she had been told was a danger to male hearts.

"I'm happy to hear there's no serious damage," he responded matter-of-factly. "Shall I assist you to rise?"

Aurora was a little surprised by this lack of reaction to her womanly charms.

She did not consider herself to be beautiful – her critical gaze could not appreciate that her beauty lay not in the excellence of each feature but in the particularly enchanting grouping of them all – nevertheless she had become used to knowing herself to be admired, and had never hesitated to use this fortuitous circumstance to her advantage.

"I would be delighted to accept the assistance of so charming a gentleman," she said with a demure flutter of her eyelashes. "I count myself indebted to you for coming to my rescue – like a knight out of a fairy story! – and will be certain to . . . *oh*!"

She found herself unceremoniously grabbed by the arms and lifted to her feet with little effort, or finesse.

Quite unused to being handled as if she were a sack of produce, Aurora was momentarily nonplussed and could only blink at the gentleman.

"Can you stand unaided?" he asked, keeping hold of her elbow to steady her, though with obvious reluctance.

Raising a hand to her brow, she swayed and fell gracefully against him.

"Oh . . . I-I beg your pardon . . . Pray forgive me! I seem to feel a little faint all of a sudden."

As her cheek was resting against the gentleman's chest, she did not see him roll his eyes.

"Of course, you do," he said blandly, his arms remaining unresponsive by his sides. "I've noticed it's a favourite past-time of your sex. Have you mastered your unsteadiness, or should I return you to the grass?"

Aurora almost laughed.

From his tone she gathered he was in the habit of having women throw themselves at him. She could sympathise with them. It was his own fault for pairing aloofness with his ridiculously attractive looks; it made one want to ruffle his composure in an entirely physical manner.

"I suppose I am a *little* better," she said uncertainly, remaining limply against him. "If only my head didn't swim so! But I can see this has been a great inconvenience for you – being obliged to stop your journey to assist a foolish female! – and not for the world would I wish to impose upon your kindness further."

Now if *that* did not make him regret his lack of gallantry, she did not know what would.

"Thank you," was all he replied; and, taking hold of her shoulders, he lifted her away from him and released her with an efficiency most women would have found insulting.

In Aurora's case, it merely brought out the thrill of the challenge. She had thought to conclude her business with him quickly and be on her way, but against her better judgement she found herself wanting to prolong their scene.

"Oh, how uncommonly strong you are, sir!" she said with breathless admiration. "I am not in the habit of allowing anyone to manhandle me in so thorough a fashion . . . and yet, I can't find it in myself to remonstrate with you."

The gentleman merely stared back at her with what she was beginning to realise was habitual reserve.

"If you would give me your direction, sir," she carried on with a determined smile, "I am certain my father will wish to write to express his thanks for you coming to my rescue."

"That won't be necessary."

"He will be most adamant in wishing to thank . . . "

"He will have to forgive me," he cut her off. "I don't make a habit of giving out my direction."

She wanted to press him further, but seeing his set expression, decided against it.

Instead, she ran a hand through her disordered blonde curls and repositioned her hat, saying: "What an untidy mess I must look! I am not usually so dishevelled, or so clumsy for that matter – though you would be pardoned for thinking so!"

She began to smooth out the wrinkles in her habit; the devil in her prompting her to draw particular attention to her curves as she did so. But when she raised her lovely dark eyes, hoping to catch a hint of admiration in his gaze, she found him regarding her with such a cynical expression that she was surprised into a laugh.

"Oh, you are no fun at all!" she protested. "Won't you offer me even the tiniest of smiles for my efforts?"

"Ma'am, you appear to have some knowledge of who I am – if your performance is anything to go by," he replied coolly. "But you don't know with whom you are dealing. Not only is any form of forced intimacy repugnant to me, but I have been about the world long enough to recognise your ploy. Content yourself that though neither myself, nor my fortune, will ever be in your possession, neither will they fall into the hands of any other conniving chit."

She had begun to feel regret for having chosen him to importune, but at this derisive speech all that fled.

"My goodness, you have a magnificently inflated opinion of yourself!" she said in quite a different voice, lifting an eyebrow. "But as Aesop demonstrated in his charming little fable about the milkmaid, you must never count your chickens before they are hatched."

He was somewhat taken aback to realise that the woman in front of him was neither as young as he had supposed, nor as provincial.

"I beg your pardon?" he said, eyes narrowing.

Aurora realised he was unused to being challenged and, fool that she was, she found his bemusement rather endearing . . . and, before she could change her mind, she acted on a mad impulse and closed the distance between them.

He watched her with guarded wariness, as if he could not decide if she was a particularly dangerous species of predator or a lap dog.

But he did not back away.

She was a tall woman, but she had to rise on her toes to be able to hover her lips in front of his. Her hand came to rest on his chest, and she felt his body tense under her fingertips.

For an instant she thought he would kiss her.

But it soon became apparent that he chose restraint over instinct. She smiled faintly and, holding his gaze, dared to do what he had not.

Her soft kiss on his immobile lips lasted only a few heartbeats, before she drew back.

Realising his hands had moved of their own volition to pull her back to him, the gentleman clasped them behind his back and offered her his most forbidding expression.

"I couldn't resist the urge to shake your masterful composure," she said with a smile, wholly ignorant of how well she had achieved her aim. "Only don't expect me to beg your pardon! I am not in the least sorry for it."

Picking up the skirt of her riding habit, she pirouetted away from him and walked over to her horse. Using the bank of the verge, she lifted a foot into the stirrup and pulled herself onto the side saddle.

"But never fear, *Sir Vanity*," she said, as she adjusted her blue kidskin gloves and then took the reins into her hands. "You are perfectly safe from me when it comes to marriage! As to your fortune . . . that I'm afraid may suffer a little. I believe the common parlance is *stand and deliver.*"

She drew out a double-barreled pistol she had hidden in the saddle and pointed it at him.

The shock on his face gave her all the satisfaction she could have hoped for, before an angry scowl transformed it into something alive with passion.

"My, my! You are not the cold fish you appear to be after all," she observed.

"If you think I'll hand over my purse, you can think again!" he warned her. "But, by all means, come and try to take it from me . . . if you dare."

"Oh, there's no need for that!" she replied cheerfully, and, retrieving something from the pocket of her skirt, held up his purse. "I was going to leave without alerting you to the fact I had taken it, but I simply couldn't allow your self-important nonsense to go unchallenged! I think the women of your acquaintance have done you a great disservice by allowing you to continue in your deceit. Perhaps next time you meet a woman you will not be so quick to conclude she is only interested in fortune and matrimony."

"You appear to be attached to one of them at least," he retorted.

"I don't count the insignificant amount that can be contained in a purse as anything to draw your censure. Why, by your own reckoning, you are a ripe pigeon for the plucking. And I have a greater need of your few coins than you could possibly imagine. I assure you, nothing but the gravest necessity drove me to orchestrate our interlude . . . though I admit I enjoyed it!"

"You are alone in that sentiment."

"That is only to be expected! I don't blame you for being a little put out."

"*A little* does not begin to do it justice," he snapped. "I give you fair warning, I intend to make you pay for your foolhardiness."

"Oh certainly! I would have it no other way. I did my best to obtain your direction so I could one day return the money to you, but you were most resistant. Would you care to give it to me now?"

"Give my direction to an adventuress! Do you take me for a fool?"

"As you wish," she conceded with a delicate shrug. "Nevertheless, I count this purse as a loan and pledge myself to repay you should our paths cross again . . . and I will even offer you a boon, for the inconvenience you are bound to suffer."

The gentleman made a sudden move towards her; but before he could take more than a couple of steps, a bullet struck the ground near his feet, forcing him to a standstill.

"I beg you don't do anything foolish," she said. "I am a fair shot and though I'll not seriously harm you, you wouldn't like to have a bullet in you for the sake of a few paltry pounds, surely?"

The gentleman glared at her, but did not move.

"Thank you, sir," she said, offering him a sympathetic look. "I knew I could trust you to be sensible. And now, I must beg your pardon for the ill-mannered way in which . . . "

"Don't think I'll spare you because of a pretty apology!" he cut her off.

A teasing smile spread across Aurora's lips. "Well, I'm heartened to know that at least you find my apology pretty – I was starting to question your manliness! And so that we are clear, I am not apologising for borrowing your purse. I am apologising for *this* . . . "

Changing aim, she fired a shot at the ground near the gentleman's horse. The animal, already skittish from the earlier shot, reared in fright and bolted, heading north.

"I can't stand to see an animal suffer," she said. "Be sure to go after him promptly or you will have a long walk ahead of you."

And with a polite inclination of her head, she trotted off in the opposite direction.

Julian de Vere, Seventh Duke of Rothworth, swore roundly as he looked after her.

He had never been more incensed in his life. He had seriously misjudged his thief, thinking her just another of the multitude of women who regularly put themselves in his way, using increasingly imaginative ways to draw his notice.

Damn the shameless hussy! How dared she question his manliness!

And damn those laughing, gypsy eyes of hers. They had made a mockery of the chaste kiss she had stolen, and he had been sorely tempted to show her how to do the thing properly.

Two

"Rory, I can't believe you stole that gentleman's purse at gun point!" said Percy, regarding his sister accusingly over the top of the steak he was sawing into. "You told me you were going to distract him, pick his pocket and be on your way with him being none the wiser!"

They were enjoying an excellent dinner in the comfort of a private dining parlour (purchased with some of the windfall discovered in the gentleman's purse), at one of the busier coaching inns on the road between Cambridge and London.

The inn had been chosen by their groom cum general factotum, John, who had decided in his prosaic way that since Aurora was set on a plan that could see them all hang, they would be less likely to be noticed in a bustling place where the coming and going of coaches never ceased.

"And almost thirty pounds at that!" Percy continued. "God only knows what the punishment would be if they caught us."

"If they caught *me*, dearest," replied Aurora, unperturbed. "You had nothing to do with my plan. And besides, how was I to know the fool would keep such a ridiculous amount in his purse? I was expecting a few coins – five pounds at most! And as for the gun . . . well, if you had heard him, you would understand why I was driven to it! He was sprouting the most conceited rubbish. And called me a *conniving chit* merely for being a woman, or so it seemed to me. So naturally I had to set him straight."

"I wish you had resisted the urge," grumbled her brother.

"You are probably correct," she conceded with a sigh. "I shouldn't have allowed him to provoke me to such a degree . . . I still don't understand my immoderate reaction! But there's no point in repining now. And, on the whole, all went to plan. Actually, I'm rather proud of myself that I still know how to pick pockets – it has been years since John taught me! Do you remember the summer I had chickenpox? I was not allowed to leave my room and John – dear that he is – spent hours every day keeping me amused."

"What I remember is the fuss Mama kicked up when she discovered what he'd been teaching you! Lord, I'd never seen her so mad."

"Yes, she was very cross, wasn't she? A shame, for if she had not banned him from showing me any more of his tricks, who knows what other useful skills I might have learnt."

Aurora was almost unrecognisable as she sat opposite her brother. She had removed the blonde, tightly curled wig she had used as a disguise earlier in the day, and had pinned her unfashionably straight, auburn locks into her customary simple knot at the base of her head.

The elegant pale-blue riding habit had also been packed away and she had put on a short-sleeved muslin dress, once a vibrant lavender that had faded to a more muted shade. Both she and her brother were dressed with sufficient quality and style to proclaim a comfortable station in life, but after the last few years of scrimping and saving, it was becoming difficult to hide the signs of wear on their clothing.

"I suppose there's no way to track him down and give the money back?" Percy asked hopefully, returning to the subject foremost in his mind.

"I would not, even if I could!" exclaimed Aurora. "Really, Percy, you seem to forget we have the solicitor's fees to pay – which will be ongoing – and all our London living expenses. We can't afford to look a gift horse in the mouth . . . especially since Mr Fitzwilliam stole a good portion of the money we had set aside for this trip, and then some petty thief in Cambridge robbed us of the rest! If I hadn't pawned my brooch, we wouldn't even have made it this far."

"George Fitzwilliam didn't steal that money," he said, reddening. "He won it in fair play. I'm only sorry I got swept up in that dashed card game! He and his university friends spend a great deal of their time playing, so I should have known I couldn't win."

"You play fair, which is undoubtedly a handicap in some circles."

"Upon my word, Rory, there's never been any suggestion of anything untoward! The play was fair – I just don't have your skill with cards." He grinned suddenly. "Lord, would I love to smuggle you into one of the gambling dens in Cambridge! You'd show them a thing or two."

"It's really just simple mathematics, and remembering what cards have come before," she replied, thinking nothing of an extraordinary talent she found effortless. "And I would be delighted to join you in a game! Particularly if Mr Fitzwilliam would agree to play against me," she added wryly.

Aurora had come to rue the day that George Fitzwilliam had befriended Percy. Her parents may not have been able to send her brother to study at Cambridge, but that had not stopped him from making friends amongst the students and visiting the nocturnal haunts of the university town. It seemed that men were particularly susceptible to embarking on imprudent friendships after-dark.

Despite Mr Fitzwilliam's noble family connections, she had always thought he had the look of a Captain Sharp about him, and she would have laid odds on him having lured her dear, unsuspecting brother into a confidence game.

At over six feet, Percy had the build of a man, albeit not one fully formed, yet his face – with its soulful eyes, sensitive mouth and fair hair falling artistically over an alabaster brow – was that of an inexperienced boy who still believed the world a place of valour and honour.

She, of course, knew better. But then she had been about the world a good five years longer than him.

Her continued silence made Percy uncomfortable and, thinking she continued to blame him, he said: "I truly am sorry, Rory. I know it's my fault you had to turn to thievery."

"Oh Percy, don't be a sap!" she said with a chuckle. "You know it has nothing to do with you. If Papa and Mama, God rest their souls, had been a little less attached to their books and sailboat, and a little more practical as to the running of a household, I daresay we could have lived quite comfortably until your twenty-first birthday."

"I suppose it never occurred to them they might be taken from us so soon."

"No," she sighed. "They could not have foreseen that." Determined to be cheerful, she added: "But at least they didn't leave us without resources! We had the books to sell."

"You *hated* having to sell off Papa's library," Percy reminded her. "You said you felt as if a piece of your heart was torn off with each sale."

"Gracious, let us not revisit the silly things I may have said in a maudlin mood! There's no point in dwelling in a past that will forever be out of our control. I prefer to focus my mind on the present . . . *that* at least I have a chance of moulding to my liking. And besides, despite our challenges, we have a great deal to be grateful for!"

"You always were incurably optimistic."

"Would you rather I brood over every anxiety and wallow in self-pity?" she asked on a laugh. "It wouldn't make one ounce of difference – apart from sinking us into a fit of the dismals! And we *are* fortunate. Why, you have now reached your majority and can claim your inheritance, and your rightful place in society!"

"We will *both* take our rightful place," he corrected, as always, her determined champion.

"I will, of course, attempt to reconcile myself to the role of sister to the Marquess of Dewbury," she said, smiling playfully.

"You, Lady Aurora, will be a natural in the role," he said, saluting her with his mug of ale. "As for myself, I can't say I'm looking forward to stepping into the late marquess's shoes."

"It's best for your case if we begin to refer to him as our father," she said gently.

Percy had always spoken of their aristocratic sire with a certain detachment, which partly arose from him having no memories of him. Aurora at least had lived for seven years in the Marquess of Dewbury's household and had some memories to guide her; although none were particularly endearing. The marquess had been a spiteful, cold man.

Thankfully, to the benefit of Aurora's and Percy's childhood, their mother's character had not allowed her to submit to his tyranny, and she had fled his house in the middle of the night with her children, never to return.

They had lived hidden away in a seaside village in Norfolk ever since, surviving on the proceeds from the sale of their mother's jewellery, and the devotion of a retired Cambridge don, who had fallen in love with the lovely marchioness, and, despite her continuing (albeit secret) married state, had been happy to claim her and her children as his own.

"Andrew Wesley is the only father I've ever known," said Percy. "It doesn't matter that he and Mama could only pretend to be married for most of my life. If the marquess had only granted her a divorce they wouldn't have had to wait until his death. As it was, they had only a couple of years to enjoy a true marriage in the eyes of God before their boating accident . . . and for that, and a myriad of other injustices he inflicted on her, I'll continue to think of him merely as someone who happened to be present at my conception."

"Must you sully my ears with such allusions?" Aurora protested theatrically. "Ladies do not appreciate plain speaking on delicate subjects, lest we succumb to our nerves."

"I only ever do so with you, Rory."

"Thank you! I'm humbled to know you don't think me enough of a lady to guard your tongue around me."

"Are you teasing me?" he asked, peering at her over the top of his mug.

"Yes, dearest," she said, eyes twinkling.

He laughed. Though he did not always take her meaning, her sharp wits were a source of great pride to him.

He returned to his steak.

After a few minutes, he looked up again and said: "You know, Rory, the Dewbury family may refuse to recognise us. I wouldn't want you to be disappointed if things don't work out how we'd like. Could you be happy to continue as plain Miss Aurora Wesley?"

"Of course, I could!" she said at once, for she knew this weighed on his mind. "Though I reject the notion that I could ever be plain! But you must not worry, dearest. I have Mama's letters and the marquess's ring. Their validity might initially be called into question, but they'll pass whatever scrutiny must be undertaken."

Percy nodded, doing his best to conceal his fears, and they continued with their dinner.

After some minutes, the habitual sounds of a busy coaching-inn suddenly grew louder, heralding the entrance of a new wave of travellers.

Peering out the window, Aurora saw that another stagecoach had arrived and the ostlers were already unhitching the horses and preparing to harness a fresh team. The coach would be off again soon and, with the coachman's warning to be quick or be left behind ringing in their ears, the weary passengers hurried inside to order their refreshments.

Aurora was on the point of looking away from the scene outside, when she caught sight of a young girl peering out of the coach window. Even from a distance she could tell that the child was frightened.

"I'm going to step out for a minute," she told Percy, and hurried out of the parlour.

As she walked out of the inn and approached the coach the face at the window disappeared.

Gently opening the coach door, she peered inside and found a girl approaching womanhood looking back at her from the shadows. Her elfin countenance was uncommonly pale, and was framed by a cluster of brown curls under a pretty bonnet with pink ribbons.

"Please forgive me for accosting you in such a manner," said Aurora with a friendly smile, "but I couldn't help noticing that you had been left behind. Are your parents with you?"

The girl shook her head.

"Surely you are not on your own?"

"No, my guardian is with me," a timid voice replied.

"Ah, I see! And is he bringing you some refreshments, dear?"

The girl shook her head again.

"Well then, perhaps you would consider joining my brother and I and sharing our dinner? I believe you have at least twenty minutes before you need to be off again."

"Oh, that is very kind," said the girl, appearing to decide that Aurora meant her no harm. "I am indeed famished, and have been for hours and hours! But Mr Wilks – my guardian, you know – does not allow me to leave the coach. I am to stay in here until we reach London and not talk to anybody."

"That seems a trifle severe. But since he is not here at present, and you are hungry, we could simply tell him that you had to step out to see to your personal needs, should he ask."

The girl shook her head vigorously. "Oh, no, I couldn't! He would be ever so angry with me . . . and besides," she added, tears gathering in her eyes, "I don't care if I die of hunger, for I'd much rather die than marry a man old enough to be my grandfather – which, no matter what Mr Wilks says, is just what Mr Regan could be, for he is over *forty*."

"Marry!" exclaimed Aurora. "But my dear child, you can't be more than fourteen."

"I will turn sixteen tomorrow and will be married before the day is out! I am an *heiress*," she confided with equal parts loathing and despair.

"I see. I take it you don't have anyone you can trust who could put a stop to this marriage?"

The girl shook her head and tried valiantly not to burst into tears.

Never one to shy away from a thorny problem, a decided look entered Aurora's eyes.

"You must not despair, dear!" she said bracingly. "Despair can only make a difficult situation worse. What we need is a plan! And I believe I have one forming that will suit our purpose. Come with me now, please. I can't leave you here . . . there is no need to look scared, I promise you! You must try to trust me . . . oh, but excuse my shocking manners! How can you trust someone without even knowing their name? I am Miss Aurora Wesley, but my friends call me Aurora." She held out her hand.

"How do you do? I am Phoebe Barton," replied the girl, shaking hands with her.

"What a lovely name! Now come down, Phoebe, and help me to find someone who can assist us with your luggage. You do have some, do you not? Yes? Very well, come along then."

In less than a handful of minutes, Aurora had swept the bewildered Phoebe out of the coach, unloaded her valise with the assistance of a helpful ostler, and ushered her into the private parlour.

Percy looked up at their entrance and regarded them with surprise. Then, remembering his manners, he quickly rose to his feet.

"Percy, may I introduce you to a new friend of mine, Miss Phoebe Barton. Phoebe, this is my brother, Percy Wesley."

Phoebe returned Percy's smile with a shy one of her own.

"Phoebe will be dining with us," said Aurora. "Her guardian appears to be an unfit person and she has been on that horrid stagecoach for hours without any refreshments! If you would see her settled, dearest, I will go and sort out a little matter. I shan't be long! Phoebe, could you describe your guardian's looks and clothing? Don't look so worried, dear! I promise, I have no intention of speaking to him about you."

Phoebe haltingly described Mr Wilks, and with a smile of thanks Aurora left the room.

"Is she always so . . . so *masterful?*" Phoebe asked Percy.

"Yes," he replied with a sigh. "Those of us mere mortals in her vicinity often feel as if we're caught up in the middle of a whirlwind. When she gets one of her ideas into her head there's no stopping her."

*　　*　　*

Aurora hurried up the stairs to her room to retrieve a small vial she had stored in her valise. It had been a gift from an old gypsy woman, who Aurora had saved from the rough attentions of the village louts, and as the gypsy had promised it had proved useful on more than one occasion.

As a precaution, she also donned her blonde wig; and once it was fitted to her satisfaction, she descended the stairs and entered the crowded taproom.

Phoebe's guardian was easy to locate owing to his considerable girth. He was a big man all round, with closely set eyes that gave him a rat-like appearance, and Aurora had no difficulty in understanding why Phoebe was afraid of him.

He was standing beside the fire, drinking his ale and conversing with the stagecoach driver, and his easiness of manner, which belied the fact that he was forcing a child into marriage, grated on Aurora. She detested him on sight and a rare anger added lustre to her eyes as she wove purposefully through the clientele in the busy taproom.

She was almost within reach of Mr Wilks when she stumbled and fell against him, knocking his ale and spilling the contents onto the floor.

"Oh, gracious me!" she cried, all remorse. "Pray, excuse me, dear sir! How clumsy I am!"

19

An ugly look descended over Mr Wilks's florid features as he turned to glare at her. "Of all the stupid, blundering . . . "

"Oh, no, you must not blame yourself!" she insisted.

"What? No! It's nothing of the . . . "

"It's nothing? Oh, you are too kind! Too charitable! But you must not tell me it's of no consequence."

"That's not what I . . . "

"Not another word in my defence, I beg you! I am shockingly to blame. As penance you must allow me to buy you another ale. And one for your friend as well, perhaps?"

She smiled at the stagecoach driver, who grinned and nodded in appreciation of her offer; and when Mr Wilks once more attempted to speak, she ruthlessly cut him off.

"No!" she said, holding up a hand. "I am determined to make recompense, kind sir! I must insist. Stay where you are, and I shall be back within the instant."

And before the bemused Mr Wilks could react, she had disappeared into the crowd.

Shortly after, she returned carrying two mugs and handed one to her victim and one to his companion, and after offering them a rambling apology that would lead any sane man to want to see the back of her, she whisked herself out of the room.

* * *

Upon re-entering the private parlour, she found that her brother had settled Phoebe at the table and piled her plate high with food from the dishes laid out for them; and the girl was consuming her meal with a gusto that led one to suppose she had not been fed for days.

"Now, we can be comfortable!" said Aurora as she took her seat.

Phoebe's blue eyes widened as they fixed on her, and her mouth fell open in astonishment.

Aurora realised she had forgotten to remove her wig. Quickly taking it off, she hid it behind her.

"A little game of mine," she said, winking at Phoebe. "I have always fancied myself something of an actress. Will you mind terribly sharing a room with me tonight, dear?"

"Oh, b-but I'm certain Mr Wilks will not allow me to stay with you, Miss Aurora," stammered Phoebe.

"Just Aurora will do," said Aurora with a smile. "And I believe you will soon discover that Mr Wilks is in no position to comment on the matter! He looks to have downed several ales already and was not at all steady on his feet when I saw him just now. I wouldn't be at all surprised if he decides to spend the night here."

"Mr Wilks is *drunk*?" exclaimed Phoebe. "But I have never seen him so before! Why, at home he regularly has a bottle of wine with dinner and is not even a *little* unsteady afterwards."

"Perhaps the journey has made him overly tired. I don't understand why he chose to exhaust himself – and you! – with an uncomfortable ride on a stagecoach, when he obviously has enough money at his disposal to hire a travelling chaise."

"He enjoys frugal habits," Phoebe explained helpfully. "Even at home in Wittering. He wouldn't even buy me a carriage to replace the one that was damaged in the carriage-house fire last year. If you can believe it, I've been driven around for months in nothing better than the old gig the servants use when going into Peterborough for their shopping."

"That is certainly very bad," agreed Aurora, containing her smile. "It gives me a very poor opinion of his character."

"Well, he deserves it!" said Phoebe with sudden pugnaciousness. "It's one thing to *want* to have frugal habits yourself, and quite another to inflict them on others. Why, I even suspect he has not paid my governess, dear Miss Winston, her salary for months and months! If she were not so much attached to me, she would have left by now."

Aurora thought this could well have been Mr Wilks's intent. It would be far easier to marry Phoebe off without her governess's interference.

"Do you reside with Mr Wilks, dear?" she asked.

"Yes . . . although I suppose it's more correct to say that he resides with me, for it's *my* house. After Papa died, I was the only one left to inherit his property and fortune. Mama died a long time ago. Papa used to say, she was so good and lovely the angels wanted her to return home to them."

"What a charming sentiment!"

"It is, isn't it? Although I suspect he only said it to make me smile."

"Is Mr Wilks your only guardian?" asked Aurora. "Are there no relatives who can champion you?"

A questioning gleam came into Percy's eyes. Knowing no part of the story Phoebe had shared with his sister, he was surprised to learn the girl needed championing.

Aurora shook her head at him, signalling for him to hold his questions.

"I don't think I have any relatives," replied Phoebe. "At least none that are still alive . . . oh, apart from my Uncle Phineas, of course – Mama's brother. He's also my guardian, but he lives all the way in Boston, which is why Papa thought it best to have Mr Wilks take care of my day-to-day needs. But he has proven himself to be a very shocking person! It's certainly *not* in my best interest to be married before I've even had my coming out, or had a chance to enjoy some dress-parties and balls. And, now I think of it, I should have allowed myself to starve and fall into a decline from which I'd never recover, for *then* he would be sorry!"

"Yes, I quite see your point," said Aurora gravely. "And it would serve him right too! But then your fortune could well end up in Mr Wilks's hands, and imagine how vexed you would be then? So, all things considered, I think it a much better idea for you to remain healthy and make your guardian sorry in some other way."

"I had not considered that," said Phoebe, looking impressed with Aurora's reasoning.

The noise coming from the taproom next door suddenly increased in volume and, a moment later, a loud crash was heard.

"I wonder what that could have been?" said Percy.

"I believe Mr Wilks's inebriation has caught up with him," Aurora replied in a calm manner, finishing off the last of her wine. "I expect he won't rise now for a good sixteen hours or so. But just to be safe we should leave early tomorrow! If you have finished your dinner, Phoebe, let us retire for the evening and get some rest."

"But what should I do about Mr Wilks?" Phoebe asked anxiously.

"You may leave him a note, dear. Tell him you have decided to visit a friend in Scotland and won't be accompanying him to London."

"But I don't have a friend in Scotland," said Phoebe, bewildered.

"Just as well!" replied Aurora. "We wouldn't want him importuning an acquaintance of yours."

"Are we to *lie*, Miss Aurora?"

"I believe some creative licence is allowed in situations such as these. Percy, would you ask John to speak to the carriage driver so that we can be ready to leave at first light? That man drives so ponderously it will be a miracle if we reach London by nightfall! It was perhaps a mistake to hire him," she mused. "But I couldn't accept the vicar and Mrs Stanton's kind offer to lend us their carriage, so there was nothing for it."

"But, Rory, surely we can't remove Miss Barton from the care of her guardian without so much as a by your leave?" said her brother, concerned by this breach of etiquette.

"Do you expect me to ask the blackguard for his permission? I don't imagine his frugal inclinations would survive any scrutiny into his scheming, and before we knew it, he would have splashed out on the hire of a chaise and whisked Phoebe away. No! For now, we have the element of surprise, and I intend to make good use of it. Come, Phoebe!"

Phoebe rose from the table, and with an apologetic smile at Percy, followed her benefactress out of the room.

Three

They reached London by mid-afternoon the following day and made their way to a small but elegant hotel in Kensington, recommended to Aurora by her vicar, who had had occasion to stay there.

Aurora had written ahead to engage rooms, and while John saw to the unloading of their luggage and Percy paid the driver, she linked her arm through Phoebe's and they entered the hotel through the glazed double-doors, held open for them by the porter.

The hotel manager was most accommodating on hearing that Aurora's young "cousin" was to be included in the Wesley party, and promised to have a trundle bed made up for her in Aurora's room; and, once Percy and John had joined them in the lobby, he escorted the whole party to the top floor (the vicar having advised that this elevated position was best for catching the breeze on a warm night).

When the manager had left them with the promise that their luggage would shortly be carried up, and Percy and John had gone off to their own room down the hall, Phoebe untied the ribbons of her pretty straw bonnet and, throwing it onto a chair, skipped over to the windows.

"Oh, what a charming outlook!" she cried, peering out over the rooftops towards Hyde Park. "May we go for a walk and explore the area, Miss Aurora? I have never before been to London."

Aurora had given up correcting Phoebe's insistence on calling her *Miss Aurora*, for she had realised with some amusement that the girl viewed her as a much older person and deserving of a deferential sobriquet.

Although she did point out: "I think perhaps *Cousin Aurora* will be more appropriate now, dear."

"Oh, yes! Of course!" replied Phoebe with a giggle. "I have never had a cousin, but already I like it excessively."

Aurora laughed. "I'm pleased to know! And, yes, we shall certainly go for a walk a little later. I have been reliably informed that it's a rare treat to watch the grand and fashionable promenade in Hyde Park between the hours of five and six o'clock. But first, I have letters to write! And you do too, dear. You had better compose a short letter to your governess, who, from all you have told me, must be anxious to hear from you."

"Yes, she *desperately* wanted to come with us, but Mr Wilks wouldn't allow it. Should I mention that I am with you in London?"

"No, it's best not to give too much away and place her in an uncomfortable position with your guardian. You may simply tell her that you have taken the opportunity to visit a friend, and that you don't intend to return home until the threat of marriage is removed. You may also mention that your uncle in Boston will be apprised of the situation. It shouldn't take you long to write it, and then make yourself comfortable and read a book while I finish my own letters."

"But I don't have any books, Cousin Aurora."

"Did you not pack any in your valise?"

"No . . . I mean, I don't own any at all."

Aurora regarded her with surprise.

Having lived with parents who had regularly travelled to Cambridge (an easy two-hour drive from their village) to purchase books, and had filled the house with them until they had become an integral part of the décor of every room, Aurora could not imagine a home without them.

"In that case, our first order of business for tomorrow will be to visit a bookstore!" promised Aurora. "It will be my present to you for your birthday . . . oh, but wait! Percy and I have a meeting with our solicitor at ten o'clock. It will have to be afterwards. For now, you may borrow one of my novels."

"If it's all the same to you, Cousin Aurora, I'd much rather unpack my dresses and get the creases out of them. Mr Wilks wouldn't allow me to bring my maid, for he said neither a maid nor governess would be necessary where we were going. But it just goes to show, doesn't it, that one should always be prepared, for *anything* can happen. And now we are to go amongst the fashionable set, and I simply can't look like a dowd!"

"I completely understand," said Aurora, doing her best to keep a straight face. "The delights of reading can't be expected to compensate for a lack in one's wardrobe."

"No, certainly not!" Phoebe agreed wholeheartedly. "And if you like," she added shyly, "I could also hang up *your* dresses . . . if you mean to change, that is?"

She cast a critical eye over Aurora's muslin dress, which was looking decidedly worse for wear after a day of travelling.

Correctly interpreting this to mean that she too was expected to look her best for their expedition amongst the fashionable set, Aurora graciously acquiesced to have her clothing unpacked. Then, seating herself at a small, well-stocked desk in the corner of the room, she spent the next hour writing her letters.

The first one was little more than a note, to inform her and her brother's solicitor that they had arrived in London and would keep their appointment with him in the morning.

The second letter was a good deal longer and was addressed to the wife of their vicar, Mrs Stanton; a woman who had not only proven herself to be a good friend to the Wesleys over the years, but since the death of Aurora's parents, had also taken on the role of maternal confident.

Aurora wrote to reassure Mrs Stanton that they had arrived safely, and then regaled her with a few anecdotes from the trip that she knew would amuse her; including a euphemistic mention of a "run-in" with a conceited gentleman who had accused her of being after his hand and fortune; and a recounting, in broad strokes, of how she had come to the aid of a young lady in something of a fix.

Her last letter Aurora addressed to Phoebe's uncle, Mr Phineas Carter. She recounted as succinctly as possible the chain of events Mr Wilks's actions had precipitated and her part in them, and adjured him to come to London with all haste and take control of a situation that had all the makings of a gothic tragedy. Her tone was polite but forceful, and would leave the recipient of the letter in no doubt that she expected him to act with all due haste on his niece's behalf.

She did not have an address to add to the letter, Phoebe being uninformed on the subject, but Aurora felt confident her solicitor would be able to send it care of the office of the *Envoy Extraordinary and Minister-Plenipotentiary to the United States,* in Washington, and someone there would know how to find Mr Carter, who from what Phoebe had told her had many business interests in both Boston and Washington.

"There! I have finished my letters," she said at last, rising. "Shall we brave the judgement of our betters and go on our walk to Hyde Park? Oh, Phoebe . . . how lovely you look in that dress! But is it not too fine for a mere outing to a park?" she asked, studying the lovely primrose sprig-muslin dress with a blue velvet sash, and matching spencer.

Clearly Mr Wilks did not scrimp when it came to Phoebe's wardrobe.

"Oh, no!" replied Phoebe with the certainty of someone who had dedicated some time to studying this particular subject. "Miss Winston used to be the governess in an earl's household before she came to live with me, and knows a great deal about London Society – it's why she was chosen to prepare me for my coming out! – and she always says one can't dress too fine when one is taking part in the Season."

Aurora realised the magnificence of her young friend's wardrobe could be better attributed to the influence of Miss Winston, and not to any benevolent leanings on Mr Wilks's part.

"But, dear, don't forget that we do not want to make *too* memorable an impression. We wouldn't want your guardian to discover your whereabouts."

Phoebe's face fell.

But she brightened almost instantly and said: "The note we left for him will send him off to Scotland, and I should think we would have at least a week or two before he discovers that I don't in fact have a friend by the name of Miss Langton living in Edinburgh."

"You have a point, but let us not become too complacent. Tomorrow I will give my solicitor the letter I wrote to your uncle and ask him to see that it reaches Mr Carter. But even allowing for no delays, it will be at least six weeks before we can expect him to arrive in England. And until that time, you will need to remain vigilant . . . but enough sermons!" Aurora went on with a smile. "I do so dislike it when others harp on about peril and caution. I hope you'll inform me if I should sink into such melancholy behaviour?"

Phoebe vehemently denied that Aurora could ever be accused of such conduct, and then proceeded to show her the outfit that she had chosen for her to wear on their outing.

Aurora had been thinking to save her best day-dress of ivory muslin with a leaf design in green silk, and matching green velvet bonnet, for a more auspicious occasion. But as her young friend seemed to have her heart set on them looking their best, her only comment was in praise of Phoebe's efforts in removing the creases.

When Aurora was dressed and they had both put on their hats and gloves, they stopped off at Percy's room to enquire if he wanted to join them.

Looking a little self-conscious, he declined the pleasure of escorting them, saying he was planning on calling on a friend.

When Aurora inquired mildly as to who that might be, he coloured faintly.

"If you must know, Rory, I'm going to see George Fitzwilliam. He's in London for a few weeks. I know you don't like him, but if you only got to know him better, I'm certain you'd warm to him!"

"My goodness, I must be a most disobliging sister if you feel the need to explain yourself to me in such a way," she said teasingly. "You are your own man and are at liberty to choose with whom you spend your time. And besides, I don't dislike Mr Fitzwilliam! He appears to be an intelligent, well-bred young man. And though I can't help but wish he would keep his excessive gambling habits to himself, rather than attempt to foist them on his friends, I don't hold it against him overly much."

"Then, you won't mind if I spend time with him while we're in London?" asked Percy, latching on to the part of her speech that most suited his fancy.

"I would never ask you to refrain from seeing him, even if I were so inclined."

Percy happily took this as approval; and after they had agreed to meet in the hotel dining room for dinner, to celebrate the occasion of Phoebe's sixteenth birthday, the ladies took themselves off.

Once they were out on the street, Phoebe observed: "It does seem a shame that Percy should have befriended someone you so dislike. Are you greatly vexed with him?"

Aurora regarded her sharply, and smiled. "But I went to great pains to point out that I do *not* dislike Mr Fitzwilliam."

"Oh, I know, but . . . well, perhaps I'm wrong, but it seemed to me that you don't like him in the least!"

"If you must be so observant, dear, pray don't allow the men of your acquaintance to suspect the truth! Most men are simple creatures and can be handled easily enough, particularly if they believe themselves superior to us."

"But surely not Percy!" insisted Phoebe.

"No, not him. Percy is one of those rare men who give credit where credit is due . . . he is, in fact, rather liberal with his credit! And though I may prefer him to be a little less trusting and determined to think well of everyone, those very qualities speak of an admirable goodness in him that few can match."

They walked on in a companionable silence, following the route suggested to them by the concierge that would take them past several sites of interest.

They did not enter Hyde Park through the gate nearest to Kensington but proceeded along the road towards Hyde Park Corner. Here they stopped outside Apsley House, which all knew was the new town residence of England's hero, the Duke of Wellington, and when they had sufficiently admired the neoclassical façade and ongoing construction works, they entered the Park through the gates adjacent to the house.

It was a fine April evening and there were many people about taking advantage of the warm weather. Phoebe's excitement was palpable as they set off down a promenade populated with all manner of persons in their finery.

"Oh, Cousin Aurora, look! That lady's hat has so many peacock feathers! Can you believe it? And that one over there is wearing the most *ravishing* shawl . . . I wonder if it's from Norwich or Paisley. Or perhaps it has come all the way from Kashmir! Uncle Phineas sent me my very own Kashmir shawl last year, but I didn't think to bring it! Did you know that Kashmir shawls are made from the hair of goats?"

"No. I am completely ignorant on the subject," replied Aurora apologetically, smiling at her charge's enthusiasm.

"Well, they are! And it's *that* that makes them so wonderfully light and warm. Whereas the replicas produced here and in Scotland are made from wool and silk."

"You are very knowledgeable on these matters!"

"Papa would often allow me to spend the day with him when he went to work. He used to trade in cloth from all over the world, before he set up his manufacturies and started to produce his own. His company became quite famous for it!"

Aurora came to a sudden standstill.

"Phoebe, please tell me you don't mean the Barton Textiles Company?"

"Have I said something wrong, Cousin Aurora? Should I not speak of Papa's company?"

"Oh, dear Lord!"

"D-does that change matters?" Phoebe asked worriedly.

Aurora did not reply for she was busy attempting to determine the increased perils of their situation. Convincing a young girl to run away from her guardian had its own legal consequences, the risk of which she had accepted willingly. However, if that girl happened to be the heiress to the largest textile manufacturing company in the country, the ramifications were amplified beyond measure.

Bringing Phoebe's anxious face back into focus, Aurora realised that even if she had known the truth beforehand, she still would have helped the girl to run away.

"Don't look so troubled, dear!" she said, offering her a reassuring smile. "I was a little surprised, that is all. Nothing has changed . . . only we will have to make certain to be *most* diligent in concealing your identity. You must promise me to never forget that you are now Miss Phoebe *Lennox*, a distant cousin of mine."

"I promise, Cousin Aurora!"

"Good girl. Now, let us enjoy ourselves, for you have gone to a great deal of effort to make us both look so very fine." And linking arms again, they continued down the crowded path.

Four

Julian De Vere, the Duke of Rothworth, was sitting beside his aunt in the ostentatious landau carriage she favoured for her daily outing in Hyde Park, and was allowing her to remind him of his responsibility to the Family.

She was a tall, robust woman in her fiftieth year, who had never married, with a generous bosom, ramrod-straight posture and no-nonsense manner. Her steel-grey hair was habitually pinned back so that it moulded tightly to her head and did nothing to soften the planes of her boldly sculpted face; and her liberal use of the hare's foot and powder, a leftover from her younger days, ensured her skin always had an unhealthy pallor to it.

Though her looks had never been thought beautiful, she had grown into them with age and was now considered a handsome woman; an impression that was further cemented by her unerring eye for style, which she indulged to the fullest with the generous allowance provided by her brother. Today she was wearing a new twilled silk redingote of such elegance that several acquaintances had already stopped beside her open carriage to express their admiration; including her nephew, who had been walking home from his club when her landau had driven past.

Quick to turn the opportunity to good account, she had requested his presence, and as he was punctilious in all dealings with his family he had submitted to her persuasion, with only a mild comment that he had an engagement and could only spare half an hour.

Taking this limit to heart, his aunt had immediately launched into what he supposed to be her favourite past-time: lecturing him.

"And furthermore, Rothworth," she now went on, fixing him with a disapproving stare, "I will not conceal from you that I have been shocked and saddened to learn that your dalliance with that actress may not be over. You are almost two and thirty years of age! You must begin to act like it. I thought we determined that all such distractions were at an end, and you would now direct your energy to finding yourself a wife?"

"Aunt Pearl, you do me too great an honour in claiming my involvement in a proposal purely of your own design," he replied composedly. "I believe you presented your arguments to me, and I refrained from contradicting you – much in the same way as I do now."

She continued to glare at him, but a glimmer of a smile entered her eyes.

"Don't think to charm me, you rogue!"

Her nephew was somewhat surprised by this allegation. He had been called *aloof, unfeeling* and, just the other day, *a cold fish,* but he had never been accused of being a rogue . . . let alone a charming one.

The Duke of Rothworth did not indulge in aberrant behaviour. He was a man known for his unshakeable composure, iron-willed discipline and high principles; a reputation that had benefited him greatly in his political career.

"I see I have surprised you," said his aunt, smiling smugly. "I am not blind to your admirable qualities, no matter what you may think."

"I do not consider being a rogue as deserving of admiration," he replied a little stiffly.

"That is your father speaking. I can almost hear him from the grave! A more pompous lobcock there never lived. I still lament that he had the rearing of you and can only be thankful he sent you to Eton before the damage became irreparable. I half suspect my sister died of boredom rather than face another moment . . . ahem . . . the point I wish to make is that your mother had natural charm and wit, and you too possess those qualities, if you would only allow them to see the light of day."

She turned from him to nod at a passing acquaintance, as she continued: "And a little spontaneity would not go astray either! Few women like to be wooed with the cold resolution of a military campaign . . . I say this to you since it appears to me you do not know how to woo a bride who will suit you."

"Without wishing to sound conceited, I don't envisage having any difficulty in finding a wife. The problem has always been the opposite – a surfeit of applicants."

As at that moment an open carriage carrying two young ladies and their mother drew up beside the landau, so that all three could try their charm on Rothworth, his point was proven for him.

After exchanging a few polite words with them, he told the coachman to drive on.

His aunt, undeterred, continued their conversation.

"You *are* being conceited. Though I am the first to acknowledge you have cause . . . was there ever a sillier woman than Lady Lutton? Does she mean to entice you to her ball with those sour-faced daughters of hers or scare you away?" After some moments of ruminating over the folly of some people, his aunt remembered her point and, placing a hand on Rothworth's arm, said: "I know my advice to you is unpalatable – I'm not such a nincompoop that I don't know that! – but I am thinking of your happiness. Can you be content with a girl who will never truly understand you, let alone love you? For how could she be expected to, when you shy away from intimacy and reveal nothing of yourself? A title and a handsome countenance are not enough to make a happy marriage."

"My expectations of marriage appear to be more modest than your own," he said, smiling lightly. "I don't hope for love, in any case."

Somewhat embarrassed at having allowed herself to become sentimental, his aunt removed her hand from his sleeve and fussed over opening her parasol.

Realising he had managed to silence her for the time being, Rothworth gladly accepted the reprieve and turned his attention to greeting the numerous acquaintances who hailed him.

Presently, while his aunt was talking to one of her friends whose carriage had pulled up beside them, Rothworth caught sight of a gentleman on foot who was well known to him, and, excusing himself for a few minutes, jumped down from the landau.

"Rupert! I didn't know you were in town! When did you arrive?" he asked, walking over with a smile of genuine pleasure.

"It's good to see you, Julian!" exclaimed Captain Rupert Torrington and took his friend's hand in a firm grip. "I arrived two days ago. My mother and sister requested my escort for the Season, and I could think of no excuse to deny them, now that I'm on furlough."

Captain Torrington was a man of above average height and looks, and was further blessed with a cheerful disposition that endeared him to whatever company he found himself in. His property in Surrey adjoined the Duke of Rothworth's and they had often run wild together as children, and when the time had come had both been sent to Eton.

"Your father does not join you?" asked Rothworth.

"No. He had a good excuse in the sudden flare up of his gout," replied Captain Torrington, laughing. "A most convenient disease for when one doesn't want to do something – I must try to acquire it! But why are you in town? When I called at your house yesterday, your butler informed me you had left to visit a friend in Lincolnshire?"

"That was my intention, but I was held up on my way north . . . and I mean that literally. At gun point, if you can believe it! I had to return to London for funds, but I hope to set out again tomorrow."

"Held up? How monstrous! Did you get a close look at the villain?"

Rothworth smiled with wry humour. "Very close. I'll tell you the whole of it tonight, if you're not engaged? Aimsley is coming to dine with me, and Helston promised to join us if he could find a way to escape his duty to the Prime Minister. You know, he is now a secretary to the great man?"

"I had heard! Yes, I shall certainly come tonight and hear more . . . ah, your aunt is looking our way. I must go and pay my respects."

"Yes, you must. Perhaps she can lecture you on some perceived inadequacy and allow me some respite."

"You underestimate me, Julian. Your aunt never lectures me. I'm a firm favourite of hers, for, unlike yourself, I am neither reserved nor unsociable, and I know how to smile!"

They walked back to the landau and Captain Torrington greeted the formidable spinster in his most charming manner, and accepted the gloved hand she extended down to him to kiss.

"Torrington, good to see you. How goes your mother? Well, I hope? And your father?"

He assured her both were well.

"I am happy to see you in town," she said. "Your character has always had a beneficial enlivening effect on Rothworth, and he will need whatever assistance you can offer him in finding himself a suitable wife."

Captain Torrington turned to look at his friend in surprise. "A wife? I had no idea you had decided the time had come?"

"I have decided nothing of the sort," Rothworth replied equably. "No matter how often the wishes of others find expression, I will consider no wish but my own on this particular subject."

"Such inflexible stubbornness!" complained his aunt. "When my sincerest wish is for his happiness and the continuation of his name."

"I give due deference to the sincerity of your wishes, Aunt Pearl, but I can't be . . . expected . . . " He petered out, his gaze on something in the distance. "No . . . it damn well couldn't be," he muttered.

His expression became so arrested that his aunt turned to look behind her.

"What is it?" she asked. "Have the cows got out of their enclosure again?"

"My God, it's that damned gypsy!" Rothworth uttered savagely; and with no further explanation rushed off down the path beside the carriageway.

"Rothworth . . . Rothworth!" his aunt called after him, shocked by such uncharacteristic conduct. Realising she was to receive no answer, she threw up her hands in exasperation and turned to Captain Torrington. "Whatever is the matter with him?"

"I have no idea, ma'am," he replied in a bemused way as he watched his friend weave through the crowds. "I believe he said something about a gypsy."

"Gypsy? Why would he go chasing after a gypsy? And in such a hurly-burly manner!"

*   *   *

Rothworth fixed his gaze on the receding green bonnet and quickened his pace.

The bonnet concealed the lady's hair and a good portion of her face, but there had been a brief moment when she had looked in his direction and a spark of recognition (and something else) had coursed through him.

It had been little more than twenty-four hours since he had last seen her riding away, and as the memory of her had intruded on his thoughts (most infuriatingly!) for a good portion of that time, he knew he could not be mistaken.

He was slowly gaining on her, and her companion, until she was a mere fifty feet away from him, crossing a junction. But then a carriage pulled up between them and blocked her from his view. He ran around it, only to find his way barred by another three carriages coming the other way. By the time he had waited for them to pass and then crossed the road, he could no longer see her.

He spent the next hour searching down various paths, oblivious to the eager greetings from several ladies of his acquaintance, and to the surprised looks that followed his unintentional snubs; the Duke of Rothworth might be reserved in his demeanour, but he was always well-mannered.

When at last it became evident that he was embarked on a useless endeavour, he admitted defeat. And, in no fine mood, he headed in the direction of his townhouse, having determined that nothing would induce him to leave London until he had caught his thief.

Five

A little after midday the following day, Aurora and Percy returned to the hotel after their appointment with their solicitor. It had proved to be a positive encounter on the whole, but as with most such legal meetings very little was settled in the room and a great deal still remained to be determined.

Mr Tadley, senior partner at the firm Tadley, Johnston & Roy, had been their mother's solicitor for many years, and their sole line of communication with the Dewbury family.

Once a year the marchioness had written to apprise the Family of the continued health of both the marquess's children and had relied on Mr Tadley to pass on the correspondence. Fearing her husband would take her children from her, should he ever discover their whereabouts, she had insisted that even her lawyer could not know where to find her and had communicated with him through her old nurse, who could be trusted to keep her secret.

Over the years Mr Tadley had proved himself to be a discreet and capable gentleman, and just as he had faithfully served the marchioness, he was now determined to do his best by her son and daughter. He had been pleased to read the correspondence Aurora had handed over to him from her mother, and believed all was in order to prove Percy's claim to the title.

Their next step, as he had explained, was for him to notify the Dewbury family solicitor that the heir to the late marquess had come forward, and to make his case accordingly.

"Was your meeting successful?" asked Phoebe, as soon as Aurora and Percy walked into the hotel room.

"Most promising!" replied Aurora.

"But it could take many months to sort out the inheritance," Percy added, flinging himself into a chair, "particularly if my claim is challenged."

"Oh, don't put too much store by that!' said Aurora. "He must inform us of all scenarios, however, he also said it could take as little as a month. In any case, we can't continue at this hotel for such a period of time – we must find rooms! And thanks to Mr Tadley's foresight, we need only choose from the properties on the list he kindly provided. But that can wait for another day! I have promised to take Phoebe to a bookstore today, and then I thought we might go to Bond Street – would you like that, Phoebe? Mrs Stanton – our vicar's wife and a dear friend – has assured me that no better shops can be found in the whole of England!"

"Oh, could we, Cousin Aurora?" cried Phoebe. "I'd love it above all things!"

"Then it's settled! Care to join us, Percy?"

He agreed to escort them to their first destination, before going off on his own explorations, and the three of them were soon catching a hackney coach to Bond Street.

They alighted at the southern end of the street and walked along enjoying the sights, until they came upon a bookstore. Here, Percy tipped his hat and bowed to them in farewell; a rather dashing, formal gesture that made Phoebe giggle and brought a smile to his sister's eyes.

"You are well on your way to becoming a London smart!" Aurora teased.

He grinned and walked off, whistling to himself.

Aurora suffered a small pang that he might be off to meet Mr Fitzwilliam again. But being a practical woman, she decided there was little point in worrying. More importantly, they had no more money left to lose, and Percy was so mortified about his one lapse of judgement that she was certain he would never again rely on IOUs to purchase his entertainment.

They entered the bookstore, and as soon as the door closed behind them the noise and bustle of the street was muted, and it felt as if they had been transported to a place of spiritual tranquillity.

It was a beautiful old shop and Aurora promptly fell in love. It was not particularly large, but the high, arched ceiling gave the space an airy, monastic feel, and allowed room for the tall bookshelves that stood like sentries down the centre and on three sides of the perimeter. They were made from oak that had mellowed with age and seemed to glow from within, adding a warmth and vibrancy to the pale light filtering in from outside. As for the books themselves, both new and old, the sight and smell of them gave her an instant feeling of coming home.

They appeared to be the only clients at present, and while they lingered near the entrance a pleasant looking man of fifty or so years walked over to them. He was holding a slim, leather-bound book that he transferred to one hand, before adjusting his spectacles down his nose to regard them with kindly eyes over the top of the silver rims.

"You look to be in need of some assistance, ladies. Is this perhaps your first time in here?" he asked in a soft, cultured voice.

"Yes, it is," replied Aurora, smiling warmly. "And yet I already know this shop is destined to become one of my favourite places in London!"

The man smiled and removed his spectacles.

"I was just the same when I first entered. This has become my oasis when I am in town," he said, gesturing about him with his spectacles. "Would you like me to recommend something to you, or do you have a book in mind?"

"Phoebe, would you prefer a novel or something more serious?" asked Aurora.

"Oh, a novel please. My governess wouldn't allow me to read anything of that nature from the lending library, and Papa's books are on the *dullest* subjects you can possibly imagine."

"Then a novel it will be! Would you direct us to the novels, Mr . . . ?"

"Mr Brinkley, at your service, ma'am."

"A pleasure to make your acquaintance, Mr Brinkley. I am Aurora Wesley, and this is my cousin, Miss Lennox."

"Delighted, ladies," he said, bowing to them in turn. "If you would follow me, I believe I remember where the novels are to be found."

He led them to a bookshelf in the far corner of the room, assured them they need only ask for his assistance should they need it, and then went to sit in one of the comfortable chairs spaced around the room to continue reading the book in his hands.

Aurora told Phoebe she could take as long as she pleased to choose her novel, and then set off on her own exploration of the shop.

After some minutes of wandering about and picking up books to leaf through them, she passed behind Mr Brinkley's chair.

"Forgive me for looking over your shoulder, sir, but is that Gauss's *Disquisitiones Arithmeticae*?" she asked.

Mr Brinkley turned to regard her with a surprised expression. "Indeed, it is, Miss Wesley. Have you perhaps studied Herr Gauss?"

"I have only read parts of the text you hold, to do with quadratic reciprocity. My father was interested in Gauss's proofs and we read them together. But that was some years ago."

"Won't you take a seat?" said Mr Brinkley eagerly. "I'd be delighted to discuss my thoughts with you . . . that is, if you would care for it, of course. I wouldn't wish to presume."

Aurora happily acquiesced and, after taking the chair beside his, they launched into a mutually pleasurable discussion that raised them both in each other's esteem.

Some half an hour later, in the midst of Aurora explaining her opinion that the reciprocity law had already been independently stated by Euler and Legendre, a bell chime heralded the opening of the front door and a small, balding man hurried in.

"Mr Brinkley, I thank you!" said the man, catching sight of them. "It was kind of you to offer to look after my shop, sir. I hope I didn't detain you from your business for too long?"

"Nothing of the sort, Mr Trill, never fear," replied Mr Brinkley. "My companion has kept me most charmingly entertained." He gave Aurora a twinkling look, then asked the bookstore owner: "And how is your good wife? I hope all is well at home?"

Mr Trill replied that it had been nothing more than an overreaction on Mrs Trill's part, which had precipitated the hurried note she had sent him insisting on his presence, and it had not taken him long to sort out the domestic emergency.

When Mr Trill had taken himself off behind the counter to go about his business, Aurora exclaimed: "I feel deceived, Mr Brinkley! You must know that I thought you worked here. May I ask, if not a bookstore owner, with whom have I had the pleasure to converse for the past half-hour?"

"No one of import," he replied diffidently. "Only a gentleman-scholar with few pretensions to learning."

"Now *that* I find very difficult to believe! No one with few pretensions to learning could have so eloquently described Gauss's reasoning. My own papa – who was a fellow of Cambridge and taught mathematics, no less! – couldn't offer me so lucid an explanation."

"But I can see from your powerful grasp of *Disquisitiones Arithmeticae*, Miss Wesley, that he is a most proficient teacher."

"He was," she corrected with a wistful smile.

Mr Brinkley nodded in understanding, his kind eyes offering her sympathy.

"Forgive me," Mr Trill interrupted from behind the counter. "I couldn't help overhearing! Miss Wesley, are you by chance speaking of the late Mr Jonathan Wesley, the book collector?"

"Why, yes," she replied, taken aback. "Papa did own an extensive library. Although it has now been mostly sold off."

"Yes, I know!" said Mr Trill excitedly. "I myself purchased several of his books at auction last year. If you will allow me to say, ma'am, your father was a gentleman of discerning taste."

"Thank you. Although, my mother too had a hand in cultivating the collection. It was a passion they shared."

"Would it be presumptuous of me to ask – and I sincerely beg pardon if I overstep!" said Mr Trill. "But do you know if your mother would consider selling any more of his books?"

"Had she been alive she would not have sold a single one," replied Aurora. "You must count yourself fortunate, sir, to have at least some in your possession. There are none left worth your while."

Mr Trill looked as if he wished to say more, but a discreet shake of the head from Mr Brinkley had him offering his apologies and scuttling off to a back room.

"I hope you will forgive Mr Trill his enthusiasm," said Mr Brinkley.

"Of course!" replied Aurora. "I'm happy to know Papa's books are being enjoyed by others, rather than gathering dust at home."

Phoebe, coming over to them just then, said excitedly: "I have found a novel by the name of *Evelina*! It appears to be most interesting, but did I choose correctly?"

"There is no right or wrong choice," replied Aurora, laughing. "Only thoughts of what will give you pleasure should weigh with you, dear."

"Will you be buying a book, Cousin Aurora?"

"Not this time," she replied. Her particular brand of scruples would not allow her to dip into the proceeds from the unorthodox loan she had acquired simply for her own enjoyment. "But I'm certain I will return before long. Mr Brinkley, it has been a delight! I trust we will meet again?"

"Nothing would give me greater pleasure," he said. "In fact, I hope you will visit me at my home. I live not far from here . . . with my sisters," he thought to add, "so you must not think I invite you to a bachelor's residence."

Aurora conveyed her pleasure at the scheme, and gave him her direction so he could send a note to the hotel with the particulars. And, after paying for the novel, she and Phoebe quit the bookstore.

They spent the next several hours pleasurably engaged in investigating the shops in and around Bond Street. It was another fine day, and the area was bustling with activity. Footpaths were crowded with pedestrians, as well as street sellers, who had no qualms in blocking the way with their carts. The streets themselves were congested with carriages, coaches and wagons, and more often than not, the speed of the pedestrians outstripped that of the vehicles.

The cacophony of the scene appealed to Aurora, and vague memories of her time spent in town as a child emerged from hibernation. She had never been partial to the quiet routine of village life. Such a life had suited her mother and Percy, but though Aurora's optimistic disposition had allowed her to find contentment, she had always looked forward to a future that would offer stimulation and greater scope for her talents.

After they had had their fill of the Bond Street shops, they ventured a little further afield and explored the streets and squares of Mayfair, peering through the railings guarding private communal gardens and exclaiming over the grand townhouses of the aristocracy.

Aurora could not help wondering which one might be the residence of the Marquess of Dewbury, and had to resist the urge to enquire as to its direction. As yet, Phoebe knew nothing of the nature of the inheritance they had once or twice referred to in her presence, and until the matter was settled Aurora was content for it to remain so.

Six

The following day was dedicated to finding accommodation. Aurora and Percy, with Phoebe in tow, visited each of the properties their solicitor had itemised for their consideration.

After making their way through the list, they decided on the second of the properties they had seen. It had a good-sized sitting-room and, though it was advertised as having only two bedchambers, there was also a study that could serve as Phoebe's room. As an added attraction, the landlady, who had her own separate rooms in the house, had informed them that for a reasonable fee she could cook their meals and organise a servant to clean.

"Phoebe, you must be used to far grander!" Aurora told her young friend with a wry look. "I wouldn't be at all surprised if you are now regretting that you chose to throw your lot in with ours."

The three of them were standing in the sitting-room, having just completed their business with the landlady and accepted the keys.

At Aurora's words, Phoebe turned from looking out the window at the small garden in the centre of the square and exclaimed: "Oh no, Cousin Aurora! This is *such* an adventure! I don't miss my old life in the least, I promise you. There is no point living in luxury if no one will allow you to do anything fun and interesting, and will only insist on you minding your lessons and taking dreary strolls around the garden."

Aurora's suspicions that the young heiress had been kept too tightly leashed were realised by this naïve speech.

"Well, dear, you are certainly out in the world now. I can only pray that your uncle and governess will forgive me!"

Upon their return to the hotel the concierge handed Aurora a note from a Miss Brinkley, which had arrived for her in her absence. Correctly assuming this to be the sister of her new friend from the bookstore, Aurora opened it and discovered an invitation to tea for herself and Phoebe for the following day.

Aurora answered her brother's enquiry as to what the message contained, and added: "If you wish to join us, Percy, I'm certain they wouldn't mind."

"No, I thank you!" he said with feeling. "I have no wish to sit through an hour or more of you and this Mr Brinkley discussing some obscure mathematical theorem. Phoebe, if you know what's good for you, you'd stay away too!"

Phoebe looked daunted.

"Oh, don't listen to him!" said Aurora, laughing. "I'd never presume to bore the Miss Brinkleys in such a way."

"You could never bore anyone, Cousin Aurora. Percy, you must not say such a thing about your sister!" Phoebe chided him gently.

Her initial shyness in his company had not outlived the first day of their acquaintance, and she now treated him in much the same way that Aurora did; a familiarity he did not appear to mind.

"You will have people thinking she is a bluestocking," Phoebe went on, "and *nothing* could be more detrimental to her chances of finding a husband. I know this is true for my guardian was most insistent that Miss Winston not teach me anything that could turn me into one, for that very reason!"

"Which guardian? *The Despicable One* or *The Distant One*," asked Percy, having adopted Phoebe's vernacular in referring to these two gentlemen.

"*The Despicable One*. But I daresay *The Distant One* holds a similar view, being a man and all."

Aurora laughed at their absurdity.

"As I have no desire to acquire a husband, I don't fear continuing my shockingly bluestocking ways. Now, I must write my reply to Miss Brinkley, but you need not tell me this instant if you wish to come, Phoebe. We will have a busy morning tomorrow moving into our lodgings, so if you would prefer to rest in the afternoon, I'm sure no one will wonder at it!"

*   *   *

On the following afternoon, having settled into their new accommodation in good time and without too much effort, Aurora and Phoebe took a hackney to the address in Hanover Square provided by Miss Brinkley.

To their considerable surprise, they were deposited in front of a smart townhouse of noble proportions.

Nothing in Mr Brinkley's appearance had led them to suppose that he was a wealthy gentleman. His manner had been unassuming and his clothing of an old-fashioned cut that, though of good quality, had not looked particularly expensive.

Aurora pressed on the ornate brass doorbell and, before the last of its echoes rang through the house, it was opened by a servant she assumed was the butler. His stature was below the average (a trait that was more pronounced when viewed beside her own queenly proportions), but he had a superior bearing and polished style that were more in keeping with such a grand residence than the owner's.

"How may I be of assistance?" he asked them in a clipped voice.

Aurora introduced herself and informed him that they were expected. He thawed a little at this information and stepped aside to allow them to enter.

Phoebe, trying not to appear overwhelmed, looked anxiously across at Aurora, and was offered a wink and a smile, before they followed the butler up the stairs to the first floor.

Here they entered a spacious drawing room, well-lit by the sunlight filtering through the large sash-windows that lined the two long sides of the room; one bank facing the square and the other the back garden.

In the middle of the room, clustered around a large settee, were arranged several comfortable looking chairs, one of which was currently occupied by a lady of middle years. Of Mr Brinkley there was no sight.

The lady rose as soon as the guests were announced and came forward to greet them.

"At last, we meet, Miss Wesley!" she said in a warm voice. "Our brother has spoken very highly of you. And you too, Miss Lennox – welcome! I am Miss Coral Brinkley."

"Miss Brinkley, I am delighted to be making your acquaintance," replied Aurora, shaking hands with her.

"Oh, do please call me Miss Coral! As the eldest, my sister is more in the habit of hearing herself referred to as Miss Brinkley. She too would have been here to greet you had she not been unavoidably delayed . . . though perhaps that is for the best!" she said with a conspiratorial look. "Being the eldest she is too used to having her own way, and we wouldn't be able to enjoy a comfortable gossip together with her taking over the conversation!"

Aurora laughed, appreciating Miss Coral's frankness. Her hostess was also possessed of a well-rounded figure, a pretty, plump face softened by age, and an abundance of hair of an improbable yellow colour, styled in ringlets.

Once they were seated and the tea had been served, Miss Coral asked: "Did you come to London for the Season?"

"Regrettably, no," replied Aurora. "We came on a matter of business."

"What kind of business? Oh, but perhaps you would prefer not to say? In which case, I shall certainly not press you," said Miss Coral, her gaze expectant.

Aurora contained a smile. "We are primarily in London, ma'am, on a matter concerning my brother's . . . "

" . . . *Wardrobe?*" Miss Coral eagerly broke in, startling her guest.

"Oh . . . no . . . Percy has little interest in fashion," Aurora assured her. "We are here so that he can claim his . . . "

" . . . *Inheritance?*" Miss Coral once more pre-empted her. Noting Aurora's surprised expression, she chuckled. "*Do* forgive me! It's so enjoyable to guess what others are on the point to saying – don't you think? It's something of a game I sometimes play."

"In that case, ma'am, you will be happy to know that you are correct," replied Aurora, eyes alight with humour. "The matter of my brother's inheritance has indeed brought us to London."

"Ah, it only took me two guesses that time!" remarked Miss Coral in delighted accents.

And to congratulate herself, she selected two chocolate bon-bons in quick succession from a silver dish on the side table beside her. Remembering her guests, she offered the dish to them just as Mr Brinkley walked into the room.

He greeted both Aurora and Phoebe, and then sat down and exchanged a few words with Aurora with evident pleasure.

Catching Miss Coral's interested gaze upon them, Aurora wondered if the lady thought there was more between her and Mr Brinkley than the reality of it.

"Pray, forgive my tardiness," a voice from the doorway declared in assured accents.

Turning in her chair, Aurora saw a lady enter, most fashionably dressed and as tall as Aurora herself, who judging from her features must be the elder Miss Brinkley. She exuded a certain strength of character that was lacking in her siblings.

"Miss Wesley, I presume?" she said, walking into the room with a brisk stride.

"Indeed, ma'am," replied Aurora, rising.

The lady looked down her magnificent nose at her guest while Mr Brinkley carried out the introductions.

"My brother has not seen fit to stop singing your praises for the last two days," Miss Brinkley told Aurora with an undisguised note of accusation.

Realising her suspicions were correct and that Mr Brinkley's sisters appeared to think he had fallen prey to her charms, Aurora replied with a disarming smile: "That must have been a great bore for you! I hope you will not hold it against me, ma'am?"

"That remains to be seen."

Mr Brinkley was looking decidedly uncomfortable at this exchange and, wishing to shield him from unwarranted conjecture, Aurora decided to give his sisters' thoughts a more proper direction.

"I too am delighted to have made Mr Brinkley's acquaintance, and to discover that he shares my love of mathematics! It is a most uncomfortable passion, for there are few who understand its attraction. And even fewer who recognise that such passion can be felt by a woman! I am used to being thought of as an oddity, however, your brother was kind enough to discuss the subject with me as an equal, and I am honoured he didn't find my interest contemptible."

"On no account must you consider yourself an oddity!" insisted Mr Brinkley. "Why some of the greatest mathematicians in times past have been women! In fact, I have found great pleasure recently in studying the work of Emilie du Chatelet and her elaborate commentary of Newtonian physics and mechanics . . . "

"Gregory, I trust you do not intend spending the remainder of Miss Wesley's visit discussing a subject in which the rest of us cannot hope to take part?" interrupted Miss Brinkley, with a look of exasperation.

"No, no, of course not," he agreed and fell silent.

Miss Brinkley then took a seat beside Aurora and for the next half an hour subjected her to an interrogation, in which her siblings were not permitted to take part; and even their occasional attempts to steer the conversation to other subjects did not sway her from her purpose.

By the time Aurora declared it was time for her and Phoebe to be off, Miss Brinkley was in possession of nearly all the information Aurora was at liberty to disclose. Though her demeanour towards her guest did not appear to soften, Aurora thought she had acquitted herself well-enough to pass whatever bar had been set for her, while still maintaining a level of ambiguity that could one day be explained away.

While Mr Brinkley saw the guests out, his sisters began to discuss Aurora as soon as she was out of the room.

"Her manners are very good," said Miss Brinkley. "I was pleasantly surprised to discover that she has none of the awkwardness that someone from her provincial background might exhibit."

"And she has such merry eyes. It makes one want to pardon her almost anything!"

"You are being fanciful, Coral. No matter how merry her eyes, if she did not also have the requisite breeding it would not make her one ounce more acceptable to a gentleman on the lookout for a wife. But, I agree, she has good ton – from her mother's side, no doubt. The Urquharts are a very old family, and even an obscure branch – which we can gather from her allusions is all she can claim! – cannot be considered contemptible. As for her father, I never heard of any Wesleys in Polite Society deriving from Norfolk. *That* will certainly be a mark against her."

"You speak as if she is on the look-out for a husband," said Miss Coral. "She gave no such impression."

"What lady of marriageable age is not?"

"*You* were never so inclined, Pearl. You were quite set against it, in fact."

Miss Pearl Brinkley waved this aside, and set out to explain to her sister in some depth why her point was irrelevant.

Seven

Outside on the front steps, Mr Brinkley was enquiring if Aurora and Phoebe wished him to secure a hackney for them when a smart town carriage turned into the street. Recognising it immediately, Mr Brinkley waved.

The young lady at the window waved back enthusiastically, while a gentleman, seated beside her, raised a hand in greeting as the carriage passed by.

"My nephew and niece," explained Mr Brinkley. "The children of my youngest sister. They live across the square."

He pointed to a magnificent, neo-classical townhouse on the other side of the enclosed garden.

"I take it, sir, that you have a third sister?" said Aurora.

"Oh, yes! Forgive me, I should have explained. My youngest sister was Coral's twin. She is regrettably no longer with us . . . hmm, how odd," he murmured, his eyes returning to the carriage.

The vehicle had jerked to a sudden stop and, as they watched, the door was thrown open and Mr Brinkley's nephew jumped out and ran back towards them.

With dawning horror Aurora recognised a countenance she had seen for the first time only a handful of days ago . . . an absurdly handsome countenance.

"I wonder what has got into the boy," mused Mr Brinkley. "He looks enraged over something . . . most unlike him."

Aurora hardly heard this.

She had but a few moments to compose herself, before the gentleman was upon them.

"You!" he thundered, grabbing her arm in a tight grip. "I see I shall be spared the trouble of engaging a Bow Street runner! What in God's name are you doing here? And how did you find out where I live?"

"Julian!" exclaimed Mr Brinkley. "What in heavens is the matter with you? Unhand Miss Wesley at once!"

"Miss Wesley, is it? A name for my thief at last."

"Do I know you, sir?" asked Aurora, looking bewildered.

"Ha! Don't think that air of innocence will deceive me. You may have fooled me once, but you'll not do it again . . . and certainly not twice in one week!"

"Have you gone mad, my boy?" demanded Mr Brinkley, frowning at his nephew with as much displeasure as was possible for someone of his temperament. "Miss Wesley is here as my guest, and I insist that you speak to her with respect. There has clearly been some mistake, but that does not excuse your conduct."

"This woman stole my purse!"

"Pardon?" said Mr Brinkley in astonished accents.

"How could you say such untruths about Cousin Aurora!" cried Phoebe, and to everyone's surprise swung her reticule and struck him on the arm. "Unhand her, you . . . you *beast*!"

"Phoebe dear, in general a lady does not hit a gentleman," Aurora instructed in a serene voice. "Only think how undignified it would be if we gave into the temptation to assault every overly-eager male who took an interest in us."

Aurora's arm was abruptly released.

"My interest in you begins and ends with seeing you delivered into the hands of a constable!" declared her accuser. Turning to his uncle, he went on: "This lady robbed me at gunpoint not five days ago."

As Mr Brinkley was looking more and more appalled by his nephew's conduct, and as Phoebe was once again preparing to spring to her defence, Aurora thought it best to quickly diffuse the situation.

"I am sorry to hear you were robbed, sir," she said. "But it can't have been at my hand, for I have been travelling with my brother and have been in his company the whole time."

"There! You see, Julian?" Mr Brinkley spoke up. "It would have been impossible for Miss Wesley to have done what you say."

"Perhaps the mistake arises from the fact that the thief was a woman with similar features and hair," Aurora suggested. "If the light was poor, it may have made it difficult to discern the details."

"Of course, that would explain it," said Mr Brinkley, his gaze prompting his nephew to agree to this likelihood.

"Her hair was blonde, and it was daytime," Rothworth ground out grudgingly.

"Oh . . . well, that certainly must be perplexing for you," said Aurora in a soothing voice, as if speaking to a child in the midst of a tantrum. "Is there nothing I can say that will convince you of my innocence, Mr . . . "

She waited for his name to be supplied.

"Where are my manners!" said Mr Brinkley in a distracted way. "If you are not averse to the idea, Miss Wesley – and no one could blame you, if you were – may I present my nephew to you?"

"I would be delighted."

"Well then, if you are certain . . . Miss Wesley, Julian De Vere, the Duke of Rothworth. Difficult though it may be to believe, he is generally held to be a gentleman of intellect and good breeding."

"Your Grace," Aurora uttered in a constricted voice as she dropped into a curtsy; almost stumbling from shock to think she had chosen a peer of the realm to detach from his purse.

Rothworth's manners forced him to offer her a bow. The irony was not lost on him.

Now that his initial visceral reaction was passing, he was beginning to realise how impossible it would be for him to hand Miss Wesley over to the law. By the look of it, she had already ingratiated herself with his uncle, and he could not deceive himself that his relative, though normally mild mannered, would stand by while he dealt with her as she deserved.

And besides, he was surprised to discover that he did not have the appetite to have her arrested. There would be little satisfaction gained by such an outcome. Better to devise his own punishment, in his own time.

Having reached this conclusion, he said with something approaching his customary composure: "I concede you may be correct, Miss Wesley. A similarity of features may have misled me . . . the resemblance is remarkable," he added dryly.

Aurora could appreciate the level of self-control it took for him to rein in what was after all a perfectly justifiable anger. She wondered what he was up to, and could only hope it did not entail her abduction and disappearance.

"It is already forgiven!" she replied, conjuring up her most gracious smile.

Just then the duke's sister approached the group, having abandoned the carriage out of curiosity.

"Clearly my odious brother has forgotten all about me!" she said with a charmingly dimpled smile. "I thought I'd join you to discover why he leapt out of a moving carriage in such a dashing manner! Dear Uncle Gregory, won't you please introduce me to your friends?"

"Of course, Charlotte," he said fondly, and proceeded to present Aurora and Phoebe to her.

Those who did not know Lady Charlotte De Vere well often made incorrect assumptions regarding her character, based primarily on her youth, her sweetly innocent expression and her short stature. What they failed to recognise in her was a shrewdness that surpassed her years.

Aurora, more observant than most, was amused to find herself being assessed in a friendly but nonetheless ruthless fashion, by a young lady who barely reached her shoulders and could not be much older than Phoebe.

"What lovely eyes you have, Miss Wesley!" said Charlotte. "I'm certain I'd have remembered you if I had seen you about town before . . . are you a new acquaintance of my brother's?"

Aurora's amusement grew. She had evidently been cast into the role of *love-interest* again (it must be a family trait!).

"I am new to London, Lady Charlotte. And as I only met your brother a few minutes ago, I wouldn't presume to count him as an acquaintance."

"You are right to be circumspect! Even those who have known my brother for years and years can't in all honesty say they are *truly* acquainted with him. Which is quite his own fault for being so inscrutable! And now, Julian," said Charlotte with a mischievous look, "would be the perfect time for you to say something gallant and assure Miss Wesley that you would be honoured if she would consider you an acquaintance."

"Your advice is misplaced," he replied. "Miss Wesley can hardly wish for the acquaintance of a man who is pressed into it by his sister."

Fearing Aurora might interpret this as a snub, Mr Brinkley felt bound to say: "I know you don't mean to imply any reluctance on your part, my boy."

"I'm willing to recognise Miss Wesley's acquaintance," Rothworth replied after a moment, but with enough hesitation to make Aurora's lips twitch. "I only point out that a forced acquaintance does not flatter either party."

His sister, rather underwhelmed by this response, shook her head at him. "You know I love you dearly, Julian, but I must say I'm beginning to understand why you are still unmarried."

Reading the irritation in the duke's eyes, Aurora hurriedly asked Charlotte what amusements there were to be had in town that might appeal to a young lady; and then she drew Phoebe into the conversation and facilitated the girls becoming better acquainted.

Her efforts bore some fruit, and by the time a passing hackney had been hailed, Charlotte had invited Phoebe to join her on her morning walk the following day.

While the girls were making their plans, Aurora said her goodbyes to Mr Brinkley and was about to do the same with Rothworth, when he surprised her by saying he would escort her to the hackney.

Thinking he wished to use the opportunity to confront her in unencumbered language, Aurora pre-empted him as they crossed the street.

"When you come to know me a little better, Your Grace, you'll realise that I like to think well of people. And so, I hope you'll humour me by allowing me to believe that the woman who relieved you of your purse was driven to it by exceptional circumstances."

He studied her profile. "She offered up a similar excuse."

"I wouldn't be at all surprised if it were the truth! And perhaps one day she may be in a position to return the money."

"I don't want the damned money!"

She glanced across at him. "Do you not? How . . . interesting."

He threw her an exasperated look. "Whether or not the money is returned is irrelevant. No amount of money could make amends for having a gun aimed at me."

"Ah . . . I begin to understand. The incident left you distressed. You may have the look of a man who can handle himself in any situation, but I suppose looks can be deceiving," she said kindly.

"The only distress I suffered arose from my inability to wring her pretty neck!"

A smile played about her lips. "Pretty? What an interesting word to describe a thief . . . *my* thief, I believe you called her earlier."

Taunting him was certainly not sensible, and yet she found it impossible to resist. Despite his resentment, there was a proprietorial quality in the way he referred to her that sparked her more primal urges.

"It was a figure of speech," he retorted.

"Which part: the *pretty,* or the *my*?"

"Both," he replied indifferently; although there was a faint query in his eyes as they held hers, as if he could not figure out why she was bantering him.

"You have been cruel to my flights of fancy!" said Aurora. "I see you don't mean to forgive her. Oh well . . . no doubt she deserves it." Walking up to the hackney, she gave the driver her direction, then turned back to Rothworth. "It does occur to me, however, that if your thief was to offer you a favour of your choosing, to make amends, it would be sporting of you to accept."

An unexpected smile tugged at his lips. "I do not accept *favours* from women I don't know, Miss Wesley."

Her eyes widened in surprise. "I meant a *respectable* and *commensurate* favour."

"Did you?"

"You know perfectly well that I did!"

He opened the door of the coach and offered his hand to help her to mount.

After a small hesitation, she took it. But as she put her foot on the step, he held her back.

She raised an eyebrow in question.

"I may consider it," he said.

"May consider what, Your Grace?"

"A commensurate favour . . . or *boon*, to use my thief's language."

Her gloved fingers tightened around his; a show of gratitude, but also of guilt, which she regretted almost immediately.

"It is kind of you to indulge me in my little fantasy," she replied with a careless smile; and, quickly entering the hackney, she let go of his hand.

Phoebe followed her in, and they were soon on their way back to their rented rooms.

It was not until that night, as she lay awake in her bed mulling over the unexpected events of the day, that Aurora realised the Duke of Rothworth had only promised to consider a commensurate favour.

He had made no mention of a respectable one.

Eight

"He's an imposter! Mark my words!" expostulated Lord Charles Dewbury, brother to the late Marquess of Dewbury and uncle to his missing heir.

He was a man of excessive bulk, incongruously attired to proclaim the dandy, and enjoyed a natural tendency towards hedonism that often led people to think him amiable. And for the most part this happened to be true. However, self-interest ruled his actions above all else, and as he did not feel the family solicitor before him warranted the same consideration he reserved for his society acquaintances, he felt able to relieve his spleen unencumbered.

"How many times over the years," he continued irately, "have we been approached by unscrupulous individuals claiming that this child or that was my brother's son? I don't understand, Woodstock, why you thought it necessary to bring us such spurious claims? They can only ruin my mother's peace and raise hopes that will never be realised. Mother, I beg you don't allow your emotions to run away with you!"

Since the elderly Dowager Marchioness of Dewbury was known to be a woman of glacial reserve, who was considered sphinx-like even by her own family, this advice seemed unwarranted.

Ignoring her son, she turned her gaze on the solicitor, seated opposite her. This gentleman had called at the Dewbury town residence a few minutes ago and, after being shown into the library, had informed them that a man had come forward claiming to be the new marquess.

"Am I to understand," she said in her cool way, "that you believe this person to be authentic?"

"I would not wish to make such a presumption at this early stage, your ladyship," replied Mr Woodstock, a competent-looking man in his fourth decade. "I only wished to apprise you in person of this latest development."

"You must have some thoughts on the matter," she remarked. "You would not have called on us today, and with so little warning, if you did not believe the case to have some merit."

Mr Woodstock adjusted his position in the high-backed leather chair.

"There may be some merit," he admitted. "The petitioner has in his possession a letter that corroborates his claim, supposedly from his mother, which goes into some detail about events leading up to the marchioness's disappearance, as well as her life afterwards. When the petitioner's solicitor visited me, he allowed me time to peruse the contents and compare the writing to other correspondence we have on file that we know to be from the marchioness."

"And what was your conclusion?" asked Lady Dewbury, her gaze appearing to contemplate the pattern of the richly embroidered black silk gown that covered her sparse frame.

"It is impossible to conclude anything without a professional assessment, which I will organise with all due haste. But to my untrained eye it seems possible that the same hand wrote all the letters."

"Correspondence can be fabricated!" insisted Lord Charles. "No sense in setting great store by such evidence."

"That is true enough, sir," agreed the solicitor. "However, the arrival of this gentleman does rather neatly synchronise with your nephew's coming of age. He would have turned one and twenty last week. And as we know from the marchioness's letters over the years, her intention was always that the boy would come forward as soon as he was of age and could no longer be legally kept from her by his father . . . or a guardian."

"We were informed that my son's wife died four years ago," said Lady Dewbury. "Why did the boy not come forward then?"

"According to the petitioner's solicitor – who, I feel it pertinent to point out, is the same man who represented the marchioness – it was his decision to stay away until such a time as he could control his own destiny. It appears he was raised to be suspicious of the intentions of . . . certain members of the Dewbury family," said Mr Woodstock, with as much tact as could be employed while speaking the truth.

"That is outrageous slander!" wheezed Lord Charles, shifting his heavy bulk to the edge of his armchair.

His whale-bone corset, which his valet had assured him was of the same construction as that of King George IV, creaked in protest at the brusque movement.

"As I'm the boy's legal guardian," he continued, "I must assume you refer to me? Are we to sit by and do nothing while this imposter goes about flinging accusations about my character?"

"As no public accusations have been levelled, it would be difficult to prove a case of slander in this instant," said Mr Woodstock. "However, should this prove otherwise in future, we will, of course, revisit the matter." After a slight pause, he continued: "I would like to raise another aspect of the petitioner's claim with you. He appears to be in possession of an antique signet ring, bearing a seal of the Dewbury crest. Is there such a ring in the Family's history?"

Lord Charles cast a furtive look at his mother.

"Am I to understand such a ring exists?" asked the solicitor when no response was forthcoming.

"My son led us to believe he had misplaced it," replied the dowager, breaking the thoughtful silence she had fallen into.

"Why, it's obvious – it must have been stolen!" interjected Lord Charles.

"How many years ago was the ring misplaced?" enquired Mr Woodstock.

Sensing a trap, Lord Charles found it convenient for his memory to desert him. "I couldn't say exactly, it was a devilishly long time ago."

"Shortly after my son's wife disappeared," answered Lady Dewbury.

"It was most likely stolen by this scoundrel!" declared Lord Charles, becoming quite red above the excessively high points of his starched collar.

"If that were the case, Charles, he could hardly claim to be a young gentleman of one and twenty years of age, which is what my grandson would now be. He would have been little more than an infant at the time the ring disappeared. Woodstock, am I correct in assuming that the author of this letter you sighted claims to have taken the ring on the night the marchioness disappeared?"

"That is correct, your ladyship," he replied, appreciative of her quick wits.

"And what of the girl? My granddaughter. Has she also come forward?"

"A woman claiming to be the sister of the petitioner has accompanied him to London."

"It's all nonsense and lies," muttered Lord Charles.

"Possibly," said Mr Woodstock. "I will do my utmost to get to the bottom of the matter, whatever the outcome. We are only at the start of the process of authentication." After a moment he continued with great delicacy: "I wished to apprise you of this new development with all speed to allow you time to adjust to the possibility – however small – that the Dewbury heir has returned and has every intention of taking up the title."

"A-adjust!" spluttered his lordship as he attempted to rise out of his chair; it took him several tries and when at last he had managed to struggle to his feet, he began to pace in an agitated way. "My good man, there's not the least need to adjust to anything without a shred of real evidence. And as yet you have presented us with nothing but the word of a . . . "

"Enough, Charles," said Lady Dewbury coolly, silencing him. "I believe, Woodstock, that you have a point to make. May I suggest you make it without further ado. Despite what my son appears to think, I am not so mentally frail as to be discomposed by whatever it is you wish to disclose."

Mr Woodstock cleared his throat. He was relatively new to his position as solicitor to the wealthy Dewbury family, having stepped into the role less than a year ago when his father, and founding partner, had passed away. He had worked alongside his father for many years and had, of course, been kept apprised of all his clients.

Still, nothing could have prepared him for legal tangle of this particular case; complicated further, in his opinion, by his father's rather lenient handling of certain dependents of the Dewbury estate.

"As you know," he began, "since the unfortunate death of my father, and the continuing ill health of Lord Heath, both of whom were named by the late marquess as executors of his will and trustees of the Dewbury estate, I have had the privilege of being appointed to serve in both roles . . . alongside yourself, of course, your lordship." He nodded respectfully at Lord Charles. "My responsibilities encompass all assets and debts pertaining to the estate. And, just as importantly, they include ensuring the rightful heir to the Marquess of Dewbury is found."

He paused to allow his words to sink in.

"Furthermore – and I say this for the sake of clarity, for I would not wish for any misunderstandings to occur – though Woodstock and Sons have been honoured to provide legal services to the Dewbury family, our contractual obligations rest solely with the marquess . . . past and present."

Another pause.

"With this in mind," he went on, "I would like to point out that the balancing of the estate accounts must be completed with all due haste, in preparation for the eventuality that this latest petitioner is successful in proving his claim."

"He's a charlatan!" scoffed his lordship. "He'll never succeed, and it would be folly to pretend otherwise."

"Regardless, I will be requesting of *all* parties that any outstanding debts owed to the estate be paid in full by the end of the quarter . . . I'm certain that, as joint trustee, your lordship must feel the rightness of this course of action," stated the solicitor, his gaze on Lord Charles; deferential but determined.

"Good God, man! What are you saying?" asked his lordship with open-mouthed disbelief.

"He is saying, Charles," said the dowager marchioness, smiling humourlessly, "that the money-well has run dry."

Nine

The next week passed pleasantly away as Aurora, Percy and Phoebe explored the sights of London and partook in what entertainments could be had within the dictates of their budget. These included: a delightful comedy in Covent Garden, which Aurora enjoyed as much for her brother's and Phoebe's laughter as she did for the events on stage; several agreeable evenings in Vauxhall Gardens, walking the lantern-lit pathways, dancing in front of the orchestra stand and watching the fireworks display; and a visit to the Tower of London where, for a shilling each, they were given a tour that took in such fascinating sights as the crown jewels and the menagerie in the Lion Tower.

They also found amusement sampling the fare of the capital's numerous eating establishments. After coming across *The Epicure's Almanac* on one of her return visits to Mr Trill's bookstore, a handy little book that listed hundreds of the best eating and drinking places in London, Aurora took them on a grand gastronomical tour. Whether it was an oyster room in Fleet Street, a chop house in St Martin's Lane, a confectioner in Piccadilly or a tea garden in St James Park, there was something new to try each day.

Their own engagements also kept them occupied. Aurora would often meet Mr Brinkley at his favourite coffee house, so they could continue their discussions on mathematics, and though she was often the only woman present she enjoyed herself immensely.

Percy would join George Fitzwilliam and his friends on their adventures about town, and was introduced to a side of London not accessible to the ladies (which his sister accepted in a philosophical light).

And Phoebe's growing intimacy with Charlotte De Vere meant they were often in each other's company.

Aurora had attended the girls' first outing to Green Park, but thereafter was content to leave Phoebe in the care of Charlotte's capable governess, and the burly footman who always followed discreetly behind whenever

Charlotte was out of doors; Phoebe was not the only heiress who needed to be guarded.

However, though a governess and a footman gave Aurora some peace of mind, she remained conscious of the risk of exposure and would often remind Phoebe that she must never divulge the details of her former life. If anyone probed into her background, she was to say that since her parents' deaths she found it too painful to speak of the past.

And should they be impertinent enough to persevere with their enquiries, Aurora taught her to hide behind her handkerchief and poke herself in the eyes, to appear as if she was weeping; a little trick she herself had used on occasion, and one that gave her not a twinge of remorse to be passing on to an innocent. After all, innocence often led to exploitation, and the sooner girls were taught the tools to survive in the world into which they had been born, the more control they would have over their own destinies.

One evening, Percy was escorting Aurora and Phoebe around Hyde Park during the promenade hour when a landau carriage pulled up beside them and they were hailed by Miss Brinkley.

Aurora exchanged greetings with her and Miss Coral and took the opportunity to introduce her brother to them. Being a personable young man, Percy spent some minutes talking to the sisters with every evidence of pleasure, and acquitted himself so well that even Miss Brinkley was drawn into a laugh at something he said.

"You are not the only one to think Prinny's horse bears too great a weight in the line of duty," chortled Miss Coral.

"We must not call him *Prinny* anymore," Miss Brinkley instructed her. "Now that he has been proclaimed king, one must show more respect."

"Oh please!" scoffed her sister. "The man is a debauched profligate, who had the audacity to put his long-suffering wife on trial for adultery! I feel no compunction to show him respect."

Miss Brinkley gave her a reproving look, and then turned back to Percy.

"Young man, I must request the pleasure of your sister's company for a turn about the park. I'm certain Miss Lennox will be happy to take your arm for half an hour or so. If you remain on the path, we will find you again shortly. Miss Wesley, would you join us?"

Aurora acquiesced to the command with good grace and, mounting, sat opposite the sisters on the backward-facing seat.

The carriage had barely begun to move, when Miss Brinkley asked her first question. "I understand, Miss Wesley, that you have taken to spending every morning in a coffee house with our brother?"

"Oh, no . . . not *every* morning," replied Aurora, a little taken aback. "But I do often meet Mr Brinkley for an hour or so to discuss mathematics. It's rare to find someone who shares my enjoyment of the subject – I hope you will not tell me I'm wrong to indulge myself?"

"Certainly not," said Miss Brinkley. "I am pleased my brother has found someone with whom he can share his ideas. I fear he rarely finds anyone's company appealing outside of his Roxburghe Club – and that is full of hardened bibliophiles who talk of nothing but their books!"

"It almost makes one wish he would develop a more interesting social addiction," confided Miss Coral. "But neither gambling, drinking nor womanising appear to hold any appeal for him. It is most lowering!"

"I wouldn't go that far," said her sister, frowning at her. "But we are certainly happy to know, Miss Wesley, that he finds pleasure in your company."

She gave Aurora such a loaded look it was impossible to pretend ignorance of her meaning.

"I thank you for the honour to which you allude, ma'am, but please don't confuse Mr Brinkley's and my friendship for anything warmer. Now, that is plain speaking indeed! I hope you will forgive me for being so forward? I only wish to spare you any unfounded hopes."

"Do you not like our brother even a little bit?" asked Miss Coral, her plump face full of curiosity.

"I like him a great deal, as a . . . "

" . . . Friend," she finished for her.

"Yes," agreed Aurora, smiling. "And, I assure you, it's the same with him. Allow me to be unbecomingly direct once more and say that I have attracted my share of male attention, and am perfectly aware when a man's regard goes beyond the line of friendship."

"Well, you certainly do speak your mind freely for one so young," remarked Miss Brinkley, eyeing her not entirely favourably.

"I'm six and twenty, ma'am, and no longer young enough to be reticent about voicing my opinions . . . though honesty compels me to confess, I never truly was," Aurora added with a droll look.

"*That* I can believe," chuckled Miss Coral. "Since you have dashed our hopes so thoroughly, are we to assume you have already given your heart to someone?"

"Oh, no!" Aurora replied. "I would rather remain unattached! I'm certain you'll both agree that being unmarried has certain advantages. It would be foolish to give them up merely for the pleasure of having a man take control of my life and liberty."

"And you are not one to put your liberty at risk, are you Miss Wesley?" a man's voice spoke from outside of the carriage.

Aurora turned and found herself looking at the mounted figure of the Duke of Rothworth. He and another gentleman had ridden up beside the landau and were keeping pace with it.

"No, Your Grace," she replied with her ready smile. "In general, I like to think not . . . but I must temper that by saying, for those I love I would do *anything*."

"How delightful to see you, Julian!" Miss Coral greeted him warmly.

"He is *Rothworth* now, and has been these last fifteen years," said Miss Brinkley. "Do try to remember!"

"He will always be Julian to me," replied her sister with a mulish look.

Miss Brinkley chose to ignore this rebellion.

"I trust you were not eavesdropping?" she asked her nephew.

"Not at all," he replied. "We merely rode up to pay our respects."

Captain Torrington broke in at this point to greet the sisters, and then, after a pointed look at his friend, earned for himself an introduction to Aurora.

From the way he coloured up when she smiled and said a few words to him, Aurora could only conclude his shyness was on her account; it was unlikely that this was the natural state of a captain in the King's army. She took this as a compliment, and while the duke's attention was claimed by his aunts, she was not at all averse to spending a few minutes conversing with the charming captain.

"Torrington!" said Miss Brinkley suddenly, breaking in on their conversation. "Rothworth and Charlotte are to dine with us on Thursday. We would be pleased if you would join us. It will be amusing to hear more about your posting in the Americas."

"I'd be delighted!" he replied promptly.

"And perhaps Miss Wesley would also care to join us?" Miss Coral spoke up, looking to her sister for support.

Miss Brinkley, however, was not one who liked to have her hand forced (especially now there was no hope of a match between her brother and Aurora), and she did not immediately reply.

As the silence surpassed awkward and moved towards discourteous, Rothworth, who had just been thinking that Aurora's presence would be unwelcome, found himself saying: "I'm certain my uncle would be pleased to have Miss Wesley's company."

"Why, thank you, Your Grace!" said Aurora. "I'm overwhelmed to know you rate my company so highly as to be certain at least *one* person will be pleased by it."

She offered him a guileless look that did not fool him in the slightest.

"Everyone who knows you must find pleasure in your company, Miss Wesley," he replied in kind.

She laughed, gratified that he had not only understood her, but had reciprocated.

'Oh no, not everyone! But I see that as a challenge to test my mettle. I thank you for thinking of me," she said to the sisters, "however, I'm sorry to say I will not be able to attend your dinner."

"Of course, you must come!" decreed Miss Brinkley, appeased by this show of reticence.

"I have plans with my brother and cousin, ma'am."

"They must come as well – there, that's settled! I promise you, you will not find my dinners contemptible."

"*Our* dinners," interjected Miss Coral, and smiled at Aurora in encouragement.

Aurora hesitated. To avoid any awkwardness, she had thought to keep her brother from mixing in polite company until his place in society was assured.

"Oh, do come, Miss Wesley!" Miss Coral beseeched her. "It will be refreshing to see some new faces around the table. One grows sadly bored of keeping the same company week after week. There is never anything new to discover in one's long-standing acquaintances! All their habits, foibles and secrets have long since been dissected for pleasure and there is little left to enjoy."

"Good Lord, Coral!" said her sister. "Do you mean to frighten Miss Wesley away?"

Aurora laughed. "Oh no, she can't frighten me away by voicing a sentiment I too have felt on occasion."

Coming to a decision, one she hoped she would not later regret, she graciously accepted the invitation.

Rothworth was unaccountably satisfied with the turn of events. This, however, disconcerted him to such a degree that he chose to ignore Aurora for the next few minutes while he concluded his conversation with his aunts, and when he took his leave, he offered her no more than a brief nod in farewell.

Ten

"Rory, what possessed you to accept an invitation on my account to a dinner party hosted by two spinsters?" grumbled Percy. "If you didn't want to watch another play at Covent Garden, you need only have said so, rather than organising such a dull evening for us."

Aurora was sitting opposite him in the hackney that was taking them to the Brinkley residence; while Phoebe was huddled against her side to ward off the chill of the damp evening air.

"I'm sorry, dearest!" replied Aurora. "I had every intention of making our excuses – in fact, I did try – but then it occurred to me that it would be a perfect opportunity for you to test your skills in a benign setting."

"What skills are those, Cousin Aurora?" asked Phoebe naïvely.

"Yes, Rory, what skills *are* you referring to?" echoed Percy with a riled look.

"Oh, don't eat me!" laughed his sister. "You must own we have not had much opportunity to mix with any truly *tonish* people. And I admit to being concerned that we might feel like fish out of water when the time comes to enter Society. This dinner may help to ease our path! There will be a duke present, and a captain, and how everyone comports themselves will be a valuable lesson to us."

"A duke? Good God, Rory, I don't like the idea of misrepresenting myself to a duke! What if the deuced fellow should take offence one day when I . . . "

Aurora coughed and rolled her eyes in Phoebe's direction.

"Ah . . . right," muttered Percy.

"Why would he take offence?" asked Phoebe, looking from one to the other.

"Oh . . . well, he may think I'm aiming above my station, or some such thing," Percy replied offhandedly.

Phoebe seemed to accept this, and they lapsed into silence for a few minutes.

Until Percy suddenly exclaimed: "I don't even own the proper clothes to be presented to a duke!"

He looked down at his dark trousers and navy coat. Both were made from serviceable wool and, though expertly tailored to his athletic form, they lacked a certain elegance.

"You look perfectly presentable," Aurora assured him. "And you have been very clever and tied your cravat in such a dashing style that not even Mr Brummel himself could have done any better!"

"What a bouncer!" he scoffed; but his smile made an appearance for he was secretly pleased with the result, which had taken him over an hour to achieve.

"You don't give yourself enough credit," insisted Phoebe. "You deserve to be amongst the fashionable set, Percy, just as surely as some stuffy, old duke. And besides Charlotte's brother does not appear to care a fig for fashion! He wears the most *comfortable* looking clothes you can imagine," she confided, delivering the perceived death blow to the duke's sense of style.

Aurora laughed. "How right you are, dear! But I think you may have been a little unfair to label the duke as stuffy and old."

"Well, I suppose *old* is not entirely correct. But stuffy most certainly is! Did you know, he intends for Charlotte to wait until she is *eighteen* before allowing her to have her coming out? It's downright gothic, if you ask me."

"Perhaps we can label him as protective, but that is one fault I can't quibble with – he has many others more deserving of my attention! But whatever his faults, I don't think he will find much to censure in you, Percy. He currently has a more eligible recipient for his ire . . . ah, we have arrived."

Before Percy could enquire further into who this *eligible recipient* might be, she quickly opened the door and dismounted. There was not the least need to disturb his peace of mind by disclosing that Fate appeared to have an ironic sense of humour, and the man she had importuned on a quiet country lane was the same duke he was about to meet over dinner.

A footman opened the front door to them and showed them upstairs to the drawing room. The three Brinkley siblings, currently the only occupants of the room, came forward to greet them and Aurora presented her brother to Mr Brinkley.

Despite Percy's reservations as to his clothing, when it came to winning over one's fellow creatures his engaging manners and good looks worked as well in a London drawing room as they did in a Norfolk village, and he was soon chatting away with Mr Brinkley about some of his favourite haunts in Cambridge.

The two of them were standing near the doors to the drawing room, not having as yet followed the example of the ladies and taken a seat, and had just accepted their drinks from the butler when the Duke of Rothworth, his sister and Captain Torrington walked in.

"Welcome!" Mr Brinkley greeted them warmly. "Come in, do come in."

Percy, caught in the process of taking a healthy sip of his sherry, turned to face the newcomers.

As his eyes landed on Rothworth, he suffered a severe shock, choked and spontaneously ejected his mouthful of sherry all over the ducal linen.

Rothworth stood frozen for an instant, before calmly taking out his handkerchief and wiping his face and cravat.

Until this moment, Aurora had not realised that her brother had seen the face of the man she had chosen to rob. With a heroic effort she stifled her entirely inappropriate laughter, and quickly came forward with her own handkerchief and handed it to Percy, who had rounded off his performance by falling into a fit of coughing.

"Please excuse my brother! He suffered from a debilitating restriction of the lungs when he was younger and on occasion the tightness can return," she said, improvising. "He will be himself again shortly. Percy, do come and sit down for minute while I get you a glass of water . . . ah, thank you, Mr Brinkley, you read my mind!"

Percy threw his sister a veiled look of accusation as he accepted the glass from her. Refusing to be ushered to a seat, he declared that he was fully recovered.

"In that case," she said, "allow me to introduce you to His Grace, the Duke of Rothworth, his sister, Lady Charlotte and Captain Torrington, so that you may beg their forgiveness for such a display. I'm certain His Grace has never before been decorated by such a deluge of sherry!"

"Not since his university days, in any case," put in Captain Torrington, grinning.

"Forgive me, sir . . . I-I mean, *Your Grace*," Percy stammered.

"It is already forgotten," replied Rothworth with his customary sangfroid.

"How do you do?" said Charlotte, recovering from her giggles and smiling at Percy. "I have heard a good deal about you from your cousin and have been wanting to meet you."

A look of confusion came over Percy. "Oh, you mean Phoebe! I hope she only had good to say . . . though I suppose that's now a moot point," he said with a self-conscious smile.

"Oh, poof! It was a rare treat to see my brother rendered speechless! I don't believe his presence has ever before elicited such a reaction . . . although, there was one particular occasion where a lady fainted at his feet. But as I believed at the time that she was play-acting, it's not at all the same thing! However, once while he was out walking with me, a woman did come right up to us, bold as you please, and slapped him . . . "

"Charlotte," interrupted Rothworth, "I hope you don't mean to catalogue all the occasions on which I have been confronted with uncommon behaviour?"

"Of course not! Only, *do* allow me to tell them about how you were held up at gunpoint by a woman not two weeks ago? Such a daring escapade! It almost makes me wish I had the nerve to . . . "

"Such aberrant conduct is not something I wish my sister to aspire to," he cut her off sternly. "The lady in question was a harridan and should be horse-whipped."

Sensing Percy tense, Aurora put her arm through his in a sisterly fashion to stop him from doing something imprudent.

"Although I don't approve of corporal punishment for animals or humans," she remarked tranquilly, "I must agree with your brother, Lady Charlotte. Only imagine how uncomfortable the lady's circumstances must have been to drive her to such behaviour. And I suspect – although it's so uninspiringly prosaic – that sometimes what can appear as daring is nothing more than a deficit of options."

Rothworth turned unfathomable eyes on her; then abruptly said to Percy: "I understand you escorted your sister to London?"

"Ah . . . yes, sir."

"I trust you took proper care of her?"

"I did my best," replied Percy, looking decidedly uncomfortable.

"I heard there was some sort of altercation en route?" pressed Rothworth.

"You certainly didn't hear it from me!" Aurora cut in. "You must be thinking of a different occasion."

At this point, feeling she had been kept out of the conversation long enough, Miss Brinkley assumed control of the party, and in a short space of time had manoeuvred them to the dining room down the hall.

Aurora found herself placed between Mr Brinkley and Captain Torrington, who had overcome his shyness and proved to be an entertaining conversationalist, and she enjoyed a delightful meal splitting her attention between her two neighbours.

Rothworth, on the other hand, appeared dissatisfied for some reason, if one was to judge from the looks he cast her way from across the table.

And this was indeed true. He thought it very bad form that his friend should be trying to ingratiate himself with his aunts' guest in so blatant a fashion. He determined to apprise him, at the earliest opportunity, that the lady was none other than his thief, and needed to be handled with circumspection.

He found his opportunity as soon as the men had finished their port after dinner, and his uncle and Percy had walked off to re-join the ladies in the drawing room. However, to his considerable consternation, when he shared his revelation with his friend, the captain laughed uproariously and declared the lady had earned his admiration with her daring.

"For God's sake, Rupert, not you too!" Rothworth said irately. "I already have enough to bear since Charlotte contrived to extract the details of the incident from me, and has been waxing lyrical about the damned woman since."

"Ah, Julian," sighed Captain Torrington, wiping tears from his eyes. "I never thought to see the day you'd be bested by a woman! I wonder what drove her to it? She must have had a pressing need."

"Apparently so, if one were to believe her," said Rothworth, unimpressed.

"Well, at least you must own there's a certain poetic justice to the whole affair. You've always despised women who fawn over you, while hiding their ambition as to your fortune. No woman has ever been so honest as to declare outright that she desires your money. How much did she steal?"

"Close to thirty pounds," replied Rothworth. After a short pause, he found himself adding, almost against his will: "She didn't steal the money, so much as borrow it."

"I beg your pardon?" asked his friend, nonplussed.

"She offered to repay me when she was able . . . don't look so incredulous! I'm only telling you what she claimed at the time. Not that I want the damned money back, even if I did trust her to be telling me the truth! She won't get away with so easy a penance."

"She stole from you but promised to give it back?" said Captain Torrington with an incredulous laugh. "You know, I'm becoming more and more interested in the workings of Miss Wesley's mind. She's a woman worthy of further acquaintance."

"Stay away from her!" snapped Rothworth with more force than either gentleman anticipated.

"Why?" asked Captain Torrington, looking surprised.

"She needs to be taught a lesson, and that does not involve you fawning over her! Leave her to me."

His friend regarded him with sudden comprehension and smiled.

"If I didn't know any better, I'd say she has already made a conquest of you, Julian. You've never before been afraid of a little competition."

"Go to hell," Rothworth muttered and walked off.

Captain Torrington's eyes stayed on the doorway through which his friend had just passed.

"Well, I'll be damned," he murmured to himself.

Eleven

The following afternoon, Mr Brinkley, Miss Coral and Charlotte called at the Wesleys's lodgings to take Aurora and Phoebe to the British Museum; an engagement they had planned the previous evening.

They were let into the house by the landlady, who had been told to expect them, and shown to the second floor. A knock on the door, then another, elicited no reaction.

The landlady was just beginning to grumble about having to get back to her baking, when they heard the front door open and quick steps on the staircase.

"Oh, I do beg your pardon for being late!" exclaimed Aurora, appearing on the landing below, Phoebe behind her. "The lending library was further away than we realised and we were on foot. Thank you, Mrs Smithson, it was very kind of you to greet our guests."

The landlady grumbled some more about having too much to do to be entertaining other people's visitors, and then took herself off in a great hurry.

"What deplorable manners!" said Miss Coral.

"Oh, don't mind that little show of gruffness," Aurora told her, coming up the last of the steps and taking out her key. "Mrs Smithson has been kindness itself to us."

"She does have a good-natured look about her," Mr Brinkley offered up charitably.

"Well, if you say so!" said his sister, clearly unconvinced. "For my part, I have observed that people who lack manners also lack the will to get along with others . . . is anything the matter, Miss Wesley?" she asked, noticing Aurora staring at the door with a puzzled expression.

"The door is unlocked," replied Aurora, testing the handle again. "I could have sworn I locked it when we left."

She pushed it open and stepped into the room . . . and instantly came to a standstill.

"Oh, no!" cried Phoebe, peering around her.

"Dear me!" exclaimed Charlotte at the same time

A scene of disorder met their collective gaze. Not a single item appeared to remain in its original location; chairs and tables had been moved, the sofa upended, and the contents of shelves and draws emptied on the floor.

Without saying a word, Aurora hurried to her bedchamber. It was no different.

She spent some minutes attempting to locate her valise and finally found it amongst the bedclothes heaped on the bed. With a sinking heart, she opened the false bottom.

Empty.

When Miss Coral entered the room a little while later, she found Aurora sitting on the bed, staring off into space.

"Are you quite alright, my dear?" she asked. "You are looking a little pale. Was anything of value stolen?"

"A ring," replied Aurora, attempting a smile.

"No money?"

"No, I appear to have hidden that more aptly . . . or perhaps it was never their target."

Miss Coral digested this comment with interest.

"Well, whatever their reason, you can't remain here now," she said determinedly. "My brother and I have been discussing your situation, and neither of us will have a moment's peace if we were to leave you here! You must come and stay with us."

Aurora's composure was slowly returning, and she rose and took Miss Coral's plump hands in gratitude.

"That is most kind of you, ma'am – thank you! But I am not at all certain we should accept your generosity. You really don't know anything about us . . . in fact, I must tell you that I have kept you purposefully ignorant of some important details. I do have my reasons, and in a month or two I'll be able to be entirely honest with you, but for now . . . well, it just isn't possible. So, you see, it would be monstrous of me to impose on your kindness."

"My dear, think nothing of it! We all have our little secrets. Yours, however, appear to be catching up with you," she turned her gaze on the disordered room, "and your safety must be the foremost priority of your friends. I am certain your brother will agree . . . speaking of whom, I believe he has just arrived."

Percy suddenly burst into the bedchamber and, on catching sight of Aurora, exhaled in relief.

"Thank God you're safe!" he said and enveloped her in a hug.

"Yes, I'm safe," she replied, patting his back. "Although dearest, if you continue to squeeze the air out of me, I can't vouch for how much longer I will remain so!"

He released her.

"Did you return here after your appointment with the solicitor this morning?" Aurora asked him. "Did you see or hear anything?"

"No, nothing! All was as it should be when John and I returned. And then I left again shortly after and walked to Bond Street to pick up some shaving supplies."

"And John?"

"I gave him the rest of the day off."

"You both left together?"

"Yes. Around midday."

"Two hours ago . . . more than enough time." She fell into a thoughtful silence.

"We will leave you now to get your affairs in order," Miss Coral's voice broke in on her reverie, "for I imagine we will be very much in the way if we remain. I'll send the carriage back for you at six o'clock – will that give you enough time to pack?"

"But I have not accepted . . . "

" . . . My invitation," Miss Coral finished for her. "I know, my dear, but you will! Mr Wesley, I count on you to make your sister see reason. No need to look flummoxed, dear boy, she will explain it all to you!"

"But your sister . . . " Aurora petered out.

"I understand you perfectly. Don't let it concern you! I know just how to handle my sister." And with a gracious nod, she swept out of the room.

"I know I should have refused her invitation," Aurora told Percy with a wry smile, "but I'm far too practical to allow pride to rule my conduct. And besides, even if I didn't have to consider your safety, and Phoebe's, there's no denying that staying with the Brinkleys will relieve us of a good deal of financial pressure."

"I'm not going to kick up a fuss over that, Rory. Makes sense, I suppose. But what I am dashed uneasy about is the fact that we keep getting robbed!"

"It isn't a simple robbery this time. The signet ring is gone and, from what I can tell, nothing else."

"You mean, one of our relatives stole the ring?" he asked, appalled.

"What else am I to think? Within a few days of Mr Tadley informing the Dewbury solicitor that you have the ring in your possession, someone breaks into our lodgings and it disappears."

"I should have put the damned thing on!"

"Language, dearest. Besides, the fault lies with our unscrupulous family. Mama did warn us there was too much at stake to trust any of them."

"I suppose my case becomes more difficult to prove without the ring?" he asked with a troubled expression.

"Oh, no, I don't believe so! It may take a little more time, but we will prevail," she replied, her smile reassuring.

However, despite the brave words delivered for his benefit, Aurora suspected the ring was vital to their chances of success. Her mother's letters alone could be contested and labelled as forgeries. But the significance of the ring and the letters together could not be ignored.

All things considered, the ring had to be retrieved; and ideally without Percy's involvement, for he had certain straitlaced tendencies that would be difficult to overcome.

*   *   *

"I could not believe my eyes, Pearl!" said Miss Coral, as she came to the end of her recital of the events that had unfolded at the Wesleys's lodgings. She was sitting with her sister in the drawing room and was in the process of pouring out the tea. "The vandalism was remarkable! If only you could have seen Miss Wesley's distress – and the fear in her dear little cousin's eyes! – I am certain you would have been greatly moved," she declared, embellishing the truth without contrition.

"I have always said that London's constabulary is too soft on crime," said Miss Brinkley grimly.

"You have indeed," agreed her sister, taking a sip of her tea.

"This is what comes of not providing suitable, fairly-paid employment to the poor. It is outrageous! I must remember to have a word with Rothworth and see that he authors a bill to address the situation."

"Yes, a good idea. It could be of great benefit in reducing *future* crimes . . . however, for the present, I don't think I will be able to sleep a wink thinking of those poor young people residing in rooms with such lax security! But what can be done?"

"There is only one thing to be done," said Miss Brinkley with great firmness.

"Oh, I knew you would think of something!" cried Miss Coral, perking up.

"Miss Wesley must turn to her maternal relations."

Her sister deflated, and struggled to suppress a sigh of exasperation.

"But, Pearl, if you would remember, Miss Wesley mentioned her mother's family resides in Scotland. There are no Urquharts in London."

"Hmm . . . most inconvenient," remarked Miss Brinkley, displeased with such inconsideration on the part of the Urquharts. "Well then," she said, after giving the matter some further thought, "in that case, they must approach their friends."

"Of course! How right you are! If only there was someone suitable. I understand Mr Wesley has a close friend in London – a young man of good birth, but a little wild. Still, a bachelor's household may be preferable to their current situation."

"Certainly not! What are you thinking, Coral? It would be ruinous to Miss Wesley's and Miss Lennox's reputations! On no account must they go there."

"But what are they to do?"

"Why, it is perfectly obvious – I am surprised it has not occurred to you. They must come here!" announced Miss Brinkley grandly.

"Here? But do you think it wise?"

"I would not have suggested it otherwise. All three are well-mannered and capable of comporting themselves with decorum. I do not hold that unfortunate incident with the sherry against Mr Wesley, for his medical condition must place him above reproach. And only consider how well Miss Wesley behaves towards Rothworth. I have never before seen a woman treat him with so much friendly indifference – it is a joy to watch, for I can see he does not like it in the least! It will be a valuable lesson to him, mark my words. Yes, I am most pleased with Miss Wesley. She is a lady of quality and nothing you say will make me think otherwise."

"I have no wish to contradict you," said Miss Coral meekly. "And now that you have put it into my head, I can see the advantages of having them stay with us. So clever of you to think of a solution! I do hope Miss Wesley will be amenable."

"Why would she be otherwise?"

"She possesses a good deal of pride and may not wish to be beholden."

"What nonsense! Still, you may be right," owned Miss Brinkley, a meditative gleam coming into her eyes. "I will write her a note. I know just how to deal with such circumspection."

Twelve

On being informed by his sister that the Wesleys's lodgings had been ransacked, the Duke of Rothworth was unsatisfied with what little detail she could offer him when he quizzed her over the matter. Deciding he must hear the whole of the story from a more knowledgeable source (one who appeared to attract trouble like no other woman of his acquaintance), he lost no time in crossing the square.

Charlotte accompanied him and together they arrived at their uncle's townhouse in time to see Percy and Phoebe supervising the unloading of the last of the luggage from the carriage.

While his sister remained outside with her friends, Rothworth entered the house and was pleased to find his quarry in the vestibule, in the process of thanking his aunts and uncle for their hospitality.

"Are you unharmed, Miss Wesley?" he asked brusquely, walking over to her.

Caught unawares, she turned towards him with a warm smile and, for a moment, he could almost believe that she was happy to see him.

"Quite unharmed, thank you, Your Grace! Were you concerned about me?" she asked, a teasing glint in her eyes.

"Not in the least," he replied, conscious that his relatives were watching. "I'm certain your redoubtable character is up to any challenge, whether of your making or not."

As this was said in a way that seemed to imply he found nothing to admire in such a character, his uncle frowned at him, while his aunts merely looked surprised at such uncharacteristic discourtesy.

"Why, thank you!" replied Aurora with unabated affability. "I have always found that allowing a challenge to overwhelm one is not helpful in the least! But really, I can't take any credit in this instance. Your aunts and uncle have come to our rescue and we will be imposing on their hospitality."

"Reconnoitring?" he asked in a low voice meant only for her ears.

Aurora's eyes widened, and for an instant he thought he saw a flash of hurt in them.

This surprised him almost as much as the feeling of remorse he experienced at having been the cause of it, and he had to remember to harden his heart against such sentimentality.

This was not a woman with whom one could let down one's guard.

"What was that you said, Julian?" enquired Miss Coral, leaning closer to him.

"He said he was *reconsidering*," Aurora answered her with aplomb.

"What are reconsidering, my boy?" asked his uncle.

"I'm reconsidering the need to keep a careful eye on a certain gypsy," he replied dryly.

"That gypsy again!" exclaimed Miss Brinkley. "What in heavens is the matter with you? Why would you bring up such a wholly unrelated subject? I must say, ever since the day you went off chasing after this gypsy person in the Park, your manners have been most uncertain."

"I was not chasing after her . . . "

"Do not attempt to justify yourself now," she cut him off. "Miss Wesley has had a trying day and is no doubt eager to rest before dinner . . . and I imagine so too are her brother and cousin," she added, as the younger members of the party entered the vestibule.

John had also entered the house and, despite being weighed down with luggage, was refusing assistance from the footman sent to help him.

"I see you have brought your man," said Miss Brinkley, and, turning to the housekeeper waiting at the bottom of the staircase, asked: "Mrs Keating, I trust we will be able to accommodate an additional servant?"

"Indeed, ma'am," replied the woman.

"Oh no!" Aurora put in quickly. "We don't expect you to house John as well. We will procure a room for him in a boarding house or the nearest mews."

"My dear, we are not like some penny-pinching households I could mention, who expect servants to be housed elsewhere," Miss Brinkley informed her loftily. "Is your lady's maid also with you?"

"I have not had an opportunity to engage one as yet," replied Aurora, speaking as truthfully as she could without going into the specifics of their straightened circumstances.

Miss Brinkley accepted this without comment. Turning to her nephew, she said: "Rothworth, if you and Charlotte wish to join us for dinner, you may return at seven o'clock."

Realising he was not to be given an opportunity to speak with Aurora now, Rothworth resigned himself to the necessity of having to cancel a dinner engagement with some colleagues; the importance of which was suddenly diminished in light of his compulsion to discover more about today's incident.

"Thank you," he replied. "You may expect us."

"May I stay to help Phoebe settle into her room?" begged Charlotte. "My dress is perfectly satisfactory for a family dinner, so there is really no need for me to go home and change! Oh, do say I can stay, my two dearest of all aunts?"

After a wry comment from Miss Coral that they were her only aunts, delivered with an indulgent smile, Charlotte was granted her wish.

It seemed to Aurora that Charlotte was often granted her wish and she was torn between admiration for her skill in achieving her aims (recognising something of herself in the girl) and trepidation that Phoebe's more compliant character could be led astray.

Had she had the opportunity to hear the conversation between the girls, a short while later, she would have realised that her unease was justified.

Once the housekeeper had left them alone in the bedchamber assigned to Phoebe, Charlotte clapped her hands excitedly and cried: "Oh, what a *perfect* opportunity this afternoon's events have created for our plan!"

"It's really more your plan than mine," Phoebe felt bound to say. "I'm not at all certain we should take matters into our own hands."

"But have you not seen how they light up when the other is in the room?"

"No – do they?"

"Yes! Why, just the other day, when Miss Wesley came to drop you off for our walk, Julian actually left his library to come and speak with her. He *never* leaves his dratted library when he is working!"

Phoebe smiled weakly, but still looked unconvinced.

Her opinion was tainted by the memory of the duke grabbing dear Cousin Aurora's arm and calling her a thief. This incident had marred his image in her eyes, and she was yet to think highly of him; though she would, of course, never admit as much to his sister, who to her mind seemed to be inordinately attached to him for no easily discernible reason.

"Oh, never mind!" said Charlotte. "You'll have plenty of opportunity to observe them in each other's company over the next few weeks – I will make certain of it!"

Phoebe was very fond of her new friend, who was a year older and represented the more worldly ideal that she aspired to. However, having been brought up very strictly, she could not entirely approve of her plans.

"If Cousin Aurora and your brother were meant to be together, then surely they would be," she suggested tentatively.

"You mean, leave it to *Chance*?" scoffed Charlotte. "That's too uncertain a force on which to pin our hopes."

"But should we have any hopes? Cousin Aurora has told me that she has no plans to marry – something to do with her father, I think, though I didn't want to pry further when she mentioned it."

"Well, my brother is similarly reticent when it comes to marriage, but that is neither here nor there!" said Charlotte dismissively, waving a dainty hand. "They can't be expected to know what's best for them when they are both so prejudiced. Poor Julian has been *grossly* hunted for years and years, and has quite naturally acquired an aversion to women seeking him out for his title and fortune . . . it's why he only has liaisons with professional mistresses," she added with an authority that would have greatly surprised her brother.

Phoebe's eyes grew as round as saucers. "Really? How do you know?"

"Oh, everyone knows! Well, at least that's what Aunt Pearl says."

"She spoke to you of your brother's *mistresses*?"

"Well, no. Naturally she wouldn't do so. I overheard her and Aunt Coral discuss the matter once. Young ladies are never told anything really interesting, more's the pity!"

Phoebe agreed with this sentiment and began to unpack her valise.

After making a tour of the room and picking up and putting down various items in a preoccupied way, Charlotte asked with studied nonchalance: "Do you happen to know if Mr Wesley has a tendre for anyone at present?"

"Percy? Uhm . . . I don't know. He certainly goes out a great deal with his friends. And sometimes he tells us the most amusing stories about their antics, but he has never mentioned any women. Why do you ask?"

"Oh, no reason!" said Charlotte airily, rearranging the flowers in a vase that the housekeeper had brought in for Phoebe's enjoyment. "I was just thinking it's a shame . . . your cousin is a handsome and personable young man, I should think he could look as high as he wanted for a wife, if his family connections were more elevated."

Having never considered Percy in this light, Phoebe was surprised by her friend's train of thought.

"I suppose so. But I don't think Percy cares for such things in the slightest! He appears to be more interested in horses than women. He once confided in me that his grand passion is to one day breed them."

"I suppose his inheritance must be substantial enough to allow him to set up his stables?" probed Charlotte.

"I couldn't say, for I never thought to ask. My governess always told me that talk of money was distasteful and that I should never show an unbecoming interest in it."

Charlotte flushed a little, though she knew the rebuke was given unconsciously.

"Of course, money shouldn't matter in the least," she said with a sigh, looking downcast all of a sudden. "But an older brother . . . well, he might take it upon himself to be beastly if one's suitor is not sufficiently capable of supporting a wife . . . even if one had a large dowry that was more than capable of supporting them both!"

Realising from this speech that Charlotte was not speaking in general terms, it finally occurred to Phoebe that her friend may have developed an unfortunate attachment to Percy.

This thought so distressed her (no doubt because Charlotte was likely to suffer a bruised heart) that it quite sunk her spirits.

As she was mulling over how to give her friend a hint that her interest was not returned, a knock sounded on the door.

The entrance of a maid, who had been sent by Miss Brinkley to help Phoebe dress for dinner, brought to a close any further private conversation; and with the versatility of youth the young ladies abandoned their cares, and happily turned their attention to deliberating over the important matters of fashion and hairstyles.

Thirteen

Dinner that night was a less formal occasion than on the previous evening. Two leaves had been removed from the table and it had been set up for a comfortable seating of eight that allowed conversation between all the parties.

Aurora found herself between Rothworth and his uncle, the young people were seated together on the other side of the table, and Miss Brinkley and Miss Coral were at the head and foot respectively.

While their wine glasses were being filled by the butler, Rothworth, determined to be civil, asked Aurora if she was enjoying the exceptionally fine April weather.

The aloof manner with which he addressed her was calculated to keep her at a distance and succeeded in rousing her inner devil. She decided to prod him a little to expose the real man, rather than suffer the detached courtesy of the duke.

"Oh, I am not unnatural in my tastes!" she replied. "I enjoy fine weather as much as the next person. And just so that we have totally thrashed out this subject and will have no cause to return to it – ever again! – tell me, Your Grace, do you also enjoy fine weather?"

His cool demeanour crumbled under the weight of his annoyance. "Are you ever capable of behaving in a conventional manner?"

"When the occasion warrants it."

"I doubt it!"

"Now, don't get on your high ropes! You will have little relief if you do, for you are not as well positioned tonight to scowl at me all through dinner – as you did last night from across the table! I can only hope it will not mar your enjoyment of the evening?"

"I did no such . . . " He broke off, honesty compelling him to leave his rebuttal unfinished. After a pause, during which he had to remind himself of the need for civility, he went on stiffly: "If my behaviour offended you, Miss Wesley, then I must be sorry for it."

"Why, Your Grace, you disarm me! How can I refuse such a heartfelt apology?"

Rothworth found his jaw clenching. "Perhaps your sense of fairness might lead you to own that no apology was necessary. If memory serves, you effected such an air of unconsciousness – and barely took your eyes off Torrington! – I admit to being surprised you even noticed whether or not I looked in your direction."

"Oh, I was conscious," replied Aurora with a saucy smile. "I simply chose to ignore you. You can't expect me to reward such behaviour by acknowledging it?"

"I had good reason for my behaviour!"

"If you say so."

"You know very well I did – and still do! – though you choose to pretend otherwise."

"Are we back to your original accusation? Very well, I will play along for the moment! Were you scowling at me so frightfully because you were afraid I would pick Captain Torrington's pocket? And abuse your aunts' and uncle's trust so unforgivably?"

"I can't know for certain of what you may be capable – though I suspect there are few limits! And I never mentioned that my pocket was picked," he said pointedly. "I can't help but wonder how you came by that information?"

"My powers of deduction are not remarkable," she replied, unperturbed. "How else was the thief to relieve you of your purse? You have an air of stubbornness about you and I doubt you would have obliged her by simply handing over your money, even at gun point. Have I guessed correctly? Did she pick your pocket?"

"Your *guess* is astonishing in its accuracy. It's almost as if you were there."

Her eyes began to dance. "It must have taken some skill for her to extricate your purse."

"Hardly! She used an age-old woman's trick and kissed me to distract me."

"Did she?" A fleeting, surprised look entered her eyes. "But perhaps you do yourself a disservice. Perhaps it was no trick at all – woman's or otherwise! And I must say, I resent the insinuation that only women employ such tactics. Do you harbour a dislike of my sex, perchance?"

"Of course not!" he replied tetchily. "Whatever gave you that idea?"

As her response would have entailed referring to a conversation that had occurred while she robbed him, she sidestepped the question.

"All I am saying is that it's *possible* the kiss was unplanned. But I am merely postulating, of course."

He studied her, frowning.

"There was little other opportunity for her to take my purse," he said, though with less certainty.

"Oh well, no doubt you are correct." And turning away from him, she joined in Mr Brinkley's conversation with his younger sister.

Rothworth damned himself for allowing her to plant a seed of doubt in his mind. What was her reason for the kiss, if not to steal his purse?

And why was it of paramount importance to him to discover what that reason could be?

While Rothworth had his head full of her, Aurora had launched into a spirited discussion with Mr Brinkley and Miss Coral on a philosophical text published some thirty years ago.

"I wouldn't have thought that *A Vindication on the Rights of Women* would be of interest to you, Mr Brinkley," said Aurora, once he had finished giving his opinion of Mary Wollstonecraft's work. "Oh, forgive me – I just realised how parochial that sounded!"

"Not at all," he replied. "It is a reasonable assumption. But what you don't account for is that I grew up in a household of four women – my father died when I was very young – so it was inevitable that I would come to understand the struggles and prejudices they faced in our unequal society."

"Oh, what a trying time we had after he read that confounding essay!" groaned Miss Coral with a shake of her head, sending her yellow ringlets dancing. "Gregory was forever pointing out perceived examples of female oppression. It put quite a dampener on my first Season, I can tell you! What girl wants to hear that she is only being thought of as a decorative possession when she receives a posy of flowers from a gentleman? It became so unbearable I had to beg Mother to forbid him to mention the *Rights of Women* inside the house!"

Aurora laughed. "Was it your mother who introduced you to Miss Wollstonecraft's work, Mr Brinkley?"

"No. Actually it was my sister, Amber. Julian's mother. She bought me my own copy and insisted I read it. I believe she did the same for you, my boy?" Mr Brinkley asked his nephew.

A smile softened Rothworth's eyes. "She did. My mother held rather passionate views on the subject. And after reading Wollstonecraft's essay I came to understand the justice of those views."

Aurora turned to regard him with palpable surprise.

"Am I to understand that you agree women should be educated in a more comprehensive manner and given the opportunity to contribute to society?"

"Yes."

"And that we are deserving of the same rights as men?"

"In essence, yes."

"And that our treatment as mere ornaments or property only demeans both sexes?"

"An outdated notion I have never supported," he returned, happy to be able to offer proof that he did not in fact dislike woman.

Aurora leaned back in her chair and studied him as if seeing him for the first time.

"I must say, Your Grace, you have surprised me exceedingly! I was so certain I had taken your measure correctly."

"And what measure was that?"

"Oh, no!" she said, eyes twinkling. "I'm not so bold as to be drawn into incivility with your aunt and uncle looking on. But I will admit that I never thought a member of the House of Lords would allow himself to be beguiled by such revolutionary philosophy . . . are you quite certain you are not attempting to bamboozle me?"

"That is not something of which I have ever been accused," he replied, a smile spreading across his features.

It was the first genuine smile he had given her and Aurora found herself quite dazzled by it. Really, the man had no business being this handsome, she thought to herself.

Rothworth was experiencing his own heady sensation under Aurora's concentrated attention; but becoming aware that the table had quietened and they were being watched, he suddenly felt the danger of paying her too much attention.

Looking across to Percy, he asked him if he had yet had a chance to box at Gentleman Jackson's salon, and before long had drawn the young man into a discussion of his preferred sports; leaving his mind largely free to dwell on the confounding woman seated beside him, and to castigate himself for being so disproportionately pleased to have earned her approval.

After dinner, the ladies took themselves off to the drawing room to set up a game of Commerce, which Charlotte had decreed was to serve as their entertainment for the remainder of the evening. Once they had left the room, the gentlemen arranged themselves at one end of the table to enjoy their port in a more convivial grouping.

When the servants had left them to their privacy, Rothworth lost no time in setting out to extract information from Percy with which to either damn or redeem Aurora, and put an end to the conflicting emotions warring within him; though at present he was hard-pressed to say which outcome he would prefer.

"I understand you are in London to sort out a matter of inheritance," he began. "Are your efforts proving successful?"

"Yes, sir," replied Percy diffidently, the memory of his disgrace from last night still fresh in his mind and making him shy. "At least, it's progressing as well as can be expected under the circumstances. We hope not to impose on your aunts and uncle for more than a few weeks."

"Do not let the duration of your stay concern you," said Mr Brinkley, smiling kindly. "We're delighted to have you stay with us."

"The Court of Chancery has been known to grind through cases at a sluggish pace," Rothworth spoke up again. "I hope for your sake it proves otherwise."

"Our solicitor advised all should move fairly quickly through the courts," said Percy. "Unless, of course, it becomes necessary for me to lodge a Petition to The Crown."

"Then, I take it a succession to a title is in dispute?"

Percy flushed and looked conscious that he may have said too much.

Rothworth sipped his drink and waited.

His patience was rewarded when, after a few moments, Percy replied: "Actually, sir, not as yet . . . but it could develop into something of that nature."

Rothworth stored away that piece of information. There could not be too many disputed claims to a title at any given time.

Since his quarry was beginning to look skittish, he then turned the conversation to other subjects; but after twenty minutes or so, as they were preparing to re-join the ladies, he said: "I went to university with a Thomas Urquhart, from St Andrews. I wonder if there could be any relation to your mother's family?"

"Very possibly!" replied Percy. "They come from Fife. My mother used to say – joking with us, you know – that she had so many cousins she could walk into any public house throughout the whole of Fife and find an Urquhart to treat her to a Scottish ale . . . that was her favourite beverage," he divulged with the good-humoured candour that two glasses of port could bestow. "No matter how many years she spent in England, she couldn't grow fond of ratafia or Madeira. When my father had occasion to travel up to Edinburgh, to the university there, he'd always return with a cask of ale for her."

"She must have been an intriguing woman to know," said Rothworth. "And beautiful too, one would suppose, judging from your sister's looks."

"She was considered a great beauty in her time, but my sister looks nothing like her! She takes after the Marqu . . . ahem . . . " Percy made a show of clearing his throat and took a drink from his port, before continuing nonchalantly: "Yes, much to her consternation Aurora seems to have inherited her looks from our father's side of the family."

"Your father was a university don, was he not?" asked Rothworth casually.

"Retired! Though we'd often tease him that considering the amount of time he spent visiting Cambridge and Edinburgh to research his proofs, he might as well have still been employed!" Percy said with a grin.

"Were your father's proofs ever published?" asked Mr Brinkley with interest. "Perhaps I have heard of them."

"I believe they were, sir, but as to the subject matter or how they were received, I couldn't say. I never could make heads or tails of anything of that nature! You must ask my sister. She'd often assist him, and they'd spend hours in his study calculating this and that. Her brain is exceptionally well suited to mathematical thinking," he added with a good deal of pride.

Rothworth felt a flicker of guilt that he had plied the boy with port and allowed him to ramble on and reveal more than he realised. He seemed genuinely amiable and decent, and it was difficult to believe he was related to a certain auburn-haired gypsy, who might look like a lady but acted like no one of his acquaintance pertaining to that breed.

Someone had to keep an eye on her, and though he might not like stepping into the role, it was his duty to do so.

And as for her brother, it was unlikely that he was as innocent as he appeared. After his reaction on first laying eyes on him yesterday, there could be little doubt that he had recognised his sister's victim.

Fourteen

Rothworth had ample opportunity to study the *auburn-haired gypsy* a little time later. The whole party had crowded around a circular table and were busily employed in a game of Commerce, buying and trading cards in a raucous fashion. Even Miss Brinkley had temporarily abandoned her dignified demeanour and was handing out counters, handling the deck and ordering everyone about with the proficiency of a seasoned dealer.

Feeling the duke's eyes on her (not for the first time), Aurora raised her own to his and offered him a challenging look.

"Do you mean to frighten me, Your Grace, by staring me out of countenance?" she asked playfully. "Such tactics will not distract me from winning your counters!"

"Few would believe it," put in Charlotte, in high spirits, "but Julian can be most devious when he is playing to win! Is that not so, brother dear?"

"I must refute both charges," he returned, smiling lightly. "Miss Wesley, it would be a useless endeavour to stare you out of countenance – even if it were possible – when you have such an uncanny ability with the cards. And, Charlotte, I may play to win – which, after all, is the object of any game – but I am never devious, for that implies a level of underhandedness that is distasteful to me."

"Oh, alright! I'll give you that," replied Charlotte graciously. "I should have said *ruthless*."

"I am willing to accept that charge."

"I wish I could be more ruthless," sighed Miss Coral. "Perhaps then I wouldn't always be left with such dismal hands! It was not at all wise of me to trade you that last card, Phoebe dear."

"Oh, I'm sorry, Miss Coral! Shall I return it to you?" Phoebe asked and attempted to hand the card back.

"No!" cried Charlotte and Percy as one; then looked at each other and broke into laughter.

"They are quite right, dear," Aurora told Phoebe. "You must wait your turn if you would like to trade again. And only to the left, remember."

"Enough talk!" announced Miss Brinkley. "I must request that you all bring your attention back to the game. Gregory, it is your turn. Would you like to buy a new card or trade with Miss Wesley?"

"I believe I'll trade," said Mr Brinkley and smiled at Aurora. "If it is not too great an inconvenience?"

"It is your right, sir!" she replied gaily. "You must not consider my wishes in the least!"

They traded cards.

"Oh, dear," murmured Aurora, her expression one of laughing dismay as she stared down at her three cards. "I truly am sorry – it appears I am done!"

She knocked on the table and offered the other players an apologetic look.

"Not again, Rory!" cried Percy.

"You have the most famous luck, Cousin Aurora," Phoebe said with considerable awe.

"Really, Miss Wesley! We have hardly begun the round," objected Miss Brinkley. "Are you certain you are content with your hand?"

"A Tricon, I'm afraid," replied Aurora.

"Well, in that case, I suppose it cannot be helped,' Miss Brinkley acknowledged. "Place your cards on the table everyone."

It soon became evident that Aurora's hand was the highest and the pot was hers, and amidst much teasing she gathered up her winnings.

They rose from the table with the arrival of the tea tray, soon after, and congregated around Miss Brinkley and Miss Coral as they served.

"I should be disinclined to play against you if I ever met you across a table at White's or Brooks's," said Rothworth, joining Aurora where she stood a little to one side. "I doubt luck has any bearing whatsoever on your play."

"Perhaps a little."

"Or perhaps not at all!"

"Perhaps," she owned with a laugh. "I am often able to calculate who holds which cards."

"I see now what your brother meant when he said you were mathematically minded."

"Did he say so? Yes, I suppose I am."

"No doubt inherited from your father . . . such aptitudes often run in families," he said, watching her closely.

She hesitated for a fraction. "I have always found that one's inclination and focused attention play a far greater role in one's achievements that any heredity talent."

"In some instances."

"I believe it's true in *most* instances. Allow me to make my case by taking you as an example!" she said in a bantering way. "It's clear from the behaviour of your sister, and that of your aunts and uncle, that smiling does in fact run in the family. However, though we must assume that you too inherited this marvellous skill, you clearly have no inclination to practice it. It's little wonder your lips have grown stiff from disuse!" she said, audaciously studying his mouth.

He resisted the urge to gratify her by smiling.

"Simply because I don't smile to an extent that satisfies your tastes does not mean I am incapable."

"Oh, I know you are perfectly capable! You were gracious enough to show me an example of it tonight. I only point out that you are out of practice. If only you would exercise your smile more regularly, you would soon be proficient and charming the world!"

"I have no wish to charm the world," he replied, a little acerbically.

"Yes, that much is clear."

"I take it you think I should?"

"Well, for the majority – and by that I mean those not blessed with your privilege and Adonis-like looks . . . "

"Adonis? You make me sound like a right coxcomb!" he objected.

"I don't see why! It's hardly an insult. Most men would be delighted with half your good looks! And you can't tell me that you have not enjoyed the excessive female attention you have undoubtedly received because of them?"

"My looks have little to do with it. A dukedom and fortune override all else."

Aurora regarded him with incredulity.

Did the silly man really have no true understanding of the magnitude of his personal appeal? It was most odd . . . but also rather endearing.

"I'll not attempt to convince you otherwise," she said. "You are free to think of yourself as an oddity with no other attractions apart from wealth and a title."

He was drawn into a smile. "I didn't say I was an oddity."

"You might as well have! But shush now!" she said playfully. "You must not interrupt my train of thought again. I was about to dazzle you with some brilliant insight when you objected to being likened to a Greek god. I was saying, for the majority, we must exert ourselves to become agreeable to others. We are not solitary creatures by nature and living as part of a society does involve some expenditure of effort."

"My *expenditure of effort* is in ample evidence when I am amongst friends," he said.

"*Male* friends?"

"Yes . . . what of it?"

"Oh, nothing!" she replied airily. "I was just remembering that you do not like women."

"I have said nothing of the sort!" he retorted.

"No, of course not. Words are quite unnecessary when actions speak volumes."

"I'll have you know," he said with irritation, "I often enjoy the company of women!"

"Really, Julian," said Miss Coral, coming to stand beside him, teacup in hand, "I don't think it is appropriate to sully Miss Wesley's ears with talk of all your paramours."

Rothworth looked down at his aunt with barely contained exasperation. "I was referring to women in general."

"But, Julian dear, it's well known that you are not partial to the company of *ladies*." Her emphasis made it necessary for Aurora to stifle a laugh. "You don't mind me speaking freely, do you, Miss Wesley? I feel as if you are almost one of the family!"

"I'm honoured, ma'am!" said Aurora. "And I am not at all surprised to hear of your nephew's reputation."

Rothworth regarded Aurora frostily. "I can assure you, I do not have a reputation as a . . . "

" . . . Misogynist?" his aunt finished for him. "Oh no, certainly not! Your mother would never have allowed such a distortion of character. I only refer to a slight – a *very* slight – prejudice against a certain set of ladies . . . usually those between the ages of eighteen and forty."

Seeing that Rothworth was finding it difficult to contain his annoyance, Aurora forbore to laugh at this rather pointed teasing from his aunt.

"Allow me to bring you your tea, Miss Wesley," he said with stiff formality and went away.

"The poor boy!" clucked Miss Coral. "He has not yet learnt to laugh at himself. His father reared him with too great an emphasis on the elevated position he would one day hold. And, worse still, the need for mastery over his emotions . . . he was a pompous old goat!"

Aurora was surprised into a laugh at this offhanded insult.

Miss Coral smiled. "As you can see, I did not like him overly much. Neither did Pearl, and yet he somehow managed to beguile our sister Amber into accepting him. She thought they would deal well together, and I must admit it turned out to be the case. She knew how to handle him and he in turn was greatly attached to her. And of course, being a duchess allowed her to champion her favourite causes, so one must conclude it was a successful union. Were your parents happily married, my dear?"

"My mother's second marriage was very happy indeed," replied Aurora.

"I suppose she learnt her lessons from the first one. I have often observed that second marriages are more successful . . . ah, Julian, you are back! Now, if you'll both excuse me, I must see if I can rescue poor Mr Wesley from my sister's clutches! She was in the throes of explaining to him her ideas on how to deal with crime in London earlier, and he must be wishing to escape by now."

Her departure forced her nephew's hand. He had had the intention of delivering the tea and leaving the ladies to their conversation, but as he could not leave Aurora standing alone he was obliged to remain by her side.

"Am I forgiven?" she asked, her laughing eyes peering at him over the rim of her teacup.

"I doubt my forgiveness means a great deal to you," he replied with reserve.

"It should not, I'll grant you that. And yet, in some absurd way, I would be made a little unhappy to know I was past your forgiveness."

"I find that difficult to believe."

"So do I!"

Rothworth did not respond, and they stood together surveying the room as Aurora sipped her tea.

After several minutes had passed, she broke the protracted silence.

"Before I retire for the evening, allow me to tell you that you need not fear my intentions." She cast him a shrewd glance. "I'm as much a stranger to you as you are to me, so I don't blame you for your mistrust – you only wish to protect your relatives, who you clearly love very much. If there was another route open to me, rather than staying here, I would take it. But the circumstances being what they are, I can't take unnecessary risks with those *I* love. I don't expect you to understand, or even to forgive," she said with a smile. "I only want to assure you that I have the highest regard for your aunts and uncle, and will do nothing to betray their trust."

Having said all she wanted to on the subject, she inclined her head and made to walk away.

Rothworth laid a hand on her arm to stop her.

"If you are determined to win my trust," he said, "then tell me why your lodgings were searched today."

"Is that all it would take to win it?" she asked with a teasing look. "Oh, don't frown! I'm perfectly happy to tell you what I know. I can't be certain, of course, but I believe it has to do with Percy's inheritance. We had a ring in our possession that would have helped to prove the legitimacy of his claim."

"Had?"

"It was stolen today."

"Does your brother's inheritance have to do with a claim to a marquisate?" he asked abruptly, surprising her.

"How, for the love of God, did you guess that?" she asked, a good deal annoyed. "I certainly never referred to anything of that nature. Really, it's most tiresome of you!"

He smiled faintly at her displeasure. "Then it's true?"

"I suppose there's no point denying it, for it will all come out eventually. I only wanted to be circumspect until we had more clarity that matters would be resolved in Percy's favour."

Realising he was still holding onto her arm, he let go and took a discreet step away from her.

"Will you trust me with the name of the title?" he asked.

Aurora hesitated, torn between a surprisingly powerful wish to confide in him and other more pragmatic considerations.

A corner of Rothworth's mouth lifted, and he said with unexpected gentleness: "You look as if you have the weight of the world on your shoulders. I'll not press you – keep your secret if it will give you some peace."

"Oh, that is unfair!" she protested. "When I advised you to practice charming the world, I did not mean *me*."

"You must be easily impressed if you believe *that* was an attempt to charm you."

"I must be indeed . . . most peculiar," she murmured to herself, looking away. After a few moments, she lifted her eyes to his again. "Can I count on your discretion?"

"You need not ask, but as we are strangers – according to you – I'll allow it. You have my word."

She smiled faintly at his arrogance. "I meant no insult, but there's a great deal at stake. I imagine you have heard of the Dewbury family?"

"Certainly," he said, frowning. "You can't mean to tell me that your brother is the heir to the marquisate of Dewbury?"

"But I do."

Rothworth held her gaze as the possibility that he was being manipulated flashed through his mind.

Her apparent reluctance to reveal the truth; her brother's supposed slip over port; even their first meeting, all could be part of some elaborate scheme to gain his trust, and ultimately his support for their preposterous claim.

"I have heard the late marquess's son is sickly and being cared for by his mother in Dewbury Abbey," he said in a noncommittal fashion.

"We are aware the Family relied on that particular rumour to explain our absence. I suppose it's more palatable than admitting that my mother abandoned her marriage. "

"And what is your role in all this?" he asked, studying her closely.

"My role? I have no role as such," she replied, a little taken aback by the question. "Apart from being Percy's sister. And surely *that* can't be disputed, if that is what you are hinting at? I should think the resemblance between us speaks for itself! We share the same Dewbury nose – see?" She turned in profile so he could judge for himself. "I have been told it's distinguished, but really that is simply a more palatable way of saying *over-large.*"

Rothworth fought against the urge to find her disclosure endearing.

"The proportions suit your face and add character," he found himself saying.

"Oh, I'm not at all concerned about it!" she assured him. "I like my nose. And besides, my vanity does not rest in any single feature. I like to think we are judged on the whole."

"I never heard of there being two children from the marquess's marriage," he said, bringing the conversation back to less personal matters.

"Did you not? Well, since I was not born a boy, perhaps I was not thought sufficiently worthy to be remarked upon. The marquess certainly never thought me deserving of his attention . . . which was just as well, for there was nothing I dreaded more than to capture his notice! Did you know him?"

"No, our paths never crossed. But my father was acquainted with him."

"He was formidable, in more ways than one."

He regarded her in silent contemplation with a look she could not decipher, and after a pause said: "If I'm not mistaken, he died five or six years ago. Why does your brother pretend to be Mr Wesley if he is now a marquess?"

"He is not pretending – and neither am I!" she insisted. "We are honouring Papa – my mother's second husband. He was the best of men and gave us the protection of his name when we were all alone in the world . . . not legally of course, for that was impossible, but as far as everyone around us was concerned, he adopted us."

"But why continue with the ruse once he died?"

"Would you have Percy go around calling himself Lord Dewbury without first proving his claim to the title?"

"He could have proved his claim before now," he returned, his expression finally revealing his scepticism.

"He could have," she agreed, withdrawing from the camaraderie that had been developing between them. "But there were other considerations at play. I can see the conclusion forming in your mind – and I don't even blame you for it! It does all sound rather fantastical. But no, this is not a fraud or a swindle."

"I didn't say it was. However, without proof it's difficult to reconcile your version of events with what I know of the case."

"What you know of the case is so limited as to be rendered entirely inconsequential," she said bluntly.

"Perhaps if you shared the particulars . . . "

"It's a tangled story," she interrupted him, "and I can't go into it at present to the extent needed to satisfy you. I really have said more than I intended – it seems the jest was on me, after all! My advice was quite superfluous, for you can be a good deal more charming than I ever supposed, when the occasion suits you. Now, if you will excuse me."

She offered him a smile as she turned to leave, but something in her eyes gave him the impression that he had disappointed her. He wished he could disregard it, for it caused him to wonder whether her implausible story could be true.

He looked across at Percy, where he sat chatting to Phoebe and Charlotte on the settee. If the boy's claim was legitimate, it would certainly set the cat amongst the pigeons. Not only was the Dewbury title one of the oldest in the land, it was also attached to a vast fortune.

And since the marquess's son was known to be sickly, it had long been assumed that when the boy died his uncle would inherit everything.

Fifteen

Having passed a peaceful night, in no small measure to the comfortable feather bed in her room, Aurora awoke with a feeling of well-being and a determination to see out the plan that had been brewing in her mind ever since she had discovered the signet ring missing.

It was time to pay a visit; one she had hoped would take place under more auspicious circumstances.

After enjoying a leisurely breakfast with their hosts, Percy and Phoebe took a hackney back to their lodgings, to continue putting everything to rights before the landlady could discover the mess, while Aurora set off on foot with John as her escort towards a fashionable address only two blocks away.

"John, are you certain this is the house?" she asked when they were standing outside a large, freestanding mansion with a multitude of baroque carvings. "I don't have any memory at all of this façade."

"Don't suppose a child takes notice of such things," John pointed out. "But I remember well enough. The grooms' quarters are round the back, in the mews."

She continued to stare up at the house in silence, and, after a minute or so, confided: "I seem to be inordinately nervous . . . quite irrational really! The worst she could do is to decline to meet with me." She exhaled slowly and flashed John a smile. "There's nothing for it but to knock and find out! Let us hope my courage does not fail."

"Your courage ain't ever failed yet. Don't reckon it will now," said John in his phlegmatic way. "You always were one to set your own course, and there's no one alive able to keep you from it. You just make sure you don't let the old harridan talk down to you! You're more deserving than any of them, Miss Aurora – you remember that."

When he called her *Miss Aurora* it never failed to make her feel all of ten years old again and in need of his counsel. There was something wonderfully comforting – and, on occasion, irritating – in having companions who had known you since your birth and felt free to speak their mind in your presence.

Aurora smiled her gratitude and, readjusting the slim package in her gloved hands, mounted the steps to the front door.

She pressed the bell and waited. The door opened almost immediately and a porter in rose-coloured livery raked his eyes over her person. Appearing to find her worthy of his attention, his demeanour softened, and he politely enquired if he could be of assistance. Aurora could only be thankful that she had had the foresight to wear her best gown.

Telling him she wished to see the Dowager Marchioness of Dewbury on an urgent family matter, she removed a calling card (freshly printed only last week) from the tortoise-shell case in her reticule and handed it to him.

Almost before she had finished speaking, the young man informed her that her ladyship was not at home.

"Am I to understand that she is not receiving visitors?" asked Aurora.

"No, ma'am. She is out of the house and not expected to return for some hours."

"Oh . . . well, in that case, there is nothing for it but to return later," she said in a determined voice. "Would you be good enough to give her my card and tell her that I shall be back at three o'clock?"

The porter promised to ensure that both the card and message were delivered.

Aurora thanked him and turned to leave.

"Oh! And one more thing," she said hastily, facing him again. "Please give her ladyship this package . . . you may tell her it is from her granddaughter."

Astonishment registered on the porter's face, before it was quickly suppressed.

Closing the door, he thought fondly of the uproar such a staggering piece of gossip would generate below-stairs, and of the central part he would play in the upcoming drama; much to the annoyance of the butler, no doubt, who had proved to be his worst detractor of late, finding fault with every task he performed and refusing to assign him any important duties that would ensure his progression through the ranks, and all because of a trifling amorous incident with one of the maids.

Yes, he would finally be able to get his own back. When pressed for details, he would be the height of discretion and refuse to divulge anything he deemed as vulgar curiosity. He smiled as he thought fondly of the butler's thwarted expression.

It was only after he had started down the stairs to the servants' floor that he thought to look at the calling card in his hand.

Lady Elizabeth A. Dewbury.

*   *   *

As Aurora walked down the front steps, she hoped she had acted wisely. She would have preferred to place the package directly into her grandmother's hands. But, then again, there was no saying the old marchioness would see her without some added impetus.

Deciding it was useless to postulate one way or the other after the deed was done, she put the matter out of her mind and re-joined John on the footpath.

"I must return at three o'clock," she told him. "My grandmother is not at home."

John gave no indication of having heard her. Eyes squinting in concentration, he watched the back of a man as he crossed the street, his mincing step accentuated by the unusually high-heeled shoes he wore.

Aurora turned to better inspect the slim figure.

Skin-tight pantaloons of an arresting yellow hue first captured her attention, and then her eyes travelled up to take in a tight-fitting coat of celestial blue, with a waist nipped in so tightly she could only suppose the man was wearing a corset.

"My goodness!" she laughed. "He does look rather gorgeous . . . or do I mean garish? I suppose he must be what they call a *fop*. The papers are always full of caricatures of such gentlemen."

"He left the house through the servants' entrance," said John. "I'm thinking a gentleman's gentleman is the closest he'll come to the title."

"A valet? He must have a most indulgent master to be allowed to dress in such a fashion! And you say he came from *this* house?"

"I did. And I've a mind to get my hands on him and ask him to explain just what he thinks he's up to," John muttered darkly.

Aurora looked across at him in surprise. "What can you mean? Is the man known to you?"

"I've a fair notion I saw that exquisite yesterday morning, as Master Percy and I left the solicitor's."

Aurora's expression turned shrewd as her eyes returned to the retreating figure.

"Ah . . . that would explain our surprise visit yesterday," she said with a frown. "They must have put a watch on Mr Tadley's office. Dash it! I should have foreseen such a move! Can you discover who his master is? I assume it's my uncle, but perhaps I have other male relatives living in the house."

"I'll go round back and pay an old friend a visit. Last I heard he was still working for the family, as head groom. Leave it with me, Miss Aurora."

"You're an angel, thank you!" she said with a grateful smile. "I don't know what Percy and I would have done without you these last few years."

John huffed to cover up his embarrassment and said gruffly: "There's nothing to be thanking me for! I gave my word to your mother I'd look out for you and Master Percy, and that's what I'm set on doing – with or without your thanks. Makes no difference to me."

"Well, it makes a difference to me, so it will have to be *with* my thanks. Now, I'd best leave you to go and speak with your friend, while I hurry back to our lodgings. I would hate for poor Percy and Phoebe to be accosted by our landlady! If she should see the state of the rooms, there's no saying how she'll react."

However, when Aurora re-joined her brother and Phoebe, a short while later, she found them quite un-accosted, and studiously working their way through the rooms to bring them back into order. With her help they managed to put everything to rights in a few short hours, and only then did she go off to speak with the landlady to apprise her of their unanticipated departure.

After thanking her for her hospitality with a generous douceur to forestall any grumbling, they left the lodgings for the last time and made their way back to Mayfair.

Aurora dropped Percy and Phoebe at the Brinkley townhouse, and then went on in the hackney and arrived at the Dewbury mansion a few minutes past three o'clock.

For the second time that day the front door was opened to her by the porter and, in rather more sombre accents than he had employed earlier, he asked her to step inside.

She was met in the large entrance hall by the butler, who cast his eye over her in a way calculated to absorb as much detail about her person as possible, and then led her up a double marble staircase to a drawing room on the first floor.

The room was magnificently proportioned and decorated in vibrant colours, which only served to accentuate the austere black attire of the woman occupying it. She was standing by the windows and gazing out at the street when Aurora was announced.

Turning in an unhurried manner, she faced her guest and inspected her in silence.

Aurora's emotions were heightened by being in the presence of her grandmother after so many years, but she had to force herself to remain still and accept the thorough perusal with an impassive expression.

She had few memories of the dowager marchioness, but what little she did remember gave her a sense that the woman had held her in affection. Still, it was unlikely that affection had survived the passage of time and all that it entailed.

The dowager's withered proportions and aged complexion, coupled with an air of gentle sorrow that seemed to emanate from her, despite her impenetrable expression, stirred Aurora's protective instincts in a way she had not anticipated, and she found she could not summon up any resentment towards the woman.

The dowager marchioness finally gestured to the settee.

"Won't you be seated?" she uttered in a colourless voice; and sat down on a crimson velvet-covered chair and waited for Aurora to comply.

"Thank you for seeing me, Lady Dewbury," said Aurora, taking her place. "I know it must have come as a shock to you, and I hope you will forgive me my boldness."

"One becomes immune," replied the old woman. "You are not the first to present yourself as my granddaughter."

"I hope I shall be the last, however! I can only imagine how trying it must have been for you to be targeted by charlatans. My mother couldn't have foreseen how you would be importuned. She would have been distressed to know of this additional pain inflicted on you."

Lady Dewbury gave no response to this. After a pause, she began to speak in a detached way, as if retelling a story that had often crossed her lips.

"My son and his wife had a volatile marriage – a regrettable state of affairs for all concerned. After one particularly incendiary argument, the marchioness disappeared with the children for some weeks. My son was naturally concerned, however, it would have been best had he resisted the impulse to hire the indiscreet individuals he tasked with finding her. Unsurprisingly, rumours began to circulate soon after. The outcome of it all was that for the last twenty years I have been plagued by a succession of *lost heirs* come to claim their inheritance . . . despite the fact that the marchioness, along with my grandson and granddaughter, have lived in our ancestral home in the country ever since their return after those ill-fated missing weeks."

"What a remarkable story," said Aurora, doing her best to keep the exasperation from her voice. "I can't help but feel relieved that my mother did not return to her marriage, if being cloistered at Dewbury Abbey for the last twenty years was to be our fate. It wouldn't have suited me in the slightest! Forgive me, I don't mean to make light of the situation, but really, it's preposterous to think we would readily have agreed to be incarcerated in such a way!"

"My grandson is gravely ill," said Lady Dewbury coldly. "It is his mother's duty to look after him."

"Yes, I suppose it would be the duty of any parent. But I don't see why *I* was also cast into such a sacrificial role? Did no one ever wonder why I never had my coming out? Or were people allowed to forget that the marquess also had a daughter?" she asked, a little wryly.

Lady Dewbury did not respond; nor did her expression give anything away.

"Your ladyship, I know what has been fabricated to keep the world ignorant of our absence," said Aurora, relenting and offering her grandmother a smile. "I promise you, I have no wish to lay blame at anyone's door! You did what you thought was necessary. My only concern is for Percy to be given a fair chance to prove his claim . . . and sending people to ransack our lodgings and take my father's signet ring is not, to my mind, playing fair."

There could be no mistaking the surprise that lived briefly in the dowager's eyes.

"I see you did not know," Aurora said with relief. "I must admit to being glad. I didn't expect the Dewbury family to welcome us with open arms, but neither did I think we would be treated so shabbily. But I don't mean to go on and on about it – I find complainers vastly boring! May I ask, your ladyship, if you had the opportunity to read my mother's letters over the years?"

"I have read all correspondence pertaining to the matter," replied Lady Dewbury coolly.

"Would you allow me to describe to you the contents of each one? It may help to prove . . . "

"That won't be necessary."

Aurora accepted the rebuff with a nod. "Well, if you ever change your mind, I would be happy to do so. When I was old enough to understand their importance, Mama began to include me in the drafting of them. And upon her death, you must know it was I who continued to write to you, to apprise you of Percy's health and our intention to return when he was of age."

"What name do you go by?" the dowager asked all at once. "You were announced as Lady Elizabeth Dewbury, but we both know that is not your name."

"That *was* my name a long time ago," Aurora contradicted her gently, "but I prefer Aurora Wesley these days."

"Elizabeth Aurora Dewbury is my granddaughter's name . . . but I suppose you already know that?"

Aurora smiled a little sadly. "I see I have not managed to convince you . . . a shame, but I suppose it can't be helped. Besides, my main objective in coming today was not to convince you, but to ascertain if you had knowledge of the ring being stolen. And, if not – which thankfully appears to be the case! – to ask you to keep other members of the family from further unconscionable behaviour. In particular, I would like assurance that Percy will not be harmed in any way . . . and surely, if there is even the *slightest* chance that he is your grandson, you too must wish to see him safe?"

The dowager marchioness held Aurora's gaze for a long while.

"No one will be harmed," she said at last. "It is offensive to me for you to suggest otherwise. No matter what you have been told of us, we do not hold our family's honour so cheap as to engage in Shakespearean intrigues."

Realising she would gain no further assurances, Aurora had to be satisfied.

"I apologise if I offended you by speaking my greatest fear. The only excuse I can offer is that I love my brother very much and would move heaven and earth to ensure his safety! As to his inheritance, I must trust in the courts and don't mean to inconvenience you further with futile petitions."

"You appear to be a lady who knows her own mind," Lady Dewbury observed meditatively. "It was the same . . . " She paused, and seemed to recollect herself. "It is not so common a trait."

"If I don't know my own mind, who will?" replied Aurora, smiling again and rising to her feet. "Thank you for hearing me out! I will leave you now."

The dowager marchioness rang the bell on the table at her elbow. "Andrews will see you out."

The butler, who must have remained waiting in the hallway, entered immediately.

"Do not forget your book, Miss Wesley." Lady Dewbury gestured to an age-worn child's book on the table. "I have no use for children's stories."

"Many years ago, my grandmother used to visit the nursery and read to me," said Aurora with a softened look. "*Goody Two-Shoes* was my favourite story, so I would ask her to read it to me over and over again. She must have been quite bored of it by the end, but she never refused me! We would sit together by the tall windows that overlooked the garden. It was a lovely outlook all year round, but spring was our favourite season. We could watch the apple tree outside the windows blossom almost before our eyes. I have treasured that book for many years as a memento from that time, and it would please me if you would accept it as a gift."

Lady Dewbury's gaze, which had remained pinned on Aurora throughout the entire interview, drifted away from her; she gave an almost imperceptible nod.

Aurora dropped into a curtsy, and then followed the butler out of the room.

Sixteen

While Aurora was visiting Lady Dewbury, Percy and Phoebe were quite unconsciously ingratiating themselves into their hosts' affections with their good-humoured antics and artless chatter. As a result, upon her return Aurora had to listen to their praises being sung by all three siblings, and though she was, of course, pleased to have it so, she was also relieved when the need to change for dinner spared her from further disclosures on the subject.

The evening passed in domestic comfort. An excellent meal, enhanced by lively conversation, was followed by a game of loo. And, later, Aurora was invited to entertain them all at the pianoforte; which she agreed to most readily as music was one of her favourite diversions.

She began by playing a country dance, her energetic execution encouraging everyone to clap along, and then followed this up by singing a few popular ballads. Her voice was warm and engaging, and her audience was so absorbed in her performance that no one noticed the Duke of Rothworth and his sister walk into the room.

"Oh, what a wonderful voice you have!" cried Charlotte when the clapping had died down. "Good evening, everyone! We thought to surprise you with a visit. I wanted to arrive earlier, but my brother wouldn't listen to reason! *See*, Julian, if not for your excessive scruples we might have enjoyed Miss Wesley for longer."

"You wouldn't wish for us to make a nuisance of ourselves by always being underfoot?" he replied, before turning his smile on the room. "Good evening. Excuse us for intruding. Charlotte insisted on paying you a short visit after dinner."

"I wanted a *long* visit, including dinner, but I was overruled," amended his sister.

"You must at all times treat the house as your own," insisted Mr Brinkley.

Charlotte cast her brother a look of *I told you so.*

"Your manners are atrocious," he told her with a fond flick of her nose.

Charlotte offered him an impish smile and, turning to Aurora, asked: "Won't you please sing another song for us, Miss Wesley?"

"I can certainly try," replied Aurora. "But I fear I have exhausted my repertoire! Although, I do know a Scottish ballad my mother taught me, in Gaelic, if you are willing to hear it?"

Her suggestion was greeted with every evidence of pleasure by all, and she began to play.

The mood of the ballad was wistful. A sweet, soaring melody melded beautifully with the soulful notes of the verses, which (if one could understand) spoke of things past and things that could never be.

As the last melancholy note died away, Aurora looked up and was surprised to see Miss Brinkley surreptitiously wipe away a tear from her cheek; while her other listeners appeared to be absorbed by their own thoughts.

"Oh dear!" Aurora laughed uncertainly. "Was it truly awful? I never could appreciate such gloomy ballads and shied away from practicing them."

"You were *magnificent*," uttered Miss Coral in choked accents, her plump hands pressed against her bosom. "I did not understand a word, of course, and yet somehow I *felt* what you were singing."

Rothworth raised his eyes from his contemplation of the carpet. "You have a way of delivering a song, Miss Wesley, so that it takes on intimate meaning to whoever hears it."

Everyone agreed with this sentiment and were soon adding their own praise, building in exuberance until Aurora had to laughingly beg them to stop before they put her to blush.

She then called on Phoebe and Charlotte to have their turn and gave up her seat to them.

While the girls decided on who would play and who would sing, Aurora poured herself a cup of tea and walked over to join Miss Brinkley on the settee.

"What a talent you possess, Miss Wesley. You remind me most powerfully of Elizabeth Billington."

"Now, I know you must be teasing me, ma'am! I have been told Mrs Billington was one of the greatest singers of her time."

"*The* greatest in my opinion. It's a shame she was taken from us recently . . . Charlotte, do not put that branch of candles on the pianoforte . . . no, dear, not there either . . . wait! I shall assist you."

While Miss Brinkley went off to help her niece, Rothworth took the opportunity to take the chair nearest to Aurora.

"I had occasion to meet Lord Charles Dewbury this afternoon," he informed her casually.

Aurora had not seen him since the previous evening, when he had questioned the validity of her family background, and she now regarded him with a good deal of surprise.

"You told me that you didn't know my uncle?"

"I did not. I imposed upon a mutual acquaintance to introduce us."

"One might well wonder why!" she declared, not entirely pleased.

"I thought it would prove useful if I cultivated his acquaintance. One never knows how I might be able to assist your brother's claim."

Aurora's surprise grew to the point of incredulity. "But you made it quite clear that you doubted the veracity of my story. Not to mention, I have never asked you to embroil yourself in our affairs! I hope you don't think I revealed our business to you with that in mind?"

"I don't think it," he replied; though he could have added *anymore*.

He had not been idle since their conversation last night. Telling himself he had a right to delve into the history of anyone residing with his family, he had initiated an investigation into Aurora's claims. It had been less than a day, but already his secretary had discovered that the Marchioness of Dewbury had been represented in a handful of matters, in the public record, by a solicitor who was not from the firm that customarily looked after the interests of the Dewbury family. And that same solicitor was representing Aurora and her brother. It was a small detail but, to his mind, important.

"There's no point denying, however," he continued, "that I hold some sway in the Lords and, if it comes to it, could be of use to you. In any case, I didn't feel I needed your permission to acquaint myself with Lord Charles. With him set to leave town, it seemed appropriate for me to seize the opportunity."

"He is to leave town?" asked Aurora, suddenly alert. "Are you certain?"

"I overheard him talking at our club that he was going to Dewbury Abbey."

Aurora sipped her tea as she wondered whether it was possible that her uncle's departure from London was tied in some way to the theft of the ring.

She would have to ask John to approach his friend at the Dewbury stables again and try to discover what he could. This man had already proven useful by disclosing to John that only the dowager marchioness, Lord and Lady Charles, and their adolescent son resided in the Dewbury town mansion; Aurora's female cousins having married and moved away.

And, most importantly, the exquisitely dressed valet they had seen earlier was indeed her uncle's man.

"What did you think of Lord Charles?" she asked Rothworth presently.

"He appears to be well adapted to indulgence," he replied deprecatingly. "In truth, I didn't warm to him, although he is widely considered to be a genial fellow. He manages to mix obsequiousness with conceit, and I have never had much patience with either trait."

"But is he a *good* man?"

"I couldn't say on such short acquaintance. I did have some opportunity to observe him in the company of his friends, and the worst I can say of him at present is that he seems to possess a weak character – a certain malleability that makes him prone to be easily led by others. That said, I wouldn't underestimate him. Greed has a way of stiffening a spine."

"I have no intention of underestimating him! I went to considerable effort today to spike his guns."

"May I ask how?"

"You may, of course," she replied with the utmost of good humour, and returned to enjoying her tea.

"I see you mean to put me in my place," he said, smiling. "Probably with good cause, but I'm not so easily abashed."

"Oh, don't smile at me in that fashion! I refuse to be charmed again into revealing my business."

"I won't say another word." His smile widened, crinkling the corners of his eyes.

Aurora eyed him with disfavour, then sighed resignedly.

"For the life of me I don't understand why I can't remain displeased with you! If you must know, I spoke with my grandmother and informed her of the theft of the signet ring. I'm happy to say, I don't believe she had a hand in it. I also suggested that she use her influence to ensure Percy's safety – I can only hope she has some sway over the relevant party!"

"Your uncle?"

"I have no wish to accuse anyone without evidence."

"But you suspect him."

"I have said nothing of the sort! I beg you stop putting words into my mouth."

"It's a simple matter of deduction. Lord Charles has the most to lose if your brother's claim to the title is successful."

"I don't deny that. However, I don't want to discuss the culpability of one peer with another."

"In other words, you don't trust me sufficiently," he said, not mincing words.

"Some matters are too delicate for general consumption," she replied.

"So now I'm relegated to the status of a *general* acquaintance – worse and worse!"

Despite his aggrieved look, she realised he was ribbing her, and her expressive eyes lit with humour.

"Perhaps not *general*. I would sooner say *reticent*. Which is why I find it simply extraordinary that you would offer yourself up in the role of confident and sponsor . . . particularly after our first meeting."

"You mean, when you held me at gunpoint," he remarked conversationally.

"I mean nothing of the sort! I was referring to the time you manhandled me and accused me of stealing your purse."

"Ah, of course! The *second* first meeting. And I did not manhandle you. I certainly wanted to! But I restrained myself with heroic effort."

"Why, Your Grace, are you flirting with me?" she asked with a shocked expression.

"If I ever do so," he retorted, "there'll not be the slightest need for you to ask. It will be self-evident."

"Oh, don't look so affronted!" she said, breaking into a smile. "I couldn't resist the urge to ruffle your composure a little."

"I think we can agree, for all concerned, it would be best if you learnt to control your urges."

"Oh, stop!" she exclaimed, laughter welling up inside her. "How can you tempt me with such blatant provocation? It is unsporting of you when I'm shackled by the propriety expected in your aunts' drawing room . . . if I were not, I would ask you which urges you had in mind."

"And I would reply: all the baser ones."

"No man has ever required *that* of me before," she responded coquettishly. "Generally, they favour quite the opposite."

He broke into a reluctant smile, though he managed to say sternly: "I see you mean to shock me."

"Would you prefer I play the innocent?"

"Good God, no! What I prefer is no play-acting of any kind."

"What are you discussing?" enquired Miss Brinkley, coming back to sit beside Aurora on the settee. "You have had your heads together for some time."

"Your nephew was instructing me on his theory on *base urges*," said Aurora, giving him a taunting look.

"Rothworth, indulging in indelicate conversation?" asked Miss Brinkley, looking greatly surprised.

"Oh no, ma'am," replied Aurora. "His Grace was speaking – with great delicacy! – about the need to *control* one's baser urges."

"Hmm . . . I should have known," remarked Miss Brinkley. "This excessive infatuation you have with control, Rothworth, should not be encouraged. One should be free to express oneself – even one's baser instincts, if the occasion warrants it."

Her companions were taken aback by this unanticipated viewpoint and exchanged a look of amusement.

"I see I have surprised you," went on Miss Brinkley. "But I speak from experience. No good will come of concealing your true nature . . . though discretion must be exercised, of course! I don't recommend revealing yourself to simply anyone, for we all must don certain masks at certain times. But in front of those closest to us – or those with whom we wish to become closer – we must be fearless and lay ourselves bare. It is the path to true happiness."

"I see, ma'am, that you are a philosopher!" said Aurora. "And I wholeheartedly agree with your sentiments."

"My aunt has always been wise beyond her years," said Rothworth.

"Oh, stop the flummery!" objected Miss Brinkley.

"Am I not allowed to show my appreciation of you after all you advised?" he countered.

She offered him a grudging smile. "Touché! And now, do not think that I wish to get rid of you, but I think it best if you take Charlotte home. I noticed my sister is looking a trifle peaky and she confided in me that she is not feeling well. We were caught in a shower this morning and I suspect it is merely a chill, but she should be in bed, and it will be easier to convince her to retire if you leave."

Rothworth agreed to it at once, and within a few minutes had said his goodbyes and marshalled his sister out of the house.

Seventeen

Aurora insisted on escorting Miss Coral up to her bedchamber. However, when she offered to help prepare her for bed, she was rebuffed and told that Lington (Miss Coral's lady's maid) was more than capable of seeing to her comfort; not that she needed any assistance, in any case, for she was feeling perfectly fine and her sister was making too great a deal out of a little headache.

But on the following morning, it was clear that her illness was more serious than they had supposed, having all the symptoms of influenza, and the doctor was called.

While they waited for this gentleman to arrive, Aurora took the opportunity to leave the house and go in search of the ingredients for a healing tisane her mother had always used when members of the household fell sick.

Phoebe insisted on joining her, and together they made their way on foot to an apothecary on Bond Street that had been recommended to them by Miss Brinkley.

They found the shop without difficulty and Aurora was able to order the dry flowers, roots and lichen she needed for her recipe. The owner was most helpful and assured her everything she required was in stock, but having fallen victim to her charm he took his time in compiling the order so he could engage her in conversation.

It was some fifteen minutes before they were finally able to leave.

"My goodness, I thought that man would never let you go!" exclaimed Phoebe. "When he offered for you to try his special pastille recipe for the *third* time, I was never closer to groaning."

"He was bored and in need of conversation," Aurora said with amusement. "We can afford to be tolerant of other people's whims for a few minutes if it will bring them a little happiness."

"I suppose so. Although it seemed to me that he took unfair advantage of your good nature. If that lady had not come in looking for a draught, we would still be listening to him try to flirt with you!"

"Oh no, not *flirt*," said Aurora with a laugh. "He only sought to banter with me to pass the time."

"His bantering looked a lot like flirting to me, Cousin Aurora."

"Oh well! It was innocent enough. And I'm a firm believer that there's no harm in a little light flirting if it will help ease our path through life."

After a thoughtful pause, Phoebe remarked: "Percy believes that a gentleman shouldn't flirt with a lady if he cares for her."

"Does he? How like him to say something so naïve! Most women would be disappointed to find themselves esteemed too highly to be eligible for a man's flirtations."

"But Percy seems to think . . . " Phoebe broke off suddenly and Aurora could not but be glad; the habit her young friend had fallen into of parroting every word to come out of Percy's mouth was starting to become tiresome.

But upon glancing at her, Aurora realised she had not simply thought better of her words; she appeared to have suffered a great shock, for all the colour had drained from her face and she was staring at something across the road with an appalled expression.

"What is it, dear?" Aurora asked sharply.

Phoebe turned her back on whatever had caught her attention and exclaimed in a whisper: "*The Despicable One*! Near the haberdashery! Oh, Cousin Aurora, what am I to do?"

It did not take Aurora long to locate the large figure of Phoebe's guardian amongst the pedestrians. He was in the company of another man, of more refined appearance but wearing just as disagreeable an expression, and together they were making their way down the street in silence.

"He has found me! Please, please don't allow him to take me away!"

"Calm yourself, dear. I have no intention of allowing anyone to take you away. Your guardian is unlikely to remember me, so if you keep your back to him he will soon move on."

"But I'm wearing my favourite pelisse," said Phoebe, raising scared eyes to Aurora. "He is bound to recognise it."

Aurora cast a look over the primrose silk garment and saw the problem at once.

"Yes, that will never do! You must take it off. Slowly, dear . . . as if you have decided you are feeling a trifle hot . . . good girl! Now, hand it to me."

Making quick work of rolling up the pelisse into a bundle, she placed her paper parcel from the apothecary on top and secured both under her arm.

"Phoebe, do you see that old hack coming towards us? When it reaches us, we are going to keep pace with it until the corner, and then we'll turn off Bond Street and leave the area. Are you ready, dear?"

Phoebe nodded with a valiant effort at courage.

Taking her arm, Aurora waited for the vehicle to draw level with them, and then started to walk, keeping its bulk between them and their unsuspecting pursuer.

As luck would have it, before they could reach the corner, Mr Wilkinson and his companion crossed the road and were suddenly stepping onto the pavement in front them, only a few meters away.

Seeing no other alternative, Aurora turned to the carriage beside them, wrenched open the door and thrust Phoebe inside. Quickly following her in, she closed the door and drew the curtain across the window.

Only after she was satisfied that they could not be seen from outside did she turn her attention to her surroundings.

"Oh, for goodness sake, not you again!" she exclaimed, her disbelieving gaze falling on the Duke of Rothworth, lounging at his leisure against the tattered upholstery beside her. "Fate appears to have a very odd sort of sense of humour to be continually throwing you in my way!"

Rothworth chose not to disclose that Fate was not to blame on this occasion. He had been setting out on foot for Jackson's boxing salon when he had seen her leave his uncle's house. The earliness of the hour, coupled with his lingering distrust, fed his sudden inclination to follow her.

Since it was easier not to be noticed in a carriage, he had hailed the first hackney to cross his path, and for the last fifteen minutes had been circling Bond Street, debating with himself on whether or not to wait for her to leave the apothecary.

He told himself it was his duty to discover if she was up to anything of which his uncle and aunts might disapprove. But the reality of it was nothing so noble . . . as he knew only too well, much to his consternation.

"May I point out that it was you who burst in on me," he responded equably.

"You have missed my point entirely, Your Grace – which shouldn't surprise me! You seem to have a predilection for arriving at a conclusion before knowing all the facts."

"But I've learnt my lesson and now shy away from drawing conclusion where you are concerned, madame. I've even learnt to not be surprised by the odd things you do. Now, do you expect me to guess, or will you tell me the reason you invaded my privacy? That's not to say that I'm not delighted to have your and Miss Lennox's company," he added with a polite nod at Phoebe.

Phoebe was huddled into a corner opposite them, and only managed a faint smile.

"Forgive me!" said Aurora, looking a little shamefaced. "I allowed my surprise to lead me into ill-mannered remarks. Phoebe and I are in fact exceedingly grateful to you! You came to our rescue at the most opportune time . . . and no, I'm sorry to say I can't explain why that should be case," she forestalled his question. "I don't wish to lie to you, so it's best if we say no more on the subject."

Rothworth regarded her in the absorbed manner of one who had come across a strange quirk of nature.

"Oh dear, I really have shocked you this time!" she said, smiling ruefully.

"I was just thinking," he said meditatively, "how peaceful and predictable my existence used to be before I had the pleasure of making your acquaintance. I really had no idea what a dull life I led."

"Not dull, surely? Perhaps a little constrained."

"There is no need to console me. I liked my dull existence."

"Did you? Well, there's no accounting for tastes," she replied, eyes dancing.

"You are incorrigible. Where would you like me to deposit you?"

Aurora sobered. "Your uncle's house. Miss Coral appears to have caught the influenza and a doctor has been sent for. We stepped out only to buy some ingredients for a tisane I hope will provide her some relief."

"I'm certainly sorry to hear that," he said. "I fear she has proven to be susceptible to any passing illness of late. I'll come with you to hear what the doctor has to say."

On their return to the house, they were met by Mr Brinkley in the vestibule and informed that the doctor had just left, and had left a draught and a long list of instructions for the care of the patient, who had indeed contracted influenza and was likely to feel very poorly for the next week or so.

"I will go up to her," said Aurora, beginning to climb the stairs.

"Can I come?" asked Phoebe. "I'd like to be of help to dear Miss Coral. Perhaps I could read to her?"

"That is very kind of you, dear, but I can't allow it," replied Aurora. "You are under my care and I wouldn't wish for you to fall sick as well."

"The same must apply in your case, Miss Wesley," said Rothworth. "We can't allow you to visit my aunt's sickroom and risk your own health. I am certain my uncle will agree with me."

"Yes, indeed!" Mr Brinkley said at once. "Coral will be well cared for by her maid. And Pearl, of course."

"But they shall need some respite," Aurora pointed out. "Particularly if a careful watch must be kept up during the night, which is often the case with the influenza when the patient is a little older. I have experience of the illness as it afflicted our household most winters, and as I am never sick it was left to me to nurse everyone. So, you see, you must not have any concerns on my account!"

And on those decisive words, she proceeded upstairs and disappeared.

"You can't allow her to put herself in harm's way," Rothworth told his uncle.

"What would you have me do, my boy? I don't think I can stop her. She is a most determined young lady," said Mr Brinkley, an avuncular fondness entering his eyes.

"Pig-headed, you mean! You must ask Aunt Pearl to make her see reason."

But when the idea was presented to Miss Brinkley later that afternoon, that she should keep Aurora out of the sickroom, she informed her brother that their guest had made herself so indispensable, and seemed to know just how to handle the recalcitrant mood that had come over the patient, that it would be counterproductive to keep her away. Not that she had any hope of being able to do so in any case, she added, for Miss Wesley was exhibiting a surprisingly stubborn streak (no doubt from her Scottish heritage) and would not be denied her share of the nursing.

Eighteen

Easter came and went without much notice from the Brinkley household. For some days, while Miss Coral's influenza was at its zenith, it was decided that she was not to be left alone. It was a particularly nasty bout, and she spent a good deal of the time in a fevered delirium.

The household settled into a routine. Miss Coral's maid would look after her mistress during the night; Miss Brinkley would sit with her in the mornings and be present when the doctor came; and Aurora would take over during the afternoon and early evening.

The Duke of Rothworth visited every day. Although his uncle was always at hand to keep him informed of the patient's progress, he never managed to hit on a time that allowed him to speak with Aurora. She was either at his aunt's bedside or out walking with Phoebe; a form of exercise that she apparently believed was most healthful when there was sickness in the house.

He did not know why it had become so necessary for him to speak with her, but when on the fourth day he arrived at the house after dinner, in the hopes of catching her before she went to bed, and was yet again told that she was unavailable as she was with his aunt, he determined to go upstairs himself.

"You wish to see Coral *now*?" Miss Brinkley asked him with surprise.

He had been shown into the drawing room moments before, to find his aunt and uncle enjoying a glass of sherry, and Percy and Phoebe playing cards on the settee.

"Yes," he replied. "I want to check on her, and speak with Miss Wesley. I shan't stay long."

"Are you certain you should, my boy?" asked Mr Brinkley. "It appears to be a most contagious illness. Only this morning Coral's maid succumbed and had to take to her bed, which is how it came about that Aurora is now sitting with her."

"Not that Lington wished to go," put in Miss Brinkley, who was looking unusually tired and drawn herself. "She is greatly attached to my sister and was determined to do her duty by her. But the moment Aurora laid eyes on her, she insisted that she go and rest. You know how it is when Aurora fixes her mind on something."

Rothworth did indeed recognise this trait; more than his aunt could imagine.

He also found it remarkable that his relatives were referring to their guest as *Aurora*, and concluded that they had been charmed (probably against their will) into abandoning the proprieties; another trait of hers that seemed to hold universally true.

"I am not at all certain you will be welcome upstairs," went on Miss Brinkley. "I myself have been banished! Aurora is concerned I am becoming overly tired and will be more susceptible to catching the influenza. And I cannot dispute her point . . . or at least I was not allowed to," she acknowledged with a smile. "But I must admit to you that I do not feel comfortable with allowing her to care for Coral all by herself."

"I should think not!" agreed Rothworth, frowning. "I will go up at once."

Percy, who had been listening to this exchange, met him at the door just as he was about to leave.

"You can count on me, sir, if you need assistance," he said in a lowered voice. "Aurora seemed to think I should remain downstairs to entertain Phoebe and bolster your aunt's spirits, but I'm at your service if I'm needed upstairs."

Rothworth smiled inwardly at the thought of a strapping young man invading his spinster aunt's bedchamber to administer succour in her hour of need. She would likely go into spasms at the thought.

"I believe your sister is correct," he advised in a sober voice. "You are most needed here."

"I'll do all I can, sir."

"Good man!" said Rothworth, and, after giving him a pat on the shoulder, left the room.

He found Aurora sitting by his aunt's bedside and reading a book by the light of one candle. The room smelled remarkably fresh for a sickroom, and he realised a window had been partially opened to let in the night air.

Aurora looked up from her book at his entrance.

"What are you doing here?" she asked quietly, smiling at him in welcome.

"I came to see how goes our patient," he replied, glancing at the sleeping figure on the bed.

"She is much better. For a day or two we were seriously worried, but all is well now. You shouldn't be here, however. It has proven to be a very contagious illness and you wouldn't wish to carry it back to Charlotte."

"I'll stay away from her for a few days, never fear. She is a robust girl and is unlikely to fare badly, in any case."

His sharp gaze took in every detail of Aurora's appearance.

Her eyes, despite their customary sparkling warmth, were tired and her complexion was bleached of its former brilliance; her dress, which did not look to be her own, was old and serviceable, and of a shape that did little to enhance the graceful figure underneath; and her lovely auburn hair had been severely contained in a single plait.

Rothworth thought she looked enchanting. But he was not at all pleased to see her looking so tired.

"I see you are passing judgement on my shocking appearance," she said with a soft laugh. "Miss Lington was kind enough to lend me a dress, for we had a little mishap earlier and my only other clothes are more suited to a drawing room than a sickroom. And I'm afraid I've had little time to dress my hair."

Before Rothworth could be so imprudent as to voice his opinion, she rose out of her chair and beckoned him over to the bed.

"Come, if you are set on taking the risk. Only, speak quietly for she is still unsettled."

He came to stand beside her and was startled to see the change in his aunt.

"Will she recover in full?" he asked with concern.

"Yes, of course. You must not fear anything of a serious nature! She may look sallow and drawn, but she will soon be enjoying her customary looks and spirits. The fever broke this morning, and I expect her to sleep more naturally tonight. For the last few days she has been very hot, and tossing and turning with it, which has not allowed her much respite, poor dear."

"Do you mean to stay with her all night? Is there no one else who can take on that duty?"

"None that will serve the purpose better than me! Miss Brinkley is exhausted and will be of no use to anyone unless she rests well tonight. Miss Lington has also come down with the influenza. And if I were to bring in more of your uncle's staff, they could well catch it themselves and spread it to the others – and then where would the household be! No, it's best if I alone look after her. I suspect it will only be for one more night. From tomorrow it should be safe to simply check in on her during the day. You must not worry," she advised, looking across at him and smiling.

For the first time since entering, he saw a red welt across her cheekbone and temple and some slight swelling.

"What happened to your face?" he asked tersely.

Taking her chin in his hand, he turned her gently towards the light.

"Oh, I had forgotten! Your aunt was delirious and flailing her arms, and I was not fast enough to duck away. The worst of it was that I was holding her lunch tray! You can imagine the mess when I tipped the dratted thing all over myself."

"It needs to be iced," he said, lightly stroking the bruise with the back of his fingers.

"There's no need. I don't regard it."

"But I do."

A quizzical look entered her eyes. "Well, if you insist. But only because I know how you like to have your own way."

He raised an eyebrow, but did not take up the bait.

"If you are going down to the kitchen," she went on, "could you retrieve the tisane I prepared earlier? I left it to infuse in a pot over the fire. I have been using it in conjunction with the draught the doctor left, and it seems to be giving your aunt some relief."

Rothworth had intended to send a servant for the ice, but the way Aurora was looking at him, with complete faith that he would carry out the undertaking himself, he found he could not disappoint her. He only wished there was something of far greater value he could do for her. She was too apt at taking other people's problems upon her shoulders, and had no one to ease her own burden.

The impropriety of their proximity suddenly occurred to him, and he forced himself to take a step away from her.

"When I return, I'll sit with my aunt until the morning. You must go to bed."

"Oh, no! I don't need . . . "

"No arguments! I'll not have you making yourself sick. And besides, I'm accustomed to staying up until the early hours of the morning, so it's not as if there will be much of a change to my routine. Now, give me a few minutes and I'll be back with your tisane and the ice."

When he returned presently, he instructed her to sit in the chair and hold a cloth bag filled with ice to her cheek.

"I dare not disobey you," she said with a docility belied by the smile in her eyes. "Your unyielding expression tonight leads me to fear the repercussions."

"I suspect there is little you fear," he observed, looking down at her with amusement.

"Now that is simply not so! I have been known to dabble in all the usual fears one comes across."

"One would never guess from your actions."

"Oh, but I never allow my fears to guide my actions! Imagine what a boring life I would lead if I allowed that to be the case. And being bored is perhaps my greatest fear," she owned, placing the iced-cloth on her cheek. "Am I doing it correctly? I wouldn't wish to incur your displeasure."

Rothworth threw her a speaking look, before returning his attention to the teapot in his hand.

"Before you go to bed, you'd best tell me how to administer this tisane."

"I'll show you," she said, starting to rise.

He placed a hand on her shoulder and held her down.

"Thank you, I'm perfectly capable of doing it myself. Should I pour out a whole cup for her?"

"She manages only a few sips at a time, so a quarter will be sufficient."

Rothworth lifted the lid of the pot and smelled the infusion.

"Good God, what's in here?" he asked with a grimace that made him look endearingly boyish.

"I can see you would make a difficult patient!" she said, smiling. "It's a mixture of violet flowers, roots of marshmallow and a little Iceland moss. It helps to alleviate her sore throat and other phlegmatic complaints. I have been giving it to her every couple of hours or so. And as for the doctor's draught, only one teaspoon every four hours."

"Is there anything else I should know before you go to bed?" he asked, putting down the teapot on a side table.

"You seem to have an unnatural preoccupation with sending me to bed! I don't know whether to be offended or flattered."

He slowly turned to look at her.

"Not so unnatural . . . but do you think it wise to bait me *now*?"

His heated gaze evaporated the veneer of decorum between them.

Aurora's breath caught in her throat.

What was she doing? Her imprudent fondness for chipping away at his self-restraint had become something of a habit, and on this occasion it had succeeded too well.

She promptly rose to her feet; too tired to regain control of the situation, and not even certain that she wanted to.

"I will be bid you good night, Your Grace. Please wake me if she should become worse." She paused at the door and turned back to look at him. "Thank you."

She was gone an instant later, and Rothworth was left alone to wrestle with his thoughts for the next twelve hours.

Nineteen

"Are you trying to kill me!" Miss Coral demanded in a rasping voice.

She was sitting up in bed, looking more like herself than she had in days, with some colour in her cheeks and her yellow ringlets tidied and adorned by a white lace cap.

"This smells like something that belongs at the bottom of a fetid pond!" she went on, glaring at the cup of tisane Aurora held to her lips.

"Yes, it's horrid, isn't it?" said Aurora. "But you have been taking it for the last five days without detrimental effects – the opposite, in fact! – so I think you are quite safe to take it this morning."

Having overslept, Aurora had entered Miss Coral's room a few minutes ago, hoping to find Rothworth still with his aunt. On finding Miss Brinkley and the doctor in his stead, she was conscious of a pang of regret; but this had been quickly brushed away and she had set about administering another dose of her tisane.

"I must have been delirious," grumbled Miss Coral. "I can't be held accountable for the peculiar things I agreed to ingest in such a state. Not that I likely had much choice in the matter! You have shown yourself to be quite the tyrant in the sickroom, Aurora dear – I hope you don't mind if I give you a little hint?"

"Now, now, Miss Coral," said the doctor, from his position on the other side of the bed, where he stood checking the pulse in her wrist. "If it had not been for Miss Wesley, you would have had a much harder time of it. Her methods have my full approval, so you must not play out your crotchets on her."

Dr Moore was a kindly man, a little past his fiftieth year, with a luxuriant black moustache that contrasted dramatically with his mane of silver hair. He was of even temperament, medium build and superior intelligence, and his grey eyes often held a spark of humour in them, even as he upbraided a patient, as he was now doing.

"But, Dr Moore,' complained Miss Coral, "you can't imagine how ruthlessly I have been nursed, when all I wanted was to be left alone to die in peace!"

"Coral, really," tutted her sister. "One would think you were still a child the way you are carrying on. I'm certain you would not wish Dr Moore, or Aurora, to think you ungrateful?"

"No, of course not. What I wish is for them to leave and not think of me at all!"

As this declaration was immediately followed by a paroxysm of coughing that left her weak and unable to grumble further, Miss Brinkley chose the moment to take the cup of tisane out of Aurora's hands and tip the whole of it into her sister's mouth.

"There! That was not so bad, was it?" she said. "It should soon begin to settle your cough."

Miss Coral glared at her.

"Well done, Miss Brinkley," said Dr Moore, giving her a warm look of approval across the bed.

Aurora was surprised to see a blush spread across Miss Brinkley's cheeks at this mild praise.

And was even more surprised to hear her respond in a girlish titter, quite unlike her: "Thank you, Dr Moore, but I hope I know how to handle my own sister!"

"I need no handling of any sort," rasped Miss Coral belligerently. "And you are free to leave, Pearl, and go about with your day – in fact, I insist on it!"

"Come, Miss Coral, this is most unlike you," said Dr Moore. "I know you are feeling poorly and out of sorts, but you should know that you owe your sister a debt of gratitude. If not for her quick thinking in wrapping you in wetted bedsheets when your fever was at its peak, it would have been much the worse for you. Miss Brinkley, you have been a worthy deputy! I have found your assistance indispensable."

"I could not have been half so useful without your guidance and support, Dr Moore," replied Miss Brinkley, her blush heightening.

Aurora looked from one to the other and began to entertain the possibility that there was more to this exchange than professional appreciation. And upon catching Miss Coral roll her eyes, she realised this suspicion could well be correct.

As soon as Miss Brinkley had left the room with the doctor to escort him downstairs, Aurora asked Miss Coral: "I have not been in the presence of your sister and Dr Moore together before, so I could well be imagining it, but are they . . . "

" . . . Smitten? I should think it was patently obvious! Pearl has had a tendre for him these last two years – though there's little chance she'll own to it! I've been doing my utmost to throw them together, but no matter how many illnesses I invent to bring Dr Moore to the house, they are both too stupid to do anything about it. I've lost all patience with them!"

"Your nephew told me you were susceptible to any passing illness – surely you have not been *feigning* all this time?" asked Aurora, torn between astonishment and amusement.

"Yes, it has been most inconvenient, I can tell you! It's no easy thing to remain in bed without real cause. I have been making great headway into my brother's library – even the dullest of his books, of which there are many! But I did not begrudge the effort, for how else was I to get Dr Moore to visit so regularly?"

"You could have simply invited him to dinner," Aurora suggested, laughing. "That is the usual way of things."

"I tried that, of course, but Pearl said it was inappropriate to breach a doctor's objectivity towards his patients with so familiar an invitation."

"Gracious! A gentleman in that profession would live a most solitary life indeed if everyone took such a view."

"Oh, it was poppycock! She only said it because she's afraid. And to some extent I understand – it's difficult to consider a change in one's circumstances at our time of life. But I never thought that Pearl, of all people, would lack courage."

"Perhaps she does not realise he shares her feelings," mused Aurora, her brow puckered in thought. "Clearly something must be done." She sank into a meditative silence for a few minutes; and then, rousing herself, asked: "Why did she never marry?"

"The simple answer is, no one offered for her," replied Miss Coral as she attempted to find a more comfortable position amongst her pillows. "I suspect her forceful personality frightened away potential suitors. And since no one came forward, she allowed herself to think that she never wanted to marry. I suppose we all tell ourselves little lies to pass through our lives with our pride intact!" she observed, and fell into another fit of coughing, though milder this time.

When it had passed, Aurora repositioned her pillows for her. Then, picking up a pretty knitted shawl thrown across the foot of the bed, she placed it around Miss Coral's shoulders.

"You look most fetching in that shawl, ma'am! Do you feel better?"

"Yes, thank you, Aurora dear. I hope I didn't offend you earlier? Regardless of what my family believes, I am unaccustomed to feeling unwell and it makes me a little cross."

"I quite understand – Mama was just the same!" replied Aurora, sitting down in the chair beside the bed. "She couldn't bear to be mollycoddled, and though ordinarily the most amiable of women, she was perfectly capable of communicating her displeasure if we went beyond the line of what she deemed acceptable."

"You must miss her greatly."

"Yes . . . and I often wish I had her counsel. But she taught me to live life without allowing regrets to become constant shadows that taint the time we have left to us, and I try to honour her memory by living according to that philosophy."

"A wise woman! I don't doubt she counted herself fortunate to have you and your brother in her life," Miss Coral said with a wistfulness that was not lost on Aurora.

Emboldened by their shared confidences, Aurora asked: "If you don't think it too great an impertinence, ma'am, why did *you* never marry?"

Miss Coral smiled a little. "I did once think myself in love with a young man – a most handsome and charming young man, if memory serves! – but, regrettably, there was never any hope of us marrying. His parents had other plans for him . . . and . . . well, then I had to have a little procedure . . . and the surgeon was not as skilled as I had hoped. I later learnt I could no longer have children, and after that there was nothing for it but to embrace spinsterhood. And I have rarely had cause to regret it, I assure you!"

Aurora took hold of her hand and gently squeezed it. "I think you would have made a wonderful mother."

"Thank you, Aurora dear. I like to think so, for I do so like children."

"And, who knows? Perhaps someday you will find someone to tempt you into matrimony!"

"Oh no, I am content with the way things stand. Besides, I don't think Gregory could do without me. He will certainly never marry, for he has never shown the slightest interest in any female and thinks only of his books! And if the heavens align and Pearl one day does marry her doctor, Gregory will need me to keep house for him."

"And if your sister remains unmarried?"

"Well, he will then need me even more to protect him from her tendency to rule his life! So, you see, things are as they ought to be."

Aurora was not at all satisfied that this held true. The wistful look in Miss Coral's eyes, when speaking of children, had given her away. And

Aurora was determined to give some proper thought to how she could best help her.

As for Miss Brinkley, an idea was already forming in her head, and she had great hopes of soon being able to bring about a satisfactory conclusion to that particular dilemma.

Over dinner that evening, she was rendered assistance in her plans for Miss Brinkley from an unlikely quarter.

While the butler and footmen were serving the first course, she said to Mr Brinkley: "I must tell you, sir, that Dr Moore is a great admirer of your sister!" She threw a smiling look at Miss Brinkley, seated beside her at the head of the table. "He was most complementary of her skill in nursing Miss Coral, and even went so far as to say that he had found her assistance indispensable."

"He was simply being kind," remarked Miss Brinkley.

"Oh, I don't think it was mere kindness," insisted Aurora. "He was kind to me when he praised my own skills, but when he spoke of *you* there was a certain warmth in his manner."

"Dr Moore has always spoken very highly of you," put in Mr Brinkley.

"He has?" asked his sister, looking surprised.

"Certainly," he replied and dipped his spoon into his soup. "He often makes some remark that indicates his regard for you. Surely you must have noticed?"

"He has never given me any cause to suspect him of being anything more than unfailingly polite – if that is what you mean, then, yes, I have noticed."

"No, it goes deeper than mere politeness. Perhaps you were not present to hear his remarks."

"And you did not see fit to tell me?" she asked, astringency entering her tone.

"I supposed you already knew," he returned, a little surprised by her reaction.

For a moment Miss Brinkley looked almost hopeful, and it quite wrung Aurora's heart.

But she then schooled her features and said matter-of-factly: "Of course, I know he holds me in esteem. I have proven useful to him on occasion when nursing Coral . . . that must be it."

"Well, naturally, that's true," said her brother. He spooned some soup into his mouth and did not see the betraying hint of disappointment in her eyes. After swallowing, he continued: "However, I was referring to a warmer regard – as Aurora alluded to. Only this morning, before he went up to see

Coral, he asked after your own health and quizzed me to ascertain if you were resting enough. He was pleased when I told him Aurora had banished you from the sickroom so you could rest."

"As our family doctor, it is his duty to do what he can to ensure all our health."

Mr Brinkley lifted his eyes from his soup and looked across at her.

"My dear," he said with his gentle smile, "I may be absent-minded on occasion, but I am not so blind to what goes on around me that I don't know that Dr Moore has a decided preference for you. I always assumed you knew and did not wish to encourage him, since you don't share his feelings."

Miss Brinkley could only stare at him in a bemused way while he returned his attention to his dinner.

Her colour became so heightened that Aurora signalled to the butler to refill her waterglass.

"Here you go, ma'am," she said, passing the glass to her. Then, leaning in a little, she added in a low voice: "A wise woman once said that we must be fearless and lay ourselves bare to find true happiness."

Miss Brinkley's dazed eyes met hers.

Aurora smiled encouragingly; and then, to give her a moment to recover from her shock, she addressed Phoebe across the table.

"Did you enjoy your walk yesterday, dear? I'm sorry I couldn't join you, but I hope Percy proved to be a fair replacement?"

"Oh, yes, Cousin Aurora!" replied Phoebe. "We had a spanking time of it – didn't we, Percy?"

"*Spanking*? What an unusual word," said Aurora, throwing her brother, next to her, a mildly censorious look. "I hope Percy is not teaching you all the cant he is picking up from his friends?"

Her brother laughed self-consciously. "No, I haven't, so don't frown at me! An occasional word may have slipped out, but quite by accident – upon my word!"

"I'm glad to hear it. And I'm glad to know you enjoyed yourself, Phoebe. Where did Percy take you?"

"We went to watch a balloon ascension in Hyde Park, and arrived just in time to see them fill up the balloon with air! It was the most wondrous thing imaginable!"

"And did you wear your new hat, dear?" asked Aurora.

The day after their near run-in with Phoebe's guardian, Aurora had taken her to a milliner and purchased a new bonnet that hugged the sides of her face and did an admirable job of concealing it.

"Yes, I made *certain* to wear it," Phoebe replied with a significant look. Noticing Mr Brinkley's indulgent gaze upon her, she added nervously: "It is quite my favourite hat now! And . . . and I imagine I'll wear it every day for some time . . . that is, u-until I find another that catches my fancy." She was blushing profusely by the time she finished.

As Aurora had discovered, Phoebe was abysmal at lying. Even a simple skirting around the perimeter of a truth, or withholding information, rendered her so uncomfortable that her sentiments were patently clear to all. Aurora found herself hoping that her letter had reached the girl's uncle in Boston, and that he was already on his way to relieve them of the evils of the situation in which they found themselves.

"And did Percy take you to Gunter's, like he promised?" Aurora asked, to distract her from her embarrassment.

"Oh, yes, he did!" replied Phoebe eagerly. "I have never eaten pastries so heavenly. Do you remember what they were called, Percy?"

"Naples Divolini, or some such thing," he replied. "And we also tried the marshmallow and an Italian cream."

"But unfortunately, we couldn't try the ices as they'd run out of ice," said Phoebe.

"The waiter told us they were expecting a ship to make harbour any day now with a cargo from Greenland," added Percy, becoming animated. "Imagine that! We'll soon be able to eat an ice cream made with ice from one of the most northern lands in the world!"

"I have always been partial to ices," remarked Miss Brinkley, making an effort to draw herself away from her thoughts.

"It would be my pleasure to escort you and Miss Coral to Gunther's," said Percy impulsively. "My treat!"

Miss Brinkley was rather touched, for she suspected he had limited resources. But though it was on the tip of her tongue to say that she must be allowed to treat him, she did not wish to put a dampener on his boyish gallantry and so declared that she would be delighted to accept his kind invitation.

"It sounds like you had a fine afternoon," said Mr Brinkley, smiling. "Did Charlotte join you?"

"Unfortunately, she couldn't," replied Phoebe. "She had an appointment with her modiste – who is apparently outrageously fashionable and in demand! But she promised she would see us tonight, when her brother brings her over after dinner."

"They are coming to visit us tonight?" Miss Brinkley asked with mild surprise. "Did you know of this, Gregory?"

"No, I don't believe so. But it makes no difference, for they are always a welcome addition. Our household is never so merry as when we have the young people together."

"I hope you are not displeased, Miss Brinkley?" asked Phoebe, sorry to think she had been the bearer of unwelcome news.

"Nothing of the sort, I assure you . . . only it is very odd. For the last two weeks we have seen more of Rothworth than we have in the last six months! And though I know he has a deep affection for Coral, I cannot believe her catching the influenza instigated his daily visits." After a pause, she added: "Though, I was never more surprised than when I discovered he had remained with her through the night! Dr Moore and I found him this morning sitting by her bedside looking worn-out but determined to remain longer. I don't know why he thought it necessary when I was there to relieve him, but he was proving stubborn, until Dr Moore added his voice to mine. He must have been more worried about Coral than I supposed . . . and yet, that does not explain his visits before her illness." She slowly turned her gaze on Aurora and regarded her musingly. "I wonder if it could it be your doing?"

"I assure you, ma'am, I have never requested His Grace's presence!" replied Aurora, taken aback.

"Of course. I'm happy to say, you are one of the few females who knows how to keep him at a proper distance. I was only speculating if it might be your company that brings him here . . . though I admit it is an unlikely conjecture."

"I'm certain Julian enjoys Aurora's company as much as the rest of us," said Mr Brinkley in gentle defence of her.

"That goes without saying. But I was wondering if perhaps . . . " She broke off, thinking better of what she was about to say. "Most likely, his reason for visiting is as simple as having few engagements at the moment. Gregory, would you pass the salt?"

No more was said on the subject, but enough had been implied for Aurora to wonder if Miss Brinkley's *unlikely conjecture* could be true.

She would be lying if she did not admit to feeling drawn to the Duke of Rothworth. He might possess enough rough edges to keep his future wife occupied for a good many years, but they were not by any means sufficiently disagreeable to nullify his finer points. Apart from a surplus of physical attractions, he personified too many of the ideals a woman could want in a man, including those most important to her: kindness and a sense of humour.

So far it had not been too difficult to keep him at a distance, for she had more important matters to occupy her thoughts. And, besides, she did not suspect him of having any real interest in her. They might banter, and even flirt a little, but she had assumed it was of no consequence to either of them.

One could admire a desirable object from afar without needing to possess it; particularly if it remained out of reach.

But if it suddenly became attainable?

She had never been one of those young ladies who dreamed of an implausible, hero-like figure sweeping her off her feet. The attractions she had felt for the few gentlemen who had elicited such a response from her had been mild and short-lived, and consequently she had come to assume her disposition was not of a type to be burdened by extravagant romantic feelings.

So, it was disconcerting to discover that one was not as immune as one had supposed.

Twenty

The Duke of Rothworth and his sister were shown into the drawing room a little before nine o'clock that evening. Aurora was surprised to find herself feeling apprehensive and wondered at her perversity. Nothing had changed between herself and the duke, and a throw-away comment from his aunt should not have the power to alter the feeling of ease and enjoyment his company had so far afforded her.

She was sitting at the pianoforte, looking through some sheets of music, when he entered; and, apart from responding to his greeting, she kept herself immersed in her task.

"Is our patient better today?" he asked, coming over and smiling down at her.

Seeing nothing in his gaze that could lead her to think he was pursuing her, her wariness receded. And though a twinge of disappointment may have taken its place, she was perfectly capable of banishing it.

What she could not know was that, for the first time in his life, Rothworth was uncertain as to whether his romantic interest would be welcome, and was acting with unusual circumspection. He was in the habit of quelling the hopes of all who pursued him as a matrimonial prize, and was now at a loss as to how to foster such hopes in the one lady he wished would display them.

"Your aunt is much better," replied Aurora. "So much so that she hopes to come downstairs tomorrow and spend the day on the settee. She is sleeping at present, but you are welcome to go up if you wish."

"I'll wait to see her tomorrow. And yourself? How are you feeling?"

"I am very well rested – thanks to you! I hoped to be able to see you this morning and find out how you fared in the night, but I'm afraid I overslept."

"My night passed without incident, which was a relief. I was, however, sorry to have missed you. I had every intention of waiting to speak with you, but my aunt was determined to send me home."

"Oh, I didn't expect you to wait for me! You must have been dreadfully tired. I only wish I had woken earlier so I could have relieved you. I don't know why I didn't! I'm normally an early riser."

"You were clearly in need of rest. I'm yet to thank you for all you have done for my aunt. I hope you know that I consider myself in your debt?"

"You most certainly are not!" she insisted firmly. "I assure you, you had no bearing on my actions whatsoever."

"I believe I know that," he responded with an enigmatic smile. "Nevertheless, you put yourself at risk for my family; for a woman you hardly know. Sacrificed your comfort, your social engagements . . . "

"How nonsensical you are!" she interrupted him. "I beg you stop before you put me out of all patience with you! Your relatives took us in when we were in need of friends and have shown us nothing but kindness. I would have had to be monstrously selfish not to lend my aid when they needed it – is that what you think of me?" she asked with an edge to her voice.

"No . . . that is not what I think of you," he replied evenly. "Have you chosen a piece you wish to play?"

"Yes," she replied with a smile that showed her approval of the change in subject. She took out some sheets of music from the folio and placed them on the stand. "*Passacaglia* by Handel. It was Papa's favourite, but it has been a while since I've had the opportunity to practice it, so I hope I can do it justice. Do you know it?"

"I can't say I recognise the piece. I'm not much addicted to music recitals."

"Then I wonder why you chose to inflict an evening of my playing on yourself?" she said with a laugh. "You must know by now that your aunts and uncle like me to entertain them after dinner. I can only hope you will not be bored!"

"I may have no love for other people's playing, but when it comes to your own, Miss Wesley, I find myself looking forward to the experience."

"Why, that is the prettiest thing you have ever said to me, Your Grace – are you feeling quite yourself?"

"No. I don't believe I am."

"I trust you are not coming down with the influenza?"

"It's not a universal sickness . . . though it appears to be just as virulent."

"You are talking in riddles! And at present I don't have the time to solve them. Your aunt is watching us with that sharp-witted look that sometimes comes over her, and I fear if I don't begin to play at once, we ourselves will become her entertainment."

"That is never a good thing," he said, smiling. "I know from experience! By all means, let us give her a more proper direction for her thoughts. Would you allow me to turn the pages for you?"

Aurora consented, and, after taking a moment to centre her thoughts on the music, embarked on a poignant performance of *Passacaglia*.

It was a rendition the like of which she had never before managed to achieve; the dance of notes across the keys had never before held such sweet synchronicity, or moved with so much feeling from one stanza to the next, in fluid waves that washed across the room and captured everyone in their wake.

Rothworth turned the pages for her, until he saw her close her eyes and play out the remainder of the piece from memory. There was something so sweet and pure in the way she allowed herself to be drawn into the music and lose herself in it, that he could not tear his gaze away and felt like a man pleasurably drowning in a sea of sensations.

The piece was over too soon for all who were privileged to hear it (including a footman who had come in with the tea tray and had progressed no further than the doorway, transfixed).

Aurora slowly became aware of her surroundings and of the sound of clapping; but it was Rothworth who caught her attention when he raised a hand, as if to touch her face, and then lowered it.

"You have . . . " He indicated to his own cheek.

Aurora realised that a tear had escaped and quickly brushed it away.

"How silly of me to get so sentimental!" she said; and then added with a smile: "At least you don't look bored."

"A man can't be bored by such virtuosity."

"That is *too* extravagant, and you know it! I play well enough, but my technique needs more practice."

"I was speaking of the feeling with which you play. Technique can be taught. What you possess is altogether more rare."

"You are going to puff me up with conceit if you are not careful," she laughed.

Returning her attention to the pianoforte, she began a lively country dance that had proved popular with her audience before.

Struck with inspiration, Charlotte begged her to stop for a moment, and then quickly pointed out that only a little shuffling of furniture was needed to make room for dancing.

She soon convinced Percy and Phoebe of her plan, and even managed to cajole her uncle into joining them; and, in a short space of time, the four of them were performing the steps of the dance in the middle of the drawing room, under the fastidious eye of Miss Brinkley, who did not condescend to join them but nevertheless felt the need to call out instructions to improve their execution.

Aurora finished the piece, then played another two requests, just as energetic, before resolutely standing up and adjuring Charlotte and Phoebe to take her place.

The girls obliged her, and though neither one was proficient, between the two of them there was enough aptitude and good humour to keep their audience entertained for the next hour. As it was then almost time for everyone to retire, Rothworth instructed his sister to say her goodbyes.

While she was planting kisses on her aunt's and uncle's cheeks and taking leave of her friends, Aurora approached Rothworth.

"May I ask a favour of you, Your Grace?"

"How can I be of service?" he asked.

"I must go out of town tomorrow for a few days, on a family matter, and I can't take Percy or Phoebe with me."

"You wish me to keep an eye on them for you?"

"Oh no! I would never expect you to involve yourself in their affairs. Percy is well able to manage for himself, and Phoebe will have him, and your aunts, to look out for her. However, in my absence, I don't wish her to leave the house, and as she and Charlotte have got into the habit of walking out together, they may take it into their heads to do so again."

"You would like me to ensure my sister does not lead Phoebe astray, is that it?"

"I wouldn't put it into those words exactly!" she objected.

"You don't need to. I understand my sister well enough. You may rest easy, I'll inform her that she must stay away from your cousin while you're away."

She threw him an amused look, tinged with exasperation. "Pray tell her no such thing! Really, I almost begin to wish I had not raised the matter with you. Can you not see it would be counterproductive to take an authoritarian stance with someone of her nature?"

"What I see is that you mean to instruct me," he remarked with a stoically sigh.

"Oh no! That would be ungrateful of me, wouldn't it?" she said, smiling disarmingly. "But perhaps a little more subtlety may be required. And besides, there's not the least need to keep them apart! I'm certain Phoebe would be glad of Charlotte's company if she came to visit her here."

"So, my task is to be subtle and not at all authoritarian – does that meet with your approval?"

"It does! I can only hope it will not prove too difficult for you," she said, laughter in her eyes. "You must think I am being overly protective, but there is a particular reason why I want to keep Phoebe safely at home."

"One you don't mean to share with me," he said in resigned voice.

"Well, no. I'm not at liberty to divulge the details at present, so I must continue to beg your indulgence."

"Then, to thank me for my indulgence, you may satisfy my curiosity and tell me where you are going."

"You seem determined to know my business! Has anyone ever told you that you are impertinently inquisitive?"

"They wouldn't dare," he replied, smiling.

"Well, *I'm* telling you. And you need not think there is anything improper in my leaving town. I am simply going to pay a visit to a member of my family."

"If you mean to visit your uncle at Dewbury Abbey," he said with a frown, "I don't think it a good idea."

"Well, you are certainly entitled to your opinion, and I don't mean to attempt to dissuade you from it."

His frown deepened. "Who will accompany you as chaperone?"

"I am six and twenty!" she said with some exasperation. "I no longer need one."

"I can't agree with you."

"Then it's fortunate you are not required to!"

He began to say something, then changed his mind and asked instead: "If not a chaperone, will you at least take a groom or footman for protection?"

"John, my manservant, will accompany me. And as he will be armed and is even more protective of me than my own brother, I shall feel perfectly safe."

Rothworth did not appear to share her confidence, for he said abruptly: "I'll escort you."

"You?" she responded with a good deal of surprise.

"I have some business to see to in the general direction of Dewbury Abbey."

"Certainly not! I can't accept your kind offer. Surely you have better things to do with your time? Besides, my visit is of a private nature and, quite frankly, you will be very much in the way."

He looked as if he wished to say more, but the general hubbub of leave-taking engulfed them, and the moment was lost.

Twenty-One

When her niece and nephew had left, Miss Brinkley took herself off to check on her sister, while Phoebe and Percy, with the help of a footman, set about putting the furniture back in its place.

With everyone otherwise engaged, Aurora took advantage of the opportunity to whisk Mr Brinkley off to his library so that she could have a word with him in private.

"Is something the matter?" he asked with concern, when he saw her close the door behind them.

"Not in the least!" she replied cheerfully. "I only have a small request to ask of you."

His face cleared. "Anything for you, my dear."

"Actually, sir, the matter relates to your sister."

"Coral?"

"Oh, no – Miss Brinkley! You see, I have recently come to suspect that she is not as indifferent to Dr Moore as she would have us believe. In fact, I imagine all that is needed is a gentle nudge and they will happily fall into each other's arms."

Mr Brinkley looked surprised and blinked several times behind his spectacles. "But she has known him for some time and never shown any interest in him."

"But she thought he had no romantic interest in her – as you saw tonight! And I must tell you that Miss Coral is also convinced they have a tendre for one another."

"Is she? Well . . . in that case, it might be possible," he said thoughtfully. "Coral is frequently unwell and as a consequence is in both their company rather often."

"I suspect," said Aurora with a wry look, 'that if we are successful in bringing about this match, the added benefit will be that Miss Coral's health will improve dramatically!"

"What can you mean, my dear?" he asked, brow furrowed.

"Miss Coral admitted to me that she has been inventing illnesses to throw her sister and Dr Moore together."

"You don't say? I never suspected it in the least."

"It was very sly and clever of her!" said Aurora appreciatively. "Unfortunately, her efforts have not succeeded – perhaps because encounters over a sickbed are too brief to be conducive to romance."

He looked struck by her reasoning. "I have never before considered the notion, but no doubt you are correct."

"I know I am! And so, I hope you can see why it's imperative that they meet in a more social setting?"

"Yes, I believe I can see your point."

"I'm happy to know you agree, sir! Particularly since the onus of befriending Dr Moore must fall on you. He seems to be an amiable man and I don't think it will be a hardship, but nevertheless it will require effort on your part, so I think it only fair to warn you."

"You wish me to befriend Dr Moore?" he asked, looking vaguely bewildered.

"If it's not too great an inconvenience?" she replied coaxingly. "Do you think you could do it?"

"I suppose it is possible . . . if you think it necessary?" he added, his retiring personality shrinking from such proactive social dealings.

"Most necessary! We must create a situation where Miss Brinkley is often hearing Dr Moore's name on your lips, and seeing him in your company. And if you could persuade him to agree to a regular dinner invitation here, all the better! Whatever we can contrive to throw them in each other's way must be attempted."

"But, my dear, perhaps Dr Moore does not wish to be manipulated in such a fashion," suggested Mr Brinkley, looking uncertain.

"He will never know a thing about it!" she replied breezily. "And really, it's for his own good, so he will one day be grateful to us. And it will be advantageous for you too, sir! I'm certain you both share many interests on which to build a friendship."

"I am not generally comfortable with new people," he owned in a self-effacing manner. "I may not be able to live up to your expectations of me, my dear."

"Dear sir, how can you talk such fustian? You were perfectly at ease when you befriended us! Your natural warmth and sincerity make your company a great pleasure, and I don't doubt that Dr Moore will think so too. Besides, he is not a stranger to you. He is a man of sense who you hold in respect – am I correct?"

"Yes . . . indeed," he replied, a little dazzled by her eloquence. "He is a most intelligent and learned man."

"Imagine the interesting conversation you will have!"

"Yes, I daresay we may. We have enjoyed a stimulating exchange of ideas in the past. One particular occasion that springs to mind is when we got to talking about the Hippocratic Corpus, and whether any of the papers had been written by Hippocrates himself. In actual fact, I was able to show him one of my own books which referred to the author . . . "

Mr Brinkley continued warming to his theme for a good while, while Aurora listened to him with indulgent interest.

*   *   *

Sometime later, once she had prepared for bed, Aurora knocked on Phoebe's door and let herself into the room. Her charge was sitting at her dressing-table while a maid brushed out her brown curls, and at Aurora's entrance she turned and smiled in welcome.

Aurora's own hair was also down; a straight and glossy mass that draped around her flannel dressing-gown, almost to her waist.

"Oh, but you do have such pretty hair, Cousin Aurora!" Phoebe exclaimed. "It has a most uncommon shine to it."

"Why, thank you, dear! I am glad that my appearance meets with your approval. In general, I fear I am not at all fashionably turned out and must be a sad disappointment to you."

"Oh, no, *never!*" replied Phoebe. After a pause, she thought to add: "You don't need fine clothes to enhance your looks like some people, and you are always dressed with the *greatest* of taste."

"One does what one can," sighed Aurora, biting back a smile as she went to sit on the bed.

Thinking she had succeeded in consoling her benefactress, Phoebe dismissed the maid and joined her.

"Did you have something particular you wished to say to me, Cousin Aurora?"

"Yes, dear, I do. You may have already heard that I'm going out of London for a few days?"

"Oh, yes! Percy told me you were going to try and retrieve his signet ring; the one that was stolen by your uncle so that you couldn't prove Percy's claim to his inheritance."

"I see he has been quite loquacious on the subject," said Aurora, surprised her brother had taken Phoebe so far into his confidence.

"Only with me," Phoebe rushed to assure her. "He knows he can trust me. I hope you are not displeased?"

"I have no objection to you knowing the truth," Aurora replied, giving her hand a squeeze. "I only think it best that as few people as possible know the details . . . for now."

"I won't tell a soul, I promise!"

"I know you won't, dear. And as you have trusted us with your own secret, it's only fair that you know ours. Speaking of which, did you write to your governess as I suggested? It has been almost a month since she last heard from you and I'm certain she must be eager for some news."

"Yes, Cousin Aurora. I gave my letter to Miss Brinkley yesterday. She promised to send it off with her own correspondence."

"Did you mention that we expect your guardian to descend on us . . . why, whatever is the matter?" she asked on seeing Phoebe's stricken face.

"Oh, you mean *The Distant One!*" exclaimed Phoebe with sudden relief. "I forgot my uncle was coming for me . . . I almost wish he wouldn't! I have tremendously enjoyed being with you and Percy."

"I feel the same way. But only think how much nicer it will be when Mr Carter sorts out your affairs! For one, you will no longer have to be afraid to walk down the street."

"I expect you're right," said Phoebe with a decided lack of enthusiasm.

"I am! But until he can sort out your affairs we must remain cautious. Which is why I must ask that you stay in the house while I'm away. I don't wish to be an ogre about it, but I will feel a lot happier leaving you if I can be certain you will be safely indoors."

Phoebe accepted her imprisonment without complaint, prompting Aurora to say that she would take her to Astley's Royal Amphitheatre as a treat, upon her return.

"And, before I forget, I have a letter for your uncle!" Aurora went on. She took a sealed missive from her dressing-gown pocket and gave it to Phoebe. "My solicitor knows to expect him and to send him to this house when he shows up. I don't believe he will reach London while I'm away, but if by chance he does you may give him that letter from me. It explains all."

A knock sounded on the door and, upon being told to enter, Percy walking in.

"Thought you went to bed," he said to his sister.

"Did you? And is that why you have come to visit Phoebe at such an inappropriate time?" she asked, lifting an eyebrow.

137

"Dash it, Rory, you make me sound like a loose-screw," he objected. "She asked me to come!"

"I did!" Phoebe rushed to say. "I wanted to warn him about . . . about something," she finished lamely.

"Secrets?" teased Aurora. "Well, then I shall leave so that you can discuss them in private. But I must tell you, dear, that it's not at all the thing to be entertaining a gentleman in your bedchamber."

"But it's only Percy. Surely there can be no objection to *him*?"

"Not by me. But I would hate for the servants to whisper about you below stairs. Or for it to reach Miss Brinkley's ears," said Aurora, rising.

"Oh . . . I hadn't considered that. I am very sorry."

"Your youth allows you a degree of leeway, dear – just be mindful in future! As for you, sirrah," she gave her brother a pointed look, "don't stay above ten minutes! And while I'm out of town, I hope you'll make time to keep Phoebe company? She must remain indoors until I return. After our run-in with Mr Wilks, I don't want to risk another close call while I'm away."

"You don't think I'd leave her alone all day long, do you?" he replied. "Besides, the ten pounds you gave me is almost gone, so I need to spend more time at home in any case."

Smiling, Aurora shook her head at this ungallant speech and left the room.

"We'd best be quick if we want to be spared another lecture," remarked Percy, taking his sister's place on the bed beside Phoebe. "What did you want to tell me?"

"It's Charlotte!" she declared tragically.

"What's the matter with her now?"

"She has fallen *in love* with you!"

"Eh?"

"She loves you, Percy!"

"Why has she gone and done a stupid thing like that? Not that I believe a word of it! Didn't she tell us, not two weeks ago, that she'd fallen in love with some dashed officer?"

Daunted by this prosaic response, she tried again to convey to him the drama of the situation.

"*That* is all over. She is determined to marry only you, and I very much fear she will persevere until she gets her own way. And I thought you should know *immediately*."

"Well, you need not put yourself in a pelter," he replied offhandedly. "I've no wish to be married, and certainly won't be popping the question to anyone any time soon."

With the sageness of her sex, Phoebe wondered at his simplicity.

"Percy, you might not *want* to marry, but that won't stop Charlotte from forcing your hand – *now* do you understand?"

Percy patted her shoulder in a brotherly way and stood up.

"If that's all that's got you in a worry, don't spare it another thought! I know how to take care of myself. George has been showing me . . . "

"The friend Cousin Aurora doesn't like?"

"Huh? Oh, yes, I suppose she's a bit wary of him. But she's got no cause to be – he's a great gun! Been on the town for years now so he knows a thing or two, and has been giving me a few pointers. I'm not a greenhorn anymore and likely to fall into the Parson's trap! As for Charlotte, you may tell her from me that she's . . . well, I suppose you can't tell her that. But I'll tell *you*, the sooner that girl is allowed to go into Society so she can suffer a few snubs, the better it will be for everyone. She's got the most dashed silly ideas in her head and not an ounce of restraint!"

"But I thought you *liked* Charlotte?"

"I do – but that doesn't mean I like the influence she's got over you! I know I promised not to tell Aurora about what happened the other week, when she escaped from that governess of hers and dragged you all over Hyde Park to chase after officers, but I didn't like it then and I still don't like it! And I'm tempted to give her a piece of my mind."

"Oh no, please don't!" exclaimed Phoebe, secretly greatly impressed by this show of manly firmness. "I promise I'll never go out with her again unless her governess is with us."

Happy to have made his point, the frown left Percy's eyes. And, after telling her to go to bed like a good girl, he bid her a good night.

It was more than he had bargained for, he thought to himself as he walked down the corridor to his own room, this feeling of being responsible for such an innocent as Phoebe. And though it was, of course, a great inconvenience, he was determined to keep a closer eye on her. There was no knowing what trouble she'd get herself into without his guidance.

Twenty-Two

Aurora found the journey into Surrey to be a great deal more pleasant than the journey they had undertaken to London all those weeks ago. There was no hired carriage or poorly skilled driver to hamper her enjoyment on this occasion; she had had every intention of hiring the one and engaging the services of the other, but Mr Brinkley would not hear of it and had insisted she use his own travelling chaise and driver.

So, the four hour journey was completed in the utmost of luxury, inside a well-sprung carriage with cushioned seats lined with velvet, and with an able coachman at the reins who knew how to drive without causing his passenger undue discomfort.

They stopped mid-morning in Esher, to break up the journey and rest the horses, but were soon on their way again at the same comfortable pace as before, and just before two o'clock that afternoon drove into Sutton Green, the closest village to Dewbury Abbey.

As soon as the carriage came to a stop, John got down from his box seat beside the driver, where they had been exchanging professional anecdotes, and went off to seek accommodation at the one hostelry the village boasted.

While she waited for him to return, Aurora peered out of the window at her surroundings. Sutton Green appeared to be a prosperous village, with a good-sized green (as the name would suggest), a cobbled high street, some shops, a Norman church and a pond, where several families of ducks had made their home. It was market day, and the street was still full of villagers and farmers as they went about their business on this fine afternoon.

John came back a few minutes later with the welcome intelligence that he had managed to secure rooms; and though there were no private parlours for hire, the common room looked to be respectable, and he had persuaded the landlord to lay out a late lunch for them.

Stirred by the thought of food, Aurora put on her straw bonnet, deftly tied the ribbon under her chin and sprung lightly from the chaise; and, while John saw to her bag, she went to thank Mr Brinkley's coachman.

"When would you be wanting me to come back for you, miss?" this individual asked politely, quite oblivious to the blonde curls peeking out from under the bonnet of his passenger, who up until they had left Esher had been auburn-haired.

"My business should be completed in two days, but in case I'm delayed let us say in three days' time," she replied.

He touched his forelock at her and with a snap of the reins set his team to navigating the busy street.

As soon as he was gone, Aurora opened her reticule and took out the clear-glass spectacles she had purchased in London and put them on.

John made no comment, merely giving her a resigned look, and led the way into the inn.

They were shown up to their rooms by a maid, so they could leave their luggage and refresh themselves; and within ten minutes had met up again and were making their way to the common room, where a few patrons still lingered over their lunch.

'That looks utterly delicious!" Aurora addressed the portly man transferring dishes from the tray he carried onto their table. "Thank you, sir, for seating us at this late hour."

"It was no hardship, miss," he replied cheerfully. "We had plenty left of the pie and vegetable pottage, seeing as my wife made extra, it being market day and all. She's known for her cooking round these parts and I've a fair hope you'll enjoy your meal. I'll bring you some wine, shall I?"

Aurora accepted his offer gratefully, and once John had ordered some ale for himself, the landlord took himself off.

"Well, you've got us here, Miss Aurora,' said John, regarding her with a sapient eye as he took his seat, "and I'm mighty interested to know what you've planned for us . . . though I daresay I'll not like it one bit, seeing you've got your wig on and those ugly spectacles."

Aurora smiled as she served him up some of the pie.

"It's best if I am not recognised here in future – it could prove awkward once Percy reclaims the title!"

"You're not meaning to put a disguise on me, are you?" he asked warily.

"Oh no! If it came to it, you could simply tell people that you liked the area and decided to seek a position up at the house."

"Can't say you're putting my fears to rest. Not when I ask myself, why does she need to keep people from recognising her in the first place?"

"There is not the least need to worry!" she said with a roguish twinkle. "I don't plan on doing anything *too* outrageous."

"I've learnt from hard experience that our definition of outrageous varies a tad, so I'll just continue to worry, if it's all the same to you. Just tell me plainly what you're plotting and I'll judge for myself."

"It is quite simple really! We will stage a carriage accident near the gates to Dewbury Abbey, late in the evening, and seek shelter at the house. I will then have the whole night to carry out a search for the ring."

"And what if it's in your uncle's room? It's as likely a place as any."

"Never fear! I have brought my sleeping draught with me. I need only find an occasion to share a drink with Lord Charles – which will be simple enough, I imagine – and he will sleep quite peacefully throughout the night."

"There's nothing simple about this plan of yours," he grumbled. "And don't go imagining it'll be a regular social call. What do you suppose that uncle of yours will think to himself when an unchaperoned young lady turns up on his doorstep, in the middle of the night?"

"But I don't mean to present myself as a young lady. I will be a governess on my way to a new position in . . . let us say, Winchester."

"It sounds like a half-baked story to me."

"You don't allow for my execution! Even you have acknowledged on occasion that I am an uncommonly fine actress."

"I meant it as no compliment! And if I'd known you'd take it as such, I'd have rather cut out my tongue than owned to it," he told her severely.

"Please don't be cross," she said coaxingly. "What would you have me do? We must find the ring."

"That ring could be in a hundred different places. Even a whole night of searching won't be enough to find it. And what about this carriage you mean to hire? Can't think the owner will be best pleased to find you've overturned it and caused God-knows what damage."

"We need only remove the bolts from one of the wheels and say that it came off. It will then be a simple matter of having the smithy replace them." She offered him a sympathetic look. "It is beastly of me to involve you in this, John, so if you would rather not take part, I will certainly understand."

"I've no intention of crying off, Miss Aurora, so don't you be thinking to go and do something foolish by yourself! But that's not to say I'm not heartily sorry I never told your brother I had my suspicions you weren't coming here to reason with your uncle – as you hoodwinked him into believing!"

"Well, I could hardly tell him the truth! It would only worry him needlessly. And it's not as if he could have stopped me – a great deal rests on the recovery of the ring! My grandmother made it clear that she does not want to recognise us, so we are left with little choice."

"Percy's case can still be made without the ring. You need only have some patience."

"I will not give them any opportunity to reject his claim. I cannot! We have no notion of what friends my uncle has in the Lords, and if they might be induced to view his claim as the stronger of the two."

The landlord returned then and placed their drinks before them. As the other patrons had finished their meals and left, he appeared inclined to linger at their table and gossip.

Once Aurora had replied to his questions regarding their destination and the reason for their journey (all easily answered with the story she had concocted), she in turn asked him: "Is there a grand house around these parts? I was told there was – *something* Abbey? And I would so like to visit it before we leave the area."

"Ah, you'll be meaning Dewbury Abbey, miss. It's a mile or so from here."

"Why, yes, that's it!"

"A fine place, to be sure, but I don't fancy you'll have a chance to visit. Not many are allowed to enter the grounds these days."

"Really? What a shame to let such a historic place go unappreciated. Why is that, do you suppose?" she asked.

"Well, I can't rightly say for sure, but the late marquess's son has always been a sickly lad and his mother moved him to the Abbey to care for him. That was some twenty years ago, and no one's seen head or tail of them since! It's said he needs careful care and ain't to be disturbed."

He then leaned in conspiratorially and added in a lowered voice: "My daughter worked as a maid up at the house and told me none of servants are allowed to enter the wing where the boy and his mother live . . . apart from the old dragon of a housekeeper. She's a nasty woman, that one! She's the reason my Jen had to leave and find work elsewhere. But none of 'em stay long that goes to work there."

"Oh? I thought all great estates needed a large, well-trained staff to keep the house and grounds in good order?" Aurora said mildly.

"You've got the right of it, miss, but there's not many there these days. Not even a butler, since the old one was pensioned off a few years back. If the Family ever visit, they bring their fancy London servants with them, and they're not there long enough to do much good to the place. My Jen said it would take a hundred people to set it to rights! It's hard work for those few left, and she wasn't sorry to leave. She's married now to a local lad and couldn't be happier."

"Oh, how wonderful! It must be a load off your mind to have her settled well."

"Just so, miss! Between us, she was ever a contrary one, my Jen and I had my doubts she'd find herself a man. She's a good girl, don't get me wrong, but she's got her mother's temper."

"We all have our little faults," said Aurora with an understanding smile. "But they say there is someone for everyone, and I'm glad for your sake that has proved to be true in your daughter's case. As for my visit to the Abbey – how disappointing!" she sighed. "I was so looking forward to seeing it, but I quite understand why it would be impossible. What a sad story! My heart goes out to that poor boy. We must hope that whatever ails him is merely a childhood complaint and will soon have run its course. I know of two similar cases where the young men in question made a *full* recovery."

"You don't say?"

"Oh, yes! So, you see, it's quite possible he will one day come out of seclusion."

The landlord agreed it was possible, and added that it would be a fine thing to have the young marquess up and about, since it was bound to bolster the local economy; and then, remembering his duties, he left them to the enjoyment of their lunch.

"You'd sweet-talk a pirate into telling you where he's hidden his gold," observed John, drawing a laugh from her.

The rest of the afternoon passed quickly as they set about preparing to put Aurora's plan into action.

Aurora took a stroll along the lane that led from the village to Dewbury Abbey, hoping to acquaint herself with the area and the house. It turned out that the house could not be seen from the road, so she was unable to assuage her curiosity on that point, but she did find a spot not far from the lodge gates, hidden from sight by a turn in the road, that would suit their purposes for the carriage accident.

John, for his part, set about gleaning what information he could from the landlord and inn-staff as to the goings on up at the house, and when this was accomplished went off to find a vehicle for hire. However, as his first task had unearthed certain troubling details, he could muster little enthusiasm for the completion of the second.

Providentially, there was not a single suitable carriage to be hired within ten miles of the village, and when they met in the busy parlour for dinner that evening, he was able to explain his lack of success with a clear conscience.

"Hmm . . . how inconvenient," said Aurora, leaning an elbow on the table and resting her chin in her hand. "And not even a gig was available?"

"No, miss," he replied firmly.

"Oh well! I suppose I must think of something else! Perhaps I can present myself to the housekeeper and see if she has need of a maid. From what the landlord told us, she appears to regularly drive her staff away – possibly to keep them from becoming suspicious – and must need a steady supply."

More appalled by this idea than he let on, John was wondering how to convince her that this course of action was inadvisable, when he saw a newcomer enter the common room.

"Thank the Lord!" he muttered under his breath.

Blissfully unaware of the large obstacle to her plans that had just walked in, Aurora remained lost in her thoughts; until a familiar voice above her head said: "Good evening."

She looked up with surprise.

Not quite believing her eyes, she slid her spectacles down her nose and regarded the Duke of Rothworth over the top of them.

"What are you doing here?" she demanded; the feeling of joy that had flared at the sight of him somewhat tempered by pique.

"May I join you?"

"Must you? It is not at all convenient . . . but I suppose you already know that?"

"Don't be concerned on my account. I would be delighted," he replied blandly.

"That is not what I meant!" She threw John a despairing look, hoping he would assist her in getting rid of the duke, but he simply smiled at him (with what she considered to be a most improper look of eagerness) and, standing, offered up his own seat.

"Please sit down, John," she said, readjusting her spectacles. "If His Grace is so determined to join us, he can find his own chair."

"But it ain't right for a duke to sit with the likes of me," John objected.

"If this duke feels it is below his dignity to do so, then he is free to find another table," she said tartly.

"I have said nothing of the sort so you may both settle down," Rothworth informed them; and, walking over to a free chair resting against the wall, he carried it back to the table and sat down.

"What are you doing here?" Aurora asked again. "Isn't Parliament in session?"

"I rearranged my schedule. It's a beautiful time of year to visit the country."

"It is! But I would like to know why you chose the same country to visit as myself? You had the whole of England to choose from! It is almost as if you followed me . . . though I can scarcely credit it, for I specifically told you I didn't want your presence!"

"And what if I did follow you?"

"Then I would be inclined to be displeased. And would take leave to tell you that your meddling goes beyond the pale!"

"I should be sorry to displease you, Miss Wesley, however . . . "

"Shhh! Don't call me that!" she said reproachfully. "I'm known here as Miss Smith."

"I beg pardon," he said dryly. "I should have realised you wouldn't do anything so commonplace as to use your given name."

A spark of humour entered her dark eyes; but she refrained from replying as, just then, the landlord came up to their table to take their order.

On seeing he had a new customer – who judging by his exquisitely cut jacket and highly polished boots belonged to the Quality – he offered him a warm welcome.

Aurora thought it prudent to explain the appearance of a gentleman at her table and offered up the information that her cousin had come to join her.

"Ah! So, you'll be escorting Miss Smith to Winchester, will you, sir?" asked the landlord in his cheerful, probing way.

"If required," replied Rothworth. Casting a quizzing look at Aurora, he asked: "Must it be Winchester, *cousin*?"

"Certainly it must!" she replied. "It is not as if a governess can have much say in where she lives. Advantageous positions don't grow on trees, you know – but I thought I mentioned all this in my note?"

"No, you did not. I suppose I should not be surprised. You have a rare talent for leaving out pertinent details," he said baldly.

Aurora had to bite down on her cheek to stop herself from laughing. "Oh well! I certainly *meant* to, but no matter!"

"If I'm to be tasked with seeing you to your destination, it matters to *me*," he said with an air of long-suffering. "Really, cousin, you must make more of a push to exercise your reason."

"Oh dear, yes, so scatter-brained of me! You are quite right to scold," she replied, getting into the spirit of the role he had assigned her. "But there were so many details to attend to before I left! So much busyness! And I was in *such* a twitter not knowing if my letter would reach you in time, and thinking I might be cast out into world all alone without a man for support! But of course, I see now that it was really quite foolish of me to leave out such an important detail – do say you forgive me?"

"All is forgiven! Now let's order," he said quickly, before he could burst out laughing.

As soon as the food and drink had been ordered, and the landlord had moved on to another table, Aurora said reproachfully: "Thank you, *cousin*. You have effectively cemented my reputation as a feather-headed female!"

"It was shocking to see how easily you rose to the occasion," he replied with an unrepentant grin. "You are a consummate actress."

"Now, don't you go encouraging her, sir," said John sternly, momentarily forgetting he was addressing a duke. "We'll be in all sorts of trouble if she gets it into her head that she has a talent for acting."

"I do have a talent for it," she said, smiling. "But rather than get into another discussion about *that*, I'd like to know why His Grace . . . "

"You'd best call me Julian," he interrupted. "To avoid complicating matters further."

"Yes, you are quite right!" she said approvingly. "I don't wish to reprimand you, Julian, after you have entered into the spirit of our little charade so beautifully, but I would like to know why you thought it necessary to follow me?"

Rothworth decided he rather liked the sound of his given name on her lips.

"It became necessary when I discovered your uncle's plans for the next few days," he replied.

"Is Percy in danger?" she asked abruptly, leaning forward in her chair.

"No, you may be easy on that count. Lord Charles's plans are of a more personal nature. They don't involve you, but they do make it impossible for you to visit Dewbury Abbey at the present moment."

"But why?"

"Let us just say that your uncle is hosting a bachelor gathering."

"That does not elucidate matters – are you being purposefully obtuse?"

"I'm being tactful."

"I agree with your cousin," John spoke up. "I've heard some talk myself today, and it's made me think we'd best come back another time."

"But it doesn't matter if he has friends staying at the house," she returned. "It may even suit my purpose better, for they will have a need for more maids."

"What has that to do with anything?" asked Rothworth, looking from her to John.

"Miss is thinking it a good idea to look for work up at the house," said John, his eyes pleading with Rothworth to make her see sense. "She plans on searching the place for something her uncle took from her."

"I really don't think it is necessary to involve my cousin in our business," objected Aurora.

"She's after the signet ring – I know," said Rothworth, taking no notice of her. "But a maid? That's the worst idea I've ever had the misfortune to hear!"

"My plan is sound," she insisted. "And would you both stop talking about me as if I'm not in the room!"

"Put aside for the moment the likelihood that you'll be caught," said Rothworth, turning a stern gaze on her. "Instead, think of the talk you'd occasion when it's one day discovered that the Marquess of Dewbury's sister masqueraded as a servant in her own brother's household."

"I'll be in disguise, of course! There will be no danger of anyone recognising me."

"Those spectacles and wig are not a disguise – they're adornments."

"Hardly!" she laughed. "You make it sound as if I use them to enhance my looks. And I'll have you know, my disguises have worked splendidly every single time I've had occasion to use them."

"Apart from one," he observed pointedly.

"Well . . . yes, I suppose in your case the matter was different," she conceded. "But you are the exception! You must have an uncommonly sharp eye for detail to have recognised me from your carriage . . . " She broke off suddenly, realising she had betrayed herself; then exclaimed in a vexed voice: "Oh, dash it!"

"You walked yourself right into that one," John remarked with a laugh, shaking his head.

"Shall I pretend I did not hear?" Rothworth asked her, smiling. "I'm willing to do so if the continuation of the ruse is important to your enjoyment."

"Good Lord, I'm not so idiosyncratic!" she replied. "But it was rather sly of you to trick me into revealing myself."

"I never had any intention of tricking you – why would I? At no point did I doubt you were the woman who robbed me. And as I knew you were aware of that fact, what was the point?"

She eyed him doubtfully. "Hmm . . . well, what is done, is done! At least I've come to know that I can trust you. When we were first introduced

I could not but be suspicious of your intentions. For all I knew, you could have wanted to see me transported!"

"I'm happy to know I've earned your trust, but what could have led you to think that I would have a woman transported for stealing my purse?"

"It is the law."

"One I have spoken out against in Parliament," he informed her gently.

"I didn't know that," she said with surprise. "I assumed . . . since you are a lord and bound to uphold the law . . . " She petered out, lost for words.

"Laws are simply the instruments men use to bring order to a world that is beyond their control. They are as fallible as the men who devise them and should be challenged if they are unjust. We can't allow any form of tyranny to stand simply because it is enshrined in law."

She regarded him thoughtfully for several moments, before saying: "You know, Julian, you have a most disconcerting way of making me continually amend my reading of your character. Before you, I was in the habit of thinking myself a good judge in such matters."

"How am I to take that?"

"I suppose you may take it as a compliment," she said, smiling. "But we have strayed from the point and I refuse to be distracted any longer! Tell me why I shouldn't visit the Abbey."

Rothworth and John shared a look.

"Oh, for goodness sake," she sighed. "I am not a child to be shielded! Out with it, please."

John shrugged his shoulders in resignation. "May as well tell her, sir. She'll be no better than a dog digging after a bone til she gets it out of us."

"Really, John, your analogy leaves much to be desired," she objected. Turning her gaze on Rothworth, she prompted: "Well, cousin?"

"Your uncle is not only hosting his friends," he said guardedly, "but also women of ill-repute."

"Whores? Ah . . . I finally understand what you mean by a bachelor's gathering."

"They call it the Siren's Ball," put in John.

"Do you now understand why it would be improper for you to visit the house?" asked Rothworth.

"But why not?" she replied. "I am hardly going to be shocked! Really, how old do you both think I am? I was half expecting you to say that he was holding orgies, or had turned the house into an opium den."

"Now, miss," said John, "don't you go talking about such things in front of His . . . your cousin."

"But my secret is already out," she returned, smiling at Rothworth. "He knows I am shockingly well-read – don't you, cousin?"

"Ovid?" he asked with a humorous look.

"Amongst others. But we digress again! Did you learn anything else that might be of use?"

"Perhaps," replied Rothworth, crossing his arms and leaning back against his chair. "But whether or not I should encourage you in your madness is another matter."

"If you think withholding information will keep me from entering the Abbey, you are mistaken. I would welcome your assistance, since you appear to know more about my uncle than I do, but I intend to search the house tomorrow with or without it."

"If your idea is to present yourself as a maid, then you are bound to fail – and then God only knows how I'm going to get you out of there with your reputation intact!"

The landlord brought their drinks over and all discussion ceased while he served. He showed an inclination to linger and draw his well-to-do guest into conversation, but the parlour was full of other patrons and his attention was soon needed elsewhere.

"I don't mean to argue with you," Aurora told Rothworth in a conciliatory tone, as soon as the landlord had left. "If you truly believe my plan has little chance of success, I will think of another. But please tell me all you know."

"You are entirely too persistent," he remarked. He sighed and rubbed a hand across his forehead. "I was playing cards last night with one of your uncle's cronies," he began, not entirely convinced he was doing the right thing. "He was in his cups and rather free with voicing his dissatisfaction with Lord Charles. It seems your uncle unexpectedly changed the date of the Siren's Ball to this weekend, and only gave his guests a few days' notice. As a result, some are unable to attend."

"Why would that be of interest to me?" she asked.

"He changed the date exactly one week ago."

Her face lit with understanding. "Right after the ring was stolen! Yes, that is certainly interesting. This gathering might serve some purpose to do with the ring. Well, that makes me even more determined to search the house."

"That's what I feared," muttered Rothworth.

"It is Thursday today," she went on, ignoring him, "and the guests will undoubtedly begin arriving tomorrow, so I must act quickly."

"You will not present yourself as a maid – that is final!"

"What an autocratic disposition you have. Luckily for you, I have decided to abandon that idea, for it occurs to me the housekeeper is bound to ask for references and naturally I don't have any . . . unless *you* would like to give me one?" she teased.

He threw her an admonitory look.

"It was worth asking!" she said, laughing a little. "I suppose we could return to my original plan: stage a carriage accident near the gates and ask for shelter overnight. Unfortunately, John was not able to find a suitable carriage, but now that you're here . . . " She drifted off meaningfully.

"I suppose you believe it falls on me to offer up my carriage?" he asked with an ironic lift of an eyebrow.

"Now *that* is a splendid idea! It is very kind of you to offer . . . ah, but I suppose your crest is on the door?"

"It is."

"Then I'm afraid it won't do. I wouldn't want anyone to know that we are using your carriage. It would invite all sorts of unwelcome speculation." She fell into a thoughtful silence, and after a minute cried: "Oh, why did I not think of it before! The *perfect* solution."

"I'm filled with trepidation," remarked Rothworth.

"You must take me as your mistress!"

Twenty-Three

"I beg your pardon?" said Rothworth, too greatly stunned to articulate further.

"Don't you see? We can say that I'm your mistress, for then we will be able to join the house-party," Aurora explained excitedly. "You yourself said my uncle toad-eats you, and if you showed up at his door expecting to be admitted he would never deny you. In fact, he would probably be delighted to have caught himself a duke!"

"I feel remarkably like a carp all of a sudden," he declared with a scowl. "And no! Under no circumstances will I allow you to masquerade as my mistress."

"I will, of course, need suitable clothing," Aurora said meditatively, paying him no heed. "A mistress's wardrobe must be more daring than anything I possess. Perhaps I could lower the bodice of my dress . . . no, that won't do! I suppose your mistresses are always dressed in the finest silks and muslins?"

"You make it sound as if I have a harem of them at my disposal," he snapped. "I assure you, I do not!"

"No, of course not – that would be wasteful."

John guffawed behind his hand, and even Rothworth was drawn into an unwilling smile.

"Wasteful is not the first word that comes to mind," he said dryly.

"But it is applicable," she insisted. "There must be only so many mistresses to go around, and for you to take more than your fair share wouldn't only be wasteful, but selfish as well."

"Since I pray never to find myself in such an alarming situation, you may absolve me of guilt on both counts."

She smiled irrepressibly. "Yes, I imagine it would be *most* uncomfortable. If I were a man, I would certainly restrict myself to one partner at a time and avoid unnecessary complications."

"I never know what outrageous thing you'll say next," he groaned, dropping his head into his hands.

"Well, I suppose you should be glad of it! How dull life would be if one always knew what others were going to say. But we were discussing what I'm to wear! I think a red silk dress would be just the thing – you do like red, don't you?"

"What man doesn't, but . . . "

"Good!" she cut him off. "I believe I saw one earlier through the window of the dress-maker's shop. And if it proves to be unsuitable, we can always drive to Guildford tomorrow and buy something there. Something daring! Or do you perhaps prefer your mistresses dressed more discreetly?"

Rothworth was momentarily fixated on the thought of Aurora in a low-cut, red gown, and had to fight to dislodge the image from his mind.

"I refuse to discuss the subject further," he said irately.

"But surely it wouldn't do your reputation any favours if I turned up looking like a dowd?"

"My reputation is not what concerns me in regard to this preposterous plan of yours! If you imagine I'd willingly subject you to the kind of attention you're bound to attract if you enter that house as my . . . as a woman of ill repute, then you will be sadly disappointed!"

"Really, Julian, this is not the time to be prudish."

"I'm not being prudish. However, since you appear to have lost your mind, I'm perfectly capable of being autocratic – as you noted earlier!"

Seeing that she had seriously disturbed him, and the mulish look in his eyes showed no signs of abating, Aurora decided to abandon the subject for the moment.

"Perhaps you are right," she said. "But then how am I to get into the house? If my ideas are not to your liking, I would be happy to consider other suggestions."

It took some moments for Rothworth to simmer down from his state of acute tension.

After a few salutary sips of his burgundy, he said: "I think it best if you leave the matter in my hands."

"You mean to steal into the house and look for the ring yourself?" she asked.

"Certainly not. I am a peer of the realm, I don't steal into people's houses."

"A poor turn of phrase, forgive me," she said, casting her gaze downward and giving the appearance of a lady abashed.

Somewhat mollified, he went on: "I will call on your uncle tomorrow and do what I can to discover information on the ring's whereabouts. Then we can regroup and decide our next steps."

Aurora nodded and sipped her wine; and as the food arrived soon after and the conversation turned to less contentious topics, Rothworth supposed her to have reconciled herself to his eminently sensible proposal.

So, it was left to John, who knew Aurora only too well, to harbour grave doubts over the sudden docility of her manner, and to wonder what plan she was hatching in that busy mind of hers.

*   *   *

On the following morning, Aurora rose early and ventured out into the village to wile away an hour before breakfast, and try to think of a scheme that would gain her entrance into Dewbury Abbey.

She had spent half the night trying to decide how best to accomplish this feat, and had at last fallen asleep on the thought that tomorrow would bring wiser counsel. But now that tomorrow had arrived, she was no closer to resolving the conundrum.

She passed the dress-maker's shop she had mentioned to Rothworth and peered through the window. It did not take her long to realise that, had he agreed to her plan, they would have had to look elsewhere for a dress; the one in the shop was of too poor quality to have made her role as his mistress believable.

Still, she thought the plan had merit and wondered if there was some way to overcome his scruples. He had looked almost repelled by the thought of her as his mistress, and she could not help wondering if there was something about her that made her ineligible for the position.

She was mulling over the possibility (a rather unpleasant one) that he did not find her sufficiently attractive, when a commotion up the street caught her attention.

Grateful to be taken away from her unprofitable thoughts, she walked towards two large wagons that had just drawn up in front of the baker's shop, from which a medley of colourful, shabby characters were descending.

Aurora had always enjoyed the entertainment provided by a travelling troupe and wondered if they were to set up in the area, or were simply passing through on their way to a larger town, where they would be certain of several days of employment.

She asked the question of an old man who was sitting in the driver's seat of one of the wagons, chewing on a length of wood that had been fashioned into something resembling a pipe.

"No, miss, we be going to the Abbey fer the Siren's Ball," he responded in phlegmy voice. "The guvn'or up there wants us fer 'is guests."

"Has Lord Charles invited you to perform at Dewbury Abbey?" she asked, incredulous of her good luck.

"'Tis what I said."

"How delightfully opportune! It just goes to show, things always have a way of working out!"

"Begging yer pardon?"

"Oh, don't mind me! Are you in the man in charge of the troupe?"

"What yer be wanting with 'im?"

"I would like to speak to him about joining you – just for tonight."

"Why?"

"Well, you see I've always had a desperate wish to perform in a troupe . . . and you wouldn't even have to pay me! In fact, I would be happy to offer you generous compensation for allowing me to come with you."

"Exactly 'ow generous are yer talking?"

"A pound!" she offered up, after a moment's hesitation.

As this amounted to a week's worth of wages for a skilled tradesman, it was little wonder the old man's eyes widened with interest.

"Must be one 'ell of a desperate wish. Do yer 'ave an act, Miss . . . ?"

"Lizzie Smith," she supplied quickly.

"Jack Wiley, at yer service," he said grandly, tipping his dusty, curly-brimmed hat.

"Delighted to meet you, Mr Wiley! As for how I can contribute to the entertainment, I have some skill on the pianoforte and also do a little singing. And I know a small repertoire of ballads and country dances that may suit this weekend's setting."

Mr Wiley cast a jaundiced eye over her. "Yer a strange one, ain't yer? Can't understand why yer'd want to perform with the likes of us, but I'm not one to turn down blunt when it's offered," he said prosaically. "We be leaving in a few minutes, so if yer want to come with us yer best 'urry."

Taking him at his word, Aurora called over her shoulder that she would be back in ten minutes and hurried towards the inn.

On entering the taproom, she requested ink, pen and paper from the servant washing the counter, and upon being given these essentials, sat down at one of the tables to write.

She dipped her pen in the ink and sat debating with herself for a few minutes whether or not to address the note to Rothworth. She decided against it in the end, and as the ink on the pen had dried, she dipped it again and set about writing to John.

When the note was finished and had dried, she folded it and handed it to the servant, with a request that it be given to her manservant when he came down to his breakfast. She then rushed upstairs and quickly packed what few belongings she had brought with her.

By the time she returned to the troupe, most of them had finished eating their baked goods and were climbing into the wagons to take their seats. On catching sight of her, Mr Wiley called out to her to sit up beside him, and so she hitched up her skirts and mounted, overnight bag in hand.

As they pulled away from the village and set off down the lane towards Dewbury Abbey, Aurora felt a twinge of regret that she had not left a note for the duke. But since he showed a tendency to mollycoddle her, she really had had no choice.

It was surprisingly agreeable to have a man so determined to protect her, but when all was said and done, she had responsibilities and they were too important to be delegated.

Twenty-Four

"She did what!" thundered Rothworth.

"Now, sir, don't you go getting yourself worked up," John advised him. "Not that I don't agree with you, mind. But there's no point letting the world know our business."

Rothworth contained himself with some effort and, casting a quick look down the corridor, ushered John into his bedchamber and closed the door.

"You're right," he said in a more moderate tone. "I'll have plenty of opportunity later to tell that blasted girl what I think of her!"

"I'll not allow anyone that's not family give Miss Aurora a trimming . . . not unless they've got a real good reason for it," said John, watching him closely.

"As neither you, nor her brother appear capable of doing so, then I will!"

"Under what authority, if you don't mind me asking?"

"My own, damn you!"

"Well, that's mighty fine talk," returned John placidly, "but you've got no real sway over her, now do you?"

"I intend to."

"Ah! Now we're getting to the heart of the matter. But will she have you? Could go either way, if you ask me, sir."

Rothworth threw him an irritated look. "I mean to keep her safe, and by God, I'll do it! You've allowed her to carry on as if the consequences of her actions are no more serious than a slap on the wrist. We'll be lucky if we can get her out of that damned house without her getting hauled up before the magistrate – and that's the least unpleasant outcome that occurs to me!"

For someone who had just been accused of negligence, John's smile contained a good deal of approval.

"Now don't you go worrying, sir. I've known Miss Aurora since she was a babe and I'll say this for her: I've never met another soul with such a talent for getting themselves out of a thorny situation."

"She appears to have many talents, and very few of them salubrious," Rothworth observed bitterly.

"That she does! Partly my fault, I expect. She always was a curious one and had me answering her questions on this and that, and teaching her tricks. I never could say no to her – which is my cross to bear! But if I can give you a word of advice, sir: you'll never win her over by ranting and raving at her, and trying to mould her into what you think a lady should be. Miss Aurora ain't one to conform if it's not of her own choosing – so you'd best give up now if that's your thinking!"

"If I *could* give up, don't you think I'd have done so by now? I appear to have no choice in the matter!" Rothworth replied with barely contained frustration.

Turning abruptly, he walked over to the fireplace and propped an elbow against the mantle to stare at the empty grate.

After a few minutes of brooding silence, he said with a degree of self-mockery: "I've no wish to mould her into anything. To my utter astonishment, I find her more perfect than any other woman of my considerable acquaintance."

"You've got it mighty bad, sir, if you're accusing Miss Aurora of perfection!"

A corner of Rothworth's mouth turned up.

"I know," he said, looking back to John and pushing away from the mantle. "A most uncomfortable condition. I count myself fortunate I've never been plagued by it before."

"You'd best get on and declare yourself so she can put you out of your misery, one way or another," said John kindly.

"She has a great deal on her mind at present. I dare not put it to the touch."

"Well, that she does. But you'll soon learn Miss Aurora always has plenty on her mind. She's one of those who can never be without some occupation. Back in Norfolk, there were always people coming to the door and looking to her to sort out their problems. And, bless her, she always would find a solution."

"Well, now she's the one in a fix – and I'll be damned if I just sit idly by and wait for news!"

*　　*　　*

Standing in Dewbury Abbey's grand ballroom and taking in her surroundings, Aurora could not help but be impressed by the Italianate frescoes that looked down on her from all sides. It seemed as if a thousand pair of eyes followed her progress. She was certain this was not a room she had ever entered in her early years, for if she had it would have made an intimidating and memorable impression on a susceptible young mind.

At present the ballroom was not only inhabited by the troupe, but also upwards of twenty servants who were preparing the space for Lord Charles's guests; cleaning, polishing, moving around furniture, hanging decorations, and also placing fresh beeswax candles in the chandeliers, which had been carefully lowered by a team of footmen.

The troupe had arrived at the Abbey several hours ago and had been directed by the housekeeper to begin setting up the stage at one end of the ballroom. They had been assigned an adjoining parlour as a dressing room, and it was there that Aurora had spent the majority of the day, helping the actors with their lines, mending costumes, dressing hair and applying face paint.

It was all rather exciting, and Aurora was so greatly enjoying herself that she regretted that her station in life precluded her from such a profession.

There were twelve entertainers in all who made up Mr Wiley's troupe: four male actors and four female; a gentleman with tattoos and two snakes that seemed to be perpetually wrapped around his body; a married couple who performed acrobatic tricks; and lastly, a monkey in cut-off trousers and a red vest that could play the cymbals when coaxed into it, but more often than not preferred to steal bits of food or climb up onto the shoulders of his colleagues and survey the room with the bearing of a sultan.

Apart from a small disagreement over the ownership of Aurora's bonnet, Mr Key the monkey and Aurora had hit it off very well, and he spent a good part of the day chattering in her ear as she went about her duties.

As for the other members of the troupe, although they had cast her a few odd looks in the beginning, they were for the most part of an egalitarian persuasion and had soon accepted her into their midst, treating her with the same free and easy manners they reserved for one another.

It was now almost five o'clock, and with four hours to go until the performance began Mr Wiley had gathered everyone in front of the stage to rehearse. He was to open the show by welcoming the audience and performing his usual comic routine with Mr Key. Aurora's set on the piano would come next, followed by the acrobatic duo, the snake-man and finally a performance of Shakespeare's A Midsummer Night's Dream.

Aurora calculated that she had as much as three hours between her performance and the end of the play in which to carry out her search for the ring, after which time the movement of guests through the house would make things rather more difficult.

The rehearsal began, and soon it was time for Aurora to sit down at the pianoforte, which had been moved from the music room to a position near the stage.

"Yer sing like an angel, Lizzie, yer surely do," said Mr Wiley, when she had finished her first ballad. "Yer wouldn't want to join us fer the 'ole of the summer, now would yer?"

"That appeals to me more than you know!" she replied with a laugh. "But regretfully I must decline. I have obligations that will keep me in London."

"We'll be back there in the Autumn, won't we, Mr Wiley?" said Mrs Lorry, the acrobatic young matron, who at present had one shapely leg encased in tight-fitting, knitted pantaloons on top of the pianoforte and was stretching. "Lizzie can join us for our theatre run."

"Oh, don't tempt me!" groaned Aurora, returning her attention to the pianoforte. "For my second song, I thought to perform *Drown it in the Bowl.* I find it rather appropriate for tonight, but you must tell me what you think!"

Her fingers played the introduction, and she began to sing:

The glossy sparkle on the board,
The wine is ruby bright,
The reign of pleasure is restor'd,
Of ease and fond delight.
The day is gone, the night's our own,
Then let us feast the soul;
If any care or pain remain,
Why drown it in the bowl.

*   *   *

Around the time Aurora was doing a fine job of entertaining the troupe and servants, the Duke of Rothworth's travelling chaise drove through the rusted gates of Dewbury Abbey and proceeded up a patchy gravel drive full of weeds, until it came to a stop outside a sprawling stone edifice that looked to be no better maintained than its approach.

The history of Dewbury Abbey was a rather long but unremarkable one. Originally known by another name, the abbey had been built during

Henry I's reign and existed peacefully for some three hundred years, until it was seized by Henry VIII during the Dissolution of the Monasteries.

It was gifted to the first Marquess of Dewbury, for services rendered to the crown in the sixteen hundreds and converted into a country house. Many of the abbey's significant structural features were saved, however, it was greatly increased in size, in the Jacobean style, using the same local stone as the original structure. In the eighteenth century, several improvements and alterations were undertaken, of which the ballroom was one, and since then it had remained in an untouched state.

Rothworth had no thoughts to spare for the historic importance of the building before him. He was wearing the same grim expression he had sported since learning of Aurora's disappearance that morning, and it took some effort for him to don the polite mask expected of him.

Turning to John, who was to act as his man and find out what he could from the servants, he told him to wait a few minutes and follow with the overnight bags. Then he opened the carriage door and dismounted.

Another carriage had arrived moments before, and while the servants unloaded the luggage strapped to the back, the occupants – two gentlemen and three ladies of questionable repute – were making their way in high spirits towards an arched stone entrance.

Rothworth followed them and entered a large vestibule, where a handful of other guests were standing about and speaking with their host.

After some minutes of raucous greetings and conversation, during which Rothworth kept to the background, the guests were led off by a footman up the oak staircase to the first floor, where the bedchambers were located, while their servants followed behind with the luggage.

As the vestibule thinned of people, Lord Charles at last caught sight of Rothworth.

"Your Grace!" he exclaimed in surprise and hurried over, his corset gently creaking with the motion. "I didn't know to expect you!"

"I'm afraid I'm importuning you. A spur of the moment decision on my part. I was on my way to one of my minor estates in Hampshire and recollected your invitation to call on you."

"My . . . ? Ah . . . yes, yes, of course," returned Lord Charles; having no memory of such an invitation, he assumed he must have been somewhat foxed at the time.

"We were at White's," Rothworth put in helpfully. And then, with a flash of inspiration (of which he thought Aurora would approve), he added: "I was sharing with you my passion for our historic abbeys, and how important I thought it was to preserve such culturally significant pieces of our past."

"Ah, yes, yes . . . I remember now! You have a great interest in preserving our history."

This was so clearly more of a question than a statement that Rothworth was hard pressed not to smile.

"Very true. But perhaps I have chosen an inconvenient time to avail myself of your hospitality?"

"Yes . . . erm . . . no, no! Nothing of the sort! Devilishly good to see you, Your Grace. I'm holding a convivial gathering for some like-minded friends this weekend . . . only it's bachelor's fare, you understand . . . may not be quite to your taste," he suggested tentatively.

"Let me put your mind at rest. My tastes can be most flexible."

"Well, if you're certain . . . I mean, I'd be delighted if you'd join us!" said Lord Charles, torn between satisfaction at the thought of being able to boast of hosting the Duke of Rothworth, and trepidation at what such a respectable personage would think of the debauchery planned for the weekend.

"I believe I shall stay," said Rothworth pleasantly. "But only for one night as I am expected elsewhere."

Lord Charles perked up at this information, for the worst of the debauchery was planned for the following night.

"Ah, good, good! I hope my humble home will meet with your approval, Your Grace."

"*Your* home?" Rothworth enquired with mild surprise. "I had not realised that congratulations were in order? Am I addressing the new Lord Dewbury?"

"No, no, sadly not . . . that is . . . the title belongs to my nephew, of course. Slip of the tongue! I've been keeping an eye on the poor boy's estates for the last few years and . . . well, one grows accustomed."

"Do they?" asked Rothworth in a lethally flat tone.

"Erm . . . ah, there's the housekeeper!" exclaimed Lord Charles with evident relief. "Mrs Ross! A moment, if you please."

It seemed to Rothworth that the housekeeper intended to pretend that she had not heard the summons, but duty must have prevailed for she slowly turned and made her way over to them.

Quite oblivious to the air of rigid disapproval emanating from her, Lord Charles handed his guest into her charge; and, after several avowals that he was honoured to be hosting His Grace, he claimed he was needed

162

elsewhere and departed in a great hurry, accompanied by the sound of creaking.

Twenty-Five

The housekeeper, a whey-faced woman of skeletal proportions and military bearing, maintained a reserved silence as she led Rothworth through the house to the first floor.

Only after she had shown him to a bedchamber did she open her mouth to inform him – in an arctic voice that left no doubt as to what she thought of his morals – that the entertainment would begin in the ballroom at nine o'clock.

Then, having condescended to provide him with this information, she turned and left the room without waiting to discover if he had any further need of her.

It occurred to him that his reputation was unlikely to recover after a visit to the household of a known hedonist. A month ago, this may have caused him some vexation, however, he found he could no longer drum up the will to care. His thoughts were wholly taken up with the recovery of a certain lady, who was fast becoming both an obsession and the bane of his existence.

Determined to find her as quickly as possible, he let himself out of his bedchamber and began a thorough search of the house. After wondering in and out of rooms, disturbing several amorous trysts in the process and enduring a good deal of understandable rancour, he at last found his quarry in the ballroom.

He entered through a door that led onto the minstrels' gallery, from which he could survey the room below, and noticed her at once, sitting cross-legged on the floor beside a woman who was contorting her body into shapes that defied nature. But it was Aurora's mop of improbably-angelic blonde curls and bespectacled face, enlivened by laughter, that held his attention and contracted his chest with a sharp ache.

It took him several moments to realise that she was not wearing a dress but rather a costume. And, judging from the Shakespearian play being rehearsed on the stage, it was likely meant to be Grecian. The flimsy material draped around her, leaving one shoulder bare, and even from this distance he could see that it did little to conceal her curves.

She appeared entirely unconscious of her barely-clothed state, as did the others in the ballroom as they went about their work preparing for the night's revelries. However, this did little to appease his irritation.

He quit the gallery, and was soon entering the ballroom through the ground floor entrance.

Forcing himself to cross the room in a controlled manner, he came up behind Aurora and said coolly: "May I have a word?"

Surprised, she looked up at him with such a degree of unconcealed pleasure that it momentarily overcame his annoyance.

"You found me!" she said, rising nimbly to her feet.

"Of course, I found you. I was hardly going to sit by and let you tumble into yet another piece of folly."

"Yes, it was naughty of me to have joined a troupe for one night!" she returned, sending him a silent message with her eyes to put him on his guard. "But, as you know, I have always wished to perform in public, so please don't scold! Instead, allow me to introduce you to the talented Mrs Lorry." She smiled down at her new friend, who was still in her contortion on the floor. "Margery, may I present you to my . . . "

"Rothworth. How do you do?" he said quickly before Aurora could introduce him as her cousin; a title that was unlikely to live up to scrutiny if Lord Charles or his friends came to hear of it.

Mrs Lorry released the leg she had wrapped around her neck and stood. Being neither old nor blind, she could not fail to respond to the handsome man before her and offered him a slow, flirtatious smile.

"Is this gent your protector?" she asked Aurora. "Or is he fair game?"

"I am neither," Rothworth replied with frosty civility. "If you will excuse us, Mrs Lorry, I have a pressing need to speak with . . . " He paused and looked across at Aurora, uncertain what she was calling herself at present.

"Lizzie," she offered up, laughter in her eyes.

"Indeed," he responded blandly; and, taking hold of her arm, propelled her away.

"Poor Margery!" said Aurora when they were out of earshot. "Was it really necessary to give her such a snub? It's not her fault that your looks lure women into throwing themselves at you . . . and for goodness sake don't say it is merely your wealth and position they want! That is nonsense. Margery knew of neither and is a married woman besides! Which just goes to prove that the temptation lies squarely with your person."

"It's not my person we are to discuss," he replied as he steered her into a small parlour off the ballroom and shut the door. Letting go of her, he placed his hands on his hips and glared at her.

"What in God's name are you wearing?"

"A costume, of course. I would have been rather conspicuous performing in a day-dress!"

"That . . . " he gestured with his hand, " . . . is improper."

"Gracious, I just had the most shocking insight into how you will one day plague your daughters. I imagine it is also how you instruct your sister. However, I am neither so you really can't expect me to allow you to take that tone with me. Besides, this costume is for *A Midsummer Night's Dream,* and it is certainly not improper! Ancient Athenians used to dress in this way, even the stuffiest and most respectable of them . . . with whom you appear to share a great affinity," she finished provocatively.

"By such reasoning, are we to walk about in animal skins, since savages too could lay claim to their own interpretation of respectability?"

"I don't imagine wearing animal skins is at all sanitary or comfortable, so even if the savages *were* respectable nothing would induce me to follow their example."

A smile hovered about her lips, beckoning him to share her amusement at their absurd exchange.

But just as she began to hope that she had managed to ease his unyielding mood, his eyes dropped to her costume again and a tense look entered them.

"I trust you have no such scruples about wool?" he said; and, taking off his coat, placed it about her shoulders. "You're cold."

"A little . . . how did you know?"

He pressed his lips together, his expression turning even more forbidding.

"*Now* what have I done to displease you?" she asked, her brow puckered.

"Nothing," he replied curtly and drew his coat more tightly across her. "The sooner we get you out of here, the happier I'll be."

"But I can't leave yet! I have had no opportunity to search for the ring."

"My dear girl, if you think I will allow you . . . "

She lay a hand on his arm, halting his words.

"Julian, I know that we both allow each other a degree of latitude, but I must tell you that in this instance you presume too much."

He looked as if he wanted to respond but something held him back.

Feeling a need to soften her rebuke, she continued with a soft smile: "You have a naturally autocratic disposition that has been bolstered by your public and private responsibilities, and I hope I make every allowance in that regard – particularly since you have proven yourself to be a good friend to myself and my brother. But I can't allow you to dictate to me. No one has that right over me."

"A husband will."

She laughed lightly. "Yes, perhaps. However, though it may have escaped your notice, I am six and twenty and of passable good looks. And yet I am still unwed."

"I assure you, I have noticed."

"Yes well, in part that is owing to the difficulty of my situation. Those who wished to marry Miss Wesley could not know that she didn't legally exist. But, for the most part, I am unwed because I choose to be." There was an infinitesimal pause. "My mother's experience with the marquess cured me of all romantic notions in regard to marriage."

"And yet she married a second time," he pointed out.

"She did . . . and I admit, she was very happy with Papa. But she was extraordinarily fortunate to find him."

"Perhaps they were both fortunate that he found a way to earn her trust."

"Perhaps," she replied, smiling in acknowledgment of his point. "However, I am not so naïve that I expect to have her . . . "

Rothworth suddenly covered her mouth with his hand, startling her. And his eyes flew to the door.

Voices could be heard on the other side.

"If they enter," he murmured, "we must give them a plausible reason for our presence here together. Do you understand?"

She nodded.

Removing his hand, he drew her over to the far wall and, pressing her back against it, used his body to shield her from view of the door.

A moment later it swung open, and the housekeeper walked in with one of the maids.

" . . . and also check all the hearths. Then you may retire for the evening. I have made it clear to Lord Charles that only his hired London servants are to deal with the guests after nine o'clock. And I advise you to lock your door . . . *good heavens!*" There was a pause, and then an incensed exclamation: "Why do they never make use of the bedchambers!"

Rothworth turned his head and offered his audience an indifferent look.

The housekeeper's scathing eyes and the maid's curious ones attempted to see past him to the lady he had pinned against the wall.

"Yes?" he said, his manner so supercilious that Aurora was tempted to laugh.

Realising she had her own part to play, she giggled rather piercingly and said in a complaining voice: "Oh fie, sir! Why did you stop? I don't care to have a gent get distracted when he's with me. Makes a girl think she ain't enough of a handful to hold his attention."

And then, grabbing hold of his head, she pulled him down for a demanding kiss.

Sometime after the door had closed with an indignant click, Aurora broke away from Rothworth's embrace (when had his arms wrapped around her?) and looked over his shoulder.

"Do you think we managed to fool them?" she asked.

"Undoubtedly," he replied.

"Yes, I think we were most convincing! I could almost feel the housekeeper's displeasure from here."

"I don't believe my credit with her will ever recover. We must hope your brother sees the wisdom in pensioning her off. And as for your performance, it did little to salvage my reputation. You appear to have a very odd impression of the type of woman who would attract me."

"I was so wonderfully vulgar, wasn't I?" she said, beaming happily.

"You need not look so pleased with yourself," he remarked, smiling down at her.

It was at this point that Aurora noticed that they were still pressed up against each other.

With a nod to prudence (though a very lukewarm one) she said: "You may let go of me now."

His forehead fell against hers for a moment; then, with a pronounced exhalation, he slowly eased away.

"That's the second time you've kissed me as part of a ruse," he observed lightly.

"In the spirit of honesty, I must tell you that you are mistaken," she said, bending over to retrieve his coat, which had fallen from her shoulders. "This occasion warranted some deception to make the plan believable, but there was no ruse intended the first time."

"That first kiss gave you the perfect opportunity to steal my purse," he noted.

"Oh, I had already stolen it by then! I picked you pocket when I fell against you. The kiss formed no part of my plan, and I still don't quite understand what came over me! Perhaps it was simply an inclination to shock you."

He regarded her in silence for a long while.

"Your inclination is a dangerous thing," he said at last. "If you were my sister, I'd confine you to the house."

"If I were your sister, we wouldn't be having this discussion."

"That much is true! And so, there are no further misunderstandings, the next time you kiss me I'll assume you mean it . . . and all that it entails."

"You are being presumptuous!"

"I am," he replied, his utter assurance sending a tremor of alarm through her. "Now," he continued, business-like, "before we're interrupted again, tell me what you have planned for tonight."

Aurora was happy to leave behind a topic that was causing her a degree of agitation that was new to her. It was one thing to have a little fun on the spur of the moment, and quite another to have the other player in your game talk of the future as if making a solemn vow.

She quickly outlined her idea to search Lord Charles's bedchamber and the library, which she had learnt he used as an office when in residence.

"For I can't imagine the ring would be anywhere else, can you?" she asked.

"If we only have a couple of hours, then those two places are the most sensible to target," he replied. "I'll meet you in the library at ten o'clock. Do you know where it is?"

"Oh yes! I managed to convince one of the footmen to give me a quick tour of the house earlier. Thank you for your coat!" she said, handing it back to him.

He took it reluctantly.

"The sooner we conclude this outlandish plan of yours, the better!" he said with astringency. "And then, I give you fair warning, I've every intention of removing you from this house, and I won't listen to a word of complaint! I fully expect this evening to deteriorate into debauchery, for which not even your extensive reading will have prepared you!"

Aurora happily agreed to all this; and after a few more minutes spent trying to convince him that playing the pianoforte and singing so early in the evening did not constitute a danger to her physical or moral well-being, she left him to find what solace he could in her words and took herself off with a sprightly step to prepare for her performance.

Twenty-Six

It would have been expecting rather too much of the well-lubricated crowd gathered in the ballroom that evening to listen to Aurora's performance with decorous attention. So, it was fortunate that she did not expect such behaviour, and was instead exhilarated to perform for persons who were just as likely to join her in singing, as they were to grab hold of the nearest member of the opposite sex and twirl them about in an abandoned fashion.

There were upwards of a hundred people there, with at least two women to every gentleman, and though the room could comfortably hold three hundred, with the stage at the far end, refreshment tables against one side and seating against the other, the space was greatly reduced. What was left was taken up by a congregation of over-heated and over-excited bodies, whose exuberance seemed to feed on it itself and rise in increasing increments.

As Aurora made her way through her selection of lively ballads, she was ably assisted by Mr Key, who sat on her shoulder and chattered his way through every song. From time to time, he made a spirited attempt to steal her spectacles and put them on, but he was always gracious enough to restore them to their rightful place when she requested their return.

He also proved to be a worthy guardian, for if any gentleman dared to approach too closely, he would screech his displeasure; and once, when an inebriated middle-aged roué dared to paw Aurora's shoulder, he sunk his small teeth into the fleshy hand as retribution.

Aurora scolded him and reminded him to mind his manners, but there was such an endearing gleam of proprietorial male arrogance in his eyes (strongly reminiscent of another male who had insinuated himself into her life) that she soon forgave him and allowed him to remain on her shoulder.

When her last song was over, she accepted her applause with a curtsy and handed over the spirited crowd to Mr Wiley. Leaving behind the uproar of the ballroom, she retreated into the relative calm of the dressing-room parlour.

It was past ten o'clock at this point, but it proved impossible for her to leave immediately to meet Rothworth.

First she had to speak with some of the actors, who were curious to hear her description of the audience; then she helpfully located one of the snakes that had gone missing, by the simple expedient of almost sitting on it; she was also called upon, rather frantically, to repair a tear in Mrs Lorry's barely-there costume, moments before she and her husband were due on stage; and, lastly, she spent some minutes coaxing Mr Key off her shoulder, and when he refused to comply had to ruthlessly manhandle him and deposit him in a trunk of costumes.

Finally, before anyone else could ask for her assistance in resolving the thousand and one little disasters that arise before a performance, she quickly let herself out the back door of the parlour and into the servants' corridor.

From there it was a simple matter to make her way to the library, which was also on the ground floor. There were many servants about, but she walked past them with a purposeful stride, as if she had somewhere to be, and hardly elicited more than a glance.

She soon reached the deserted part of the house where the library was situated and entered. Her gaze immediately landed on Rothworth, sitting in a leather chair, glass in hand.

"Drinking while on duty?" she teased.

"A prop," he replied, laying down the glass on a table beside him and standing. "I had to have some reason to be in this room in case someone entered. Why are you still wearing that dratted costume?"

"You have a very odd fascination with my clothing!"

"It is the 'lack of' that concerns me," he muttered to himself.

"Pardon?"

"I was speaking to myself. . . something I appear to succumb to in your presence."

"Papa was just the same! Don't let it concern you, it's quite common when one gets on in years."

"Minx."

She smiled at him impishly. "I'm sorry I'm late. I had a temperamental monkey to deal with."

"I take it that isn't a euphemism?"

"No!" she replied, bursting into laughter. "He is a perfectly charming little fellow, despite his brazen possessive streak. Have you had a chance to begin searching?"

"I've been all over the desk and found nothing . . . though I felt like a loose-screw, rifling through another man's papers!"

"You will soon grow accustomed," she said consolingly.

"I have no wish to! It's hardly a talent I want to cultivate."

"But only think how useful it might prove should you want to discover the secrets of your Parliamentary colleagues."

"Good God, what do you take me for? I'd no more search through a colleague's desk than I would . . . "

Her smile halted his outburst.

"Are you ribbing me?" he demanded, doing his best to resist her infectious humour.

"A little! You were looking so fraught and serious when I entered that I couldn't help myself."

"Stealing has a way of depressing my amiability."

"Then let me assuage your conscience! It is not stealing to recover something that was stolen. But if you prefer to return to the ballroom, I'm perfectly happy to continue the search by myself."

"I'm not leaving you alone in this house of depravity! Let us not waste any more time. We have little of it left as it is."

She agreed fully with this sentiment and began to walk around the room, inspecting various decorative items for signs of hidden compartments.

Rothworth meanwhile checked behind the few paintings on the walls, and when no secret safe or cavity was revealed turned his attention to the shelves of books. The Dewbury library was not as extensive as the one left to him by his forebearers, however, it still covered two entire walls of the high-ceiling room and posed a daunting challenge for the time they had available.

As her own search had not yielded anything of interest, Aurora soon joined him in pulling books off the shelves and checking within their covers.

After half an hour, and several bouts of sneezing, she exclaimed: "There is so much dust! I would be astonished to learn these shelves have been cleaned in the last decade."

Rothworth handed her his handkerchief as another sneeze overcame her.

"Thank you," she wheezed, emerging from behind the fine linen.

"You have the look of an angelic urchin," he remarked, and, reaching over, adjusted the spectacles on her nose. "It's rather disconcerting. You are far from one and too old for the other."

"Would you prefer me to play the grand lady?" she asked, putting on a lofty accent; but then ruined the effect by screwing up her face for another sneeze.

"A rather demented grand lady," he replied, smiling at her predicament. "I think we had better leave this room before you announce our presence to all and sundry."

"Yes, let's! It seems I am allergic to dust . . . or at least this quantity of it! And besides, I have a feeling the ring is not in here."

"You couldn't have had this feeling earlier and spared us a fruitless hour of searching?" he asked, pardonably annoyed.

"It is best to be thorough! And now at least we can move on with a clear conscience."

"I don't know how you contrive to do it, but you make the irrational sound perfectly reasonable."

"A compliment?"

"I couldn't say."

Going to the door, he opened it to check the corridor. Apart from the distant sounds of revelry, it was empty. He beckoned her over and held the door as she passed before him.

"Do you know where your uncle's bedchamber is located?" he asked.

"Yes," she replied, setting off towards the main staircase that would take them to the first floor.

"Let me guess: your obliging footman?"

"They are always kind enough to be obliging," she said over her shoulder, smiling.

"Is there anyone you can't turn to good account?"

"Gracious, I'm not omnipotent! But I do find most people are amenable to persuasion as long certain conditions are met. It is then a matter of discovering the correct conditions for each individual."

"You would make an excellent political hostess," he remarked. "And that *is* a compliment."

"Why, thank you!" she said, greatly pleased. "I believe I should like that. However, there is little hope of Percy pursuing a political career. He is more suited to an active life out of doors, and not even my affection for him can credit him with more than a modest interest in weightier concerns."

Rothworth refrained from correcting her misunderstanding. The words had slipped out before he could stop himself, and though his inference was blindingly clear to him, Aurora's apparent unconsciousness only served to highlight the depth of her disinterest in marriage.

It was a novel experience, and he did not at all care for it. It was perverse of Fate to dangle, just out of reach, the one woman he wanted above all others.

Quite oblivious of the duke's mental perturbations, Aurora led them up the deserted staircase to the first floor, and then turned right down a corridor. The stone walls here were decorated with the original carvings of the old abbey, and the light from the candles in the wall-sconces caused a myriad of shapes and shadows to further embellish their surface.

This was the oldest part of the house and though a carpet had been put down on the floor, there was an all-pervasive chill in the air that not even the heat of a warm spring evening could dispel.

After walking past several closed doors, they turned around a final corner, beyond which the corridor came to an abrupt end at the door to Lord Charles's rooms.

Aurora had just put her hand on the door-handle, when they heard a voice from the direction of the stairs say: " . . . yes, yes! You do it! I'll get a group together and bring them to my brother's rooms just as soon as I can."

"Your uncle," Rothworth whispered against her ear.

"As you wish, sir," said another voice; also male, but higher in register. "As soon as it is in my possession, I shall go immediately and hide it as we agreed."

"It's a nice little hidey-hole that priest hole – good that you remembered its existence! Hadn't thought about it in years! It will serve nicely to explain how it remained lost for so long."

"It will indeed, sir. It was clever of you to think of it."

"Thank you, Pipell! Just as soon as you put me in mind of it, I knew at once what must be done."

The voices were growing louder and as there was no chance of retracing their steps without being seen, Rothworth propelled Aurora into Lord Charles's bedchamber and closed the door.

"We must hide," he said.

"Under the bed?" she suggested, going over to this grand edifice, which stood on its own plinth.

"There's not enough room."

"Behind the curtains? No – you are too large! Oh dear, we seem to be in a little bit of a fix," she said, biting her lip.

Rothworth smiled at such wonderful understatement and rubbed a hand across his face. He was clearly becoming as demented as her, for despite the risks they faced he was enjoying himself immensely.

"Come, we may have better luck in the next room," he said, leading her into the adjoining anti-chamber.

This turned out to be a large dressing room. As with the main room, here too oak panelling covered the walls from floor to ceiling. The space was filled with several wardrobes and chests, two large mirrors that angled towards each other so one could see one's back view, as well as a crimson velvet day bed and a collection of occasional tables, all strewn with various items necessary to a man of fashion.

"Good grief!" she exclaimed, momentarily taken aback by all the opulent extravagance. "This looks more like a lady's boudoir than a dressing room for a gentleman."

"Look there," said Rothworth, pointing. "A door in the wainscoting."

"Perhaps there is a secret passage behind it – how delightfully opportune that would be!"

But when they opened the door, they discovered nothing more interesting than a small closet space, no more than three by five feet, with rows of shelves stacked with neatly folded small-clothes.

Aurora peered inside doubtfully. "I don't wish to be missish, but must we? I have no particular desire to skulk around my uncle's undergarments."

"It will have to do."

Quickly stepping into the confined space, he roughly pulled her up against him, her back colliding with his chest.

She let out an exclamation at the impact.

"Shhh," he blew against her ear.

And, leaning over her, pulled the door closed and plunged them into darkness.

His awareness of the contact of their bodies was instantly heightened, and he could do nothing to stop his muscles clenching with desire.

He swore silently.

His one consolation was that the woman nestled so intimately against him could have no idea of the devastation she was inflicting on his body.

And Aurora was indeed oblivious, but not so much from innocence, rather from being occupied with her own predicament.

She felt positively engulfed.

From shoulders to thighs, she was pressed against a warm, hard male body.

Thrills danced across her skin and played havoc with her senses. Nothing in her limited experience of men had prepared her for this. She had enjoyed a few kisses and embraces over the years, but no man had ever made her feel so *wild*.

"I don't think this is a good idea," she whispered into the darkness.

The hands that were still gripping her arms tightened, as if to stop her fleeing.

"No, it bloody well isn't," Rothworth ground out, shifting his weight as far back against the shelving as he could.

It made little difference. They were pinned together, with no room to move in any direction.

Thankfully – or not (she could not quite decide) – Lord Charles and his companion soon entered the main chamber and diverted her attention.

" . . . with any luck, we won't need to come back to this infernal house again this year," Lord Charles's muffled voice declared. "A colder, more uncomfortable place I'm yet to visit. And no matter what that devilishly unpleasant bailiff says, it would take more than regular maintenance to set it to rights. It would take tens of thousands! The other properties at least make enough to pay for themselves. But this pile of stones is a constant drain, and I'll not waste good money on it!"

"Very wise, sir. It is fortunate that you need only come here for your Siren's Ball."

"Quite right, Pipell, quite right. The one thing the house is good for is privacy! And, I must say, it's damned gratifying to think my little gathering has grown to be such a success. Did I tell you, I had both Espley and Thorrington call on me to convince me to keep to the original date? And a score of others wrote with the same intention. I wished to oblige them, of course, but needs must! There was no time to lose with that damned upstart making a claim on the title."

"Indeed, sir. It was a stroke of brilliance on your part to bring the event forward so that the ring could be found in front of an audience."

"You're the only one who truly appreciates my abilities, Pipell. The moment you mentioned the Abbey, I immediately perceived the way forward! The more witnesses the better, as you said. Couldn't very well say I found the ring when I was alone – Mother's already mighty suspicious! Made me a rather insulting speech, I don't scruple to tell you. All but accused me of stealing my own brother's ring! I'm a reasonable man, Pipell, but I won't have my own mother accusing me of being a thief! Couldn't say that to her, of course – she could make things very difficult for me, blast her – but I *wanted* to say it! I've as much right to that ring as anyone else in the family . . . more, in fact!"

"Indeed, you do, sir. If all was fair in the world the title would belong to you by now."

"It *should* belong to me. My nephew is likely dead. Why else would he stay away? I don't dispute that my brother had a nasty temper – even I often wished I could avoid him – but he's been dead five years. Why wouldn't the boy come back by now if he was still alive? *I'm* certainly no danger to him, no matter what that impudent solicitor implied!"

"Certainly not, sir. No one could doubt that you have only the best of intentions towards the boy. As you know, I have always believed that he must have died, being so sickly and all."

"Yes, yes . . . well, that's what my brother always said. But if you ask me, I think he came to believe his own Banbury story. How could he possibly know? Hadn't seen the boy since he was a babe!"

"The servants, sir, always remember him as being weak and unhealthy. I have heard them say there were fears for his life on several occasions, although it was all hushed up."

"They say that, do they? Didn't realise you knew any of the old servants, Pipell? Thought they'd all left before you became my valet?"

"Regrettably, sir, not all servants are as discreet as I am. Talk in the servants' hall has a way of being passed on."

"I don't doubt it! Well, I suppose if anyone would know it would be the servants . . . and yet, the Scottish woman wrote every year to tell us he was in fine health."

"She must have been disseminating, sir. Only think how many childhood illnesses he would have had to navigate to reach adulthood."

This insinuation against her mother's character so outraged Aurora that she thought longingly of boxing the silly man's ears.

"Far be it for me to speak ill of the dead, sir," the valet continued, "particularly since your brother thought he was doing what was best by inventing that story about his wife and son, but I can't help feel he placed you in a most awkward position. Knowing his son was unlikely to survive, it seems only fair that he should have declared you his heir."

"You're right, Pipell – he should have! If he knew his son was so sickly, then why the devil didn't he?"

"Why, indeed, sir."

"You know, he never liked me. I wouldn't put it past him to have tried to keep me out of the succession."

"Very possibly, sir."

"The damned impudence!"

"If you will indulge me one suggestion, sir?"

"Yes, yes, of course."

"Perhaps, as soon as this latest pretender is sent on his way, it would be wise to apply to the Lord Chancellor to have you declared your brother's heir. After more than twenty years, it is not an unreasonable request."

"We tried, remember? Mother won't hear of it!"

"Indeed, sir. However, perhaps her ladyship will be more amenable to so sensible a path after the shock of this latest assault on the Family?"

"Don't know about that. She was downright unpleasant the last time you told me to bring it up. I'm damn well persecuted by all the women in my life! My wife's barely said a word to me since I told her I was coming here, rather than escorting her to the Wolsey ball. One weekend out of the whole year I can't dance attendance on her, and she gives me the cold-shoulder! Is that fair, I ask you?"

"Indeed not, sir . . . as for your mother, sir, I am certain when your claim to the title is sanctioned – which all your friends in the Lords must think only just and reasonable – she will become accustomed, and will be happier knowing the succession is assured, rather than continuing with this uncertainty."

"There might be something in what you say, Pipell. You're a dashed perceptive fellow, that's certain! Don't know what I'd do without you."

"Thank you, sir. I am honoured you think so." There was a short pause. "Shall I fetch your jewellery case now, sir?"

"Eh? Oh, the ring . . . yes, yes we'd best get on with it."

Aurora felt Rothworth tense as they heard the click of heels enter the anti-chamber, followed by the sound of a draw opening. After a few moments, it closed again and the heels retreated.

"They have the ring," she whispered, turning towards him.

"Be still!" he murmured, his breath fanning across her cheek.

"Pretty thing, isn't it?" Lord Charles's voice filtered through to them. "Been in the family over three centuries. Damned impudent of that Scottish woman to run off with it! I admit, I didn't quite like your plan to retrieve it, but when all's said and done you probably had the right of it. Here, take it . . . you know what to do."

"Most assuredly, sir."

"You have proven yourself indispensable, Pipell – I shan't forget it!"

"Thank you, sir."

"Yes, yes, credit where credit is due. And if I didn't mention it before, I must tell you that your suggestion to book a troupe at the last minute was inspired. That taking little songbird went down a treat, and so did the lady-contortionist – most edifying! But perhaps next year we could dispense with the play. I'm not entirely . . . "

There was a click of a door closing and the voices faded away, leaving silence behind them.

"They're gone," whispered Aurora.

"We'd best remain a while longer to make certain no one returns," said Rothworth.

"But we don't have a moment to lose! They intend on hiding the ring *now*," she said, turning in his arms to face him.

He grunted as if in pain. "Would you be still!"

"Did I hurt you?"

"Just don't move!"

An intensity disturbed the air between them, vibrating with all that was possible.

She found it difficult to draw breath.

His desire to kiss her communicated itself without the need for words or sight, and was matched by her own inclination. Only the knowledge that he would place greater emphasis on the act than she was willing to allow held her back.

Still, she wavered from one moment to the next, motionless in his arms, and the silenced stretched on.

"I don't suppose I can convince you not to follow them?" Rothworth asked at last in a colourless voice.

"No," she laughed lightly, relieved he had broken the tension.

She pushed back against the door and all but fell out of the closet in her hurry to escape his proximity.

"Are you coming?" she asked, blinking to adjust to the light.

"I don't appear to have a choice."

"Of course, you do! I'm perfectly capable of going alone."

"Yes, I thought you were going to say that," he said on a sigh. "Come then. But stay behind me in case they see you. I can talk my way out of discovery, but you are another matter."

"Oh, don't worry about me! I can pretend to be your light-skirt again."

"Never again!" he avowed fiercely. "I meant what I said earlier. If you want to kiss me, you need only ask . . . but be prepared for the consequences."

Walking off, she said: "You have an excessive attachment to rules and restrictions. It can't be at all good for you."

"I have only one excessive attachment," he said under his breath, and followed her.

Twenty-Seven

They saw Lord Charles's valet when they were almost at the head of the staircase. He was disappearing down a corridor in the opposite wing of the house.

Of Lord Charles there was no sight.

"You stay with the valet and find out where he plans to hide the ring," Aurora told Rothworth. "I'll follow my uncle and do what I can to distract him to give us more time."

"You can't mean to do so yourself? He's bound to remember your face the next time you meet."

"I shan't approach him myself. Now, go quickly before you lose your man!"

And without giving him time to object, she ran lightly down the stairs.

Rothworth stared after her for a few moments, then, swearing under his breath, hurried after the valet.

He followed him around the first corner, where his own room was located, and then more cautiously around a second corner, in time to hear a door close at the end of the corridor. Walking over to it, he placed his ear against the wood.

Faint sounds came from within.

After muttering to himself that he hoped Aurora would appreciate his efforts, he ran a hand through his hair to tousle it, skewed the angle of his cravat, and then threw open the door and stumbled into the room in an inebriated fashion.

The valet was in the process of pulling shut a concealed panel in the oak wainscoting, but at this rude interruption, he twirled around and let out a dainty shriek.

"Who the hell are you?" slurred Rothworth. "And what are you doing in my room?"

"Y-your room? But, sir, you are quite mistaken. These are the Family's private quarters. I must insist that you take your leave at once."

"You don't say! Must've taken a wrong turn . . . bad form . . . accept my apologies!" He offered the valet a deep bow that almost toppled him over.

Having accomplished what he had set out to do, he staggered from the room and proceeded down the corridor, singing a song he had picked up in Cribbs Parlour.

He entered his bedchamber soon after and found John waiting for him.

"Nice little ditty, that," said the older man with a chuckle. "Didn't think that be something Your Grace would know."

Sobering, Rothworth threw him an exasperated look. "Both you and your mistress appear to think I'm a strait-laced prude! I'll have you know, I've done my fair share of hellraising. And just because the time came for me to put aside frivolity for more rational concerns, that does not mean I've turned into a bloody prig!"

"No, sir," agreed John, grinning.

"Damn your impudence! Did you learn anything useful from the servants?"

"Nothing that be useful to Miss Aurora tonight. Though I did hear some talk about master Percy. The servants all think he's insane, and that's why he's kept hidden from the world. The marchioness – God bless her soul! – would turn in her grave to hear it. The sooner we put that rumour to rest, the better."

"Good God, yes!" agreed Rothworth grimly. That would be grounds to strip him of the title."

*   *   *

After parting from Rothworth, Aurora had rushed downstairs but had not been in time to catch sight of her uncle. She assumed he had returned to the ballroom, and since she had no intention of distracting him herself, she took the servants' corridor back to the dressing-room.

As the play was still underway only four of the troupe were making use of the room. Mr Lorry, the acrobat, was in deep discussion with the snake man as they sat together drinking from a bottle between them. Mrs Lorry, still in her tight-fitting costume, was lounging on the sofa eating an apple and flicking through a periodical she had found on one of the side tables. And one depressed-looking monkey was sitting on top of a stack of hatboxes and playing disconsolately with a piece of ribbon. Until the moment he saw Aurora, at which point he screeched in delight and bolted over several trunks and pieces of furniture to climb up onto her shoulder.

"Yes, I missed you too," she told him. "But there is not the least need to screech in my ear . . . no, you may not have my spectacles. Please put them back . . . what a good boy! But not another word, if you please. I have important matters to accomplish." Quickly making her way over to Mrs Lorry, she said: "Margery, I need your assistance!"

"'Ow can I 'elp, Lizzie?" replied the contortionist.

"I warn you, it's a strange request and I don't doubt you will have many questions, but I can't answer them at present. I'm in something of a hurry!"

"What's got you stirred up?"

"I need you to distract Lord Charles and keep him from going upstairs."

"Can't see it'll be a problem. The fat fribble's been ogling me 'alf the night."

"I don't expect you to do anything below your dignity, of course! But do you think your husband will approve?"

"Oh, Tom won't mind anything I 'appen to take into me 'ead to do," said Mrs Lorry carelessly. "We only married for convenience, to give us respectability. For 'ow long do you want me to distract this lord?"

"As long as you can! Thank you! Just as soon as I have some matters sorted out, I promise to repay your kindness."

"Oh, Lord bless you, Lizzie, there's no need to repay me for 'elping out a friend." She threw her half-eaten apple onto a table and rose lithely to her feet. "Besides, it's getting downright boring sitting back 'ere with all the fun 'appening out there."

"You're an angel! I can only hope he does nothing to insult you," said Aurora, leading her towards the servants' corridor.

"Never you mind, I know just 'ow to 'andle 'is sort . . . don't go forgetting you've got Mr Key on your shoulder."

"Gracious! I did forget! You, sir, will need to stay here . . . no, don't argue. I promise to let you play with my spectacles when I return."

With a little more persuasive reasoning, much to Mrs Lorry's enjoyment, Aurora at last managed to convince Mr Key to abandon her shoulder and take up the discarded apple she was offering him as inducement.

"So, where's this lord then?" asked Mrs Lorry, when they had entered the servants' corridor.

"I think in the ballroom. He is mustering a group of people to take upstairs to one of the bedchambers."

"Ah . . . 'e's of that persuasion, is 'e?"

Aurora looked at her blankly.

"Oh, no!" she laughed as understanding dawned. "At least, not as far as I am aware. I can't go into his reasons at present, but they are not lewd."

"You're not stealing, are you?" Mrs Lorry asked in a manner that showed it did not matter to her one way or the other.

"No! I can promise you *that*."

They had by this time reached the double doors that led to the ballroom.

"I must return upstairs," said Aurora. "Will you be alright?"

"'Course I will! I can 'andle meself, never you worry. Run along."

With a final thanks, Aurora hurried off.

As she ran up the stairs to the first landing, she saw Rothworth pacing in the corridor, and John leaning against the wall and watching him with engrossed interest.

"I should have known you could not keep away from an adventure!" Aurora greeted John.

He gave her a look of fatherly forbearance and would have replied, but Rothworth beat him to it.

"Finally!" he exclaimed. "I was beginning to think God only knows what had happened to you!"

"What could possibly happen to me in a house full of people?" she asked, vaguely surprised.

"In *this* house, anything!"

"I tried to tell him you'd be along soon enough," put in John, "and none the worse for having gone off alone, but the young fool was set on fretting."

Quite unused to hearing himself described in such prosaic terms, Rothworth cast him an annoyed look.

"I am perfectly unharmed," said Aurora breezily. "But what happened to you, Julian? You look as if you've been pulled through a briar bush backwards."

"I'm in character," he responded gruffly, running his hands through his hair to bring it back into some order. "I had to convince that valet I was in my cups when I burst in on him."

"Oh, how wonderfully inventive of you! I wish I had been there to see it."

"Hardly a difficult task," he muttered, more gratified by this praise than was wise.

"Did you see where he hid the ring?"

"I've a fair notion in which part of the wall to look for the priest hole mechanism, but it may take us some time to find it. Did you manage to delay your uncle?"

"Yes. Only I can't say for how long Mrs Lorry will be able to keep him distracted."

"Then let us go."

Rothworth led them down the corridor to the marquess's rooms and on reaching the closed door put his ear against it. On this occasion no sounds came from within.

After a precautionary knock, he opened the door and found the room to be empty.

"Wait around the corner," he told John, "and if you see anyone coming whistle a tune. I'll leave the door open so we can hear you."

John nodded his agreement and turned to retrace his steps, while Rothworth showed Aurora the wall where he had seen the priest hole.

The wainscoting here was of a similar design to that in Lord Charles's rooms, only it was more intricately carved and provided many opportunities for a door mechanism to be hidden.

After a few minutes of pressing on the carvings, to no avail, Aurora said musingly: "Perhaps the mechanism is not hidden in the wainscoting."

She took a few steps back and considered the wall as a whole.

"Why is that candle in the wall-sconce beside you unlit?" she asked Rothworth. "All the others in the room have been lit."

"You may have a point," he replied.

Inspecting the wall-sconce, he pushed on it in several places, and then tried pulling it; but it did not move.

Joining him, Aurora put her hand on the ornate metal and turned it clockwise. A soft click sounded from within the wall, and the outline of a secret panel was suddenly revealed.

"We did it!" she exclaimed.

" *You* did it," he said, smiling at her delight.

They pushed on the panel and peered inside. There was not enough light to see clearly so Rothworth went to collect a candelabra from a table by the windows.

Returning, he walked into the priest hole and held it aloft.

The space was revealed to be big enough for a bed and a small table, adequate space to house an occupant for a few days. However, what had originally been designed to hide persecuted Catholic clergymen had at some point been converted into a storeroom, stocked full of what looked to be French brandy.

"If I wanted someone to see me find a ring that is meant to be lost," said Aurora, dropping to her knees on the dusty floor, "I would place it under one of these racks . . . but no . . . it appears my uncle had other ideas."

"You forget your uncle is a man of considerable girth," said Rothworth. "He would have an apoplexy if he attempted to crawl on the ground as you are doing."

"I still have not managed to lay eyes on him!" she said, rising to her feet. "Is he really so large?"

"More so than the king."

This unfavourable comparison to George IV made Aurora look incredulous. "Gracious, that large! I suppose one must feel sorry for him."

"By all accounts, he brought it on himself so I wouldn't waste your sympathy on him."

Placing the candelabra on the ground, he began to pull bottle after bottle from the racks and check under each one. Aurora joined him in the task.

After having inspected several rows, Rothworth was in the process of pulling out a bottle when something that had been lodged underneath fell to the ground and rolled to a stop at their feet.

They stared down at a heavy-looking gold ring, with the crest of the Dewbury family emblazoned on its oval face.

Aurora picked it up and put it on her middle finger.

"I *knew* we would find it!" she said exultantly.

Raising her gaze to Rothworth, she threw her arms around his neck and hugged him.

"Oh, I do apologise!" she said, quickly releasing him before he had a chance to return the embrace. "I forgot that you are not fond of shows of affection."

"I have never said anything of the sort," he replied, looking at her a little strangely.

"Have you not? Perhaps it's an impression you convey . . . although, I distinctly remember you once saying you disliked forced intimacy."

"You are mistaken, I am not . . . "

A whistled tune suddenly reached their ears and they looked towards the door.

In a flash, Rothworth picked up the candelabra and propelled Aurora out of the priest hole. While she set about closing the secret panel, he returned the candelabra to its place and went to close the door to the bedchamber.

Coming back to her side, he took hold of her arm and led her over to the windows.

"What are you doing?" she asked. "Shouldn't we hide?"

"I noticed earlier that there's a ledge outside that we can stand on."

"You took the time to plan for that?"

"Considering your propensity for getting yourself into difficult situations, I thought it prudent to know how to exit the room quickly." Opening the casement window, he swung a leg over the sill and stepped through to the other side. "Take my hand."

He seemed determined to help her and so she refrained from telling him that she was perfectly capable of climbing out of a window by herself. Besides, it was rather appealing to be treated with such care and consideration.

The ledge on which they found themselves was deep enough to allow two people to comfortably stand abreast. However, the drop to the ground was another matter. Though no more than fifteen feet, it made Aurora's head swim when she looked down and she had to hastily grab onto Rothworth's arm.

"Perhaps I should have mentioned earlier," she remarked, fixing her eyes on his face, "I am a little terrified of heights."

"Surely not?" he said without thinking.

"I'm sorry to disappoint you, but it's quite true!"

He smiled at her disgruntled expression and, tugging her gently towards him, manoeuvred them out of view of the window. When his back was up against the wall of the abbey, he tucked her head under his chin, so she could not see the drop, and put his arms around her.

"I've got you," he said into her wig (wishing it was her own hair) and was rewarded by feeling her relax against him.

Aurora found there was something infinitely safe about being held by him in such a fashion. She could have quite happily remained in his arms indefinitely and left the world to sort out its problems without her.

"Thank you, I'm much obliged to you," she mumbled against his coat. "Although I don't want to make you uncomfortable. If you would rather not hold me . . . "

"I beg you rid yourself of this infernal notion that I am somehow against intimacy."

In her case, quite the opposite happened to be true. Never before had he spent so much time thinking about how to orchestrate contact with another person; an accidental touch, a held hand, a stolen caress. All small moments in time that somehow held greater meaning for him than all the years of his life put together.

"I'm sorry if I mistook the matter," she said. "I didn't mean to offend you."

"Quiet now," he warned softly. "I can hear them."

They fell silent, listening to the rumble of voices from within; too distorted to be understood but conveying the impression that a large group had entered the bedchamber.

"We can't remain here," he murmured against her temple after some minutes. "We can be seen from the drive."

Not having paid much attention to her surroundings, Aurora lifted her head from its comfortable position against him and looked about.

The marquess's rooms were at the end of the wing, the ledge finishing a few feet to the left of them, where it tied into the façade. To their right, it continued on, passing the bedrooms in this part of the house and coming to an end at the central block of the Abbey.

"Had I been thinking more clearly," he continued, "I should have positioned us on the other side of the window. This ledge appears to continue all the way to my room."

"I expect it was my fault for distracting you with my odious fears," she whispered back. "But we need only crawl past the window."

"Can you manage it?"

"Of course. We have no other choice."

While she spoke, she turned her head so that her lips were close to his ear; and her cheek ended up resting against his jaw.

He stilled at the contact.

When he showed no inclination to move, she asked: "Shall we start out now?"

"It would be wise."

They carefully lowered themselves onto all fours, then Rothworth indicated for Aurora to go first, and she started to crawl, keeping her gaze on the wall beside her.

It was no easy task, however. She was wearing long drapes of flimsy muslin that tended to catch under her knees and impede her progress; and on one occasion she heard an ominously loud tearing noise.

It was hardly an opportune moment to inspect the damage, so she kept crawling; until Rothworth said that they had gone far enough and helped her to rise, positioning himself between her and the edge.

As she was re-adjusting her costume, she discovered a large split in the material. A side seam, almost from thigh to hem, had come apart and revealed the length of one shapely leg.

"Oh, dash it! I ripped my costume," she sighed.

"Yes," agreed Rothworth in a strained voice.

Having been privy for the last few minutes to a sight he had no right to behold, he had himself tightly leashed and the effort was causing him considerable discomfort.

Aurora gathered the two separated sides of material into her fist, and they continued on for a few more yards, until they reached the window to Rothworth's room.

It was unfortunately closed, and seeing no other alternative, Rothworth began to undo his cravat.

Aurora watched with fascination as the tanned skin at the base of his throat was revealed, and for several moments did not even think to ask what he was doing.

This soon became evident, in any case.

He quickly wound the cravat around his right hand and with a jabbing punch shattered one of the mullioned window panels. Then, carefully reaching through the hole he had created, he opened the casement window from within.

Turning to Aurora, he swept her up into his arms before she could protest.

"What are you doing?" she asked, startled.

"For the sake of your modesty – and my sanity! – I think it best if you don't attempt to climb through any more windows."

"Thank you, Julian," she said demurely, enjoying his discomfort more than was seemly.

Had he not already been uncomfortably aware of the fact that she was not wearing any draws, he would have discovered it at this point.

He muttered something under his breath, of which she only heard the word *purgatory*, and after readjusting her in his arms, threw a leg over the sill and stepped into the room.

Thinking he had endured more than any man could possibly be expected to, he all but dropped her onto her feet and took several decisive steps away from her.

"I hope, after all that, you managed to hold onto the ring?" he asked with more severity than the topic warranted.

She raised the hand that had been clutching the fabric of her costume together and showed him the ring, still safely on her finger.

188

"I can't thank you enough for helping me to retrieve it," she said. "It was a wonderful adventure, wasn't it?"

"One I'm glad is over! Now I can get you out of this curst place. Here . . . take my great-coat."

He strode over to where he had thrown this garment upon the bed and, bringing it over to her, helped her to put it on, and then buttoned it all the way up to the neck.

The door opened abruptly just as he was finishing the top button and John walked in.

"Have you never heard of knocking?" asked Rothworth, pardonably annoyed.

"Well, sir, seeing as I thought you were elsewhere, I didn't see the need," John replied with unruffled composure. "How did you manage to slip away?"

"Out the window, in the most dashing style imaginable!" Aurora replied. "And look, John . . . we found the ring!"

"Well, well! I'm mighty glad, Miss Aurora."

"And now she must leave," said Rothworth. "Have my carriage brought round and take her back to the inn. You may tell my coachman to return here afterwards. I must remain until the morning so as not to raise suspicions, but I expect to leave here no later than eight o'clock and shall come pick you up."

"I'm happy to fall in with your plans," said Aurora, "but first I must thank Margery and say my goodbyes."

Rothworth did his best to convince her to leave immediately, however, she could not be budged from her determination to take her leave of her new friends.

Realising further discussion was pointless, he gave in. And, while John went off to the stables, he escorted her downstairs. They encountered a few surprised looks in the servants' corridor, which they ignored, and were soon entering the changing-room.

As the play had finished, the whole troupe was crowded into the space.

Aurora spotted Mrs Lorry and, walking over to her, said gaily: "Margery, you did a marvellous job! How did you manage to distract Lord Charles?"

"Aw, it was nothing!" replied Mrs Lorry. "I just did a few of me stretches and positions for the guv'nor and his friends. Told 'em it was part of me act to go into the crowd. He was proper appreciative too! I'd 'ave 'eld onto him for longer if a little, toadying man in yellow breeches 'adn't come over to whisper in his ear and take him away."

"His valet," said Aurora grimacing with disgust. "Horrid man! He appears to have a talent for persuading his master to follow his lead."

"Did you find what you were looking for, Lizzie?"

"I did, and I shall be eternally grateful to you for your part in it! But now – sadly! – I must be off. Julian," she glanced at Rothworth beside her, "wishes to take me home."

"I'm sure 'e does," said Mrs Lorry saucily, earning for herself one of the duke's cooler looks.

Aurora embraced her warmly. Then, after retrieving her overnight bag and saying a general goodbye to the troupe and accepting their good wishes, she allowed Rothworth to escort her to the door. But before they reached it, a piercing shriek came from across the room and a ball of fur hurled itself towards her.

Rothworth thrust her behind him and caught the creature mid-flight.

"Oh, do be gentle with him!" cried Aurora, grabbing hold of his arm. "He will not hurt me."

Rothworth looked dubious, but allowed her to free the monkey from his grip.

To show his appreciation, Mr Key wrapped his arms around her neck and clung to her.

"I am much obliged to you," she told him, "but you need not strangle me, you know . . . there, that is much better."

"I see you have another admirer," observed Rothworth.

"He has become rather attached to me for some reason," she replied with a laugh, stroking the monkey under his chin.

Her words were discovered to be only too true when she attempted to hand him back to his master. Mr Key categorically refused to let her go and even Mr Wiley could not convince him to release her.

At last, and rather desperately, for the creature was becoming more and more agitated, Aurora exclaimed: "Please don't pull him, Mr Wiley! You will hurt him . . . perhaps you would consider allowing him to come with me? I would be willing to compensate you for your trouble."

Mr Wiley gave her a crafty look. In his own way, he had become fond of her and would have been happy to oblige her in any request, as long as it caused him no trouble of any kind.

"I might be convinced . . . fer the right amount," he said significantly.

"What if I was to offer you another pound?"

"Don't rightly know, Lizzie. Got a lot to consider, yer see," he replied, brows drawn together thoughtfully. "Me act don't work without Mr Key. Can a pound compensate me fer that? Can't say it does. Not even close."

Aurora was aware of how much – or rather, how little – she had remaining in her purse and, knowing she could not offer him anymore, was gravely disappointed.

One glance at her was all it took for Rothworth to decipher her emotions.

"What do you want for the monkey?" he asked the troupe leader brusquely.

Mr Wiley considered his question deeply.

Finally, in accents that showed he thought he was being magnanimous, he replied: "I've a soft-spot fer our Lizzie . . . I'll take five pounds."

The collective intake of breath of those gathered around them was cue enough as to how outrageous a sum this was.

"I'm sure you would," drawled Rothworth. "I'll give you two."

"Four. Yer wouldn't want to leave without yer woman's pet, now would yer?"

Rothworth forbore to correct his misunderstanding. "I shall give you three and not a penny more, you conscienceless scoundrel."

Mr Wiley, rather pleased by this form of address, and even more so with the riches offered to him, put out his hand to seal the bargain. Rothworth made no attempt to hide his sardonic smile as he shook hands with him.

Withdrawing his purse from the inside pocket of his coat, he paid the man his bounty, and hoped no one would ever get to hear that he had been so idiotic as to pay three pounds for a damned monkey. They would undoubtedly laugh themselves rigid.

Without another word, he led Aurora out of the room.

"I don't know how to thank you," she said simply, when they were in the servants' corridor again.

Temporarily relieved of her spectacles by Mr Key, the full force of her expressive eyes brought him to a standstill.

"You have nothing to thank me for," he replied curtly. "It was the most expedient way to get you out of the room."

"That is certainly a valid reason. And yet I don't believe it was *your* reason."

"You must allow me to be the judge."

"I am too much indebted to you to do otherwise! And I will not even chastise you for being untruthful . . . or accuse you of kindness."

"We must keep moving," he said, turning away from the challenge in her eyes. "The carriage will be out front by now."

"Oh, I forgot to return the costume!"

"Keep it. I paid enough for the monkey to cover the cost of a hundred costumes!"

He then took her arm again and hurried her down the corridor.

They exited the house through a side entrance and saw the carriage coming up from the stables, with John seated beside the driver. As soon as it had drawn up beside them, Rothworth opened the door and handed Aurora in.

But before he could shut the door and send her on her way, she surprised him by leaning over and giving him a quick peck on the cheek.

Sitting back against the plush, pale blue upholstery, she said primly: "That was not a kiss; simply a gesture of gratitude. It does not count!"

Twenty-Eight

The Duke of Rothworth arrived at the inn shortly after breakfast the following day. He found Aurora and John enjoying the sunshine on a bench in the small garden at the front of the building, amongst several rambling rosebushes.

It was a picturesque scene, had he been inclined to admire it, however, his attention was on the lady sitting amongst all this rustic charm, who greeted him with a smile that could brighten the most overcast of days.

The spectacles and wig were gone, her auburn hair was pinned up in a simple style, and her primrose cambric day-dress, with its short sleeves and high neckline, revealed only a modest quantity of flesh. All in all, apart from one small monkey, who sat like an adornment on her shoulder and observed the world with superior self-assurance, she gave all the appearance of a respectable young lady.

No one would have guessed, Rothworth reflected cynically, that underneath her veneer of propriety lurked an audacious spirit capable of turning a man's life upside down.

"Better!" he declared, walking up to her.

"I take it you didn't approve of my spectacles and wig?" she said with a laugh. "Was I such a fright with them on?"

"You must know that most would find you attractive whatever you decided to wear."

She was about to ask him if he agreed with the majority, but caught herself in time. It was best not to broach a subject that might lead them down a path she was not ready to navigate.

She lightly thanked him for the compliment and, after picking up the bonnet on the bench beside her, placed a gloved hand into the one he held out to her and allowed him to assist her to her feet.

John observed this interchange with a sapient eye and left them to their own devices, declaring he needed to see to the strapping of the luggage onto the back of the carriage.

He completed this task in a mechanical way, and then climbed up to sit beside the driver and set out to extract from this unsuspecting individual as much information on his employer as John considered pertinent to the future happiness of his mistress.

Meanwhile, unsuspecting of John's well-meaning exertions on her behalf, Aurora had taken a seat inside the carriage and was settling the monkey beside her on a nest she made out of the carriage blanket.

Once this was accomplished, she returned her attention to Rothworth and asked him how Lord Charles had reacted to the disappearance of the ring.

"I didn't see him again," he replied, taking the backward-facing position, opposite her.

"Did you not return to the ballroom after you saw me off?"

"I had no desire to! I went in search of food and drink at one point, since no one answered when I tugged on the bell-pull, but that's all."

He did not think it necessary to share with her that he had been accosted twice on this errand. Once on his way to the kitchens by an inebriated beauty with wandering hands, who had lost her way to the ladies retiring room (or so she said) and had insisted on his escort. And a second time, on his return, when a group of damsels, led by the same beauty, had overtaken him in the corridor and insisted on joining him in his bedchamber.

He had had to overcome years of breeding and resort to incivility to extract himself from their tender attentions; by which time a fair portion of the food on the tray he carried had ended up on his person and left him in no pleasant mood.

"What a tame evening it must have been! I am inclined to feel sorry for you," she said teasingly. "I had such visions of you joining in the revelries."

There was a pause.

"And did these visions afford you pleasure?" he asked.

His tone, more than his words, alerted to her to his meaning and she was shocked into a nervous laugh.

She looked so adorably uncertain how to respond that he could not regret the devil that had prompted his words.

"I never thought I'd see the day you would be rendered speechless," he said, regarding her knowingly through hooded eyes.

"I was not expecting you to say such a thing to me!" she said accusingly, then quickly changed the subject.

She rambled on for some minutes on a variety of topics: the charming scenery; the comfort of the carriage; the odd little man manning the first tollgate; and even the remarkable shine of the duke's top-boots (was it due to blacking made with champagne? she enquired); until, at last, she ran out of inconsequential chatter and fell silent.

"For goodness sake, why did you let me prattle on in that inane fashion?" she asked all of a sudden.

"It was not my place to stop you when you seemed inclined to it."

"It was beastly of you! I now feel like a veritable fool."

Rothworth suddenly left his seat and came to sit beside her.

"Do be careful! You almost sat on Mr Key," she chided gently as she picked up the monkey and placed him on her lap.

Rothworth impatiently moved the carriage blanket to the seat opposite, and then plucked the monkey out of her hands and deposited him on it.

Mr Key regarded him with patent disapproval. But before he could do more than squeak his displeasure at his rival, Aurora quickly gave him a piece of the bread roll she had had the foresight to salvage from breakfast.

"You have a particularly intent look about you," she remarked, turning back to Rothworth. "Should I be concerned?"

"That's for you to decide," he said, and took hold of her hand.

Her eyes widened with surprise.

"Julian, surely you are not so provoking as to . . . you can't possibly be about to do what I think you are?"

"Aurora, listen to me . . . "

"Oh, that is most unfair! You choose *this* moment to call me Aurora for the first time? And in such a charming way that it quite makes me lose my wits! I beg you say no more!"

"Will you not even hear me out?" he asked with such feeling that she returned his grip convulsively.

"Of course, I will," she said earnestly. "I will listen to anything you have to say to me. Only, I'm afraid you expect a response that I may not be able to give you – and then where will we be? If you find yourself unable to forgive me, will we become polite strangers who nod to each other at parties, but who otherwise refuse to have anything to do with one another? Quite frankly, I'm not sure I could bear it!"

"Upon my honour, no matter what you choose to say to me, I'll not turn my back on our friendship."

"Oh, Julian . . . must you be so wonderful?" Tears suddenly welled up in her eyes, and she had to wrench her hand out of his and search around in her reticule for a handkerchief. "Now look what you've done – I dislike crying excessively!"

She dried her eyes, took a few fortifying breaths and then offered him a determined smile.

"What would you like to say to me?" she asked.

Not even the most optimistic of suitors would have thought this an auspicious occasion in which to declare himself; and though for a moment the seasoned politician had been supplanted by a man deeply in love and no longer able to hide it, Aurora's obvious distress had dampened all ardour.

Rothworth berated himself for his precipitateness. His aunt might lecture him on the need for spontaneity when wooing a woman, but Aurora was no ordinary woman. If he allowed his analytical mind to consider the problem, it became obvious that what was needed was a concerted campaign based on subtlety and patience, and one that addressed the cause of Aurora's prejudices against marriage.

Had he not been convinced that she was not indifferent to him, the task ahead would have seemed daunting to say the least.

Changing tack, he leaned back into the corner so as not to crowd her.

"I hope you'll not mind if I remain beside you? I get ill facing backwards," he lied.

"I don't mind in the least," she replied, though she would have preferred him to move; his proximity was playing havoc with her senses.

"How many marriage proposals have you turned down over the years?" he asked in an amused voice.

"Gracious, I was not expecting *that* question. It would be very ill-bred of me to divulge the number."

"Shall I guess? Five? Twenty?"

"Twenty? I should hope not!" she laughed shakily. "The number is closer to your first guess. I have a knack for adapting myself to my company, and that leads some men to create a false image in their minds of who they believe me to be . . . and sometimes they even imagine themselves in love with me. But it's not love at all, merely a passing infatuation."

"And you think I have made the same mistake?"

"I did not say that," she replied, becoming a little flustered. "For one, you have never told me that you . . . that you hold me in that sort of regard."

"You appear to not want any such declarations," he pointed out with a sangfroid she found irritating.

"That is a mighty cool way of letting me know your sentiments!"

"Is it? Would you prefer a man to embarrass you with exuberant speeches of undying love?"

It was disconcerting to discover that she was not averse to such speeches, if they came from him.

"No, of course not," she replied.

"Then it's fortunate I have no intention of being so *de trop*," he said equably. "Nor need you fear that I will force a marriage proposal on you. I believe I know your sentiments on that subject only too well."

Since she herself no longer knew her own sentiments, she was uncertain how to respond to such ready acceptance.

She would in all likelihood have to refuse him if he asked her to marry him, for her long held views were not so easily put aside, however, she discovered herself to be so contrary as to wish he had made more of a push to overcome her scruples.

For the remainder of their journey she managed to respond cheerfully to every unexceptional topic he introduced; and though she never initiated one herself, and tended to sink into thoughtful silences when he was not addressing her, overall she thought she acquitted herself well.

She could now look forward to their ongoing friendship without the need to be concerned about further uncomfortable confrontations.

It was what she wanted after all.

And as for the uncommon feeling of dissatisfaction that had come over her, well, that must surely be due to the fact that she had stayed awake most of the night, replaying in her mind their adventures . . . and their embraces.

Twenty-Nine

They arrived at Hanover Square at around two in the afternoon. Rothworth escorted Aurora into the house and stayed only to pay his respects to his aunts and uncle, and accept an invitation to dine there that evening. He then headed back to his own residence to take care of certain matters that had occupied his thoughts for the last few hours.

As soon as he walked through his front door, he instructed a footman to track down his solicitor and tell him that his attendance was required as a matter of urgency. And while he waited for this trusted retainer to arrive, he went in search of his sister.

He found her in the music room, practicing on the pianoforte; a surprising circumstance, for her governess was nowhere to be seen so it appeared to be of her own volition.

"Good God, I can't believe my eyes," he said, smiling. "What sort of virtuous quirk has come over you, Charlotte? I thought you disliked applying yourself to your music?"

"Julian!" she cried and rushed over to embrace him. "Did you hear me play? I'm attempting to instil my performance with the same *feeling* as Miss Wesley's."

"It was very well done."

"Why, thank you, kind sir! But what are you doing home? Did you manage to sort out your affairs so quickly?"

"To some extent."

"You never did explain what took you out of London?"

"A private matter, as I believe I mentioned at the time," he said with a pointed smile.

"Oh, I don't mean to meddle! I'm only asking because, according to Phoebe, Miss Wesley was also out of town at the same time . . . perhaps you chanced to see her on the road?" she asked, giving him a saucy look.

"You are being pert," he said without heat. "Why would you think I would meet up with her?"

"Oh, no reason! Although it did occur to me that you might *want* to."

He turned her around and propelled her back to the pianoforte. "Your practice is a more important subject on which to concentrate your attention."

"I wish you would stop treating me like a child," she objected, sitting down on the stool with something of a flounce. "Surely it is *most* important for me to know who you will choose to be my sister-in-law?"

"That is plain speaking!"

"Am I wrong?" she asked, facing him.

A smile entered his eyes. "*Precipitate* is the word I'd use."

"Oh, as to that, I'm sure you need not fear that Miss Wesley will refuse you."

"Why would you say that?" he asked, regarding her in a fixed way.

"Because, dear brother, I'm not a ninnyhammer! It has been quite obvious for days that you are both madly in love."

His brow creased at this brash declaration. "You will someday learn, Charlotte, that love is not always enough. Any number of circumstances may make it impossible to hope for a happy conclusion."

"But it must surely be the most important ingredient? Every obstacle can be overcome if love is present," she insisted, the naivety of youth prejudicing her judgement to think only in absolutes.

"I shall certainly do all I can to make it so!" He lowered his gaze to hide the stab of emotion that had come over him, and only when he had mastered himself did he look back up. "Don't allow me to disturb you further – continue with you practice. I have some business this afternoon that needs my attention, however, we are dining across the square tonight so be ready to leave by quarter past six."

With a smile, he quit the room; leaving his sister to wonder what could possibly have occurred between him and Miss Wesley to have put such a fierce look in his eyes.

*   *   *

Earlier, at the Brinkley residence, John had taken Mr Key with him to the stables, so the household could be prepared for his appearance, while Rothworth had escorted Aurora into the house. Here they had found Miss Brinkley and Phoebe on the staircase, making their way up after having seen Dr Moore to the door just minutes before.

The new arrivals had been greeted with pleasure and a volley of questions, and, upon the duke's departure soon after, Aurora had been swept upstairs so that her companions could continue quizzing her; while

Mr Brinkley, who had heard the commotion through his library door and come out to join them in the vestibule, book in hand, had in his unobtrusive way been just as eager for her time and had followed them to the drawing room.

Miss Brinkley was keen to learn what business had kept Aurora busy the last three days and, after calling for tea, sat down on the settee and beckoned her to sit beside her.

"Was your trip successful?" she asked without preamble.

"Most successful," Aurora replied happily.

"Oh, thank goodness!" exclaimed Phoebe, clapping her hands together. "Now Percy can be comfortable."

"I understand you visited Sutton Green," said Miss Brinkley.

Aurora was faintly surprised that her destination was known, then realised the coachman must have reported back.

"Why, yes, ma'am, I did. I have family in the area."

Miss Brinkley waited expectantly for further information.

"Forgive me," Aurora responded with an apologetic look. "I know it's an imposition, my being so secretive and all, but I must beg your indulgence a little longer. I'm hopeful all will be resolved soon and then I will be at liberty to share the details with you."

"It has to do with your brother's inheritance?"

"Yes, ma'am – which is why I must be cautious."

"If you feel you must keep the details to yourself, I for one will not make a push to discover them – I dislike meddlers!"

"Thank you," said Aurora, smiling inwardly.

"When Rothworth informed his uncle that there was no need to send the coach back for you, since he had some business in the area and could convey you back to London himself, it occurred to us that he might in some way be involved in your affairs?"

"Well, I certainly had no intention for him to be!" returned Aurora. "He was determined to be useful, however. And I must admit, though at first I did not at all appreciate his meddling, by the end I was exceedingly grateful for it."

"Rothworth imposed himself on you?" Miss Brinkley asked with great surprise. "Without invitation?"

"Yes! Shocking, isn't it?" Aurora laughed. "I suppose his autocratic disposition – I hope you won't mind my making mention of it? – leads him to think he can insert himself into the affairs of others, with or without their permission."

"I see," was all Miss Brinkley could reply to this.

She was not in the habit of thinking of her nephew as someone who acted in such a way; not only did he generally hold the world at a distance, but he was also known to be punctilious in all matters of etiquette.

While Miss Brinkley was distracted by her thoughts, Aurora asked Phoebe: "Have you had any news from your uncle, dear?"

"Not as yet, Cousin Aurora. But Mr Brinkley was kind enough to explain to me – using the wonderful globe in his library! – that it takes up to thirty days to travel from New York to London, so we shouldn't expect him for another few days yet. Isn't that right, sir?"

"Indeed, my dear," replied Mr Brinkley, smiling at her indulgently.

"I must thank you both for looking after Phoebe in my absence," Aurora said gratefully. "And I hope Percy stayed home and made himself useful? He promised me he would!"

Percy was a firm favourite with all three of her companions and they were quick to jump to his defence, making Aurora laugh.

"I had no idea he had become such a paragon in a few short days!" she said. "I take it he's not home at present?"

"I persuaded him to meet his friends for a few hours," replied Miss Brinkley. "I do not hold with young men kicking their heels at home. Besides, Phoebe and I were occupied with callers . . . ah, before I forget! Aurora, this arrived for you just after you left town."

Reaching over to the rosewood table at the back of the settee, she picked up a sealed note and handed it to her.

Aurora did not recognise the seal on the wax. Opening it, she quickly scanned the contents.

An eyebrow rose in surprise.

"Good news I hope?" asked Mr Brinkley.

"Yes . . . an olive branch, if I'm not mistaken," she replied distractedly, and re-read the note.

Miss Brinkley leaned closer to Aurora to see if she could read the signature. This, however, proved impossible without her spectacles.

"And do you welcome this olive branch?" she asked, righting herself.

"Oh, yes!" replied Aurora, looking up with a smile. "My grandmother requests that I visit her."

"I didn't realise you had family in London, Aurora dear?" said Miss Coral as she walked into the room, leaning on her maid's arm.

Her plump figure had grown a little thinner over the last few days and she was still weak, but having heard through the efficient channels of communication that exist in all great houses that Aurora had returned, she had insisted that Miss Lington dress her with all due haste and escort her downstairs.

Aurora rose, thinking to take Miss Lington's place, for the lady's maid was herself looking unsteady on her feet after her own bout of the influenza. However, the possessive glint in her eyes made it clear that any assistance would not be appreciated, and so Aurora restricted herself to asking how Miss Coral was feeling, and if she had been taking her medicine.

"It's good to see you, Aurora dear, but if you insist on treating me like your patient, I'll be wishing you to Jericho! And no, I didn't take that poisonous smelling concoction you left for me. My brother insists that Dr Moore continue to visit me daily, so I have all the quacking I can bear! You will be doing me a great service if you never refer to my dratted illness again – I am heartily bored of it!"

"Still crotchety, I see," remarked her sister, shaking her head.

"Coral, you must know," Mr Brinkley said gently, "that Aurora has only your best interests at heart?"

"That I know only too well!" replied Miss Coral, unmoved. "And though I'm sure I'm much obliged to her, she must focus her well-meaning efforts on another unsuspecting victim."

Aurora laughed, accepting these strictures meekly, and promised to abide by her wishes.

"Good!" declared Miss Coral and, sitting down in a comfortable winged chair, waved her maid away when she attempted to fuss over her. "Phoebe dear, if you could pass me the blanket over there . . . thank you! Now, tell me," she said, looking back at Aurora, "*do* you have family in London? I thought they were all in Scotland?"

"Actually, ma'am, my father's family is in London. But . . . well, the truth of the matter is, they have not wanted to recognise us, and I didn't feel it would be appropriate to claim kinship in light of that."

"Are they a ramshackled lot?" asked Miss Coral, bristling at the thought that anyone might find Percy and Aurora anything less than delightful. "Perhaps it is *you* who shouldn't recognise *them*."

"I'm afraid they are utterly respectable," replied Aurora, smiling.

"Then what possible reason can they have to not recognise you?"

"It has been many years since they last saw us," replied Aurora carefully, "and – perhaps understandably – they are concerned we are not who we say we are. Fortunately, my business over the last few days went so well that I now believe I can put those concerns to rest."

"What will you do if they still refuse to recognise you?" asked Miss Brinkley.

"Then we must let the courts decide. Although that is the longer path and I had hoped to avoid it."

"You will always have a home with us," said Mr Brinkley, surprising both Aurora and his sisters. "If you should want to continue to live here," he added diffidently.

"Thank you, sir! But we can't continue to impose on you," replied Aurora, touched by his generosity.

"It would be a pleasure! We have more than enough room here – don't we, Pearl?"

"Indeed," said Miss Brinkley. "I'm certain we would be pleased to have them live with us, but whether or not that would be best for them is another matter." Seeing the butler enter the room just then, with the look of one who had something to impart, she asked: "What is it, Levington?"

"There is a female caller downstairs, ma'am, enquiring if Miss Wesley is home to visitors."

"Did she not give you her card?" asked Mr Brinkley, surprised that his normally exacting retainer had come up without this information.

"No, sir," replied the butler. "I did explain that I am not in the habit of conveying messages for individuals who do not provide their names, however, the lady was adamant."

"*Is* she a lady?" asked Miss Brinkley.

"Most assuredly, ma'am. A lady of the first consequence, if you will allow me to conjecture. And one who does not appear to be in the habit of having her wishes contradicted. Rather than continue to exchange words with her on the front steps, I asked her to step into the downstairs parlour while I came to apprise you of the situation."

"How odd!" said Miss Coral. "At the very least we should let her come up so we can assuage our curiosity. Unless you have an objection, Aurora dear?"

"None! Though for the life of me I can't think who she might be. I'm not known in London."

"You may show her in, Levington," said Miss Brinkley. "But I intend on giving her a piece of my mind at such ill-mannered conduct."

When the time came, however, this rebuke proved impossible to administer. The butler returned and stunned them all by announcing the Dowager Marchioness of Dewbury.

Aurora rose at once and walked over to the slight figure, clad in black, that stood on the threshold.

"Your ladyship," she said, dropping into a deep curtsey. "How did you find me?"

"I have my ways," Lady Dewbury replied with reserve; and then looked past her to the other occupants of the room.

"Allow me to introduce you to my hosts," said Aurora quickly. "Mr Brinkley and his sisters, Miss Brinkley and Miss Coral. And my cousin, Miss Phoebe Lennox."

The dowager nodded at each in acknowledgement.

"I am not aware of any branch of your mother's family with the name Lennox," she remarked, her penetrating gaze returning to Aurora.

"Quite a distant relation," replied Aurora.

A moment later, her eyes widened as she was struck by the implication of the dowager's comment.

"Won't you come in, Lady Dewbury?" said Miss Brinkley, recovering from her astonishment. The dowager marchioness was unknown to her, but everyone had heard of the wealthy Dewbury family. "Tea will be served any moment and we would be delighted if you would care to join us."

With a look, she sent Levington out of the room to hurry along the tea preparations, and to add to the order whatever delicacies could be found to impress their exulted company.

Aurora accompanied Lady Dewbury to the settee and placed her beside Miss Brinkley, while she took the chair opposite.

Mr Brinkley, who had risen at the dowager's entrance, also retook his seat, saying pleasantly: "You may not know this, your ladyship, but I had the privilege to be acquainted with your husband."

"Were you, sir?" said Aurora, regarding him with surprise.

"Oh yes, my dear. He was a most interesting man – you would have liked him. We were members of the Roxburghe Club."

"My husband was a great lover of books," acknowledged Lady Dewbury, her eyes softening. In the next instant, she retreated from her reminiscences and continued in a cool voice: "I trust you will forgive me for my unorthodox visit. It occurred to me that if I gave my name I risked being turned away." Her gaze drifted to Aurora.

"I would never refuse to see you, your ladyship," Aurora said hastily. "I hope my own conduct did not give rise to such an impression?"

"When you did not respond to my note, I assumed the worst," replied Lady Dewbury.

"I am very sorry indeed! But, you see, I only just received it! I was out of town until this afternoon."

It appeared as if a great weight lifted from the old woman at these words.

"I admit . . . that pleases me to know," she said in an unsteady voice. "I assumed I had succeeded in pushing you away . . . as I once did your mother . . . I had no reason to hope that . . . that . . . "

To everyone's horror, the dowager marchioness's remote façade crumbled before their eyes and tears began to roll down her lined cheeks.

Aurora instantly dropped to her knees in front of her grandmother and took hold of her hands.

"Oh, I did not take it to heart in the least!" she assured her. "I quite understand how horrid it must have been for you to have charlatans imposing on you all those years. I promise you, I don't blame you for being suspicious of me. I would certainly have been the same if I were in your shoes!"

Mr Brinkley averted his eyes to give them privacy, and, standing, caught his sisters' and Phoebe's attention and indicated that they should leave the room.

Phoebe dutifully rose.

But Miss Brinkley frowned and shook her head; while Miss Coral simply turned back to the interesting goings-on.

Caught in the awkward position of not knowing whether to leave or sit back down, Mr Brinkley and Phoebe were saved by the arrival of the tea tray. Phoebe then said that she would pour, and Mr Brinkley designated himself to carry the cups for her.

After some minutes of concerted effort on the part of everyone to put the dowager at ease with tea and small talk, their efforts suffered a setback when the door to the drawing room burst open and Percy rushed in.

"Rory, you Trojan! John just told me you retrieved the signet ring!"

Six pairs of eyes turned on him.

He suddenly became aware that there was a stranger in their midst. "Oh, I beg pardon! I-I'm very sorry . . . I didn't realise you were entertaining. I shall leave at once."

"No, Percy, don't go!" said Aurora, standing. "I would like to introduce you to Lady Dewbury."

Percy's expression stiffened perceptibly and the smile died from his eyes. The memory of the way his sister had been treated by her ladyship was still fresh in his mind.

"Of course," he said politely and, coming over, offered Lady Dewbury a bow. "How do you do?"

Having slowly risen to her feet, the dowager was staring at him with a fixed expression and appeared not to have heard his civil greeting.

The teacup and saucer in her hand began to rattle, and Aurora quickly took possession of it before it could spill.

"Are you, alright, ma'am?" she asked anxiously, for what little colour had been in the old woman's face had vanished. "Perhaps it would be best if you sat down?"

"Thank you," Lady Dewbury replied in a trembling voice as she allowed Aurora to guide her onto the settee, her eyes never leaving Percy's face. "I . . . I never expected the likeness to be so very great."

"Do I resemble my father?" asked Percy, taking a seat beside Phoebe.

"A little. But I am speaking of my husband . . . your grandfather."

"Well, well," muttered Miss Coral, greatly enjoying herself. "It's a good thing I insisted on coming down!"

Her sister, who had barely managed to contain her curiosity up to this point, now exclaimed: "Good Lord! Do you mean to say, your ladyship, that Aurora and Percy are your *grandchildren*?"

Lady Dewbury offered her a distracted look. "Yes, of course."

That simple admission was enough to ease the worries that had occupied Aurora's mind for years.

Yet it had an entirely different effect on Miss Brinkley. Unimpressed by the cavalier delivery of such a momentous revelation – and all that it implied – her large bosom heaved with displeasure.

Her brother, observing the signs with trepidation, rushed to say: "How unexpected . . . and delightful! You ladyship, you will no doubt wish to be alone with your grandchildren and so we will leave you for a few minutes."

He gave his sisters as commanding a look as he could manage and once again rose to his feet.

They ignored him.

"Do you mean to imply that Percy and Aurora are your *natural* grandchildren?" Miss Brinkley asked bluntly.

A haughty look transformed the dowager's countenance. "Their birth is perfectly legitimate, I assure you."

"But if they were not born on the wrong side of the blanket," said Miss Brinkley, "why did you not recognise them until now?"

"Really, Pearl," her brother protested weakly, sitting back down, "that is none of our business."

"It *is* our business! We have all grown attached to Percy and Aurora, and it is useless to deny that they have had an uncomfortable time of it since coming to London. I, for one, would like to know why they were not welcomed into their own family, but had to rely on the kindness of strangers?"

Aurora was touched by this unexpected championing, but felt driven to say: "I'm afraid, ma'am, the matter is rather complicated. My grandmother is not to blame for the situation we found ourselves in."

"Thank you, child," said Lady Dewbury, "but it is quite impossible to defend the indefensible. Rather than assume the worst, I should have made an effort to look into the veracity of your claim when I first became aware of your existence. Allow me to say," she continued, looking at the siblings in turn, "that I am deeply grateful my grandchildren have had you to look out for them."

The words were spoken stiffly, as if she was not in the habit of apologising; nevertheless, they were sincere and Miss Brinkley, always scrupulously fair, accepted them in a forgiving spirit.

"I am certain my brother and sister will agree with me," she replied, smiling a little, "that it has been a pleasure to have them stay with us. And dear Phoebe as well, of course!"

"A great pleasure," agreed Mr Brinkley. "The house has never been merrier!"

Miss Coral had been silent for some minutes, searching her memory for an elusive detail that was pricking at her consciousness, and now suddenly cried: "Ah, I remember! I knew there was something familiar about the Dewbury name! Years ago, there was talk about the missing heir – remember, Pearl? It was all over the papers! But then the boy and his mother turned up and went to live in the country due to his ill health – have I remembered it correctly, your ladyship?"

"That was what was reported," Lady Dewbury conceded with circumspection, duly noted by her audience.

"Exactly how many grandsons do you have?" asked Miss Brinkley, eyes narrowing as an incredible suspicion entered her head.

"Only two," replied Lady Dewbury, knowing perfectly well where this was headed. After a pause, she added portentously: "My youngest son also has a son."

Phoebe drew in a sharp breath and her eyes flew to Percy. He offered her a twisted smile.

"Percy, when you spoke of your inheritance," said Miss Brinkley, "did you mean . . . were you referring to . . . " She floundered with incredulity.

"What my sister is attempting to ask, Percy dear, is: are you the heir to the Marquess of Dewbury?" interjected Miss Coral.

Percy turned to Aurora for guidance. She in turn directed a questioning look at her grandmother.

A rare smile appeared on the dowager marchioness's lips.

"In point of fact," she announced, "my grandson is not the heir. He has not been for some years now. Allow me to present to you Lord Henry Percival Phillip, seventh Marquess of Dewbury."

Thirty

"If I had known all it would take to prove Percy's identity was for my grandmother to take one look at him, I would never have gone chasing after that wretched ring!" Aurora told Rothworth that evening.

She glanced up the table to where Lady Dewbury was seated. Her ladyship had been invited to stay for dinner *en famille* and was at present, in her undemonstrative way, profoundly enjoying conversing with her grandson.

"Can you believe it!" continued Aurora with a humorous look. "We could have spared ourselves a great deal of bother."

"And yet, I would not have wished to be spared," replied Rothworth.

"Whyever not?" she asked; at once eager to know his answer and yet wary it might complicate matters.

"I seem to have acquired a passion for . . . let us call it, adventure. Your influence, no doubt."

"Oh."

She was oddly disappointed by his response.

But then, she was not feeling herself tonight. Ever since Rothworth had walked in with his sister, an unfamiliar agitation had taken hold of her.

He, on the other hand, appeared perfectly unconscious of all that had passed between them, to the point where she almost doubted the embarrassing interlude in the carriage had occurred; which made it doubly imperative that she put the matter out of her mind.

If only his presence at her side was not making the task so utterly impossible!

She found it galling that he was looking especially attractive this evening. His dark good looks were somehow more overpowering than usual. And a coat of navy blue, paired with biscuit-coloured pantaloons (both more tight-fitting than the style he usually favoured), showed to great advantage his lean, well-muscled frame and brought back fond memories of a dark closet.

And his valet must have done something new with his hair. She had never before noticed the way the candlelight picked out amber highlights in the dark waves.

As for his compelling blue-grey eyes . . . they were gently laughing at her.

She realised she must have been staring.

"You're making me blush," he said. "Is there something out of place with my appearance?"

"No!" she replied too quickly. "Excuse me, my thoughts were elsewhere – you were saying?"

"I wasn't."

Amused by such a direct rebuttal, a smile tugged at her lips. But her amusement did not stop her from scolding herself over her misplaced wits.

Perhaps she was simply tired. Or perhaps (if one was inclined to hypothesise) now that her brother's future was all but settled, there was nothing to distract her from thinking about her own.

She felt oddly out of control when she was in the duke's company, and almost wished he would disappear from her life and leave her in peace.

Almost.

Sensing the unsettled state of her mind, Rothworth was pleased that his strategy appeared to be working. It was not his intention to spare her (she had certainly not spared him!) but though a base part of him wanted to press his advantage and disconcert her until she forgot all reason and begged him to take her into his arms, he found he could not do it.

Not yet, in any case.

Silently berating himself for being a fool, he offered her a reprieve and filled the charged silence by saying: "I suppose we must now call you Lady Elizabeth?"

"Oh no, please don't! Miss Brinkley has already attempted to address me as such, and I don't like it in the least! But she and my grandmother are adamant I must take up my title, and so we have agreed on a compromise. I am to be known as Lady Aurora . . . but I hope I will always be Aurora to my friends," she said with a smile.

A slight tension in his expression made her wonder what she had said that was not to his liking. But before she could question him over it, Charlotte's laugh across the table drew her attention.

Charlotte was seated between Percy and Phoebe, and both girls were absorbed by something that Percy was telling them. But in contrast to Phoebe's unaffected enjoyment in listening to her friend, Charlotte was playing with one of the curls framing her face and her laughter had a distinct coquettish quality to it.

It occurred to Aurora that the girl was trying out her womanly wiles. She found it rather amusing, however, when she glanced at Rothworth she could see he was displeased.

"She is simply unfurling her petals," she told him. "Don't make more of it than it is! She will soon grow weary of so unresponsive a beau as my brother, and move on to a more worthy flirt."

"My sister should not be flirting in the first place," he said sternly.

"Gracious, you have some odd notions! I'm not at all certain you are suited to raising such a vivacious sister. Surely you wouldn't wish to deprive her of the joy of knowing herself to be admired? Or of engaging in some perfectly harmless flirting? It should be a requirement of any girl's education."

"I can't agree! She should have more decorum."

"Did you at her age? I'd wager you enjoyed plenty of rather less innocent diversions! And have you ever noticed that no one ever talks of decorum when referring to a man?"

"It's not at all the same thing."

"Perhaps," she conceded. "But it should be! Men are granted as much license as they wish to pursue whatever amuses them, while women are constrained by rules in every direction and expected to limit their enjoyment. I personally don't think that is fair – do you?"

She was surprised when he took the time to properly consider his response.

"The word fair is not applicable in such an example," he replied, after some moments. "But then, fairness is an idealistic principle that has little basis in reality."

"I disagree! I think we all *feel* if something is fair or not. The feeling may be idealistic, but it is very real. Whether we then act on that feeling is another matter. Often it is our lack of endeavour to change the *un*fair that results in a reality we do not wish to inhabit . . . which is regrettable, for only think how peaceful and pleasant our society would be if fairness was distributed in equal measure to all!"

He smiled, studying her. "It has occurred to me on more than one occasion that you are a woman out of your time."

"I'm not sure I would describe myself as such," she said, returning his smile. "Perhaps I'm simply well-read enough to know that our way of life is not the only model. And, as you may have guessed, I have no compunction about speaking my mind! Others probably think as I do, but perhaps don't

211

feel able to express their thoughts. If all of us spoke up for what we wanted, or did not want, imagine how powerful a force for change that would be!"

"A force for change can have both positive and negative consequences. One must be careful what one wishes for! But that in no way lessens the persuasiveness of your arguments," he said with admiration. "And, what is more, I am beginning to realise that I would be a fool to not make use of your opinion on the bills I sponsor."

He saw that he had surprised her. And also saw the moment she decided she should not take him seriously.

He had no time to convince her of his sincerity, for his uncle asked them a question and the conversation became more general to include him.

Over the next hour Rothworth sat back and watched as Aurora charmed her host with her knowledge on all manner of subjects he raised for her consideration. He also noted how she drew the others around the table into discussions that were of interest to them, and through the force of her personality ensured their enjoyment of the evening.

She was a consummate hostess, he thought to himself, and only needed the right setting for her talents to shine. He could provide that for her. By his side, she could entertain prime ministers and ambassadors, princes and politicians; and he had no doubt that she would excel in the role, and also greatly enjoy herself.

However, though it was tempting to entice her with this vision of the future, he refused to do it. If she came to him, it had to be for him and only him.

It was not until the dessert course was served that he at last managed to reclaim Aurora's attention.

"I've been thinking that your brother is not the only one who can claim a family resemblance," he said, glancing at Lady Dewbury. "There is something of your grandmother in you."

"Really? I'm flattered you think so!" she replied. "Anyone can see my grandmother was a great beauty in her day. But I think her eyes are more similar to Percy's than mine."

"Yes. Your eyes are your own . . . gypsy eyes," he said as an afterthought.

She was drawn into a laugh. "How fanciful you are!"

"I've never been called such before."

"Then you must hide it well in front of others." After a slight pause, she asked: "Why do you call them gypsy eyes?"

He offered her an enigmatic smile. "I must decline to answer you. I've a fair notion you won't want to hear my reason."

"Is it so uncomplimentary?"

"Quite the opposite . . . but whether or not you will think so has me in something of a quandary."

"Oh, now you are toying with me! You can't say *that* and then not tell me your reason."

"I had not intended to say as much."

"Well! That is most unsatisfactory . . . and curious. I have always thought my eyes are a most common shade of brown."

He regarded her leisurely over the top of his wine glass in a way that set her pulse racing.

"My dear girl, there is nothing common about you."

"You know, Julian," she said softly, "for someone who does not approve of flirting, you do it remarkably well."

A corner of his mouth lifted; the only acknowledgement that he had heard her.

This private interlude was suddenly and rudely interrupted by a high-pitched screech, quite out of place in a gentleman's household.

The whole table was shocked into silence; and, a moment later, Mr Key bounded into the room and launched himself onto the table.

Pandemonium ensued.

Miss Coral, Phoebe and Charlotte screamed; Miss Brinkley cried *An Animal!* and jerked to her feet, startling the dowager marchioness into dropping her wine glass; and a footman, in the process of placing a blancmange on the table, recoiled in fright and ended up tipping the whole wobbly dessert over the Duke of Rothworth.

Frightened by all the loud noises, Mr Key ran across the table and took his place on Aurora's shoulder to twitter anxiously into her ear.

"Oh, I beg your pardon!" Aurora said with dismay, fighting back her laughter. "It's all my fault! Mr Key adopted me while I was out of London and I meant to explain it all earlier, but with all that has happened it quite slipped my mind. Oh, Julian! Your clothes – I fear they are quite ruined!" she exclaimed, using both hands to scoop up bits of dessert off him.

"I am becoming inured to the experience of having foodstuff thrown over me," he remarked stoically.

The mortified footman attempted to apologise and offer his assistance, but was waved away.

"No need to say another word," Rothworth assured him. "No training could have prepared you for having a wild beast let loose at the dinner table. I know at whose door to lay the blame."

"Yes, it's quite unforgivable of me!" agreed Aurora, her top lip firmly between her teeth to hold back her smile. "There . . . that is the last of the blancmange."

Picking up her napkin, she dabbed at the stains to his coat and waistcoat; until he gently pried the napkin from her hands.

"That won't be necessary," he said, his tone impassive. "See to your monkey."

Across the table, Percy was guffawing behind his hand, shoulders heaving. Having heard from John that a monkey had joined the household, no shock tinged his appreciation of the scene.

And now that she had recovered from her fright, Miss Coral was also enjoying the unexpected entertainment, and it was all she could do to stop herself from dissolving into a fit of giggles.

On the other hand, Miss Brinkley did not look to be amused in the slightest. She had suffered a lapse in her dignity, as well as stains to her clothing from the spilt wine. And when Phoebe and Charlotte begged to be allowed to hold the monkey, she was quick to dampen their hopes by declaring that on no account must they handle an animal that could very well bite them.

"Oh, no, ma'am! He is quite tame," Aurora assured her. "He was raised as part of a troupe and is used to being around people. Only, he is a little twitty at the moment because he is frightened . . . aren't you, Mr Key?" she said, stroking the monkey lovingly.

"Is that a capuchin or a vervet?" enquired Mr Brinkley with interest, adjusting his spectacles and leaning over to peer more closely at the monkey.

"Gregory, that is neither here nor there!" snapped his elder sister with exasperation. "More to the point, what is that animal doing *here*?"

Aurora rushed to offer a sanitised explanation of Mr Key's presence. And the moment she was finished, the table erupted with questions.

Into this uproar walked John.

"I'm sorry, Miss Aurora," he said, out of breath from running. "The little rogue was scaring the horses, so I took him back to my room, but he got away from me."

"Never mind!" she said. "I should have sent for him sooner."

"But what do you mean to do with him, Aurora dear?" asked Miss Coral.

"You cannot go about town with a monkey," said Miss Brinkley. "You will be thought deranged!"

"She is a Dewbury," the dowager marchioness spoke up. "They would not dare to judge her. If anything, they will think her an original."

"I have no plans to walk about town with Mr Key on my shoulder, so we need not put my credit to the test!" Aurora assured them. "John, please take him to my room and watch over him until I can come up."

Mr Key, however, did not appear to like this suggestion. Alarmed by the arrival of the one who had kept him from his mistress, he bounded off her shoulder, scurried across the floor and climbed to the top of the curtains.

Phoebe and Charlotte immediately left their seats to try and coax him down, but neither theirs, nor Aurora's efforts could convince him to descend. It was not until Mr Brinkley had the good idea to hold up some grapes, did he finally agree to leave his perch and take up position on his host's shoulder.

"What a fine little fellow," said Mr Brinkley, stroking the monkey and handing him more grapes. "They are very clever, you know. You must bring him down to the library tomorrow, when he is not so overwhelmed. I have always been fascinated with his kind."

Aurora could see that Miss Brinkley was on the verge of a scold. Quickly thanking Mr Brinkley for his assistance, she picked up Mr Key, handed him to John and ushered the girls back to the table.

Miss Brinkley was painfully conscious that she was entertaining a dowager marchioness, and, not wishing to leave her with the impression that they were a hurly-burly household, she took the reins of the conversation firmly in hand and steered it away from talk of primates.

While their elders were discussing the rumours that Napoleon's health was fast deteriorating, Aurora took the opportunity to quietly say to Rothworth: "Have I sunk myself beyond redemption with your aunt?"

"I didn't think anything could alter her good opinion of you," he replied, smiling, "but I fear you have sorely tested her to the limit by introducing a monkey into her circle."

"Then I'd best make reparations with all possible haste! There's nothing for it but to feign an illness and call the doctor."

"I can see from the disreputable glint in your eyes that you have news to impart, and wish me to inquire further into your oblique reference."

"I'm appalled I am so easy to read!" she said on a gurgle of laughter.

"I have many weeks experience of you now and am generally considered a fast learner . . . particularly in matters of self-preservation."

"How odious you are! I'm tempted to withhold my news. But you may come in useful, so I'll forgo my petty revenge. Prepare to be happy for your aunt! I have learnt that Miss Brinkley and Dr Moore are enamoured. And we are going to help them to seize the moment – Carpe Diem!"

Rothworth stared at her uncomprehendingly. "A romantic connection? Aunt Pearl?"

"Keep your voice down! And don't look at me as if I need to be admitted to Bedlam. She deserves love as much as anyone."

"I'm not disputing that. Only, if it were to happen, don't you think it would have happened by now?"

"Our capacity to love does not dimmish as we age! Time has no bearing on that particular equation. And besides, there's no point saying *if it were to happen*, for it has already happened! Really, you say some peculiar things on occasion. It's as if you are simply observing life from a safe distance, trying to rationalise it, rather than jumping into the mud along with the rest of us."

"Aurora dear!" Miss Coral addressed her suddenly, making her start guiltily in case they had been overheard. "I was telling her ladyship that I don't believe you have a ballgown – am I correct?"

"Yes, ma'am. I have never had a need for one."

"You shall have a need very soon," said Lady Dewbury. "I intend to hold a ball for you and your brother before the end of the Season. It will be the perfect opportunity to introduce you to the ton. I hope the idea pleases you?"

It would have been disingenuous to demure at so splendid an offer; not that it even crossed Aurora's mind. She would have thought herself a very odd sort of creature not to find enjoyment in the idea of a ball in her honour.

She declared herself delighted and insisted on being allowed to help her grandmother with the planning.

Percy thought a ball more of a chore than a pleasure, however, he was perfectly ready to fall in with whatever plans his grandmother and sister thought necessary.

"Also, I feel I should mention, your ladyship," said Miss Brinkley, "Aurora does not have a lady's maid."

"That will certainly need to be remedied!" responded Lady Dewbury. "I shall take care of it."

Aurora suggested that she could do without a maid for the present, but was overruled. And as she suspected her life was about to become a good deal busier, she decided they were probably right.

After dinner Aurora entertained the party with music and singing, and the dowager marchioness was able to judge her granddaughter's talent; a talent she herself had fostered, as she reminded Aurora, by engaging a music instructor for her when she had turned five; and though Aurora could not recall the memory she was perfectly ready to claim it, since it appeared to afford her grandmother pleasure.

Before the party broke up plans were made for Percy and Aurora to visit their grandmother the following day and meet their cousins and aunt. Their uncle, the dowager explained, was in the country visiting Dewbury Abbey, and was expected to return in a day or two.

Aurora's eyes could not help seeking out Rothworth's, and a current of amusement passed between them.

If amusement had been the end of it she would have been spared a sleepless night. But no, she was not so fortunate, for another emotion had also ridden the current between them and made a mockery of the word *friend.*

Thirty-One

"Can I come in?" Aurora asked from the doorway of Miss Brinkley's bedchamber, having just knocked and peered inside.

"Do you have *that animal* with you?" asked Miss Brinkley warily.

"Oh no, ma'am! I would never bring him to your room. Percy and your brother have him in the library and are attempting to teach him tricks."

"In that case, you may enter," said Miss Brinkley. She was sitting at her dressing table, ready to apply her usual liberal dusting of white face powder. "Come and tell me what happened when you met your cousins and aunt today. Were they kind to you?"

"My aunt and her daughters were a little stiff, but perfectly polite. I think they need a little time to become better acquainted with us. As for my cousin William, he doesn't appear thrilled to be cut out of the succession. Although, I could be doing him an injustice," she said with a humorous look. "He may have been suffering from some digestive complaint that made him appear pinched and sullen."

"Your grandmother must not have approved of his lack of manners."

"I believe you're right. She gave no outward sign, but I had the distinct impression she was displeased. As we were leaving, I heard her ask William to grant her a few moments of his time, and in *such* a colourless voice that it put the poor boy in a quake! I almost felt sorry for him. He is sixteen and I think at least part of his manner could be attributed to that awkward adolescent stage. Even Percy at sixteen made me want to box his ears!"

"I have heard it can be a trying age," said Miss Brinkley as she dipped the hare's foot into the pot of powder and prepared to dust her face.

"Dear ma'am, would you allow me to apply your cosmetics tonight?" Aurora asked hastily. "My mother taught me well, I promise you! And I have a small gift for you – Pear's White Imperial Powder." She showed Miss Brinkley the box in her hand. "Mama wouldn't be seen without it! It leaves a very fine, pearly finish that looks most fetching – may I try it on you?"

Miss Brinkley needed a little persuasion, but Aurora managed to convince her at last; and a few short minutes later stepped back to admire her handiwork.

For the first time in years Miss Brinkley's face was not caked with a stark white powder that dried her skin and served to deepen her lines. Her skin appeared dewy and fresh, and a very light application of rouge and lip colour lent her a youthful bloom.

Aurora also insisted on redoing her hair, which her maid had pinned back tightly in her customary style. Masterfully overriding Miss Brinkley's objections that she was too old to be changing her hair, Aurora re-pinned it in a looser style that better flattered her angular features.

"How lovely you look, ma'am!" exclaimed Aurora.

Miss Brinkley assessed herself in the mirror and raised a hand to pat her hair.

"Is it not too youthful a look for someone in my time of life?" she asked doubtfully.

"Certainly not! It looks charming on you!"

Miss Coral poked her head through the door just then to ask if they were ready to go down and enjoy a glass of sherry before dinner, and was invited to give her opinion on her sister's transformation. Catching Aurora's prompting look, she declared that she had never seen her sister look more beautiful.

"Fudge! I've never been beautiful in my life," retorted Miss Brinkley. "And I don't imagine that at fifty years of age I will suddenly become so."

"There are many kinds of beauty," said her sister. "Yours is distinctly your own!"

"We both know you are simply offering me a salve for my ego."

Miss Coral insisted that was not the case; and, seeing they were settling in for a comfortable bicker, Aurora left them to it and went off to prepare for the ruse she had decided on that afternoon.

Descending to the first floor, she came upon Rothworth leisurely making his way up the staircase.

"What are you doing here?" she said, joining him on the first-floor landing. "I thought the Lords was in session tonight?"

"It is. I was able to accomplish my part early," he replied. "Does that displease you? You don't look entirely happy to see me."

"Nonsense! I was simply surprised. In fact," she said warmly, "you may prove useful to my plan! Is Charlotte with you?"

"I left her in the library. My uncle is explaining his globe of the world to your cousin and brother, and Charlotte wanted to join them. Not that she

219

has ever shown the slightest interest in geography, so I don't delude myself it's due to a sudden studious bent," he said, smiling. "Dare I ask, what is this plan you refer to?"

At that moment the sound of Miss Brinkley's and Miss Coral's voices filtered down from above, and Aurora only had time to say: "Just follow my lead. And for goodness sake don't drop me!"

As the sisters came into view on the staircase, still bickering, Aurora executed a graceful trip on the carpet runner and launched herself into Rothworth's arms.

"Oh, how clumsy!" she cried.

"I feel a sense of *déjà vu,*" he muttered against her hair, and readjusted her in his arms so that he held her more securely against him.

She contained her laughter and frowned up at him in warning.

"Are you alright, Aurora dear?" asked Miss Coral as the sisters rushed to her side.

"I . . . I believe so. Although my ankle is a little sore."

She tentatively put down the foot she was holding aloft and flinched.

"Rothworth, you'd best carry her," commanded Miss Brinkley. "Put her on the settee in the drawing room."

"Certainly," he said, lifting Aurora into his arms with little effort.

"You are too kind," she said demurely.

His fingers dug into her flesh, tickling her as punishment for her impudence and making her squirm. She had to bite down on the insides of her mouth to stop herself from giggling.

"Miss Coral," she said over the duke's shoulder as he walked off with her, "I would be grateful if you would ask Dr Moore to come as soon as he can. I'm afraid it's the same ankle that I have previously injured and I would appreciate his opinion."

Miss Coral caught the twinkle in her eyes and, divining her intent, answered readily: "Of course, Aurora dear. At once!"

"But must we bother Dr Moore for something so trivial as a sprained ankle?" Miss Brinkley asked her sister. "The poor man was only here this morning! Gregory is already importuning him by insisting he call on you on a daily basis even though you are almost entirely recovered."

"Of course, he must come," replied Miss Coral. "If Aurora has a weakness in her ankle, Dr Moore's opinion will be invaluable!"

Miss Brinkley's reservations were overborne, and the doctor was sent for.

Whether he was already in the area or had allocated certain priorities in his own mind, Dr Moore arrived within half an hour and was taken up to see the sufferer, who at this point was surrounded by well-wishers. Her brother, the Miss Brinkleys, Mr Brinkley, Phoebe and Charlotte, all hovered around where she lay on the settee, her foot raised on a cushion and a cloth bag of ice on the afflicted ankle.

Only Rothworth was standing to one side, leaning against the wall with his arms crossed over his chest, and observing the tableau before him with a satirical expression.

Aurora was looking remarkably buoyant for one who was meant to be in pain, and was fielding questions with the ease of a seasoned politician; not lying so much as avoiding the truth.

As Dr Moore set to work discovering the extent of her injuries, Aurora suggested, her gaze on Rothworth, that everyone should sit down to dinner without her so that it did not spoil.

Rothworth did not disappoint her and soon had everyone out of the room, telling them they should give Aurora and the doctor privacy.

"Mr Brinkley, could you stay a moment?" Aurora called out as he was leaving the room. "I have something particular to ask you."

"Of course, my dear," he said, coming back to her side. "What is it?"

"Just one moment please, sir," she replied. "I believe Dr Moore has finished examining me." She turned her smile on the doctor.

"Well, I don't know what to tell you," he said, regarding her from under his dark eyebrows. "Your ankle appears to be strong and healthy, and there's no swelling to speak of. Does it still pain you?"

"Hardly at all," she replied, rolling the ankle. "The ice must have done the trick! Let me try to put some weight on it." She swung her legs off the settee and carefully rose to her feet. "Oh, it is feeling much better! Forgive me for asking you to come for such an inconsequential injury . . . I only wish there was some way to make it up to you."

She threw Mr Brinkley a speaking look.

He smiled back at her a little vacantly.

"Mr Brinkley, were you not saying just the other day that you wished to invite Dr Moore to dinner?" she said, giving him a prompting nod. "Perhaps tonight would be the perfect opportunity, so that his evening is not entirely wasted on my account."

"Hmm? Oh . . . yes!" he answered with sudden understanding. "A splendid idea! Dr Moore, I'd be pleased – and my sister too, no doubt . . . ah, my *sisters* – if you would join us for dinner. If you are not averse to the idea, of course?"

The doctor showed himself to be most willing and ran a hand through his silver mane of hair.

The matter thus happily settled, Aurora accepted Mr Brinkley's arm for support (at the last minute remembering her injury) and they made their way to the dining room.

They entered to find everyone seated, the first course laid out, and an extra chair already placed near the head of the table, beside Miss Brinkley.

"We hoped Dr Moore might be convinced to stay for dinner," said Rothworth, earning for himself an approving look from Aurora.

"How is your ankle, Aurora dear?" asked Miss Coral, winking quite blatantly at her.

"It hardly bothers me at all," she replied with an admonitory look, grateful that Miss Brinkley was too focused on Dr Moore to notice her sister.

"I thought that might be the case," said Miss Coral smugly. "Dr Moore, we are delighted you could join us! We placed you between my sister and I, for we are such old friends, are we not?"

"Really, Coral," said Miss Brinkley, her manner self-conscious, "I'm certain Dr Moore does not consider us in so familiar a light."

"But you are quite mistaken!" the doctor responded, his black moustache twitching with his smile. "I shall be most disheartened if you mean to deny our connection, Miss Brinkley."

"I-I would not dream of doing so," she replied.

"May I say how lovely you look this evening?" he told her, taking his seat.

She was surprised into a titter, which she quickly brought under control; but there was no way to control the blush that bloomed across her cheeks.

Observing this exchange from across the table, Aurora took her seat beside Rothworth and sighed contentedly.

"I expect we shall have a wedding before Christmas," she said quietly.

"Are you not presuming too much?" he asked.

Something in his tone made her look across at him sharply and re-examine her words.

"I . . . I did not mean between *us*."

He gave her a faintly surprised look. "Naturally. Seeing as I haven't asked you to marry me, that would be nigh-on impossible. Unless you know of some other way the deed can be done?"

"I just thought . . . when you said . . . oh! You are ribbing me, aren't you?"

He broke into a grin. "Yes."

"You *fiend!*"

"The temptation was overpowering. Particularly since you're set on throwing my aunt on the matrimonial pyre, when you yourself don't believe in marriage."

"I have never said that!" she exclaimed. "It's not that I don't believe in the ideals of the institution, I simply have an issue with the laws surrounding it. They are geared towards binding a wife to her husband, financially and otherwise, including taking away her rights over her own children. Why, if you consider the matter rationally, it's more advantageous to be a mistress than a wife!" Noting his startled expression, she smiled. "Oh dear, I have shocked you again. I didn't mean that *I* was going to embark on that path."

"I'm glad to hear it!" he replied. "One never knows with you. As for your other points, I could show you that such obstacles are not insurmountable – if you would allow me?"

She held his gaze for a few moments, then turned away to pick out a bread roll from the basket on the table.

"How did we stray onto such a dismal topic?" she remarked. "I should know better than to allow myself to become impassioned over dinner. It's a practice I don't hold with, for it quite ruins one's appetite!"

Thirty-Two

On the following day, Aurora and Percy met with Lady Dewbury and their respective solicitors to begin the process of resolving Percy's inheritance.

Lord Charles was notably absent.

Having arrived home on the previous evening to be greeted by the news that his mother had started proceedings to declare *the upstart* as the rightful heir to the Dewbury fortune and title, and to add insult to injury was to hold a ball to introduce him and his sister to Society, Lord Charles's anger had soon given way to dejection.

It had been a trying few days for his lordship. The run of bad luck had begun when his valet had somehow managed to misplace the signet ring while hiding it; a damnable inconvenience that had wasted precious hours of a weekend that should have been devoted to pleasurable pursuits, rather than accusations and unhappy musings.

Then, the prime article of questionable virtue that he had been hoping to entice into his keeping had rejected him, with little consideration for his vanity, in front of several gentlemen who did not count discretion as a one of their attributes.

And now, to top it all off, his long-lost nephew had reappeared to usurp his place as head of the family.

All in all, he thought life damnably unfair.

Consequently, as soon as the difficult interview with his mother had drawn to a close, rather than face the discontent and recriminations of his wife and children, he had abandoned the comforts of hearth and home for those of his club, and there had proceeded to drink himself into blissful oblivion, with a few cronies who knew just how to perk up his failing spirits; until, in the early hours of the morning, it had taken four of the club's brawny footmen to half-carry, half-wrestle his bulk into a hackney coach and send him home.

Only the porter had been awake to witness his ignoble state as he staggered through the front door and up the stairs to his room. But within a few short hours the whole household was aware that Lord Charles had been dipping too deeply and had cast up his accounts into a potted palm on the landing.

It was therefore unsurprising that his mother did not expect the pleasure of his company when she welcomed the lawyers and her grandchildren into the library. In his absence the meeting was carried out with the utmost of civility and professionalism, and it was fair to say that no one missed his presence; all five participants each delighted in their own way with how matters were settled.

Upon their return to the Brinkley residence, Aurora decided to make good on her promise to take Phoebe to the equestrian circus at Astley's Royal Amphitheatre.

Her brother, still jubilant from the interview with the lawyers, offered himself up as their escort, even though he did not hold out much hope for such childish amusements, and the three of them were soon on their way to Lambeth.

After spending the afternoon watching daring acrobatic feats on horseback and re-enactments of famous scenes of war with dozens of horses (which even Percy found exciting), they returned to Hanover Square several hours later in high spirits.

Aurora was the first to descend from the hackney and saw at once that there was some sort of commotion at the front door.

Levington, looking more flustered than she had ever seen him, appeared to be refusing entry to a lady and gentleman who were arguing with him, and each other.

"There is no Miss Barton in residence," he was saying in beleaguered accents, "as I have repeatedly told you, madam."

"I know for a fact that she is here!" cried the woman, thumping the tip of her parasol on the ground for emphasis. She was a diminutive lady in her thirties, dressed with neat propriety and holding herself very erect. "I demand to see her at once and I'll not leave this spot until I do! And as for you, sir," she went on, turning to the gentleman beside her, who despite his current harassed state had a competent air about him. "If you are indeed Phineas Carter – which I'll not accept without first seeing proof! – then all I can say to you is, you have been negligent in the extreme! I wrote to you months ago begging you to come and relieve Mr Wilks of his duty, and what did you do? Nothing! Not a single thing! I hold you personally responsible for my poor Phoebe's disappearance."

At this point Phoebe herself descended from the carriage and, catching sight of the woman, cried: "Miss Winston!"

Quickly running up the shallow steps, she threw herself into her governess's arms.

"My dearest, you are safe!" exclaimed Miss Winston, clinging to her with surprise and relief. "I did not dare hope!"

"But I wrote to tell you I was perfectly safe? Did you not receive my letters?" asked Phoebe, taking a step back and smiling at her.

"I did, but I could not be certain that you had not been coerced into writing them."

"Oh, not at all! Cousin Aurora did have to prompt me to write them, but her only thought was to spare you unnecessary worry. But how did you find me? I was so careful not to mention anything that might give away our location."

"Your last letter was franked by the Duke of Rothworth. I needed only to find out where he lived."

"Oh, how thoughtless of me! I should have known Miss Brinkley would have her mail franked by her nephew."

"Well, whoever she is, I'm greatly indebted to her for it! How could you disappear like that without a word of warning to me? Not that I blame you for disappearing, dearest, for what else could you do when that horrid man all but kidnapped you! Only I wish you had confided in me."

"But I had no notion of escaping when I left you, dear Miss Winston," replied Phoebe. "All that came later, after I met Cousin Aurora and Percy. And I've had the most wonderful adventure, so I can't regret any of it!"

This was going too far for Mr Carter.

He was at the end of his tether after a tense journey that had taken him across the Atlantic in record time, and that had led him to this house to find his niece's governess there before him, pounding on the door.

On discovering his identity, the hysterical woman had lost no time in abusing him, and since he was not in the habit of being taken to task by anyone, let alone someone in his employ, what had remained of his good humour had deserted him.

He now scowled down at Phoebe and said with some heat: "Not regret it? Let me tell you, young lady, anyone with a modicum of delicacy most certainly would! It's a shameful business all round and I'm appalled that you can treat it so lightly!"

Phoebe, noticing him for the first time, was taken aback and stared up at him.

"Uncle Phineas? Oh, it is you!" she exclaimed, breaking into a smile. "I remember you with a long, curly beard so I couldn't be certain at first.

Although Cousin Aurora did tell me to expect you, so I suppose I should have guessed – pray forgive me for being such a goose!"

Mr Carter seemed to relent a little at this disarmingly naïve speech.

"Who is this *Cousin Aurora* you keep referring to?" enquired Miss Winston. "You also mentioned her in your last letter, dearest. But you don't have any cousins that I know of."

Seeing the time had come to present herself, Aurora hooked her arm through Percy's and together they climbed the steps.

"A small deception on our part," Aurora told Miss Winston, "but necessary as a precaution. How do you do, ma'am?" she went on, smiling in a friendly fashion and shaking hands with her. "I'm Aurora Wesley . . . oh, forgive me! Aurora *Dewbury*."

"You must be the woman who summoned me here," said Mr Carter, looking unimpressed. "I received a most impertinent letter from you!"

"Oh dear, I fear it was! And I do sincerely beg your pardon," said Aurora. "Having just rescued your niece from a situation in which she should never have found herself, I was not in a conciliatory mood when I wrote to you. Also allow me to apologise to you, and Miss Winston, for taking matters into my own hands without your prior approval. Circumstances dictated that I act quickly."

"I for one am willing to forgive anything," said the governess, "if you would tell me, Miss Dewbury, how my charge came to be . . . "

"Oh no, Miss Winston!" Phoebe interrupted, looking proudly at Aurora. "Not *Miss* but *Lady* Aurora. And this is her brother, Per . . . " She broke off and looked across at Percy. "Have you decided if it's to be Percival or Henry?"

"Do none of you know your own names?" protested Mr Carter, eyeing Aurora and Percy with disfavour. "What sort of havey-cavey family have you fallen in with, Phoebe?"

"They're nothing of the sort!" she objected.

Before she could further fire up in defence of her friends, Charlotte suddenly rushed up the steps to join their small congregation.

She had been keeping an eye out for Phoebe's return from a parlour window and, on catching sight of her, had hurried downstairs, poked her head into the library to tell her brother she was needed across the square, and then had dashed out of the house.

"Oh, Phoebe, did I do wrong?" she now cried. "This woman came to the door asking for Phoebe Barton and I was so surprised she knew that you were . . . well, *you* know . . . that I foolishly blurted out your direction."

Phoebe assured her she had acted correctly and introduced her to her governess and uncle.

"Are you certain you are Lady Charlotte and not some other derivative?" asked Mr Carter sarcastically.

Charlotte, taking exception to his tone, said to Phoebe in an audible whisper: "I take it this is *The Despicable One?*"

Phoebe shook her head.

"*The Distant One?*" Charlotte said with surprise. "You poor thing!"

Mr Carter's scowl deepened.

Phoebe threw her a warning look, fearing Aurora might be made unhappy to know that she had gone against her wishes and shared her secrets with her friend.

This was not lost on Aurora, and she could barely hold back her laughter. Realising the situation required more diplomacy than could be achieved standing on the front porch, she invited everyone to step inside.

Levington, despite what his superior expression might have led one to suppose, was enjoying the farce being played out, but at Aurora's beseeching look he stepped aside and allowed them to enter.

"Dearest," Miss Winston said quietly to Phoebe, as everyone made their way into the vestibule, "is this the young man you wrote to me about?" She indicated to Percy. "The one in whose pocket you have been living all these weeks?"

Phoebe reddened, conscious that Percy might overhear.

"Yes, but I-I didn't write to you *about* him," she whispered back; although she was sadly conscious that she may have, quite innocently, made several references to him in her last letter.

Miss Winston huffed and speared Percy with a disapproving look.

He had been quite oblivious up to that point, but this captured his attention, and he became uncomfortably conscious that he had somehow earned the governess's ire.

"What sort of adventurer are you, sir?" she asked him. "Fixing your interest with an heiress not yet out of the school-room!"

"Eh?" he responded blankly.

"Miss Winston, please don't," begged Phoebe, mortified.

But her governess had held onto her concerns for too long to be able to keep a prudent tongue in her head.

"Did you come to Phoebe's rescue so you could ensnare her for yourself?" she went on angrily. "I should think you would be ashamed!"

"You quite misunderstand the matter, ma'am," said Aurora.

"Indeed, you do, dear Miss Winston," Phoebe said agitatedly. "Percy would never take advantage of me – or anyone! He is the kindest, most wonderful gentleman of my acquaintance."

Finding more to alarm her than comfort her in this speech, the governess asked: "Then what *are* his intentions towards you?"

"I don't have any!" Percy insisted.

"Of course, he doesn't," agreed Charlotte, linking her arm through his. "He is *my* admirer."

After a stunned pause, Percy rather ungallantly pulled free of her hold. "I'm not anyone's admirer!" he said in appalled accents.

"Perhaps we could go up to the drawing room and continue this discussion over tea?" suggested Aurora, voice quivering.

No one heeded her, for Charlotte cried out at the same time: "But how can you say that when I *know* you are devoted to me? Why, you punched Lieutenant Ross on my account!"

"For the love of . . . " Percy sighed with exasperation. "That loose-screw had his arm around you and was trying to force his attentions on you. Any gentleman would have come to your aid! But it doesn't follow that he must be dotty on you – that's just addlebrained! *Now* do you understand?"

This was too much for Charlotte's emotional state. Having spent a good part of her waking moments over the last week or so wallowing in her infatuation and feeding her imagination with improbable scenarios, the truth, delivered with such blunt force, was most unpalatable.

She burst into tears.

"You bungled that," Mr Carter informed Percy.

Miss Winston, for once finding herself in agreement with Phoebe's uncle, glared at Percy. "Most badly done, indeed! Anyone can see the poor girl has a tendre for you."

"I do not!" retorted Charlotte, emerging from behind her handkerchief and throwing the governess an irate look.

"Mutton-headed thing to have done," said Mr Carter, shaking his head at Percy, but not unkindly. "You're too green to know it yet, my boy, but you'll soon learn women can't stand to have their delusions shattered with honesty."

Miss Winston at once took exception to this unflattering portrayal of her sex; Mr Carter stood by his point; Percy attempted to defend his actions to both of them, and was assisted in this by Phoebe; and Charlotte loudly proclaimed that she was perfectly indifferent to immature young men who had no hope of catching her fancy.

No one heard Rothworth walk in and cast an inauspicious eye over the scene that greeted him.

Aurora, her lip firmly between her teeth, was the first to notice his arrival and sent him a look of such hilarity he feared she was about to dissolve into laughter.

A smile briefly touched his eyes as he sent her a warning look.

Turning back to the combatants, he said in a dispassionate voice that brought all conversation to a halt: "Charlotte, if you cannot comport yourself with the dignity befitting the name De Vere, then I suggest you return to your governess and do not venture out of the house until you have learnt some self-restraint."

His sister blinked at him several times, as if coming out of a trance, then quickly dried her eyes and assumed a haughty expression.

"Pray excuse me," she said. "I was not prepared to meet with Percy's duplicity today, and momentarily allowed my emotions to overcome me."

"Dare I ask what she means by that, Dewbury?" Rothworth enquired mildly, his eyes still on his sister.

When no response was forthcoming, Aurora prompted her brother in an unsteady voice: "Dearest, I believe His Grace is speaking to *you*."

Percy started and looked sheepish.

While Mr Carter and Miss Winston, having had no idea they were in the presence of a duke, regarded Rothworth with new appreciation,

"Sorry, sir. Forgot!" said Percy. "Still getting used to the dashed name. As to what your sister is referring to, you'd best ask her to explain. She's decided she knows the truth of it, and it wouldn't be gentlemanly of me to contradict her."

"Ooh!" exclaimed Charlotte, eyes flashing. "How *dare* you!"

" . . . though, I daresay," he went on quickly, "I may be partly at fault. And if that's the case, then I'm sorry! I never intended to mislead anyone."

"You never did!" cried Phoebe, incensed on his behalf. "Charlotte, if you dare to allow your brother to think Percy has acted dishonourably, why I'll . . . I'll tell him the *truth*," she said with awful meaning, leaving her friend in no doubt that she would disclose their clandestine visit to Hyde Park and Lieutenant Ross's improper advances.

Charlotte huffed audibly, and after a short inner battle said with the air of one suffering persecution of the cruellest form: "I must have mistaken the situation . . . Percy is blameless."

"I never doubted it," said her brother, unimpressed. "I believe you owe Lord Dewbury an apology."

"*Lord* Dewbury?" asked Mr Carter with sudden interest. "You never told us the boy was a lord, Phoebe?"

"What does that have to do with anything?" Miss Winston demanded, bristling again. "I hope you're not suggesting that we should be pleased he compromised Phoebe simply because he is a lord?"

"Good God, woman, I said nothing of the sort!" replied Mr Carter, his own temper flaring. "And I'll have you remember, as Phoebe's uncle and guardian I don't have to justify myself to her governess!"

"No one was compromised, I assure you," said Aurora, stepping into the fray. "I have acted as Phoebe's chaperone from the moment we rescued her."

"You are barely more than a girl yourself! And are you to be trusted?" demanded Miss Winston, weeks of fear on her charge's behalf making her both courageous and quarrelsome. "For all we know, you may want an heiress for your brother."

"I admit, the unusual circumstances could lead you to doubt my intentions," said Aurora, keeping her voice as reasonable as possible, "but I promise you, I have only ever wanted to safeguard Phoebe from a forced marriage."

"That is easy enough to say *now*," retorted Miss Winston. "And since Mr Carter does not seem inclined to question your veracity . . . "

"Enough!" Rothworth declared in a cold voice. "You must be overwrought, ma'am, for I can think of no other explanation as to why you would question Lady Aurora's word?"

Miss Winston would have liked nothing better than to give the fine-looking duke a piece of her mind, but there was something implacable in his gaze that kept her words at bay.

Aurora inwardly rolled her eyes at Rothworth's high-handed tactics.

She was on the point of trying to smooth things over, when Miss Brinkley's voice suddenly declared from above: "If you must all congregate in the vestibule, I would ask that you lower your voices. My sister has been unwell and requires her rest."

Turning as one, they saw her standing on the landing, looking down at them with displeasure. Apologies were offered as she descended at a regal pace and came to join them.

Aurora carried out the introductions; and then apologetically explained, in broad strokes, why it was that they had had to pretend that Phoebe was her cousin.

Miss Brinkley accepted her disclosures with equanimity, only observing: "You have an unusual capacity for finding yourself in improbable situations,

Aurora. You may wish to consider a less sensational path in future. Public life can be most censorious." She flicked a look at her nephew. Before he could do more than tense, she had moved on and was saying to Mr Carter and Miss Winston: "I would be pleased if you would join us for tea, or a glass of sherry. I imagine you still have many questions, and Lady Aurora will no doubt wish to do all she can to set your minds at ease. Percy, you are, of course, welcome to join us, however, I hardly think our discussion would be of interest to you – perhaps you have your own engagement?"

Gratefully accepting this lifeline, Percy remembered an appointment with a hat maker and, taking his leave of everyone, all but ran out the door.

"Phoebe," continued Miss Brinkley, "I'm certain Charlotte would be obliged to you if you would take her up to your room so that she can refresh herself. You may then join us in the drawing room."

Though neither girl was much inclined to spend time in the other's company at present, they did not dare contradict her and dutifully started up the stairs.

Miss Brinkley and her guests followed after them.

"Your aunt was magnificent!" said Aurora, hanging back so she could speak with Rothworth privately.

"She has always been a woman of masterful poise," he replied. "Unlike others I might mention! At one point I feared you were going to go into whoops. What a reprehensible sense of humour you have."

"Oh, dear, I know!" she agreed tragically. "It was shockingly uncivil of me. Not to mention, it made it quite impossible for me to attempt to pacify them. I can only be thankful no one but yourself noticed."

"Why did you not tell me you had come to the rescue of Miss Lennox? Did you think I would disapprove of your actions?"

"Would you have?" she asked with a faint smile.

"I'd have made every allowance to understand them."

Her smile widened. "Even at first? I think you forget how much you disliked me in the beginning."

"I have never disliked you . . . and there lay the problem."

She returned his steady gaze, uncertain how to react to this admission.

"She is not Phoebe Lennox," she remarked, looking away and starting up the stairs. "Her name is Phoebe Barton – as in Barton Textiles."

"Good God!" he exclaimed, following her. "Her governess is right to call her an heiress."

"I didn't know it at the time, of course. And yet, even if I had, I *still* would have saved her from that horrid guardian of hers." She threw him a challenging look over her shoulder. "She was so frightened of him she was on the point of agreeing to marry a man almost three times her age – I had no choice! If there is one thing I can't stand, it's people who look away when they see injustice. I refuse to become one of their number."

He laid a hand on her arm to halt her steps.

"I would have done the same myself, so there is no need to bite off my nose."

"I have become impassioned again, haven't I?" she said with a sudden smile. "Boring you rigid, no doubt!"

He experienced a physical ache in his chest on seeing her smile at him with such easy comradery; and it occurred to him that being nothing more than her friend was likely to kill him.

He dropped his hold on her and continued up the stairs.

"You may be as impassioned as you please with me. And *boring* is not a word I'd ever use to describe you."

She laughed. "Dare I ask what word you would use?"

He stopped and looked back to where she was standing. "Vexatious. Fearless. Enchanting . . . Unattainable."

"Oh . . . " she breathed, her smile fading.

"Oh, indeed," he replied and continued up the stairs.

Thirty-Three

Three hundred and twenty-one gilt-edged invitations were sent out for the Dowager Marchioness of Dewbury's ball, and gratifyingly all but five acceptances were received back.

Of the four regrets that came in, two were owing to the invitees being out of the country, one couple was in hourly expectation of enlarging their family, and the fourth was still eschewing social gatherings in the aftermath of a particularly humiliating *crim. con.* that had been picked up by the papers.

As for the one invitation that elicited no response, since the elderly gentleman in question had rather suddenly tossed off his mortal coil this oversight was deemed entirely understandable.

For the many who did not receive the most coveted invitation of the Season, they were left to envy those who had; and to reconcile themselves to having to learn second-hand the details surrounding the sudden re-emergence of the young Marquess of Dewbury, and his miraculous recovery from the mysterious childhood ailment that had kept him confined to the country for most of his life.

Some had always maintained that it must be madness that afflicted the boy, and now at last Society would be given the opportunity to ogle, prod and judge for itself. And so, even before it had even begun, the Dewbury Ball was declared a great success; uniting exclusivity and mystery, two attributes of great value to the ton.

It had been almost six weeks since Aurora and Percy had been welcomed into their family and the time had flown by in a whirl of activity; mostly to do with legal matters, estate business, preparations for their formal presentation at court, and a handful of select engagements to begin introducing them to Lady Dewbury's close acquaintances.

While the lawyers were sorting out the financial details of Percy's inheritance, Lady Dewbury had taken on the responsibility of furnishing her grandchildren with entirely new wardrobes, including their costly court presentation garments. There was not a day where they did not have appointments at glove makers, milliners, modistes, tailors, cobblers and even jewellers; a circumstance that afforded Percy little pleasure and Aurora much.

Lady Dewbury had attempted to convince her grandchildren to move into the family mansion (since it was Percy's by right), but they had decided to remain with the Brinkleys for a while longer, as Aurora wanted to be near Phoebe until the girl had settled into her new life.

With a little manoeuvring, Aurora had managed to persuade Mr Phineas Carter that, since the Brinkleys had many aristocratic connections, it was in Phoebe's best interest to remain with them and have Miss Coral prepare her for her coming-out next year. This idea had greatly appealed to the spinster, particularly since (as Aurora had pointed out to her) Phoebe was in need of maternal attention and guidance, which Miss Coral was uniquely placed to provide.

And as Mr Brinkley and Miss Brinkley were also attached to Phoebe, this solution was seen to benefit them all.

As for Mr Carter, he was glad to have one of his problems so easily resolved, for he had many others to see to before his return to Boston. He had a busy few weeks removing Mr Wilks as Phoebe's guardian, starting legal proceedings against him, and engaging a firm of solicitors to oversee Phoebe's interests in his absence. No one could doubt that he had his niece's best interests at heart. He may have been too complacent in the past, but now he was meticulous and rigorous in carrying out his responsibilities to her.

Between him, Aurora and the Brinkleys – and even Percy, who was becoming remarkably protective of her – Phoebe's future seemed assured.

A happy conclusion was also reached for Miss Winston (after Aurora interceded on her behalf) and she was allowed to continue as Phoebe's governess; and since she had lost her belligerence as soon as her fears for her charge had been put to rest, and had begun to act like a sensible woman, no one found anything objectionable in her continued presence.

Aside from wishing to be near Phoebe, Aurora and Percy chose to remain with the Brinkleys as neither of them wanted to live under the same roof as their uncle and his family.

These relatives may have come to view them with resigned tolerance and treat them as their station deserved, but there remained an undercurrent of friction between the male members of the family (namely Lord Charles, his son and Percy) that would have made living together quite a miserable experience for all concerned. And as Aurora and Percy did not want to eject them from the house without sufficient warning, while matters were being sorted out, it was thought best to keep the living arrangements as they were.

However, though they did not move into the Dewbury mansion, they were often there; whether for regular dinners *en famille*, or instructive visits where they were taught the ins and outs of the household, or, in Percy's case, meetings with the house and land stewards to begin familiarising himself with his various estates and responsibilities.

While Percy was diligently busy with one such meeting, Aurora went to visit her grandmother to help her to finalise the arrangements for the ball, which was to take place the following day.

After a couple of hours of inspecting rooms together and issuing instructions, Aurora could see that the elderly dowager was getting tired and persuaded her to go and rest, saying that she herself could finish the last few remaining tasks with the housekeeper's assistance.

It was several hours before Aurora felt able to leave, happy in the knowledge that the preparations were almost complete. She was making her way through the house to the front door, pulling on her gloves as she went, when she passed one of the parlours on the ground floor and saw Lord Charles wedged into a chair too small for his bulk, and studying a glass of brandy in his hand with a forlorn expression.

"Uncle Charles! Why are you sitting all alone in the dark?" she asked, coming into the room and going over to the windows to draw back the curtains.

He looked up and blinked a few times against the light to bring her into focus.

"Ah . . . it's you, my dear," he said, attempting a smile.

Despite some initial coolness on his part, Aurora had quickly become a firm favourite of his. He was always partial to pretty women, and particularly if they knew just how to take his jovial banter and respond in kind.

As for Aurora, she did not hold his lapse in judgement over the signet ring against him, laying the blame at another door. And just as soon as she had cemented her favoured position in his esteem, she had set about convincing him that a new valet was just the thing that was needed to lift his spirits and give him a more positive outlook on life.

Lord Charles was already cross with Mr Pipell over the loss of the signet ring (which had somehow since been found, delivered to his mother and was now on the finger of its rightful owner) and her suggestion had fallen on fruitful ground.

Aurora had noticed a beneficial change in him as soon as the manipulative Mr Pipell had left his service and a more respectable valet had taken his place. And as she was always one to look for the good in people, she was very ready to admire her uncle's agreeable traits and forgive him his less salubrious ones.

"Come now! It's a fine day outside," she said bracingly. "You can't sit here all alone, drinking yourself into a stupor. It would give anyone a fit of the dismals!"

"Nothing else to do," he replied glumly. "I'm of no use to anyone anymore."

"What rubbish! Forgive me, Uncle Charles, but it's just not true! You are an important member of the family, and your experience and wisdom benefits us all. Who else but you can advise Percy and me on how to navigate the pitfalls we face in Society? You know your mother does not enjoy going out in the evenings – and has not done so for many years – so she may not be up to snuff . . . at least, not in the way that *you* are."

Lord Charles looked struck by this reasoning. "Yes, yes, I'm a knowing one, certainly. Been on the town for more years than I care to count! Have many friends too and could help to ease your way, my dear."

"There, you see! You are indispensable to us."

"There might be something in what you say," he agreed pensively. But after a few moments he fell into dejection again, saying: "But it's not the same, my dear. I used to oversee all the estates! They were forever dragging me into one meeting after the next and asking for my opinion . . . but not anymore."

"Well, if you are being truthful with yourself, Uncle Charles, you'll admit that you are not at all suited to such responsibility!" Aurora informed him, not mincing words. "I visited Dewbury Abbey the other week and found it to be in a shocking state of disrepair. You have many fine qualities but managing estates does not appear to be one of them! And besides, I imagine to a man of your gregarious nature the task must have been vastly boring?"

"Perhaps, perhaps," he sighed. "I can't say I enjoyed stepping into my brother's shoes when it came to estate business . . . I did my best, though!"

"Certainly," she offered up; not wishing to be drawn into a debate on this ambiguous point. "But you must not become disheartened if your talents lie elsewhere. We can't all be proficient at everything! But I agree, you certainly need an occupation. Only, let us find you one that will benefit both yourself and others."

"But what, my dear, what?"

She thought for a moment, and then said baldly: "I have heard that you enjoy entertaining – is this correct?"

"Yes, indeed! I have always been partial to a convivial gathering."

She smiled inwardly. "Well then, off the top of my head – and this is only one idea of many! – how would you feel about helping to plan an event at Dewbury Abbey in the summer? A masked ball, perhaps?"

"No, no, my dear! Devilishly uncomfortable affairs! Those dashed masks never stay on, and more often than not end up giving one a nasty rash," he said, shuddering. "A costumed ball, on the other hand, well, that allows people more scope to choose what suits them . . . and we could have a theme! Oriental, perhaps," he added, warming to the idea.

"Famous! Already I can see you will be indispensable in helping to plan all sorts of marvellous entertainments for us," she said with her lovely smile. "But for today, I have another more urgent need of you! I must beg your escort, for I need to walk to Bond Street to purchase a book."

"Walk all the way to Bond Street?" he said, horrified. "We'll catch a hack, my dear."

"Oh, no! We must walk." She cast her eye over his awe-inspiring girth. "It's only a few streets away and we both need the fresh air and exercise. It can become our regular outing – you know how much I enjoy your company! You tell the most amusing stories."

Lord Charles perked up at this and let out a chuckle. "I do tell a fine story, don't I? And no one appreciates them more than you, my dear – especially the salty ones! You're not the least bit missish," he said approvingly.

"The saltier the better," she agreed, laughing. "Now, let me help you to rise."

He went to finish his brandy, but Aurora quickly swiped the glass out of his hand and put it down on a table.

"You know I don't like you drinking too much, Uncle Charles. Not only is it not good for you, but I've noticed your stories are not nearly as funny when you are not sober. I would like a charming companion on our walk, not a sloshed one! Now, come!"

After several tries, they managed to get him to his feet and, with only a small delay to retrieve his cane, hat and gloves, they set out for Bond Street.

Linking arms with him, Aurora adapted herself to his laborious pace and they were soon enjoying a tête-à-tête.

The conversation started innocently enough. Aurora told him about her court presentation, the week before, and regaled him with her irreverent opinions of the palace, the princesses and the people in attendance.

She then moved on to talking about how much she had enjoyed their evening at the opera last night, and as Lord Charles was surprisingly conversant in all matters of music, he delighted her with his own assessment of the music and performers.

But from there things deteriorated in tone, for he then fell to reminiscing about his younger days, when he had been slimmer and considerably better looking, and the various opera singers that had enjoyed his attentions.

Aurora found his amatory adventures so amusing that she soon developed a stitch in her side from laughing.

"Infamous behaviour!" she exclaimed, trying to sound severe, but failing. "It seems that in those days pursuing actresses and opera singers was all you gentlemen could think about!"

Lord Charles chucked. "Still is, my dear, still is! The forces of attraction have a way of distracting one to the point of imprudence . . . ah, speaking of which," he went on in a more serious tone, "that puts me in mind of something I wanted to say to you. May not be my place, but I want to spare you unnecessary pain if I can."

"That sounds terribly ominous!"

"No, no – devilishly awkward subject but not as bad as all that! It's to do with the Duke of Rothworth. I've seen you in each other's company a good deal over the last few weeks and . . . well . . . I don't say it's *not* a coup, getting him to dance attendance on you – because it is! Tremendous achievement when you consider all the caps that have been set on him."

"You quite mistake the matter, Uncle Charles," she insisted, colouring a little. "We are simply friends."

"That might be, but I'd wager there's more to it on your side," he said, peering at her with surprising shrewdness.

"Oh, no!"

"No use denying it, my dear. Seen it for myself – you light up when he enters a room! Which is why I thought I'd better put a word in your ear. Wouldn't want you to be made unhappy."

She was touched by his concern, but also rather disturbed that she had so easily betrayed herself.

"Thank you, Uncle Charles, but I assure you I have no expectations towards His Grace," she said firmly.

"Good, good – better that way! Don't say he's not a fine catch, mind you. The ladies all seem to like that handsome face of his, and his name and fortune are almost as old as ours! I'd be mighty pleased to welcome him into the family, no doubt about that. But that don't mean he'll make you happy – most unlikely, in fact! Thing is, he's too much of a cold, reserved fellow for you, my dear. Barely ever cracks a smile! And is such a dull dog besides."

"But he's not dull in the least!" she felt bound to protest.

"His great passion is *historical abbeys*," announced Lord Charles damningly, as if that clinched the matter. "But, what's more unpardonable, is that he keeps trying to engage me on the subject! Why, just the other evening when we dined with those relatives of his, he pinned me down for longer than I care to remember and droned on and on about the subject. What the deuce have I ever done to make him think I care a fig about buttresses and barrel vaults?" he asked disgustedly.

Aurora's lips twitched. Rothworth had developed a rather reprehensible habit of teasing her uncle; one she had had to take him to task over since it sorely tested her self-restraint, and she feared she would one day disgrace herself by succumbing to a fit of the giggles.

"That is certainly a mark against him," she agreed sombrely. "But in general, I think His Grace is excellent company. And I find it exceedingly odd that he has a reputation for being cold and unemotional. In my experience, he has a rather exuberant set of emotions, including a perfectly healthy temper and a shockingly inappropriate sense of humour!"

Lord Charles appeared surprised. "Does he now? Never would've guessed! Always looks so starched up and proper . . . though, come to think of it," he mused, "he must have some spirit in him, to be able to keep L'Incomparable by his side."

Aurora felt a tremor of shock course through her.

"Who is L'Incomparable?" she asked casually.

Lord Charles belatedly remembered to whom he was speaking and tried to change the subject.

"Yes, that horse is a very fine specimen," she agreed, forcing a jovial tone, "but I won't let you distract me! Is L'Incomparable a courtesan? You must not think you'll shock me by telling me the truth. I already assumed His Grace kept a mistress – it is the way of things."

"You're a sensible girl," he said approvingly. "Should've known you wouldn't kick up a fuss. She's an actress – the toast of Paris and London! And the loveliest creature you've ever laid eyes on . . . " He was brought up short by a stricken look in her eyes. "But of course, she's nowhere near as lovely as you, my dear!" he put in quickly.

"What flummery!" she laughed carelessly and slapped him lightly on the shoulder. "You're a terrible liar, Uncle Charles, but if I had a need of your words, I would greatly appreciate them. However, as I said, I've no claims on His Grace other than those of friendship, so I can hardly expect him to forgo his entertainment on my account . . . that would be illogical. . . and *stupid.* . . in fact, I'm delighted that he has found such a charming mistress to cater to his whims – they are often unreasonable, and I don't envy the poor woman in the least!"

Lord Charles patted her hand; but it was unclear if he was congratulating her on her ability to view the matter in such a philosophical light or commiserating with her.

Thirty-Four

A torrent of rain fell over London that evening and continued into the next day, with an impressive accompaniment of lighting and thunder. The mood of the weather so perfectly matched Aurora's own that she felt almost glad that the sun refrained from showing its cheerful face.

She decided to take her breakfast in her room and brood in privacy, rather than subject anyone to her ill humour. However, brooding was not a natural state for her, and she soon grew impatient with it, and herself.

She was the one who had insisted that friendship was all Rothworth could expect from her, and it made not the slightest sense that she should now resent the fact that he had taken her at her word.

A little after midday, having had enough of her own company, she forced herself to go downstairs and find a book to read.

The house was unusually quiet. Miss Coral and Phoebe had an appointment with a modiste that morning, and, as for the others, she assumed they must be in their rooms resting before the ball that evening.

She walked into the library expecting to see at least Mr Brinkley, bending over his books, and was arrested by the sight of her brother in private conference with the Duke of Rothworth.

They rose at her entrance.

"Good day to you both!" she said in as bright a voice as she could manage. "Although I suppose that's a rather inapt greeting considering the tempest outside. I didn't know you were to visit us today, Your Grace?"

Rothworth's eyebrow rose infinitesimally at this form of address; he had become used to hearing *Julian* from her when they were in private.

"Your brother and I had some business to discuss," he replied.

Coming over, he took her hand and raised it to his lips. He had begun performing this small gesture of late and she had done nothing to dissuade him, but today it grated on her nerves, and she had to exercise considerable control to stop herself from pulling her hand away.

His smile dimmed as he looked into her eyes.

"Is anything the matter?" he asked. "You don't appear to be in spirits."

At this, she did remove her hand and stepped away.

"How unchivalrous of you!" she replied lightly. "I'm a little tired from all the preparations for the ball, nothing more. I hope you still mean to attend? My grandmother has told me repeatedly how fortunate we are to have earned your patronage, and I begin to fear we couldn't manage our way in Society without you!"

"You would manage quite easily without me – as I am regretfully aware. But yes, I'll be attending tonight. Will you save your first waltz for me?"

"I would be delighted. Grandmama insisted on hiring a dance instructor for us – she refuses to believe our mother's training is sufficient! – so I trust you won't find me lacking." Unable to continue holding his gaze, she turned to her brother and asked: "Percy, what have you done with Mr Brinkley? I hope you didn't banish him from his own library?"

"Of course not," replied her brother, grinning at her in a way she found rather incongruous. "He took Mr Key down to the kitchen to discover what foods he prefers. He told us he's been reading up about the diet of monkeys and wanted to do his own research."

"I see I should prepare myself to be supplemented in Mr Key's affections – whoever rules his stomach, rules his heart! Already, he has begun to prefer sleeping in Mr Brinkley's room . . . it seems all males have an astonishing capacity to divert their affections from one subject to another," she said, forcing a smile. "What business did you and His Grace have to discuss?"

Percy's eyes slid away from hers and he found a sudden interest in readjusting the sleeves of his smart new coat. As this garment had been made by the great Weston himself and was of impeccable fit, it did not deserve the fussing to which it was now subjected.

Had she not been so preoccupied with her own thoughts, she would have been put on her guard.

"I was recommending a secretary to him," Rothworth replied in Percy's stead. "He will benefit from one now he has taken on the responsibilities of his title."

"That was most thoughtful of you," she said, looking across at him briefly. "I shan't disturb you both for long. I came only for a book."

She walked over to the shelves, picked up the first volume within reach and headed towards the door.

"May I speak with you in private?" Rothworth asked as she passed him.

She turned to him rather reluctantly. "Now?"

"If you are able to grant me the time."

"Could it wait? I don't wish to be disobliging but I'm somewhat occupied at present."

With an amused look, he gently pried the book from her hands and read the title.

"I had no idea my company ranked below *Agricultural Principles in the Midlands*. I am duly chastened."

His tone provoked a smile on her unwilling lips.

"Lord, Rory!" said Percy, frowning at her. "Surely you don't mean to put off His Grace so you can read some dull book?"

"I never said any such thing," she replied. "I was speaking of other matters when I said I was occupied . . . but, if it's important, they can wait for a few minutes. What would you like to say to me, Your Grace?"

"I'll leave you!" said Percy quickly.

"There is no need," she insisted.

"I have to prepare for the ball."

She regarded him cynically. "You have a good six hours to prepare, and I've never known you to take longer than twenty minutes to dress for anything!"

"Hopkins insists he needs the time," replied Percy, laying the blame on his new valet without compunction. "Says he wants to trim my hair."

Aurora raised an eyebrow but said no more to convince him to stay.

As Percy passed Rothworth on his way out, he went to give him a pat on the shoulder, paused mid-way and then quickly lowered his hand, appalled that he had attempted such a familiar gesture.

It was left to Rothworth to save him from embarrassment by shaking hands with him and saying: "I shall see you tonight."

"I look forward to it, sir."

Percy then surprised his sister by giving her a quick kiss on the cheek on his way out of the room.

She looked after him with a perplexed expression. "He seems rather pleased over something."

"Perhaps he is excited about tonight."

She laughed a little at this. "Unlikely! He admitted to me that he is nervous to be served up for general consumption. Although I couldn't say why! So far, everyone our grandmother has introduced to us has been polite and welcoming."

"He'll soon learn that the Marquess of Dewbury is welcome wherever he goes."

"As is the Duke of Rothworth, I imagine."

"Yes," he agreed, smiling.

"Speaking of Percy," she said as something occurred to her, "did he repay you the thirty pounds we owed you?"

"The money you stole?"

"Borrowed!" she corrected him with a playful look; then remembered his perfidy and quickly sobered. "Percy has been meaning to give it to you from the moment the lawyers released his funds. It's been playing on his mind, poor dear – he is shockingly respectable."

"Unlike his sister," he said with some amusement. "You may rest easy, he did attempt to give me the money, but I refused . . . I'm waiting to call in the boon that was offered to me."

She busied herself with repositioning a Sèvres porcelain ornament on a side table beside her.

"Of course. Is that why you are here? To claim it now?"

"Good God, no!" he said sharply. "My wish to speak with you has nothing at all to do with that boon – it's imperative you understand that!"

She looked back at him, puzzled by his vehemence. "Then why *do* you wish to speak with me?"

"Won't you be seated?" he said, indicating to one of two chairs in front of the large desk in the centre of the room.

She walked over and seated herself, while he retrieved some documents from the desk. After casting his eye over them, he handed them to her without a word and took the chair next to hers.

Brow furrowed, she glanced down at the papers in her hand.

"Contracts?" she asked.

"Of a type. I had my solicitors draw them up. Please take your time reading them. I think matters will become clear . . . you will understand once you've read them."

She was surprised to see him looking ill-at-ease.

"As you wish," she said, and began to read.

Her perplexed expression soon smoothed out and her face became a mask of impenetrability.

She turned the page.

After ten minutes or so, she put down the documents. He did not know what reaction he had expected, but it was certainly not what she now offered him: utter blankness.

"If I understand correctly, Your Grace," she said in a calm voice, "you are proposing to transfer over to me property and funds – rather excessive funds – to be held in my name . . . upon our marriage?"

"Yes." He watched her intently, trying to interpret her response.

"And if we have children," she went on, "and I decide to live apart from you, or even to divorce you, you have written an affidavit that you give permission for the children to reside with me."

"Yes."

"And is this affidavit legally enforceable considering the law gives the father all rights over the children?" she asked with mild curiosity.

"There's no clear precedent," he admitted. "My solicitors did all they could to alleviate your concerns, however, they informed me it's possible the affidavit could be discounted, depending on circumstances. I can only pledge you my word that I'll stand by it!"

The intensity of his vow caught her off guard.

"Thank you . . . I understand the value of that," she said softly.

She felt herself relenting towards him and had to quickly harden her heart before sentimentality overruled reason. Looking away, she took several moments to reassemble her armour.

"Thank you, Your Grace," she said at last, offering him a polite smile. "I can't but appreciate the lengths to which you have gone to allay my concerns regarding marriage. But it does beg the question: why?"

"Why?" he repeated dumbly.

He had a sense that she was furious with him, but his wits appeared to have temporarily deserted him and he could not for the life of him work out why.

"Is this," she held up the documents, "meant to be a marriage proposal?"

"You may call it that . . . if you wish," he said carefully, the words coming thickly to his tongue.

"May I? How charmingly original. But again, I must ask – and forgive me if I'm being particularly obtuse – why?"

"You need ask?"

"Clearly I do! Why do you want to marry me? Is it because you think I'll make a suitable wife for a politician? Or because I don't stand for any of your nonsense? Or because you like the colour of my hair? In a word, *why*?"

He felt as if he were sinking into a quagmire and could not see his way clear. "All that, of course . . . and more!"

"More?" she asked interestedly.

"Damn it, Aurora, I love you!" he burst out, and, leaning forward, took hold of her hands.

"Do you? Perhaps we understand the word differently," she said, allowing her anger to show at last. "Tell me, Your Grace, did you also draw up a generous contract for L'Incomparable when you courted *her*?"

She could see that she had disconcerted him, for he stilled and did not immediately respond.

All at once she found it unbearable to be in his presence and, wrenching her hands out of his, rose abruptly and rushed out of the room.

She felt as if she was suffocating.

Jealousy was a new emotion for her, and she was staggered by its insidious power; one was wholly at its mercy.

She marched out the front door with little thought to where she was going. The rain had eased from a torrent to a shower, but it was still strong enough to quickly soak through her clothing. She hardly noticed; until Mr Brinkley's butler ran after her with an umbrella and begged her to take it.

She thanked him in a mechanical way and continued walking.

How dare he presume she would be willing to share him with another woman!

Had he been thinking about his mistress when they had been together at Dewbury Abbey?

In the closet?

"Ergh, I detest jealously!" she cried out suddenly, startling a man hurrying past her in the opposite direction.

She picked up her pace, as if to run away from her emotions. Within minutes, she was entering St James Park and setting off down one of the paths towards the river. There was no one about, only her and the swans, and the stillness soon served as a balm for her soul.

Just as she was beginning to find a measure of peace, a voice called out her name, and, looking around, she saw Rothworth jogging towards her.

He had no umbrella, his hair was plastered to his head, and he was unusually pale . . . but he was smiling.

Aurora wanted to hit him.

"I don't want to talk to you," she stated as calmly as she could and continued down the path.

He caught up and matched her pace.

"I must apologise," he said. "I made a hash of things!"

She looked across at him and saw that he was still smiling. "And that amuses you, does it?"

He had the effrontery to outright grin at her.

"Do you realise, until now, you had not given me any indication that you were suffering as much as I was – not once! So, you'll have to forgive me if I'm rather overjoyed about it."

"Is this meant to be an apology?" she asked, becoming riled despite her best efforts. "If it is, it's an appalling attempt! Do you seriously mean to tell me you are delighted that I am suffering?"

"No . . . yes! I'm trying to tell you I'm elated beyond reason to finally know that you love me. And not just as a damned friend!"

"Of all the pompous, self-congratulatory . . . " She looked straight ahead once more and twirled her umbrella so that it blocked him from her view. After a moment of inner struggle, she could not stop herself from saying: "I don't see how you can think that I love you."

"You're jealous," he said simply.

She twirled the umbrella around to reveal him, her eyes snapping wrathfully.

"You ask me to marry you – if handing a woman a contract can be called a marriage proposal! – and all the while you have a mistress in your keeping. I would have to be an imbecile not to be jealous! But I promise you, I shan't suffer this ghastly emotion for long." Turning her gaze back on the path, she increased her pace. "So, if you would just leave me alone and be on your way, I'd be much obliged to you."

"I'm never leaving you! Do you hear me? Never!"

"I hear you perfectly well, there's no need to shout!"

"Good. Because now that I know you love me there's only one way this is going to end."

"And how is that exactly?" she asked pleasantly. "In a cosy *ménage à trois*?"

"For the love of God . . . would you stop and look at me!"

He pulled her around to face him and almost had his eye taken out by the umbrella.

He grabbed hold of the handle. "May I?"

She nodded, thinking he wished to hold the umbrella over the both of them; but instead, he plucked it out of her hand and threw it down the shallow bank beside the path.

Aurora followed its progress as it rolled several times and landed in the mud by the river. She threw him a look that said she thought he had lost his wits.

Taking hold of her shoulders, he peered intently at her through the rain.

"Allow me to make something very clear to you, you daft woman – I don't have a mistress! I've lived like a bloody monk for months! Ever since you came hurtling into my life like some damned whirlwind and upended my well-ordered existence with your meddling and managing."

She returned his heated gaze in stunned silence.

Somewhere in the recesses of her mind, it occurred to her that her hold on reason must be more tenuous than she could have ever imagined, for Rothworth's decidedly unloverlike words had evaporated all the perfectly valid arguments she had constructed to protect herself.

"You know, Julian," she said at length, "your language is utterly atrocious. I thought you were known as a paragon of civility?"

"You've turned me into an undisciplined, emotional fool!"

The passion in his blue-grey eyes was tempered by a look of such longing that it quite took her breath away.

She lifted a hand to smooth his wet hair away from his face. "I always knew you weren't a cold fish."

She suddenly found herself hauled up against him and kissed with a thoroughness that proved just how right she had been.

After several minutes, he pulled away and said with something of a growl: "Now *that's* how you kiss a man if you want to distract him – not those chaste pecks you gave me! And for the record: *no*, the documents I gave you were not a marriage proposal, they were meant to set the ground for one. And if you ever want to hear that proposal you're going to have to earn it! I meant what I said: the next time you kiss me it will be given freely, and I'll know you understand all it implies . . . and, it doesn't count if I'm the one kissing you!" He kissed her again to prove his point. "So, take as long as you need to go through those documents with your solicitor . . . no, don't interrupt! You *will* seek his counsel – I insist on it! I want you to understand exactly what you'll be getting yourself into, because I tell you now, I'll not stand for any regrets in future!"

"Julian, you are being quite ruthless," protested Aurora, thrilled to be addressed in such masterful terms.

His eyes, which she had suspected from the first were capable of flashes of passion, warned her that she was about to be kissed again.

Sadly, before he could carry out this gratifying threat, a gruff voice shattered the moment by demanding: "Is this gentleman molesting you, Miss?"

Aurora started, and broke free of Rothworth's arms.

She had only an instant to perceive the park ranger, standing under an umbrella and looking censorious, before the sodden ground beneath her feet gave way . . . with a little shriek she slid down the shallow bank, arms flailing, and landed on her posterior in the mud.

The shock and indignity of her situation was too much for her gravity and she burst out laughing.

Rothworth thought she looked demented; drenched to the bone, covered in mud, no hat or gloves, her long hair coming out of its pins and plastered about her, and all the while laughing uncontrollably.

It was the most beautiful sight he had ever seen.

He walked down the slope and offered her his hand.

"Oh, you shouldn't have come down!" she cried. "Your beautiful boots are now ruined."

"You should see the state of you!" he returned, grinning. "And besides, someone once counselled me that I should jump into the mud and stop observing life from a safe distance."

"How wonderfully literal of you," she replied, gazing up at him with such raw emotion that he knew he would never forget this moment for as long as he lived.

Taking hold of her hands, he attempted to pull her up; but the mud sucked on her clothing and would not let her go. He tried again, more forcefully, lost his footing and landed on top of her, flattening her.

She let out a faint groan.

"Are you hurt?" he asked sharply, attempting to shift his weight off her.

"No . . . " she replied, gasping. "You merely knocked the breath . . . out of me a little."

"See here," yelled the ranger, "I'll have none of that business in my park! This ain't a fancy house! You get off her this instant, mister – you hear me?"

"What the deuce does he think I'm doing to you?" said Rothworth exasperatedly.

Sitting back onto his knees, he helped her into a sitting position.

"Whatever one does in a fancy house, I imagine," she replied, dissolving into laughter again. "Only, I had no idea they catered for a mud perversion!"

"It shall certainly be one of mine from now on." Reaching out, he moved a wet tendril away from her eye and tucked it behind her ear. "Let's get you home before you catch your death of cold."

"Oh, I stopped being cold a while ago! But to make certain I'm warm enough on the way back, perhaps it's prudent for you to kiss me again. I'm not initiating the kiss, you understand, only suggesting a sensible course of action."

He took her head in his muddy hands.

"Sensible? You don't know the meaning of the word," he muttered and kissed her.

They ended up lying in the mud again.

This proved to be the last straw for the ranger's sensibilities, and he became belligerently vocal with his disapproval.

Rothworth raised his head and sighed. "We'd better go before that man has an apoplexy."

"Hmm," she nodded, disorientated.

"You certainly look like a gypsy now," he said tenderly.

After giving her one last, quick kiss, he managed to get them both to their feet, retrieved one of her shoes that had stuck in the mud, and then helped her back onto the path, with some assistance from the ranger, who was only too happy to expedite their removal from his park.

Having said a cheerful farewell to this indignant individual, Rothworth took off his coat and draped it over Aurora's shoulders to keep her warm, and, putting an arm around her, they set off for home, trailing mud in their wake.

After some minutes of silence, Aurora asked: "Did you know that people thought L'Incomparable was still your mistress?"

"Yes," he admitted, looking at her to see her reaction. "Belinda refuses to accept that it's over between us. She thinks she'll be able to change my mind, and in the meantime is telling anyone who'll listen that we're still together. We're not!"

Aurora accepted this with a smile. "She doesn't know you well at all if she thinks to change your mind with such tactics. Were you generous enough with her on parting?"

"An emerald necklace."

"Oh, that's a wonderful gift!" she said approvingly. "Then, perhaps the problem is that the poor woman is seriously attached to you and is deluding herself. It's unfortunate, certainly, but it can't be allowed to continue."

Rothworth had visions of Aurora marching into L'Incomparable's apartments and instructing her on how to rid herself of her delusions.

"Forget Belinda!" he said quickly. "I'll handle her. Had I the least notion that the story would reach your ears I would have dealt with it sooner."

Thunder rumbled above their heads, and, within moments, a deluge of rain followed. Rothworth held his coat above Aurora's head and they dashed across the square to the Brinkley townhouse.

The butler opened the door to them with evident relief, which was quickly followed by shock at their appearance.

Rothworth ushered Aurora inside, but he declined to enter himself. He instructed Levington to have a hot bath taken up to her room, then briefly raised her hand to his lips in silent farewell and left.

Aurora stayed looking after him for some time, a muddy puddle forming on the marble floor around her feet.

"Shall I see to your bath now, Lady Aurora?" prompted the butler, taking in her distracted state with an interested eye.

"Hmm? Oh, thank you, Levington . . . but first, I will need to see my solicitor. Immediately."

Thirty-Five

The Dewbury Ball was in full swing by the time Rothworth arrived, a little after ten o'clock that evening. He was impatient to see Aurora and had hoped to arrive earlier, but the inclement weather and the sheer numbers of carriages dropping off Lady Dewbury's guests, conspired against him.

He was looking *very fine* according to his sister, who had had an opportunity to admire his appearance when he had come into the drawing room to say his goodbyes to her. Not yet being out, she was not allowed to accompany him to the ball and had been sulking most of the day. However, her grievances had been forgotten on seeing him in his cream waistcoat, black velvet coat, and black knee-breeches and stockings.

Exclaiming that he would be the most handsome man there, she had added that if a certain lady was present, she would find it exceedingly difficult to refuse him anything tonight.

What he thought of this sally she was never to know, for he had distracted her by promising to dress with even greater elegance for her own coming-out ball next year; and as he had then proceeded to provide a detailed and marvellous description of this longed-for event, she had been in raptures by the end and had seen him off in the best of spirits.

Over an hour later, Rothworth entered the Dewbury mansion and almost immediately caught sight of Captain Torrington.

The captain, who was privately delighted that the Season was drawing to a close, was there playing escort to his mother and sister, and on seeing his friend, called him over to join them in the line winding its way through the house to where Lady Dewbury was welcoming her guests.

There was a good deal of noise around them, with many conversations going on at once, as well as acquaintances calling out greetings to them. During a lull in these exchanges, the crowd shifted and Rothworth overhead his name mentioned by a matron in gold satin, a few feet ahead of him.

" . . . yes, he was at the opera," she was saying to her friend. "And the sister and brother too . . . the new marquess is most handsome – the image of his grandfather, they say! . . . The sister? Well, I won't say she isn't pretty, for she is – in a common way, you understand – but I was surprised at how free she was with her smiles . . . yes, indeed! *Particularly* when the duke was nearby, if you take my meaning . . . mighty comfortable in his company . . . not at all conscious of how high she was aiming!"

Captain Torrington had also become aware of the conversation and raised an eyebrow at Rothworth. He would have spoken, but Rothworth shook his head at him and moved so that his friend blocked him from view of the women.

"He danced attendance on her all evening," went on the lady. "But he's done the same before with any number of girls . . . *they* all had youth and beauty on their side . . . he is merely amusing himself until he tires of her . . . I'm not the only one who thinks so. Lady Placket and Countess Strossberg – did I mention the countess is a friend of mine? – were kind enough to share their thoughts with me."

The woman's friend said something behind her fan, and the two of then tittered.

"One can't help feeling sorry for her," the lady in yellow continued. "She's bound to suffer a disappointment . . . of course, some might say it's only what she deserves for her presumption, but *I* would not be so severe . . . does her no credit, however, to think she can appear out of nowhere and ensnare him . . . worthier girls have failed. My own Lara once stood up with him to dance, did you know? He was most gracious . . . such refined manners . . . "

The queue began to move again, the crowd shifted, and the two ladies drifted off.

Rothworth stepped to the side to allow others in the line to overtake him. Captain Torrington joined him; he could see his friend was struggling with a rare anger.

"You're taking their babble mighty hard, Julian," he observed. "What do you care what some inconsequential tattletales say about you?"

"I don't – though Countess Strossberg is neither inconsequential, nor generally considered a tattletale. But I'll be damned if I'll allow anyone to speak of Aurora in such terms!"

"You're on a first name basis now, are you?" the captain asked with a meaningful smile.

"Rupert, if you don't rid yourself of that blasted smirk we're going to come to blows," snapped Rothworth. "You're speaking of my future wife." Seeing he had surprised his friend, he added with uncharacteristic hostility: "And the sooner you get used to the idea and direct your outrageous flirting at someone else, the better it will go for you!"

The captain laughed and put up his hands in a gesture of surrender.

"It took you long enough to realise you were in love with the girl! When's the wedding?"

Having already said more than he wished, Rothworth ignored the question and moved back into the line.

"Go and catch up with your mother and sister," he said. "I'll see you inside."

Captain Torrington raised both eyebrows at his dismissal, and, smiling with what his friend considered to be a maddening amount of cocksure amusement, went off.

By the time Rothworth presented himself to Lady Dewbury he had himself back under control.

The dowager marchioness – who due to her age was receiving her guests while seated, flanked on one side by Lord and Lady Charles and on the other by Aurora and Percy – received him with a genuine smile of welcome. Having spent several weeks observing him and her granddaughter, she held certain suspicions that she was eager to see come to fruition.

While her family exchanged greetings with the duke, she cast her gaze over Aurora and thought to herself that if anything could drive a man to propose, Aurora's appearance tonight would cement the deed. She herself, though she had few prudish pretensions, had been a little startled on first laying eyes on her granddaughter, when she had arrived for dinner earlier in the evening with her brother and the Brinkleys.

Aurora's eye-catching red velvet dress had been cut daringly low across the bosom and fitted rather closely to her tall, shapely figure; none of which should have been a surprise to the dowager, for she had approved the design, however, she had not imagined that the dress, once on her granddaughter, would entice the imagination to such a degree.

But there was more to Aurora's allure than simply her clothing. Her burnished hair had been loosely curled and pinned to fall dashingly over one creamy shoulder; her dark, expressive eyes held glints of humour; and her mobile face was alive with some inner happiness.

All in all, she was destined to leave a lasting impression on all who saw her tonight.

Thinking of a different kind of impression, Lady Dewbury addressed Rothworth: "My grandchildren have been at my side for over an hour and must be in need of rest and refreshment by now. Would you be good enough to escort them in, Your Grace?"

"It would be my pleasure," replied Rothworth, understanding her.

Before she left, Aurora took pity on her aunt and uncle, who had been standing at their post for as long as anyone, and told them she would send over a footman with some iced champagne for them.

She earned a heartfelt look of thanks from Lady Charles; while Lord Charles, who was sweating profusely, made her smile by offering her a comical grimace of misery from behind his handkerchief, as he went to wipe his brow.

With Rothworth on one side and Percy on the other, Aurora began the descent into the sunken ballroom. The impressive space, which appeared to be constructed wholly out of marble, was lit with the light of a thousand beeswax candles and was already full to overflowing with guests.

It was a glittering sight, especially when viewed from above, and, together with the sound and heat emanating from the room, someone who had never before attended such an event could be forgiven for being overwhelmed.

Aurora barely noticed.

It was impossible to know how to act towards a man once you had rolled around in the mud with him, and inevitably she had suffered from a few qualms before Rothworth's arrival. But these had been displaced by exasperation as soon as he had greeted her with barely more than a nod, and had then proceeded to act as though they hardly knew each other.

She had stolen several glances at him to better understand his mood, and each time he had caught her looking he had offered her such a bland, polite expression that she could have happily throttled him.

She resolved to take her lead from him and, maddening though it was, to act as if nothing out of the ordinary had occurred; but that did not preclude her from needling him a little.

"I hope you realise, dearest," she told her brother, "that His Grace has been enlisted to lend us countenance? It seems our grandmother fears we can't survive on our own merit and need a mature, stalwart sponsor to take us under his wing."

Rothworth did not react.

"I did wonder why I was asked to be the third wheel," Percy replied cheerfully. "I imagine I'm very much in the way!"

Aurora looked across at him with surprise. She had not said a word to anyone about what had passed between herself and Rothworth.

"Why would you think you would be in the way?" she asked cautiously.

Her brother's smile told her that he was not going to fall for any prevarication.

Understanding dawned and she turned from him to Rothworth. "In the library, were you speaking to Percy about *me*?" she asked.

"You may have come up," Rothworth replied evenly.

"We also spoke about secretaries," put in Percy, grinning at her. "I happen to agree with His Grace on both subjects . . . so do Miss Brinkley and Miss Coral. And I suspect Grandmama does too! As for Mr Brinkley, he's been rather pre-occupied with your monkey and as yet may not have realised which way the wind was blowing."

"Enough, you brazen whelp," Rothworth said mildly.

"You discussed me with *everyone*?" Aurora asked him indignantly, trying to keep the annoyance from her expression, given that hundreds of pairs of eyes were watching their progress from below.

"You have the matter in reverse," he replied. "Everyone found it necessary to bring up the matter with me . . . or rather, my aunts did, no one else would have the effrontery. You brother's counsel is the only one I actually sought."

Before Aurora could ask him to explain further, they had finished their descent into the ballroom and were surrounded by a throng of people, all eager for a few words with the young marquess and his sister.

As Rothworth set about establishing their characters, nothing in his expression or language hinted at anything more than avuncular interest in his new friends.

However, several of the more observant guests noticed him, with little more than a cool look, depress the pretensions of any gentleman who showed too blatant an interest in Lady Aurora; and they also saw the proprietorial way he placed a hand on her back to remove her from the vicinity of those same gentlemen.

"I have the distinct impression we are being scrutinised," Aurora remarked, a while later, as Rothworth led her onto the dancefloor for the first waltz of the night.

She was a little irritated with him for keeping her at a distance all evening. But since she possessed a healthy appreciation of her own self-worth and was not given to irrational flights of fancy, she had not once been tormented by the idea that he might be regretting what had passed between them earlier in the day.

She assumed he had either adopted his reserved society manners out of habit, or something had occurred to put him out of temper.

When he took her gloved hand in his and put an arm around her waist, she regarded him with wry amusement. But he avoided her gaze, and so her subtle attempt to bring his incongruous behaviour to his attention proved unsuccessful.

"Did you not expect some scrutiny?" he asked, his eyes fixed on a point above her head.

"I can't say I gave it much thought," she replied.

"You and your brother have come back from the dead – or near enough – to successfully claim one of the most coveted titles in the kingdom." He began to twirl her past the other couples. "I should have warned you that you would be notorious for a good while . . . or at least until you've been dissected on the altar of Society's curiosity," he added somewhat bitterly. "You must take care not to give them any fodder or you'll only prolong their feeding frenzy."

"Oh, they don't frighten me!" she said. "And I don't even begrudge them their curiosity . . . but you misunderstood! I was not referring to Percy and me being scrutinised, rather *you* and me. Several jaws dropped almost to the ground when you led me onto the dancefloor."

"I rarely attend balls," he said, as if that explained matters.

"And now you astound the room by condescending to dance with me – I'm honoured!"

"I have no aversion to dancing."

"Naturally," she said with great irony. "Which leaves me to conclude that your aversion is to my company."

He glanced down at her sharply. "You know that's not true."

"I thought I did," she said with a pensive smile. "But something has put you out of temper and I can't help but wonder what?"

"Forgive me . . . I don't like to have you so exposed to people's judgement," he said, looking away again.

"You must not take it so to heart! *I* don't."

She had hoped to prompt him into letting down his guard, but his expression remained impassive and he did not respond.

"You do it beautifully, by the way," she said after a pause, undaunted. "Dancing, I mean."

"As do you."

"Thank you! I'm happy to know you don't find my efforts contemptible. Why do you not attend balls?"

"I feel remarkably like prey," he admitted after a pause, his disgruntled tone making her smile.

"Well, you may have a point! I couldn't help but notice the number of ladies who follow you about the room. They put me forcibly in mind of that

German story – *The Pied Piper of Hamelin*. Most uncomfortable for you! Have they always made a nuisance of themselves?"

"One fainted in front of my carriage once. My man barely managed to keep the horses from trampling her. Another time, a mother and daughter followed me to the races and bribed the stable manager so they could enter and be there when I visited my horse after the race. One of them – I scarcely remember who! – was wearing the most monstrous hat, and Pegasus had the good sense to eat half of it. You should have heard the screeching! She had to be bodily escorted from the stables before the horses could kick down their stalls."

"How . . . enterprising!" she said on a gurgle of laughter. "I now understand your reaction the first time we met. I don't blame you in the least for thinking me a conniving chit!"

"You *were* conniving, just not in the way I imagined," he pointed out, unable to hide his amusement. He glanced down at her again. "I don't encourage them, you know."

"I know," she replied with a soft smile.

He tore his gaze away from her.

"While I think of it," he said, "I must thank you for saving me earlier. Lady Anne is more determined than most."

"The girl who accosted you? Well, that's certainly one word for her! I'm afraid I was a little rude, but really, a torn sleeve is the least she deserved. Does she always drape herself over you in that vulgar fashion?"

"She has been known to." A smile touched his lips. "You were remarkably effective in detaching her. I could have used your help on a few other occasions I don't care to remember."

"If I must continue to trip and tear the clothing of every woman who shows an interest in you, I'll soon acquire a shocking reputation for clumsiness! Don't get me wrong, I'm willing to sacrifice myself for a friend, I only point out I'll become a social pariah in the process."

"A friend?" he said with sudden harshness, his eyes locking with hers. "You expect too much of me!"

"How?" she asked, baffled.

"If you think, after this afternoon, I'll allow you to see me as something so lukewarm as a *friend* . . . " He broke off as he struggled to recover his sangfroid. "I've given you a reprieve, nothing more!"

"Really, Julian, I find you incomprehensible at times," she protested. "From the way you've been acting tonight you can hardly expect me to have guessed how you felt. One minute you're cool and remote, as if we hardly know each other, and the next as if you used to dangle me on your knee when I was a babe! Not to mention, you have barely looked at me all evening."

"God's teeth, woman! Can't you understand why I dare not look at you?" he demanded; and for a moment he allowed her to see behind his controlled veneer.

She felt scorched.

"You'll be set upon by every gossip-monger in attendance if I looked at you as I wish!" he said savagely; his hand splaying across her back and pulling her closer.

"I'm not so poor-spirited as to be afraid of a little gossip," she insisted somewhat breathlessly.

"You don't understand," he sighed, schooling his features and looking away. "What you've never appreciated – and I thank the heavens for it! – is that I'm considered one of the biggest matrimonial prizes in the kingdom. If there's even a hint of something between us, there'll be a good deal of disappointment and jealously in some quarters. And until they see a formal engagement notice in the papers, they'll feel at liberty to lash out at you, any which way they can . . . *you* will be the one to suffer, not I. And I can't allow that."

"But I can't suffer if I don't care what they say of me," she pointed out.

"Don't ask me to lay you open to insult, or to tarnish your reputation – I won't do it!"

All this angst was, of course, highly gratifying; however, Aurora saw no reason to prolong it.

"Then it's fortunate we need not wait! My solicitor visited me earlier and we discussed the documents you gave me in some detail – as you insisted! So, you see, I don't need the reprieve you so thoughtfully . . . "

"Don't!" he cut her off. "I'll not have you rush your decision – not when I know your thoughts on marriage only too well! I've been tormented for weeks thinking I might never be able to convince you to put your trust in me; I can wait a few more days to give you the time to be certain. For when you come to me, love, it must be without any reservations."

"But, Julian, I have already made up my mind!"

"I think it's best," he said, his voice implacable, "if we don't speak again tonight."

Recognising futility when she came across it, Aurora decided to hold her tongue; only pointing out in a droll voice that if he wanted to avoid gossip, he might consider not holding her so tightly against him.

He immediately put a few inches of space between them, and they finished the rest of the waltz in silence.

*   *   *

"My nephew appears to be in a surprisingly inauspicious mood," Miss Brinkley remarked, as she watched Rothworth's retreating back.

As soon as the waltz had finished, he had escorted Aurora to where his aunts were standing, in conversation with a group of middle-aged matrons, and with barely a word to anyone had taken himself off again.

"He is," agreed Aurora with a secret smile.

"What have you been doing to the poor boy?" asked Miss Coral, stepping away from her friends to join them where they stood a little apart.

"Why would you think I had anything to do with it, ma'am?" asked Aurora wide-eyed.

"Don't act all innocent with me, Aurora dear. I have lived with you long enough to know there is a good deal of mischief and mayhem in that pretty head of yours. And besides, it has been obvious to me for some time that no one can drive my nephew to distraction as you can."

"I truly don't mean to . . . at least, not *often*," Aurora corrected herself.

Miss Brinkley regarded her with a good deal of comprehension. "I cannot blame you for tormenting him a little. Rothworth has always been too complacent when it came to women – they do make such fools of themselves over him! – which is why some turmoil and uncertainty will do him good."

Aurora remembered that the sisters had spoken to their nephew in regard to herself, and had probably guessed a good deal of what lay between them.

"I only ask," went on Miss Brinkley, "that you do not keep him in this state for too much longer. I fear he has lost all interest in his parliamentary responsibilities, and he must turn his attention to the crime bill I want him to sponsor . . . and Dr Moore also has some thoughts on a bill for the compassionate treatment of the insane," she added.

For the last few weeks, the good doctor had not been far from Miss Brinkley's thoughts, and though he could not attend tonight, owing to an unexpected birthing, he was still casting his influence over her. The splendid gown of silver lace and silk that she wore had been designed with him in mind, and her hair had been pinned into a flattering style that had found favour with him in the past. But though he might be in her thoughts, not by one look did Miss Brinkley betray that she missed his presence.

"Is Julian's suit not prospering, Aurora dear?" asked Miss Coral. "Has he not been able to overcome your aversion to marriage?"

"Do you mean to have him or not?" Miss Brinkley enquired outright.

"I can't imagine my life without him," replied Aurora, deciding there was no point in dissimulating. "My mind is made up, but he is trying so hard to be noble that he refuses to listen to me! He will not even look at me for fear he will somehow besmirch my reputation. I had no idea my reputation was balanced so precariously on the precipice of disaster that a mere *look* would be enough to destroy it!"

"That is certainly ridiculous," scoffed Miss Brinkley. "Did he really say so?"

"Yes! Something about not giving Society any more fodder."

"What does that mean?" asked Miss Coral, overcome with confusion.

"I couldn't say for certain," replied Aurora, "but he appears to think that by showing a preference for me in public he will lay me open to insult . . . or something of that nature – his reasoning was rather convoluted. And the upshot is, he will now barely glance in my direction!"

"That must be difficult to do when you're wearing *that* dress, Aurora dear, "observed Miss Coral, looking her over appreciatively. "Dear Phoebe told me earlier, as she was seeing us off, that you were *all the crack* – apparently it means the height of fashion – and I must say I agree wholeheartedly. It is a most modish creation – not to mention, exceedingly enticing! It reminds me of a dress I once wore, oh, many years ago! Red as well," she said with a fond, reminiscent smile. "It led to a great deal of naughtiness . . . which, I freely admit, I enjoyed excessively."

Aurora laughed behind her fan.

"Coral!" exclaimed Miss Brinkley, frowning at her sister.

"What? I didn't go into any detail! And, besides, it's not as if we need fear such behaviour from Julian. I'm certain *he* would never be tempted into such wickedness."

"No," sighed Aurora regretfully. "He has a most exasperating amount of self-control."

"That is too true," said Miss Brinkley. "I believe you know my thoughts on his father."

Their conversation was interrupted at this point by Mr Brinkley, who walked over to claim his dance with Aurora.

Though he had a dislike of balls – or indeed any large social gathering – he had insisted on coming to show his support. He had been hiding for most of the night in one of the alcoves behind a potted palm, with another gentleman of introverted leanings, but as Aurora had insisted on reserving a quadrille for him, and as this dance was about to begin, he had plucked up the courage to leave his sanctuary.

Aurora suspected much of this and was greatly moved by his exertions on behalf of herself and her brother. She accepted his arm with every evidence of pleasure and spent the next half an hour on the dancefloor doing all she could to make the experience enjoyable for him.

When he escorted her back to his sisters, she thanked him prettily and, knowing it was his preference, suggested he might wish to re-join his friend, as this gentleman appeared to be waiting for him so that they could continue their conversation.

When her brother had gratefully retreated to his alcove, Miss Coral returned to their conversation as if no interruption had occurred.

"You know, Aurora dear, it occurs to Pearl and me that Rothworth's fixation with safe-guarding your reputation would be superfluous if only he would get on and propose to you – as we thought he was on the point of doing days ago! Do you know what could be keeping him?"

Aurora rolled her eyes expressively as she fanned her flushed cheeks.

"If you can believe it, I am to have a reprieve so that I can come to know my own mind."

"Good Lord," said Miss Brinkley with exasperation.

"Exactly so, ma'am," agreed Aurora. "He appears to have mistaken me for a child who needs to be protected from herself. Fortunately for the both of us, I have no intention of tolerating such nonsense! I have always believed it's best to set out as you mean to go on, and he will soon learn that he will not always get his own way with me."

"What will you do?" asked Miss Coral all agog.

Aurora smiled and looked from one sister to the other. "I have a plan, but I shall need your help."

"I trust it will be nothing outrageous?" said Miss Brinkley.

"Oh no, not outrageous!" Aurora assured her.

"Indiscreet perhaps?" suggested Miss Coral, looking at her with amusement.

"Well, I wouldn't call it *discreet* exactly. But it will be entirely respectable!"

"It's not that we don't trust you, Aurora dear, but sometimes it does seem as if your definition of respectable differs a little from Society's."

"Which is why, dear ma'am," Aurora replied with aplomb, "I shall need you and Miss Brinkley to keep me from doing anything too shocking!"

Thirty-Six

For the last hour Rothworth had been sitting at one of the dozen card-tables that had been set up in a parlour, just off the ballroom, for the entertainment of the guests. He was playing faro with a recklessness that was unusual for him, but that seemed to serve him well on this occasion, for he was holding the bank and had a substantial pile of winnings in front of him.

He did not see Aurora enter the room, or notice her make her way over to where Captain Torrington stood behind him, watching the play with several other gentlemen.

The captain smiled at Aurora in welcome and made room for her beside him.

After a few minutes of studying the game, she asked him quietly: "Does His Grace always play so recklessly?"

"I've never seen him do so before. Something has riled him tonight, I believe," replied the captain, sending her a speculative look.

"Yes, I know! I hope to soon save him from further aggravation. But, first, I'm afraid he is bound to become a little more riled. I tell you this because I may need to call on you to aid me – may I count on you?"

"I look forward to it!" he replied. "And shall probably enjoy it more that I should."

Aurora laughed, and the sound brought her to Rothworth's attention.

He turned and looked up at her, frowning. "What are you doing here?"

His tone so lacked its customary civility that several persons noted it with surprise.

"Why, watching the play, Your Grace," she replied, offering him an artless smile.

He turned back to the game without another word and to all appearances seemed to forget that she was there; but those watching noticed that his play became more ferocious (though they could only guess at the reason) and by the end of half an hour he had either driven away the other players at his table or won most of their money.

"You've the devil's own luck tonight, Rothworth," complained a gentleman with whiskers as he threw his hand onto the table and stood. "There's no winning against you – I'm out!"

"I must be done as well," said the last remaining player, an obese, elderly lady with a jovial face supported by several chins.

If her proportions had not drawn the eye, then her purple turban, decorated with ostrich plumes that curled about her head in startling profusion, would have done so.

"I've had a great deal of pleasure losing to you, my dear duke," she went on, "but I've learnt to limit myself to two thousand a night."

"Please accept my apologies, Mrs Jameson," said Rothworth, standing and going over to help her to rise out of her chair. "You will certainly have the opportunity to recoup your losses from me in the future. My luck can't hold out against your skill forever."

She chuckled and rapped him on the knuckles with her fan.

"Flatterer! I've nowhere near your abilities and don't I know it! You must find yourself a more worthy adversary . . . and I hope you won't mind me saying, I would greatly enjoy seeing you get your comeuppance!"

"Allow me to be your champion, Mrs Jameson," said Aurora stepping forwards and drawing everyone's eyes. "I believe we were introduced earlier, ma'am?"

"Yes, indeed!" replied the elderly lady. "After you so nimbly tripped over Lady Anne's train! I must tell you, I appreciated your ability to catch yourself before you could topple her . . . or do I mean *restrain* yourself?" She chortled, pleased with her own wit. "But what is this I hear? Do you seriously mean to take on Rothworth and win?"

"I mean to try," replied Aurora. "From what I've observed, he plays with a certain laxity that is crying out to be exploited."

Mrs Jameson was delighted by this audacity. "The young lady has thrown down the gauntlet, duke! What do you plan to do about it?"

"I have had enough of cards for tonight and must disappoint her," he said indifferently. "But allow me to escort you back to the ballroom, ma'am."

"I am rebuffed!" Aurora exclaimed tragically, eliciting smiles from several gentlemen. "I should have kept my opinion of His Grace's play to myself. But what is to be done, ma'am? Only one of us dares accept your challenge."

"Surely you don't mean to refuse to play Lady Aurora?" Mrs Jameson pressed Rothworth.

"As you yourself pointed out, ma'am, my luck is in tonight, and it would be ungentlemanly of me to relieve the lady of her money."

"You had no such compunction about relieving me of *mine*," retorted Mrs Jameson, provoking an outburst of laughter from the group that had formed around them.

"You, ma'am, are a seasoned gambler," Rothworth replied smoothly. "I don't take money from babes."

"Oh, I'm determined to make you eat your words, Your Grace!" said Aurora. "And to assuage your fine sensibilities we will not play for money . . . we will play for a kiss."

A shocked silence followed this pronouncement.

Aurora saw the tell-tale clench of a muscle on Rothworth's cheek.

"If His Grace bests me," she went on blithely, holding up an arm encased in white silk, "he will earn for himself a kiss on my hand."

A few low chuckles were heard as people realised she was toying with their assumptions.

"And if you win, Lady Aurora?" asked a gentleman.

"Why, the same, of course," she replied demurely. Her eyes returned to Rothworth. "So, you see, Your Grace, your scruples are unnecessary. If you win, I forfeit nothing of value."

However, if *she* won, they both knew what she forfeited . . . a lifetime.

"You will have to excuse me," he said, abominably casual. Turning to Mrs Jameson, he offered her his arm. "Shall we, ma'am?"

The elderly woman looked from him to Aurora and back again. There were undercurrents at play here and she had every expectation of being wonderfully entertained by these two young people.

"Thank you, duke, but I think I shall remain and see if Lady Aurora can find someone else on whom to test her skill."

"Perhaps Captain Torrington wouldn't be averse to the challenge?" said Aurora.

"I am at your service," he replied at once, bowing gallantly.

On lifting his head, however, he encountered a look of such suppressed violence from Rothworth that he felt a moment of hesitation.

"Don't desert me now, captain," Aurora murmured.

"Never," he replied quietly. "But I don't hold any hope of surviving with my skin intact."

Aurora winked at him; and taking a seat at the card-table, asked: "Do you have a preference for a particular game, Captain Torrington?"

"Lady's choice," he replied.

"In that case, let us play *Vingt-Un*." She glanced at Rothworth, and her smile was just for him as she said: "I like the odds."

Captain Torrington agreed to it and went to sit opposite her, but as he reached his seat Rothworth casually thrust him aside and took the chair for himself.

"I believe the lady wishes to pit her skill against someone who actually has a modicum of skill," he remarked, prompting some laugher.

Captain Torrington looked relieved that he had got off so lightly, and, after good-naturedly accepting the jibes sent his way, settled down to watch the game.

"You do realise," Rothworth told Aurora, his manner insouciant, "that some might consider the card-room a male-domain . . . though I am not inclined to agree with them." He directed a nod of deference at Mrs Jameson.

This lady had retaken her seat, ordered a drink from a passing footman, and looked to be happily settling in for a bout of entertainment.

"It did cross my mind," replied Aurora. "But when your aunts came in to play a game of whist, I knew I need have no qualms in following them."

She gestured behind him, and for the first time he saw Miss Brinkley and Miss Coral playing at a small table with two of their friends.

Sensing her nephew's eyes on her, Miss Coral looked up and offered him a jaunty wave, before returning her attention to the game.

Rothworth turned back to Aurora, and she thought she saw a glimmer of a smile in his eyes.

"You appear to have thought of everything," he remarked.

"Thank you!"

"It wasn't a compliment."

"It is to me."

"You are impatient and impetuous."

"And you are too used to having your own way."

"I'm surprised no one has been driven to throttle you by now," he said with the greatest amiability imaginable.

The ready laughter leapt into her eyes. "Do you mean to distract me with sweet words, Your Grace?"

"Whatever it takes to win. Can I order you a drink? Champagne, brandy? Laudanum?"

"It is kind of you to offer! Lemonade will suffice. Your play may be reckless, but the luck appears to favour you, and I have no wish to give you any advantage. I play to win tonight."

"Don't think I mean to reward you with an easy victory," he warned.

"I would expect no less!"

A footman was called, and the drinks ordered.

Aurora shuffled the cards and laid one in front of Rothworth and another in front of herself; his card being the highest, he took on the role of dealer.

He reshuffled the pack and dealt them two cards each, one at a time.

"Do you stand?" he asked.

"Another please."

She checked the new card and decided to stand.

Rothworth drew one additional card, then threw up his hand on the table . . . twenty-one.

She nodded graciously in acknowledgment of his win. Captain Torrington put himself forward to keep score and the play continued.

Once the whole pack had been dealt, Rothworth's score won him the first round.

In the second round Aurora took over as dealer on winning a hand with a *Natural Vingt-Un* of an ace and a ten; but Rothworth once again won overall with the highest score.

They were partway through the next round when a suspicion that had been growing in his mind became a conviction. Aurora was trifling with him.

She was using considerable skill to allow him to stay just ahead of her in the scores. Had he not already reached such a conclusion, he would have certainly done so on looking up and encountering a smile of great innocence from her.

"You either play to win or don't play at all!" he told her severely.

Aurora laughed, delighted; she had been waiting for this moment.

"Is that what you really want?" she asked, bracing her arms on the table and leaning forward. "If I win, I will claim my prize freely?"

"But a different *prize* to what was agreed at the time.

"No specifics were discussed."

"Was my demonstration not sufficient explanation?" he asked.

Remembering the passionate kiss, Aurora felt the heat creep into her cheeks.

Their audience, listening with avid interest, wondered what exactly was being exchanged between them.

"Nevertheless," Rothworth went on, "I concede your point."

"You do?" she said with an arch look. "Even if it means abandoning your cherished *reprieve*?"

"You have forced my hand."

"I had to."

"Do you plan on ever doing anything I ask of you?"

"If I find it reasonable. You would do no different!"

He grunted noncommittally. "May I suggest we return out attention to the game? I'm going to need to be on my mettle if I hope to win."

He went on to win the third round; but only by one hand. And thereafter, as he had suspected, it went very much the worse for him. To murmurs of admiration and the occasional applause, Aurora won four rounds in quick succession.

They were coming to the end of the next round, evenly matched in points, and she had only to win the hand to win the game.

This, however, appeared to be unlikely.

Rothworth was holding, and was seemingly very satisfied with his hand, while Aurora had already picked up four cards and was reaching for a fifth, greatly increasing her chances of going bust.

Rothworth raised an eyebrow. "Five?"

She merely smiled and turned her attention to her hand. Slowly, one by one, she lay down her cards.

Two. Three. Four. Five. Seven.

Exclamations of astonishment and clapping erupted all around them.

"Your calculation of the odds is astonishing," Rothworth told her through the noise, regarding her as if she were a rare and wonderful creature.

"You must know I had added incentive tonight," she returned. "And now, Your Grace, I would like to claim my prize . . . if you are amenable?"

Rothworth got to his feet and stood perfectly still, his gaze inscrutable.

Aware of their interested spectators, Aurora threw them a humorous look as she walked over to Rothworth, and, taking hold of his gloved hand, placed a prim kiss on the back. His fingers tightened around hers for an instant.

And then it was over, and she was stepping away and accepting the raucous congratulations being lavished on her.

After some minutes of dealing with her admirers, she at last had an opportunity to turn back to Rothworth, who had not moved from her side.

"Did I work hard enough to earn my proposal?" she asked softly, eyes alight with laughter as she replayed his words back to him.

"Indisputably. You appear to have a talent for grand gestures."

"I had no choice when you were being so noble and tormenting us both in the process."

He took hold of her hand and raised it to his lips, surprising her with such an intimate gesture in front of an audience.

She was even more surprised when he began to inexorably pull her towards him; the intensity in his eyes doing odd things to her pulse . . .

. . . then suddenly Miss Brinkley and Miss Coral appeared from nowhere and tugged her out of his reach.

"Lady Dewbury is looking for you, Aurora dear," declared Miss Coral. "We will take you to her!"

"Rothworth, no doubt you will wish to call on Lady Aurora in the morning," Miss Brinkley informed her nephew; leaving him in no doubt that she expected him to make a formal proposal at this time or incur her deepest displeasure.

He did not respond.

His gaze was entangled with Aurora's and neither of them appeared to be paying any heed to their surroundings.

"Ahem . . . yes, well, we'd best be going!" declared Miss Coral, beginning to lead Aurora away. "And the sooner the better, Aurora dear," she added in a lowered voice, "for it's just those sorts of looks that get a girl into trouble – believe me!"

The sisters escorted Aurora to the door with gentle ruthlessness and were about to pass through it when Rothworth's raised voice halted their progress.

"Lady Elizabeth Aurora Dewbury . . . "

Aurora slowly turned around.

"Oh, good lord," muttered Miss Coral. "Surely he is not going to do it *here*."

"In public? He wouldn't dare," said Miss Brinkley darkly.

The crowd of onlookers parted to allow Rothworth a clear path to Aurora.

"Yes, Your Grace?" she said.

He walked over to her and, taking hold of her hands, raised them to his lips; his eyes never leaving hers.

"I promise to spend my life making certain you never regret putting your trust in me . . . will you marry me, love?"

"Yes, Julian," she replied with a dazzling smile.

To the sound of loud cheering from the assembled company, Rothworth drew her in for a kiss not often witnessed in the ballrooms of the *haute ton*.

"That will be quite enough," stated Miss Brinkley, thrusting them apart. "Congratulations are certainly in order," she told the room in a carrying voice, "but first you must all excuse us, for we should go at once and inform Lady Dewbury of the happy news."

She threw her sister a look; then linked her arm with Aurora's and walked her out of the card-room.

Miss Coral did the same with her nephew.

They managed to get the besotted couple across the length of the crowded ballroom, up the stairs, and along the corridor to the library without once halting their determined pace.

When they arrived at the library, Miss Brinkley gestured them inside, told them strictly that they would get no more than half an hour of privacy, and then shut the door on their bemused expressions.

"You had better wait here and stop anyone from going in," she told her sister. "I will go and apprise Lady Dewbury of the spectacle Rothworth and Aurora have made of themselves. On the whole, I have reason to believe she will be pleased."

"Undoubtedly!" retorted Miss Coral. "Julian is the catch of the decade! I wouldn't be at all surprised if she wanted to announce the betrothal tonight."

"Yes, you may be right. The sooner the better with those two! If I'm not back in half an hour you'd best go in and chaperone them. When it comes to Aurora, I no longer trust Rothworth to act with restraint."

"No indeed," chuckled Miss Coral. "I knew we would need to guard *her* from her own actions, but never once did it occur to me that we would also need to look out for Julian! Who would have thought he would do something so rash and improper?"

The sisters shared a smile of triumph.

*   *   *

Inside the library, Rothworth had pulled Aurora into his arms in a ruthless fashion and was kissing her as if he would never let her go.

After some minutes he drew back with a guttural laugh, amazed at his own desperation.

"You'll have to pardon me if I'm too rough. I've been wanting to do that from the moment I left you this afternoon – a lifetime ago!"

"I do hope you mean to do it again?" she returned.

He laughed and groaned in one; then kissed her eyelids, her nose, and, softly, her lips.

Too softly for Aurora's liking.

She put her arms around his neck and crushed herself against him, deepening the kiss.

Rothworth was the first to pull away.

"Enough, love! We only have a few minutes. We can't . . . *I* can't . . . " With his hands buried in her hair, he dropped his forehead to hers, his breathing ragged.

Rather dazed, Aurora allowed him to hold her until they had both calmed a little.

When she finally looked up at him, she said with a good deal of amusement: "Would you have ever believed it possible that you would one day marry the woman who held you at gunpoint?"

"I could only hope! Don't you know I've been yours from the moment you stole my purse and my heart along with it?"

"Liar!" she laughed. "You were ready to wring my neck that first day."

"I was. But I could have just as easily kissed every lovely inch of it."

"And I could have easily let you."

"I know! Your eyes gave you away. It was torture."

"My gypsy eyes," she teased. "Do you remember, I asked you once why you call them that and you told me I wouldn't want to hear your reason – why was that?"

"In the carriage, on the way back from Dewbury Abbey, you made it abundantly clear that all you wanted from me was friendship. Had I answered you, I'd have been going against your wishes."

"What a fool I was! Can you tell me your reason now?"

He smiled at her eager expression.

"I call them gypsy eyes because they exert some strange, mystical force over me." He cupped her upturned face between his hands and held her gaze with renewed intensity. "But most of all, because I can see my future in them."

"Oh Julian! I never guessed you were a romantic."

"I'm not," he said, revolted by the idea. "I'm a realist who knows how to recognise good fortune when he comes across it. I hope you'll not expect pretty speeches from me?"

"Never."

"And I'll probably always be an authoritarian who likes to get his own way – can you bear it?"

"I imagine so."

"And don't think I'll forget about that boon you owe me! I have every intention of claiming it, whether it's six months or twenty years from now."

"A commensurate and respectable boon," she reminded him, eyes twinkling.

"You may be certain of one thing, my enchanting girl: it will in no way be respectable."

THE END

Dear Reader

I hope you enjoyed AURORA; I had such fun writing it!

It will come as no surprise to those of you who know Georgette Heyer's books that Aurora bears a striking resemblance to the heroine in The Grand Sophy (my favourite GH story!). Both are blessed with irrepressible optimism and a can-do-attitude, which are two of my favourite qualities in a person. I couldn't wait to explore a character who had a plan for every situation and never allowed life to get her down for long.

There is a multi-generational romance theme in my previous novel, APHRODITE, and I wanted the same theme in AURORA (my hero's aunt has her own romantic moment). After all, why should only the 20, or 30-somethings have all the fun! I'm a great believer in finding love at any age. My own grandmother had 3 husbands, and met the last one when she was in her 70's, so it's never too late!

Thank you for coming with me on my writing journey. And if you're in the mood, I would be delighted if you would leave me a review on Amazon and Goodreads.

xDG

DGRampton.com
Facebook.com/DGRampton
Instagram.com/fortheloveofjaneausten

The Regency Goddesses Series

The novels in the Regency Goddesses series are standalone and can be enjoyed in any order. They share only one minor character (have you spotted them yet?).

Chronological order:

Artemisia – Book 1 (1812)
Aphrodite – Book 2 (1820)
Aurora – Book 3 (1821)

"Delightful, funny and filled with clever conversation. Two thumbs up!"
A. Sockwell

"There are so few Regency novels that are this well-written, with such strong characters, a good plot and sexy, but clean relationships."
C. Sparks

"An enthralling Regency romp full of endearing and meddlesome characters, a stubborn hero and heroine, and hilariously entertaining mix-ups and tangles!"
Austenesque Reviews

"Truly witty, delightful characters .... the author has mastered the art of satire with a heart."
Dragonlady

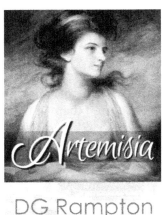

ARTEMISIA

#1 Amazon Best Seller, British Historical Literature

'You forget yourself, your lordship. You have no rights to allow or disallow anything I may choose to do. You have, in fact, no claim over me whatsoever – a circumstance for which I thank the Lord on a daily basis! I am not your ward, or your dependent, and I will not allow you to speak to me in that odiously overbearing fashion!'

High-spirited Artemisia Grantley, niece to the Duke of Wentworth, has never made any attempt to conform to the feminine ideal expected of a lady of quality; nor has she ever had the benefit of an unfavourable opinion formed against her. But when the Marquess of Chysm enters her life, it seems to her that his lordship is always at hand to witness her shortcomings and bring them to her attention.

As she reluctantly embarks upon her first London Season, a scandalous family secret and a conspiracy that stretches all the way to Napoleonic France threaten to entangle her with the one person she could happily throttle.

DG Rampton

No. 1 Kindle bestselling author of ARTEMISIA

APHRODITE

#1 Amazon Best Seller, Regency Historical Romance

"I fail to see why you expect me to put up with your acerbic charm? Others of your acquaintance might be inclined to do so, but I, strange creature that I am, will not!"

When the beautiful Miss April Hartwood arrives in London to be introduced to Regency high society, she hopes for some fun and frivolity after a life spent in rural obscurity in Cornwall. Unfortunately for her, her grandmother has other ideas...marriage. Lively and strong-willed, April does not appreciate being compelled to catch a husband, yet she finds herself courting the affections of the Duke of Claredon, while struggling with a wholly inappropriate attraction to the insufferable Mr Royce.

In the lead up to Christmas, in the year 1820, a delightfully devious campaign is orchestrated to bring together two people destined for one another, regardless of the obstacles to be overcome and the inconvenient tendency on the part of the protagonists to resist their attraction...until they are finally brought to realise they cannot escape fate, or the meddling of one determined grandmother.

An Adaptation of North and South

ELIZABETH GASKELL

NORTH AND SOUTH

Brought to you by Manor House Books, this classic novel has been adapted for a modern readership by bestselling historical romance author D.G. Rampton.

Set in Victorian England, North and South by Elizabeth Gaskell was first published in 1854. This adaptation stays true to the dramatic social commentary of the original, while bringing into greater prominence the love story at its core, which is reminiscent of Jane Austen's Pride and Prejudice.

Uprooted from her idyllic existence in the South of England, Margaret Hale moves with her family to an industrial town in the North, where she develops a passionate sense of social justice upon witnessing the hardships suffered by the local mill workers. Her views often bring her into conflict with wealthy mill-owner John Thornton, who befriends her family. But their turbulent relationship masks a deep attraction that cannot be subdued, and a bond that only strengthens when tested by the vagaries of fate.

** Exclusive to Kindle **

Printed in Great Britain
by Amazon

21184773R00161